A Deal with
a Stranger

MARTINA MUNZITTU

ISBN: 1493721453
ISBN-13: 978-1493721450

Cover Design by Siv Lien

To those who wanted to leave before the time

Chapter 1

Clara had long suspected that Paolo was going to propose soon. They'd been together for four years, and recently he'd been trying to tell her something, but always postponed at the last minute. He would get nervous, his hands would go cold and sweaty, and his words would get tangled. This was a clear signal that what he wanted to say was important, but perhaps, he didn't quite know how to say it. Clara had decided to make things easier for him, so she'd suggested, on this occasion, that they ought to go for a romantic walk by the mountains. He loved being outdoors, and particularly hill walking.

To be honest, Clara wasn't that keen on mountains, but since her strategy was to make Paolo happy and comfortable, she felt she ought to make a small sacrifice. Surely it would pay off? One Sunday afternoon, they headed towards Monte Arcosu, a nature reserve located in the south-west of Sardinia. It was a beautiful warm day at the end of May, and the sky was so bright and blue that it was impossible to imagine that clouds could ever be scattered up there.

"What happens if we bump into an angry wild boar?" Clara asked, as they approached the reserve.
"The boar is more likely to be scared of you. He'll probably run away in the opposite direction." Paolo accelerated his car on the steep narrow road.
"Last time we came here I was chased by an ugly-looking wasp. It was gigantic, almost like a hornet. I hated it." Clara shivered at the thought.
"It must have been the perfume you were wearing."

"I wasn't wearing any perfume, nor make-up for that matter." Why would a girl wear perfume to go rambling, she wondered. The fact was that the awful insect had decided to chase her, out of the dozen people she was with. Nothing to be flattered about, maybe it knew she was afraid of stinging insects? Perhaps her fear had emanated irresistible pheromones? Whatever it was, she just hoped that none of those nasty bugs would fly in her direction today.

"You're still thinking about that insect?" Paolo laughed. "If you want to be scared of something, I can think of all sorts of other dangers you could find in a forest." He always liked to tease her.

"It's the buzzing they do, that's the unpleasant thing. If those flying little monsters were silent, they wouldn't be so frightening." Clara was thoughtful. "What other dangerous animals could be in these woods then?"

"I can think of many. Hungry boars, clumsy deer, angry wild cats, menacing eagles, hissing snakes. Even the fish, they could jump out the river and attack you."

Was Clara supposed to take him seriously?

"But the most dangerous species is the one we always underestimate." He continued speaking softly.

Clara's look was inquisitive.

"Homo sapiens." Paolo stopped the car.

"Great, all I needed was a bit of reassurance." Clara shook her head.

Paolo left the car and headed for the visitors centre where he purchased two tickets. Clara opened the door and let the warm breeze in. The scenery around her was delightful, despite the many fires that struck the Sardinian forests; this area was intact and still very green. Monte Arcosu felt like a solid rock mountain, its pale stone was particularly visible at the top, where its rugged appearance reflected the sun rays. Further down, towards the base, it was covered with thick vegetation, mostly bushes of various shades of greens, yellows and rusty colours.

"Mediterranean maquis," explained Paolo as Clara looked. "Those shrubs there consist of many types of plant life, myrtle, juniper, heather, and *corbezzolo*, also called strawberry tree." He inhaled slowly and added: "Can you smell their scent in the air? The maquis is what gives the forest this delicate perfume."

Clara closed the door and they carried on driving on the unfinished road.

She admired her boyfriend, he was so knowledgeable. Sometimes she wondered if he spent his reading time going through encyclopaedias, rather than fiction. Paolo seemed to know a lot about nature, the arts, science, and history. She liked the fact that he was a man of culture and she could learn a lot from him.

"We'll go to the top, so you can admire the waterfall," said Paolo.

The road became steeper. On her left, Clara could see the rocky side of the mountain, whilst to her right, she could admire the green scenery, bushes of various shades of green, but not as luscious as in winter. Gradually, the shrubs turned into trees and the forest started to appear. The car was moving slowly inside this green tunnel, surrounded by vegetation. Holm-oaks and cork trees stood tall and strong, close to each other, the sunrays could barely squeeze in between.

"Now that I think of it, we may not be able to see any water, once we reach the waterfall." Paolo seemed thoughtful.

"Why's that?" Clara was intrigued. What was the point of going to a waterfall if the water wasn't there?

"Drought. It hasn't rained for so long." Paolo shook

his head. "We can try it, but you should get ready for a possible disappointment."

Great, that's all she needed. She'd looked for the perfect setting for Paolo's proposal, and now nature had decided to throw some obstacles in her path.

They reached the end of the road, and parked the car in a small lay-by. Clara grabbed her picnic basket, they both left the car and started to walk along the path. Gradually they arrived in the heart of the forest; it felt much cooler under the shade of the trees. Everywhere around them was quiet, even the birds were barely audible. They'd met nobody on the way, and probably the wild boars and deer were hiding from view. There was an infinite sense of peace. The sunrays were playing between the trees, creating magical beams of light, conferring the foliage different shades of green and extra brilliance.

They crossed a small wooden bridge, but Clara was disappointed to see that no water was running in the stream. The bare stones on the riverbed were of various sizes and shapes, she tried to imagine what it'd be like when the water was gliding over them.

As they carried on walking, Paolo pointed at various bushes, using their Latin name. He'd already told her before; she just wished she could remember them.

"These are oleanders!" Clara said with pride. At least they were easy to identify. She was also able to spot some willow trees and an alder; not bad.

When they finally reached the water fall, all Clara could see was a large round rock at the top. There was no water running from it.

"I'm sorry." Paolo seemed disappointed.

"It's not your fault."

"Let's go and sit at the top of the rock, so we can

admire the view."

Clara followed her boyfriend, and they sat on the cream-coloured stone. It'd been warmed by the sun, but felt comfortable enough.

"What's in the basket?" Paolo always had a huge appetite.

"Since we came after lunch, I only brought some pastries, and a thermos flask of coffee."

"Sounds good."

Paolo suddenly got up and decided to go down where the water would've hit the ground, if it'd been running. He picked up an unusually-shaped stone, and started to examine it. Clara thought that from the top, he looked taller than he was. He'd have been pleased to know. He never quite accepted the fact that she was as tall as him. Men liked shorter women, and Clara was always careful not to wear high heels in his company. And in any case, even if he wasn't tall, he still had a muscular and fit body. He liked to play football and go to the gym, unlike her. And his face, it was just so kissable, she thought. With his square jaw line, full lips, and well-proportioned nose. His olive skin seemed tanned even in winter. Yes, what a gorgeous boyfriend she had. And didn't they say that the good wine comes in the small barrels?

Clara wondered if Paolo was going to propose now. After all, this was a very romantic spot. He was in his element, between mountains, trees, and wilderness. Was he going to kneel down and ask her? Or would he do it while standing up?

"Damn! I left my camera in the car!" shouted Clara.

"Don't worry; we can come back here another time." Paolo smiled. "Perhaps, when there's actually some water in the fall."

No way. If Paolo was going to propose on this day,

on this spot, Clara had to seal that memory with her camera. But she couldn't tell him that.

"The view is magnificent, I must take a picture." Clara got up. "I'll walk back to the car."

"Let me come with you."

"No, you better watch that basket. I'll be back in no time."

"Why are you taking your handbag with you? All you need is the car keys."

"Ladies always carry their handbag. It gives us a sense of security." Guys couldn't possibly understand this.

"OK then. But stick to the path, otherwise you might get lost," he said with tenderness.

She kissed him on the cheek and started to walk.

Her steps were decisive and her feet kept cracking on the occasional twigs. The breeze was light and made the leaves rustle. She kept looking at all the shades of browns from the tree trunks, their branches and the soil itself, as well as the various greens of different foliage. Clara always thought the nature had a fantastic way of matching colours; they just seemed to be in perfect harmony, even the ones she would never herself, wear together.

She decided to walk inside the woods. She felt even closer to nature, that way. She suddenly heard an unusual noise, coming from behind a massive oak tree. She moved to her right and saw a middle-aged man who was standing under a large branch of the oak. He was tying something around that branch, it looked like a rope. Clara approached the scene quietly and saw that the man was standing on a small stool and tying that rope around that branch, with great care. He was now checking the knot. What was he actually doing, she wondered. And why was her stomach churning? She only ever had this sensation when she felt danger. Danger of what? This man hadn't even seen her. Oh no. It couldn't possibly be the case? This guy wanted to hang himself. Was this likely? Or was she over-reacting? She took a second look. His movements were slow and carefully planned; he was now inserting his head through the loop and feeling the knot. She had to act quickly: she was too far from Paolo to call for help, and she hadn't seen any other people around. She had to stop this man now, before it was too late. She ran towards him and shouted:

"Stop it! Stop it! Whatever you're doing."

The man looked up in disbelief.

"Where have you come from?" He seemed agitated as he removed the cord from his neck.

"I... I just came here for a walk, and I saw you."

The man slowly came down from the stool, trying not to lose his balance. He looked at her with embarrassment. His hands were shaking and he was extremely pale.

"Can you go back the way you came and pretend you never saw me?" His voice was trembling.

"How can I?" Clara didn't know what to say.

"Has anyone ever taught you to mind your own business?"

"Yes. But this is *my* business now." Clara was confused. "If I hadn't seen you... then you'd be right. But because I saw you, it's now become my business too." Why did her tongue get twisted when least needed? She could've done better than that.

The man sat on the stool and held his head between his arms.

Clara approached him, with slow steps.

"Perhaps you'd like to talk?" She sat on the ground next to him.

"I'd like to be left alone, " he mumbled.

She looked at him. He must have been in his late fifties, and similar age to her father. His face was leathery and darkened by the sun, obviously a man who worked outdoors, perhaps a farmer, or a builder. His hands were cracked and had many rough bits. His eyes were dark and looked terribly sad.

"What's your name?" she asked.

"Peppino."

"Signor Peppino, why were you trying to kill yourself?"

He didn't reply straight away. He put the cord down, in front of him, and stared at it.

"You're just a girl, you don't want to know." His voice was faint.

"You're wrong. I do want to know. What happened? Why do you want to do such a horrible thing?"

"Life isn't worth living." He exhaled heavily.

What could she say to that? She didn't want to start a debate on life and why it was worth living. In fact she was too young to understand things like that. Perhaps she could try and dissuade him from the idea of death, at least?

"I once heard that people who commit suicide, go straight to hell." Her tone was serious and convincing, she thought.

"My life is hell anyway, what difference would it make?" He was holding his face between his hands, and spying through his fingers.

"Oh, there's hell and hell. They say the one after death is truly awful." Clara was trying to imagine it. "Every time I look at the picture of the Final Judgement by Michelangelo, I get the creeps. Some awful images there." Clara's body quivered at the idea. "Not to mention

Dante's Inferno. If you read that, it would definitely put you off wanting to die."

"I don't know about these things. I barely finished elementary school." He seemed confused.

"I'm sorry, I wasn't trying to show off at all. In fact, I had difficulty studying history of art, or Italian literature. I always had bad teachers in those subjects."

Signor Peppino wasn't reacting. She had to try something different. But she was no counsellor; she had no idea what to say in these situations. She'd only ventured into the forest to retrieve her camera. Paolo must be wondering what had happened to her. This hadn't been her plan at all. All she wanted was to immortalise the moment her boyfriend proposed to her. This stranger was ruining everything. Why hadn't she just stayed put and let Paolo make his proposal by the waterfall?

"Since my wife died, a few months ago, I feel lost. I just can't see any point in living." His voice was broken.

"Do you have any children?"

"Two girls. One is twenty-two and the other twenty-four."

"When my grandmother died, I was only fifteen. It wasn't her fault, but I was very angry." Clara's voice was soft and her gaze was lost. "I shouldn't have been angry, but I was. Because she left us, and she couldn't be with us any longer." She turned her head towards Signor Peppino, and looked intently into his eyes: "If she'd taken her life away, like you plan to do, I'd have been *furious*. I'd have hated her. Do you want your daughters to be mad at you?"

"Of course not!"

"Do you love yourself more than you love your daughters?"

9

"No, they come first; always." There was no hesitation in his response.

"Then you have to live *for* them. If you can't live for yourself, do it for them." Clara didn't know how these words came out, but they just kept flowing. "Your girls have already lost their mother, if they lose their father too, they'll be devastated. They *need* you."

"I never thought about it that way." Signor Peppino seemed baffled.

"It's the only way to look at it." Clara sighed and added: "Perhaps you thought you no longer had a role in life, but you have. You're a father first of all, and you've got a duty towards your daughters. Then you're a brother, a son, a cousin, a friend and so on. All these people you're related to, care for you, and you can't just dump them like that! They'd all be very upset if you did. They'd all wonder what they did wrong, why they couldn't help you. They might even feel guilty. Is this what you want?"

"Perhaps you're right." His voice was reduced to a whisper.

"Not *perhaps. Surely*, I'm right." Clara touched his shoulder and continued: "I'm going to take that rope now. And when you get up, I'll grab the stool as well. "

His sad eyes were filling with tears. Clara was touched and she wiped them with her tissues. Thank God she'd taken her handbag with her, where she had at least three packets. She suddenly felt close to this man, who was so hurt and vulnerable.

"Can I do anything to help you?" She kept wiping his cheeks. Tears were rolling gently, unstoppable, on his wrinkled face. Clara wondered if the lines on his skin were caused by the grief or by hard work under the sun. Both probably.

"You've done enough." He snuffled. "I promise, I

swear to you, that I'll never try to take my life again."

Could she trust him? Should she get his contact details and make sure that he was still alive the next day? Should she follow him? Somehow, he sounded sincere.

"I trust you. I think you're a man of honour and won't cheat me. Nor your family, or friends." Clara believed in her instincts, they'd never failed her.

They sat in silence for a few minutes. She felt that Signor Peppino needed to cry, and she wasn't going to hurry things. He sobbed gently, while she kept offering her tissues. It was the first time she saw an older man cry. She hoped that her father and her grand-father would never suffer this way.

"Thank you, stranger." Signor Peppino's voice was croaky. He got up, and handed Clara the stool. He smiled and waved goodbye.

Clara was tempted to hold him and talk to him for a little longer, but perhaps enough had been said.

She was confused as she walked back to the fall. Her relaxing Sunday afternoon had turned out to be different from what she'd expected. Did she just save someone's life? Could she be proud of herself on this occasion? Not to mention that instead of one camera, she was now coming back with two items, the wooden stool and the rope.

"What happened to you?" Paolo was pacing around. "I was getting worried."

"If you were so worried, why didn't you come and look for me?" She hurried towards him. "I was gone for ages, someone could've attacked me."

"I didn't want to leave our food basket behind, unprotected… you know with all those hungry boars, and deer."

"I need a hug, Paolo." Clara dropped the two important items to the ground, but kept her handbag. She then threw her arms around his torso, and held him tight.

"What's the matter?" He was concerned.

Clara told him everything, her tears flooding his shirt. She thought that the incident hadn't affected her, but she was wrong. She suddenly felt very heavy, almost as if Signor Peppino's burdens had been unloaded onto her. His whole life was now crushing her shoulders. Paolo was caressing her back and consoling her.

"I can't believe it. What an awful thing to happen." He kept stroking her." Just as well you're taking tomorrow off work."

"Yes, I never work on my birthday." She sniffled. "I'm going to treat myself tomorrow, I think I need it."

"I was going to tell you something today, but I guess it'll have to wait." He seemed serious.

A suicide attempt and a marriage proposal all in the same day didn't sound like a good idea to Clara. Once she was married and became a mother, she couldn't tell her daughters that the day her husband proposed she'd also rescued a man from death. It wasn't romantic at all. Better keep things separate.

"You can tell me tomorrow, on my birthday." She looked at him and tried to smile between her tears.

Chapter 2

Clara had just enjoyed a warm relaxing shower. She put her cream bathrobe on, walked to her bedroom and checked the clock: 10:45. She had fifteen minutes. *Fifteen minutes!* Where had the time gone? What was she thinking? She was getting married at 11:00 and she'd only managed a shower.

"Mamma! Mamma, come here!" she shouted from her bedroom.

"I can't my darling; I'm getting ready." Mamma shouted back from the other bedroom.

"Where's my hairdresser? And my beauty therapist?" Clara was still screaming.

"Oh, they must have forgotten to come," answered Valentina, from the kitchen.

"Will someone come here and give me a hand? I'm supposed to be the bride!"

"I always tell you not to leave things to the last minute," reproached Mamma from the distance. "Even on your wedding day, you wanted to have a lie-in."

"The photographer is here," shouted Dino, her brother, from the corridor.

This wasn't happening. How could Clara be so disorganized? She wasn't even dressed yet, her hair was a mess, and her face looked puffed up. She was supposed to look stunning on her special day. She quickly searched for the dress inside the wardrobe. Only to find out that it'd fallen off the rail and it was crumpled into a huge fluffy bundle.

"Can someone help me with the dress? Is Zia Carmela around? Can someone get an iron for her?"

"I'm not ironing on your wedding day! You must be joking." Her great-auntie had strong objections.

13

Clara resigned herself to having to wear her dress as it was. Luckily Valentina came to the rescue and helped her with the zip behind.

"Oh no," whispered her sister. "Two buttons are missing from the collar line."

"That can't be right. I checked the dress before I collected it from the shop!" Clara was stupefied.

"I'm sorry, sister, but it's true. The zip only goes up to a point close to the neck, but the collar is missing two buttons." Valentina looked up as if to invite some form of inspiration. "I'll find two safety pins."

"No way! I'm not having safety pins on my dress!"

"Where the hell am I going to find two small ivory buttons at 10:55 on a Sunday morning?"

"Safety pins will do." Clara sighed, as she started to feel the panic coming.

There was a knock on the door.

"Can I come in? I'm the photographer."

"I'm not ready yet," Clara replied frantically.

"But we're late. I'll have to take you as I find you." The photographer rushed in armed with a disposable camera.

"My hair is a mess and I'm not wearing my make up yet." Clara suddenly looked at his camera. "I'm not paying 800 euros for my wedding service, for you to use one of those!"

"My apologies, but my professional camera stopped working last night." He seemed embarrassed. "However, these toy cameras are pretty good."

"Go and get a decent camera. Otherwise, you're sacked."

"Clara, Clara, will you come out? All the family are waiting in the living room to see the bride, before we go to the church." Mamma was calling.

"And the bells are ringing. It's 11.00 now and everybody is waiting for you before Mass starts." Grandpa, Nonno, conveyed his message with a serious tone.

That was it. Clara had to come out. With her brown curls scattered on her shoulders, rather than tied up, as she'd hoped for. Her face was nowhere near as glamorous as her make-up trials. And her dress neckline was undone. Valentina hadn't even found one safety pin. She slowly walked towards the living room, where a dozen familiar faces were expecting her. To her surprise, there was no applause. People whispered to each other in disapproval, and looked at their watches. Why wasn't anyone smiling? She looked at them, one by one, but they all seemed disappointed, dissatisfied with her appearance. Until she noticed a girl on the left, a blonde girl, probably in her twenties. She was wearing a blue hat with a delicate veil over her eyes, and she was smiling. But her smile was a teasing one, like *La Gioconda*'s smirk. Who was that girl? And why was she wearing a veil? A veil was the bride's prerogative on this day.

"Hurry, hurry, bambina mia. We're very late." Mamma grabbed her arm and led Clara towards the front door. The procession of people followed.

As they left the palazzo, Clara turned round to find Papà. He was supposed to give her away to Paolo. Where was he?

"Papà couldn't come today, so I found someone else," whispered Mamma.

"What do you mean? What was more important than my wedding day?"

"Football. He just couldn't miss that match." Mamma seemed uncomfortable as she introduced Papà's substitute: "This is Signor Peppino, we found him in the woods and he agreed to give you away."

"It would be a pleasure for me." Signor Peppino grabbed Clara's arm.

"But… but you haven't even changed. You're still wearing those outdoor muddy clothes…" That's all Clara could say.

As they walked towards the church, the blonde girl appeared next to Signor Peppino, and continued to smile, below her blue veil.

"Who's invited you? Are you one of mine, or one of Paolo's?" Clara whispered.

The girl continued to smile. Clara was losing her patience. It was normally a two-minute walk from her flat to the church. Why were they taking so long today? And why were the roads wet and full of mud? Her dress was getting dirty, so she lifted her skirt only to notice that she was wearing her black leather boots. How could she? How could she wear black boots under her ivory wedding dress? How could she be so distracted and forget to put her matching satin sandals? The bells kept ringing and were going faster and faster, louder and louder. Why didn't the priest stop them? People were chatting but she couldn't understand a word, the noise was too much. It was a drill in her head. She screamed, until her voice became louder than the bells. She screamed again, until she woke up. Her alarm clock was exploding.

"Clara, are you all right?" asked Mamma through her bedroom door.

"Yes, Mamma." She touched her nightshirt, just to make sure it wasn't her wedding dress. "I just had a nightmare." She could feel the sweat on her neck.

"Fancy that, a bad dream on your birthday. I'll make you a coffee."

Clara's head was still hurting. She could've sworn that the church bells were ringing for real. She gently got out of bed, put her slippers on and walked towards the window. She lifted the shutters and let the sunshine through. She opened the window; she could do with some fresh air. Cars were racing by below, but luckily, on the fifth floor, she felt closer to the birds than to the people on the street. She checked the sky, she wanted no clouds on her special day. There was only a solitary one, shaped like a soft sheep, which posed no threat. Before going to the kitchen, she opened her wardrobe, just to make sure that there was no wedding dress hanging there. She sighed with relief.

What can you buy with one hundred euros? Not much nowadays, thought Clara as she kept staring at those peach sandals. They cost seventy-five euros, but the matching handbag, cleverly placed next to them on the glass stand, cost fifty-four. They went so well together, handbag and sandals, they were made for each other, it would've been a sin to separate them. And yet, Clara could only afford one of the two, as she'd only allocated one hundred euros for her own birthday present. She had to make a choice, and face the big dilemma of picking one against the other. No-one should ever be put in such an awkward position.

Clara paced around the shoe shop. She was enchanted by the variety of colours and shapes, and slowly breathed in the scent of the soft leather. Perhaps one day, she'd become rich and she wouldn't have to make such choices ever again? But for now, she'd have to take a short break and think about it.

She left and walked under the porticoes in Via Roma, paying attention to the passers-by. She was always curious to spot the latest fashion trends, and especially eager to find new colour combinations she hadn't thought of. That lady with the brown linen suit, for instance, was wearing a light pink cotton blouse under her jacket. Two colours she never would have put together, brown and pink, and yet, she looked good. Clara tried to see if anyone was wearing peach, she needed some inspiration for the soon-to-be-hers handbag or shoes. It was the end of May, the morning felt hot even in the shade, and the huge white ferries in the port seemed so bright, with the sunlight reflecting from them. The traffic was heavy on the paved via Roma, and no matter how uneven the surface of the road, the cars kept racing on it, testing their suspensions to the limit.

"One cappuccino, please," she ordered as she got to the bar.

She was tempted by the pastries displayed on the glass counter. The chocolate bigné looked delicious, but so did the millefeuille with crème patissière. She was sure she could smell their perfume even through the glass. OK, maybe calling it perfume was excessive, but it was such a divine scent, that it managed to stimulate all the five senses, somehow. Anyway, she'd already had her birthday cake for breakfast, so she shouldn't get distracted.

Clara never liked having her drinks too hot, so she grabbed her teaspoon and started stirring. If only she could have a piece of Mamma's cake now, with her cappuccino! She had enjoyed her birthday cake very much. In fact, it was irresistible. Clara always thought it should be used as a bribe. If you wanted someone to tell you a secret, present them with a slice of Mamma's cake, and they wouldn't be able to stand their ground. They'd tell you even more than you wanted to know. Why was she still thinking of cakes anyway? She had a sip of cappuccino, but it burnt her tongue. No problem, she could wait; today she was a free woman. No work pressures on her birthday.

"Have you ever dreamt of someone you don't know?" Clara was addressing the woman behind the counter.

"Yes. I always dream of a tall young man who comes on his horse and takes me away from this place." She smiled. "It's just that parking a horse in via Roma isn't exactly easy."

"I never thought we could dream about people we don't know. Make them up, I mean." Clara meant to be serious, didn't this lady understand?

"Of course, haven't you ever dreamt of places you've never been before?" She pressed the button on the espresso machine, and the creamy coffee descended into the tiny cup. Another heavenly aroma wafted under Clara's nose, as the espresso was delivered to the man beside her.

"I've recently dreamt of a beautiful lady I've never met," interrupted the guy as he looked at his coffee.

"What was she like?" asked Clara.

The assistant behind the bar crossed her arms and listened carefully.

"A tall blonde lady, with blue eyes."

"Was she wearing a hat with a light blue veil which partially covered her face?" Clara's tone was intrigued.

"No, she was naked." The gentleman sipped his coffee and winked.

"Will someone take me seriously today?" Clara raised her hands.

She was still thinking about her weird dream. What could it mean? It obviously reflected some form of

19

anxiety, perhaps the fear that Paolo might not propose today. After all, the actual proposal part was only something you saw in movies. It wasn't really done much these days. Anyway, there was a funny side to the dream, something she could tell her beloved boyfriend later on, after he'd proposed, of course.

As she stirred the froth in her cappuccino she pondered: the sandals, or the bag? She already had thirty-nine pairs of shoes, did she need another pair? But these were peach; she didn't have any sandals of that colour. And, in any case, of those thirty-nine pairs of shoes, she only actually wore thirty-five, maybe. Some were uncomfortable, others too tight. Yes, because, believe it or not, since she'd put on a few kilos, even her feet had grown! One size bigger. People didn't believe her, and her family thought it was just an excuse to buy more shoes, which it was. But the truth was also that her feet were now just a bit wider. Those sandals in that shop had fitted perfectly; they felt like velvet gloves caressing her newly-fat feet. They had to be hers.

By the time she got home, Clara had twenty-five euros left and a total of forty pairs of shoes. She could have bought some flowers with those extra euros, but Paolo always got her a bouquet for her birthday, so she'd decided to keep them for another occasion. She put away those twenty-five euros, in the internal pocket of her handbag. They shouldn't be mixed with the other spending money, they were meant to complete her present, sooner or later.

As she walked through the front door, an out-of-tune and out-of-time choir of four people started to sing 'happy birthday'. She smiled to see her family re-united for lunch and kissed everybody on the cheeks, except Nonno, who didn't like displays of affection.

"You made lasagne Mamma, that's fantastic." Clara was delighted. The whole flat smelt of wonderful food.

"And your favourite second course as well, octopus salad." Mamma was always proud of her cooking.

"Thank God it's not my birthday," commented her sister Valentina, with a disgusted face.

The whole family sat at the table. Mamma had used the bohemian china, the crystal glasses and the best cutlery. It was a special occasion, after all.

"I never understood why you don't like octopus," Papà wondered.

"It's a revolting animal. It just looks like a giant spider!"

"Stop it, stop it, please." Clara didn't want anyone to ruin her meal with unsettling images.

"You're a spoilt little girl," reproached Nonno as he shook his head. "You should've experienced hunger during the war."

"Oh Nonno, please. Don't start again," pleaded Valentina.

"We used to eat all sorts of things."

"Nonno! It's my birthday. I don't want to hear about what you ate during the war. Nor how often you ate it. Another time, please."

"So, when are you seeing Paolo today?" Mamma placed the first portion of lasagne onto Clara's plate.

"After he finishes work. We're meeting at Monte Urpinu at eight-thirty."

"Do you have any idea what he's bought you?"

Valentina's eyes were lighting up.

"Well, I guess it'll be the usual bouquet of flowers, for a start." Clara paused as she sipped from her glass of wine. "But I'm also expecting another surprise."

"What's that? Come on, tell us." Valentina had always been curious.

"I suspect, although I shouldn't say this…" Clara looked up and her cheeks blushed slightly.

"You're killing me. Spit it out!" Valentina got up threatening her sister with her fork.

"Paolo's been a bit nervous recently. Yesterday, he was about to tell me something, and then he stopped himself…"

Mamma and Papà looked at each other, whilst Valentina seemed more and more intrigued. Nonno was sitting quietly and looking thoughtful.

"I think, or rather, I hope, that tonight, on the occasion of my birthday… he will ask me to marry him," Clara whispered. Perhaps she'd dared too much by saying it?

"Oh, you mean, he'll give you an engagement ring?" Valentina was still waving her fork. And then suddenly she looked away. "Don't eat that octopus in front of me!"

"This is wonderful news bambina mia!" Mamma was almost in tears. "I'd be very proud to be Paolo's mother-in-law. He's such a gentleman, such a good boy. You couldn't have chosen better!"

"I'm not your bambina any more, Mamma. I'm twenty-five today. Pretty grown-up." There was a hint of pride in Clara's voice, she felt ready to leave the nest.

It was 20:10 and Clara was almost ready. She wanted to wear her new sandals for Paolo, but it was difficult to find clothes that matched peach. Her cream trousers didn't seem to fit and she realised that her hips felt a bit rounder than last time she'd looked. In the end she opted for a pair of stretchy black trousers, and a black blouse with a stylish chiffon collar and sleeves. Peach and black should go well together, she thought. She wore a little mascara, although she was lucky enough with her big brown eyes and long eyelashes not to need much make-up. Her shiny brown curls were scattered on her shoulders, and some rebel ones leapt forward towards her cheeks. The problem was always the lipstick. Paolo hated lipstick, as it tended to leave marks everywhere, but Clara had found a new stay-on lipstick. It was more pink than peach, but it'd have to do. Her lips were full and heart-shaped, a little bit of colour was just right. Now she felt complete, ready to observe the full masterpiece reflected in her wardrobe mirror. She looked smart, almost chic. Black was definitely slimming. Normally she could've worn anything, but in the last year she started to put on weight and had now reached sixty-five kilos. In fairness, this isn't a lot if you are 1.60 metres tall, but since the age of seventeen she'd always been 1.60 metres tall and had always weighed fifty-five kilos; those ten extra kilos seemed like a ton of bricks. They made her look fuller in the hips, bum and tummy. However, why her chest hadn't grown proportionally was a mystery. Those extra kilos should have spread out more evenly.

"Valentina! Can you please come here?" Clara needed a second opinion. Tonight was going to be special.

"Yes?" Her sister appeared at the door.

"How do I look? Pretend to be Paolo, please."

Valentina stretched her legs, stood up on her toes and

paced stiffly around the room.

"I'm Paolo now. Let's take a look."

"He doesn't walk that way. Stop it." Clara was amused.

"Yes he does. He's always so rigid and straight."

"Only when he's preoccupied with something."

"You look very nice, sister." Valentina was now examining every detail. "He won't be able to resist you tonight."

"Do you think he'll notice that I've put on weight?"

"Since yesterday?"

Clara gave her a tough look.

"Have you? I've never noticed." Valentina sat on the floor, cross legged. "Can you give me some of your extra kilos, if that's the case?"

"If only. I wish I could have a figure like you. You're so skinny, and tall. I can't even believe we are sisters!" Clara raised her arms in frustration.

"No, no. Don't go there. I may be slimmer than you, but I've got a face full of spots for a start." Valentina dragged herself up and looked in the mirror. "I am a spotty eighteen year old. With small eyes and a big nose. At least you don't get called Pinocchia!"

"What? You never told me they call you Pinocchia!" Clara was shocked. Her younger sister was being called names in school. "Is it because of your nose?"

"And my legs. They say that they are long and wooden, like broom handles. Why do you think I always wear baggy jeans?"

"How awful. Poor little sister, being bullied by your school friends."

"Oh no, I'm not bullied. We all call each other names. But not face-to-face; just behind our backs. So nobody gets upset. After all, we're all adults now."

Why was there always so much traffic in Cagliari? It was taking ages, driving from her home to Monte Urpinu. Clara had picked this spot because four years ago, this was the place where Paolo had kissed her for the first time. So many romantic memories, their walks hand-in-hand during the summer, their sitting in the car watching the city lights on winter evenings. And tonight, on her birthday, if Paolo was going to propose, this had to be the place. Not that he'd seemed that pleased, when she suggested it. In fact, he wasn't keen at all. He'd said they should meet somewhere else, but he wasn't specific; he hadn't really given it much thought. Men didn't pay attention to these important details.

As Clara drove up the hill, she wondered what sort of a day Paolo had had. They worked for the same company, but he was in the personnel section, while Clara worked for the director general. She knew how busy and stressed Paolo would get at times. As she reached the top of the hill, there he was. Standing on the belvedere, with his hands in his pockets. She parked the car, and as she walked towards him, she could see that he was looking at the sea in the distance. She wondered why he wasn't holding a bouquet this time. Perhaps he'd got something more special for her, that didn't need to be that visible? She quietly went behind his back and tapped him on the shoulder.

"Happy Birthday Clara!" His voice trembled slightly and he turned towards her.

"Isn't this romantic?" Clara opened her arms almost as if to introduce the scenery. She felt that the whole panorama had been organized especially for them.

Paolo hugged her and invited her to sit on the bench. She held his arm and sat, while crossing her legs. She waved her right foot, hoping that he'd notice her beautiful peach sandals, but he didn't say anything.

"So, how was your day?" He was looking towards the sea.

"Very busy. I had a great day so far. I walked around via Roma in the morning and got myself a present. Then had a lovely lunch with the family. Mamma made me this chocolate cake, just fantastic. It was about ten centimetres of light cocoa sponge, with two layers of crème-patissière in the middle, one vanilla flavoured and the other plain chocolate." She paused and closed her eyes. "Mmmhh... pure heaven!"

Paolo was listening and looked preoccupied. He must be quite nervous, Clara thought. It was only natural, he was about to make a marriage proposal, it wasn't something people did every day. Perhaps she ought to be quiet for a few minutes, and give him time to organize his thoughts. As far as she was concerned, she could enjoy the view while he mentally practised what he was going to say. She hoped very much that he was going to be poetic, not just the usual 'will you marry me' stuff, but something more creative. Paolo could be inventive, if he only made an effort. She breathed calmly, she could smell the pine trees behind, and the delicate breeze was caressing her curls. But most of all, she was taken by the view in front of them. In the distance, the Poetto sea looked still, almost lifeless, preceded by the even quieter salt marshes. Just below, a wide green area was interspersed with trees and shrubs, and to her right, far away, the tall city buildings served as a reminder that they weren't on an isolated spot. The beauty of being up high was the ability to perceive the magnitude of the sky, that infinite blue dome, which was becoming darker and more mysterious at this sunset time. What a pity that the bench they were sitting on wasn't a revolving one, since the red and orange sky was waiting just behind them.

"I've got something to tell you, Clara." Paolo finally looked at her, and cleared his throat.

"I'm ready." She turned back at him with a wide smile.

Chapter 3

Paolo seemed agitated. Clara knew that this was normal, even in such a calm man. She kept smiling, to make things easier for him.

"I've been meaning to talk to you for ages, but I just didn't have the courage." His voice was low.

Clara nodded and kept smiling. Her heartbeat started to accelerate; here was the moment every girl longed for. Nothing was going to spoil it. Paolo looked away again and sighed:

"I am leaving you," he said quietly.

Silence fell in between them, Clara wasn't quite sure she heard it correctly.

"You mean... you're leaving me *here?*" What else could he mean? "To go where?"

"Clara, please." He sounded slightly annoyed.

"I'm not sure I understood. Can you say it again?"

"*I am leaving you. Like a boyfriend leaves his girlfriend.*"

He had pronounced each word with extreme clarity, there could be no misunderstanding this time. Clara felt dizzy for a few seconds; her heart had stopped beating altogether. Thank God she was sitting. Paolo took her hands, and held them:

"I'm sorry to have said it this way. I guess that no matter how you say it, it still sounds awful." He looked up with frustration. "I prepared for this moment so many times. I tried to think of ways of saying it that would be less hurtful, but I couldn't find one." He paused and then added: "Say something please, say something."

Clara's tongue was twisted in her mouth, she couldn't quite move it, perhaps the shock had affected her brain, and its signals to the rest of her body. She was incapable of articulating words. Words, words, what was there to say anyway?

Paolo shook her shoulders and tried to get some reaction from her; it worked.

"Of all days, did you have to dump me on my birthday?" she managed to say.

"I know, I know, it's terrible. But I've been meaning to do this for ages."

"Is that supposed to make me feel better?" She pulled her hands away.

"Oh God, I'm digging a deep hole in here…"

"Is this why you didn't get me any flowers? It's my birthday, after all."

"I… I just thought it'd be bad taste, to get you flowers and then… leave you." Paolo was definitely in trouble now.

"And you didn't notice my brand new sandals! Don't you even look at me these days?" Her tone was now furious.

He leaned towards her and tried to hug her.

"Don't you dare touch me! Or I'll make a scene here in Monte Urpinu. And everybody will know!" She felt like screaming, and hitting him and kicking him, but she was a lady, after all. Ladies don't attack men in public. Although newly-dumped-girlfriends have every right to. Paolo was quiet now, he'd better be. He'd done enough damage for the day. There he was, her beloved man, looking pale and uncomfortable, almost sad. What right did he have to be sad? *He* was the bad guy! So many thoughts were passing through Clara's head, but one was predominant:

"Why? I need to know why you're leaving me."

"I'm no longer in love with you." Paolo's reply was immediate; he didn't even have to think about it. Was Clara so obviously unlovable?

"How did you fall out of love? Did I do anything wrong?" She was inquisitive now. People just don't fall out of love, for no reason. It's just something that doesn't happen, it can't.

"To be honest Clara, I don't know." He paused, he was carefully looking for the right words. "We've been together for four years and in recent months I noticed that, somehow, I was getting used to you."

"Is this a bad thing? Because I am very much used to you!" Her voice was rising.

"I mean... this sounds horrible, but... you don't have that magic effect on me any more." Paolo was treading on dangerous ground. "What I mean is... I care for you, like a very good friend. But I don't feel that I look forward to seeing you every day, I no longer get excited when I hear your voice."

Clara was listening carefully, and every word Paolo said was an extra stab in her wounded heart. The torturer persisted:

"Clara, I do care for you and you're a great person. You don't deserve this and I'm being a bastard here. I know it. But, at the end of the day, I don't fancy you any more, this is really it."

For a second Clara regretted asking for explanations. Ignorance was definitely bliss at times. But she wanted more:

"What's wrong with me?"

"Nothing is wrong with you. You're a pretty girl, your big brown eyes and your soft skin... However... you've put on a bit of weight recently..."

That was the worst thing he could say.

"Do you think that I'm fat? Are you leaving me because I'm fat?" she asked in desperation.

"No, of course not. But to be honest, I preferred you

when you were slimmer…"

That was it. Her boyfriend, her Paolo, was leaving her because *he thought* she was fat. How low could a man get? What a worm! She'd heard enough now. Time to go. But one last thing needed to be sorted.

"What shall we do about work? What shall we tell our colleagues?" Her tone was distant.

"Let's just say that it was a mutual decision to split up. That we grew apart with time, or something like that." Again, his answer was quick. He'd thought this one through as well.

"Fine." She just wanted to get the hell out of there now. Monte Urpinu had never felt so inhospitable.

Clara drove back home on autopilot. It was almost ten in the evening and the family were probably still up. She desperately wanted to cry, but Mamma would be very upset if she saw her in tears, so she decided to keep all emotions inside. She could probably last for an hour at most, and then the volcano would have to erupt. What was she going to tell her parents now?

Since she got home early, could she get away with it and quietly sneak into her bedroom? She tried to unlock the front door with the utmost care, but Valentina happened to be in the corridor. Typical luck.

"Clara, you're already home! How come?" She was carrying her books.

"Hey Clara, look who's here! Zia Carmela! Come and say hello, she's got a surprise for you," shouted Mamma from the living room.

Clara was in no mood for visitors, let alone visitors with surprises. How strange, Zia Carmela didn't buy her birthday presents, usually. She didn't believe in them, like her brother, Nonno.

"Hello Zia Carmela," said Clara as she joined the family, who were comfortably spread out on the corner sofa.

"You look a bit pale, my dear." Zia Carmela kissed her on the cheek and handed her a big box wrapped with shiny silver paper and a red satin bow. "This will make you smile."

"What is it?" Clara's head felt fuzzy.

"It's an engagement present," whispered her great-aunt.

"What's going on here?" Clara looked at her parents, Valentina and Nonno, who all appeared perfectly happy, as they sipped their coffee.

"I told your Zia this afternoon." Mamma had a grin on her face. "I told her that Paolo was going to propose to you tonight, and she couldn't wait. She just went out and got you the first engagement present." She looked at Zia Carmela and they smiled at each other. "Come on, open it. Don't keep us waiting. We're all dying to know what's inside."

Clara had to sit down; the world was definitely spinning now. She carefully placed the large box on the floor. Things were looking pretty bad. There she was, at the centre of attention, surrounded by intrigued familiar faces. Nonno was the only one looking serious, as he smoked his pipe. His eyes were interrogating Clara's; he knew that something was up. Papà was still holding his paper, pretending to be interested in the latest local news. Mamma was nervously moving her hands on her lap, while Zia Carmela was simply enjoying her coffee. Valentina was sitting next to Clara, cross-legged, on the floor. The eye-tour was over, she had to talk.

"I can't open this present, I'm sorry."

"What? Why?" Mamma's voice was broken with surprise. "What's the matter?"

There was an embarrassing silence. Clara was wondering whether to tell them or not, maybe she should leave it to later? But it looked as if everybody was waiting for something.

"Paolo and I split up tonight."

"Nooo! That can't be right!" shouted Mamma.

Zia Carmela had to put her cup down, as her hands started to shake.

"What happened?" asked Papà.

Clara didn't want to cry in front of the family, but that heavy knot on her throat was preventing her from talking.

"Emergency procedure!" yelled Valentina as she got up. "I need to make a drink for Clara. Hot chocolate?"

"Definitely yes," mumbled Clara.

"Make a drink for me too." Nonno was chewing his pipe. "A mirto liqueur, please. Double."

"So, are you going to tell us what happened?" Zia Carmela had an exasperated tone.

"There isn't much to tell. Paolo told me tonight that he didn't love me any more and we should separate."

Again there was silence, broken only by Valentina, who was stirring the hot chocolate in the kitchen. Did she have to be so rough with that teaspoon? Was there a patent somewhere for rubber teaspoons?

"Have you ever slept with Paolo?" enquired Zia Carmela.

"Excuse me, but that's none of your business!" Clara was indignant.

"Well, you know what they say… once you've slept with a man, why would he want to marry you afterwards?" Her great-auntie knew it all.

"Times have changed. This is no longer the case. I can assure you, as a man," intervened Papà.

"In fact, times have changed so much that boyfriends will leave you if you *don't* sleep with them," contributed Valentina as she carried the hot chocolate to the living room.

"How dare he? How dare he leave my daughter?" Mamma stood up and waved her arms in the air. "That worm! I treated him like my own son Dino. And look what he does? He leaves my daughter!" She was very agitated now and her voice kept rising. "What a bastard! I knew that he wasn't to be trusted. I always suspected he was no gentleman!"

"Mamma, only today at lunchtime you said how much you liked him!" exclaimed Valentina. "Make your mind up please!"

"Be quiet. Show some respect for your mother," reprimanded Nonno.

"Will you excuse me? I'd really like to go to my bedroom now." This was getting too much for Clara. "Zia Carmela, I'm really grateful for your present, but I can't accept it. Is there any way you could take it back to the shop and have a refund?"

"No way. They'll never take it back." She seemed rather annoyed. Her forehead was corrugated and her nose and lips looked even thinner when she was disappointed. Her eyes were hidden behind fragile round glasses. "But I'll keep it for the future. Sooner or later you or Valentina will get engaged at some point, so it'll come useful." She got up and sighed heavily.

Zia Carmela looked even taller and slimmer now, and had her hair gone whiter? Perhaps it was the absurdity of the situation.

"That is... in the hope that neither of you becomes a spinster like me." She hugged Clara firmly, picked up the box from the floor and said goodbye to the family.

When the alarm clock went off the next morning, Clara's head was thumping. She had cried for forty-eight minutes and then ran out of tears. Her pillow was still damp and her bedroom bin was full of wet tissues. She'd asked so many questions to an invisible Paolo, but none of the answers she'd come up with had satisfied her. Still now, in this bright sunny morning, she couldn't quite understand why Paolo had left her. Had he been giving her hints or signs that she'd ignored? Was she so blindly in love with him that she couldn't see that he didn't care for her? Or perhaps, there was something seriously wrong with her that would make any boyfriend run away? That thought really hurt her, it was sharp and cruel.

Clara dragged herself to the kitchen, where her Mamma and Valentina were having breakfast.

"Please don't mention Paolo, nor my break-up. I'm not in the mood. Let's just have some peace and quiet," she muttered as she slumped on the kitchen chair.

"Are you well enough to go to work?" Mamma seemed concerned.

"I don't really have a choice. I've got to go."

"I think it'll do her good," said Valentina. "It'll be a distraction from her problems."

"What? With Paolo in the office next door?" questioned Clara.

Mamma and sister looked at each other; there was little they could say to console Clara. But Mamma had been to the bar round the corner and got some fresh pastries.

"Have one of these with your caffelatte."

"I'm only going to have one, and that's it. Just because you got them especially for me." Clara paused and then continued with a sad tone: "Mamma, from now onwards, no more cakes, sweets, ice-cream, and other nice things for me. I'm going on a diet. The fun is over."

She arrived at work at 08:30 sharp. She parked her Punto in the courtyard and swiped her card at the entrance. She liked to be on time, as the head of personnel was always on the look-out for staff that didn't do their thirty-nine hours a week. She wouldn't want to give him the satisfaction of noticing her being late, would she? The receptionist was on the phone, but she waved. Clara took the lift to the eighth floor. She turned right and went straight to her office. Her colleague Marcella was already there scribbling some notes. When she saw Clara she suddenly got up, came towards her and kissed her on the cheek:

"Happy birthday. Did you have a nice day yesterday?"

"Don't ask," Clara took her jacket off and sat at her desk.

"In fact you don't look too good." Marcella came closer to Clara. "Your face is all puffed up. Have you been crying?"

Gianna turned up at the door and shouted:

"How's our birthday girl today? We missed you yesterday."

"Shut the door please," whispered Clara.

Gianna obeyed instantly. Something was up.

"I've got some bad news." Clara took a deep breath.

"Paolo and I broke up yesterday."

"What? Are you sure? I saw him ten minutes ago and he looked fine!" Gianna was always very tactful.

"What happened?" Marcella looked worried.

"Well, there are two versions of the story," Clara crossed her arms.

"We're listening." Gianna sat on Clara's desk.

"The *friends* version, which is the *real* version, is that Paolo dumped me because he no longer loves me." Clara had to stop because the knot on her throat was coming back, like a traitor who hits unexpectedly. "The *work* version is that we both agreed to split up as it wasn't working out."

Marcella and Gianna looked at each other in disbelief.

"I can't... understand this," said Marcella. "He just looked so in love with you. Is he going mad?"

"He's certainly lost a few screws up there. You just don't dump a girl like Clara. He's going to find it really hard to replace you." That was Gianna's contribution.

Clara was silent, she was afraid to talk. The tears were approaching, and the minute she'd let them out, the whole office would be flooded.

"I don't want to sound nasty, but I'm sure that Miss shake-your-bum next door is going to jump at the opportunity straight away." Gianna whispered, pointing the finger at the opposite wall.

"Who? Teresa?" Clara was alarmed.

"Come on, Gianna. I never saw her flirt with Paolo." Marcella was coming to the rescue.

"She flirts with everybody. And she's always had a soft spot for Paolo, we know that. Why do you think she hates Clara so much?"

"I never realized that I was hated!" Clara was all the more confused as she looked blankly at the wall.

37

"Well, it's true that her skirts tend to be a bit too short for work." Marcella was now in deep thought. Was there any further evidence?

"And her tops too tight. For someone who's got such large boobs." Gianna was merciless.

"Come on, you yourself would want such large boobs, admit it." Marcella was now smirking.

"Who wouldn't?" Gianna had to agree.

"Stop it please. What's going on here?" Clara's headache was getting worse. "Are you telling me that Miss Shake-your-bum has got an interest in my boyfriend? Or rather, my ex-boyfriend?"

"Yes, and you'd better watch her. No man at Technosarda has been able to resist her charms, so far. Single or married."

It was 17:30 and Clara was happy to leave work. She decided to go for a walk and clear her head. Monte Urpinu was banned for a while, so she opted for another hill in Cagliari: San Michele. The view was just as spectacular from there, and most of the pathways were uphill and for pedestrian access only. Good exercise, ideal for her post-dumping slimming resolution. Besides, this oasis of green represented a comforting refuge for her troubled soul. As she almost reached the top of the hill, she was breathless, so she decided to sit down. Exercise was good, but not too much in one go. Her heart had already been weakened by Paolo, no need to cause a premature failure. In truth, she could've gone up a little further and reached the castle remains at the very top, but this spot was just as good.

She enjoyed the view of Cagliari, the city where she

was born, and maybe destined to stay for ever. The streets below felt alive, the tall buildings glowed in the light of the sun, but most of her attention was drawn towards the sea. Clara liked water, and no opportunity was ever missed to pay her respects to the Poetto sea, even from the distance, starting from the Devil's Saddle promontory. She then turned towards the Santa Gilla lagoon, in the hope of spotting a cormorant or a pink flamingo, but it was too far. She kept listening to the birds singing, but had no idea as to what birds they were. They just sounded good, and in tune, unlike her family yesterday when they'd sung her happy birthday. She reflected on the day just gone.

When she'd bumped into Paolo at the photocopier in the corridor, he'd smiled at her. He'd seemed mildly uncomfortable, what a cheek. She'd pressed the button for 100 copies, instead of 10, and only realized when it was too late. Then her boss, the director general, what an unpleasant character he was. Now, *he* was fat, in the real definition of the word. Fat and tall; and his size was proportionate to his stupidity, which never failed. She hated Mr Big-idiot, because he had this habit of asking her do work, which was naturally to be expected from a boss. But what was less nice, was to do work, undo it, and do it again. That morning Clara had written the letters of invitation for the board of directors' meeting. Mr Big-idiot had checked them and asked Clara to post them straight away, only to find out later on that he'd missed out one agenda item. So, just before lunch he'd asked Clara to send off a second set of letters, with an extra item on the agenda. Clara had felt bad in asking Ernesto, the office junior, to go to the post-office again, luckily he was always so polite and compliant. But when Clara came back from her lunch break, Mr Big-idiot had realized that he should have sent the budget document together with the letters. Would Clara send a third batch, enclosing the document? Of course, otherwise, how was she supposed to fill her time? Thank God for incompetence, she thought. At least the director general kept her busy.

Marcella and Gianna had been very supportive throughout the day; these were the two only friends at work she could rely on. Miss Shake-your-bum had been lurking around; Clara wondered if she already knew that Paolo was a free man. Somehow she seemed ready for the attack, her demeanour felt ultra-confident and her fake smile was stuck to her face with super-glue. Teresa was definitely an enemy, she even smelt like one. Were her hips swaying a bit more than usual today, or was Clara being paranoid? And how did she manage it, even when wearing flat shoes?

Chapter 4

Clara was still feeling the pain. Neither thinking about work, nor the view seemed to make it any better. They were right to talk about a broken heart, because hers felt like it'd been shredded to pieces and Paolo had trampled on them. She could just imagine her poor little heart inside, bleeding, and pleading for mercy, while he was slashing it into smaller bits. It was too much; she had to get away from it. What could it make it better? The enlightenment came soon: shopping. Of course, why didn't she think of it before? She didn't even take another look at the panorama, her healing mission was overdue. She walked briskly down the slope, towards her car.

She got to via Manno, her favourite shopping area of the city. On each side of the street there were shops selling all sorts of interesting things, such as shoes and clothes. Clara still had twenty-five euros left and was now determined to spend them. In fact, considering the traumatic set of circumstances, she might even spend more.

She pondered whether to go up the hill visiting the shops on the right, and then come back down, stopping at those on the left. But, maybe she might like to go further and see the other shops in via Garibaldi too? What was best? She decided to criss-cross via Manno, one shop to the right, one to the left, and so on. She was going to make sure she didn't skip a single window. The road was quite busy, it was meant to be a pedestrian area, except for taxis, police cars, and buses. But mischievous scooter riders were present all the time. Some of the shoppers were already carrying multiple bags, and she didn't want to arrive home empty-handed.

As she looked at the clothes, she was disconcerted to find that she couldn't get excited about anything. What was wrong with her? Normally she wanted to buy the entire boutique. But her real test came when she reached her usual shoe shop. Now, there was bound to be something she liked. She carefully examined all shoes and sandals, in all their shapes and colours, but the little voice 'buy-me, buy-me' that she was used to hearing, was not speaking today. What was the matter? Had they suddenly started to produce rubbish shoes? Junk clothes? She walked out feeling annoyed. It wasn't her day, really. Why bother looking at the other shops now? She may as well go home.

She reached Piazza Costituzione, the roundabout was busy and noisy, with cars waiting to race past, at the traffic light. Motorists in Cagliari just seemed so impatient: some kept pressing the accelerator just to show that they were ready to go; others liked to push the horn for no reason, sometimes only to encourage the car in front to move off one second before the green light appeared. She never understood them; they seemed to constantly chase each other, not minding for an instant the vulnerable pedestrians. And once they got to their destination, they'd get out of their cars, looking and acting perfectly relaxed. Perhaps they were just hurrying to get to the bar to enjoy their coffee. While Clara waited at the traffic light she spotted a young beggar. He was wearing purple baggy trousers, dirty trainers and a long-sleeved yellow shirt with a hole on the chest. What a combination of colours, she thought. His hair was in a mess, rasta style, tied up in a massive bundle behind his neck. But his face looked young and gentle.

"Any heavy coins in your pockets? Just give them to

me," the guy was shouting.

Clara looked away. Beggars always made her feel uncomfortable. Should she give them money or not? What if they spent it on drugs? Or alcohol? Was she really helping then?

"Come on, give me your spare coins. You don't want any holes in your pockets!" he kept yelling, as he crossed the road towards Clara. Should she turn round and leave in the opposite direction? Perhaps she could give him some money after all; maybe he'd buy a panino, or a pizzetta. He did look rather skinny.

"Hey, beautiful girl, don't run away. I only want your spare change." Yes, he was talking to Clara, no way out now.

"I'm not running away, the traffic light is green and I intend to cross." She felt proud for her politically correct reply.

"I'll cross with you then." He put his hands in his pocket and followed her.

Oh no, why were people looking at them? Did they think he was her friend? Wasn't it obvious that they had nothing in common?

"Hey, beautiful girl. Let's make a deal. If I guess how much you have in your purse, in spare coins, can I have them?" He seemed rather cheeky.

Clara was taken aback and stopped. She had lots of small coins, and there was no way he could guess. In fact, even *she* didn't know how much she had in change.

"OK then. You must guess exactly. Not a cent less, nor a cent more." Her look was defiant.

"Fine." He smiled, shook his rasta hair backwards and looked up. "You have two euros and seventy-five cents."

"Shall we check?" Clara was amused, as the guy seemed ultra-confident. She took the purse from her handbag and counted her coins. She had all sorts, five cents, ten cents, twenty cents, but not a single one euro coin. The total came to two euros and seventy-five. Surprise, surprise.

"How did you know?" Her eyes quizzed him intensely.

"Inspiration?"

"Well, I guess I just have to give them to you. You've earned them." Clara handed him the money. She was still puzzled. "Are you usually that good with numbers?"

"I never get it wrong." He held the coins tightly in his right hand.

There was a mischievous look in his face. That kind of expression of someone who knew something that she didn't.

"Thank you." He put the coins in his pocket, tightened his red sack on his back and walked away.

Clara had intended to spend her money that evening, but not quite that way. Anyhow, she hoped now that the young beggar would use those coins reasonably. Not that someone could buy a lot of drugs or alcohol with two euros and seventy-five cents. She was still at Piazza Costituzione, wondering where to go. As she faced the imposing Bastione building, she considered whether to go up there. She hadn't been for a while; it now appeared as if shopping wasn't such a good idea after all, and anyway, it was too early to go home and face Mamma's concerned face.

She took a good look at the white limestone edifice, with its grand arch at the top and double staircase at the front, one to the right and one to the left. How many steps, she wondered. She should know, as Papà used to take her and Valentina up there for a stroll, when they were younger; this was their Sunday afternoon pastime. Sometimes even Nonno would come. She used to count those steps and always reach the terrazza before Valentina. Nothing to be proud of, since she was just older and had longer legs... She wondered if she could go up the stairway, all the way to the Terrazza Umberto, without stopping. Was she fit enough? She tried it, but she had to stop four times. Still, not too bad. The terrazza was very ample and open, and she paced slowly, to catch her breath. The view over the city was almost 360 degrees. Even from here, she could admire the Poetto sea, shining under the evening sun. She looked down, towards the traffic below and remembered how, many years before, this was the spot that some people picked to commit suicide. Yes, it was incredible, how some human beings could have the courage to throw themselves from up here. Wouldn't they be scared?

She suddenly remembered Signor Peppino. How was he doing now? Did he still think about ending his life? He did promise that he wouldn't try to commit suicide again. But how could she be sure of that? Perhaps she should've got his phone number after all. Maybe she should've found out about his daughters and spoken to them. But was this fair? Was she supposed to interfere with people's lives in this way? She kept looking down. The piazza below felt very distant, and daunting. What courage would it take to jump from up here? People who did such thing, they must be absolutely desperate. Extremely unhappy, maybe the way she was feeling now.

"I wouldn't do it, if I were you," a soft female voice spoke behind her back.

"Do what?" Clara turned round.

"It's a rather messy business," said the girl who was facing Clara. "Broken bits of body, blood splattered everywhere. Definitely bad taste."

"Do I look like someone who's about to commit suicide?"

"You were thinking about death, and looking down."

"Wow, we've got someone who can read my thoughts!" Clara looked at the girl. Tall and blonde, with long straight hair, she looked of similar age to Clara, but was definitely prettier. In fact, she was beautiful, almost too beautiful. There was something familiar about her. Her big blue eyes were expressive and tender looking, her nose was small and proportionate and she had soft round lips and perfect white teeth. She moved very gracefully as she came closer to Clara.

"Death should not be taken lightly. And it should never be seen as the solution to your problems," the mysterious girl continued.

"Can we lighten up here? Change of subject perhaps?" Clara was feeling uncomfortable; it wasn't her style to talk to strangers, even if she was friendly by nature.

"What do you want to talk about?" the girl asked.

"I don't want to talk about anything. In fact, I'd rather be left alone, if you don't mind." Clara turned her back to the girl, and looked at the view.

"No need to be rude, just because your boyfriend left you." The stranger was now pacing up and down behind Clara.

"Do we know each other?" Clara was shocked as she couldn't remember where she met this blonde.

"I'm Lucilla." She extended her hand towards Clara who automatically shook it.

"So, Miss Lucilla, do you go round the streets chatting

to people you don't know?"

"No, I'm usually very selective whom I talk to." She had such calm, relaxing voice. Clara could almost fall asleep. Yes, she must be dreaming.

"How do you know about my boyfriend?"

"You just look like someone who's been recently dumped." There was no emotion in her voice, despite the fact that what she said didn't sound very nice.

"And how does a 'dumpee' look like then?"

"They walk slowly, looking down. It seems as if their shoulders carry the weight of the entire planet. Their eyes are lifeless, with a hint of desperation."

"Wow. So everybody in via Manno has noticed?"

"No, they don't care really. But the beggar did." Lucilla still sounded calm.

"How long have you been following me?" Clara was getting suspicious.

"All your life."

How was Clara supposed to take that?

Lucilla continued: "That silver Punto you've got…"

"Oh, now you know even what car I drive!" Something definitely wasn't right. "Could you see my dumpee look even through the windscreen?"

"Get rid of it." Lucilla's sentence sounded like an order.

"No way, I adore my car. It's my first one!" protested Clara.

"It's not good enough." Lucilla was now moving away.

"Good enough for what?"

There was no answer. When Clara turned round, Lucilla had gone.

Clara finally got home and was still puzzled. Had it been a weird day, or was everything normal? Maybe the fact that she was still upset about the split-up made her perceive the world in a different way. Strange things seem to happen when you get emotional, perhaps she should just forget about it and start all over again.

The entire family was in the kitchen, the heart of her home. Nonno had just cut a piece of focaccia and had left the crusty bits for Clara, on her plate, while Papà was opening a bottle of wine. As Clara went in, the kitchen went quiet.

"Please, don't mention what happened yesterday. I'm trying to forget." Clara crossed her arms.

Everybody sat at the table, except Mamma who was draining the spaghetti. Valentina broke the silence to talk about her maths teacher, and Clara was glad that the attention was being focussed on someone else. She looked at her Nonno. His hair was almost white. His beard and moustache were slightly darker, and made him look wise. He always kept his facial hair well-trimmed and liked to wear nice clothes. His grey waistcoat matched his trousers, and his watch chain was hanging from the side pocket. It was almost summer, and he still wore waistcoats, everybody teased him for that. Valentina was still talking, while Mamma was pouring the tomato sauce on the pasta. Papà was listening carefully as he filled the glasses. Clara liked the fact that he always paid attention to his children, he seemed to take an interest in everything they did. She knew how much Papà missed her older brother Dino, who now had a family of his own. Papà was sipping his wine and unfolding his napkin. He had a gentle, calm nature and never liked to hurry. Unlike her Nonno, Papà had lost all his hair and was practically bald. When they were little they used to call him 'light bulb', because his scalp would shine in the sun. His face was oval and he had bright dark eyes, masked by round glasses. His spectacles made him look like the intellectual in the family, which he, no doubt, was.

"The pasta is overcooked." Valentina had only had one bite.

"I was hoping you wouldn't notice," apologized Mamma. She looked rather frazzled.

"This isn't nice. Your Mamma has taken all the trouble to cook and all you can do is to criticise," reproached Nonno. "And anyway, I like it this way. I don't have to chew so much."

"I don't want to add insult to injury, but… it's also a bit insipid." Papà had very high standards when it came to food.

"I know, I know. I just can't quite concentrate today." Mamma sounded agitated as she put her fork down.

"What's the matter?" asked Clara.

"You know what the matter is. I'm so upset, I just can't accept what Paolo has done to you!" Her voice was already going up.

"Mamma, let it go. There's nothing we can do."

"I can't understand this! I seem more upset than you! And I didn't even like that guy!" She banged her fist on the table.

"Come on, Maria. Clara's young, she'll find someone else!" Papà touched her arm trying to calm her.

"When? When? She's twenty-five now. At her age I was already married and had two children!" she seemed more and more exasperated.

"But times are different now. People don't get married so young," commented Valentina.

"Exactly, that's the problem. By the time she finds another boyfriend it'll be two to three years, then they probably won't marry for another five to six years, by the time she has her first child she could be retiring!"

"Thanks very much!" Clara felt angry. "This is a great encouragement for me! Precisely what I need to hear!" She tried to shut her ears with her hands.

"Stop it Maria." Nonno's voice was stern. "Clara is still young and it's better that she's alone, rather than going out with that ... worm!" He dabbed his lips with the yellow napkin. "Sometimes bad things happen for a reason. She'll probably be grateful for this, in the future."

Mamma went quiet. Her father was her father, she'd always obey him. Papà secretly hoped that he'd have the same effect on his wife, one day.

"By the way, the pork escalopes are tough," remarked Clara.

Revenge, sweet revenge. And yet, it didn't make her feel any better.

Chapter 5

Clara had managed to sleep well that night. No matter what the trouble was in her life, it was almost impossible to suffer with insomnia. However, she had cried again, before falling asleep; but this was part of her plan. She had decided to adopt a new strategy to cope with her pain. Since she was bound to bump into Paolo at work and be reminded of him all the time, she couldn't afford to break into tears every ten minutes. It wasn't really practical and it was damn embarrassing too. So, she'd decided that she'd put on a brave face for the days ahead and pretend that everything was fine. She'd lock inside herself, every negative, sad, desperate feeling she had, packing everything in tightly and securely, during her waking hours. However, before going to sleep every night, in the privacy of her own room, she'd open the door of the prison and release all those sentiments. She'd cry for however long she needed to, shamelessly, freely. She could then fall asleep and start again. It's not that she would cry-on-command. The tears were ready to get out by then, it was just a matter of relaxing for a second, and they'd break every possible barricade she'd carefully put up. On her first night as a single girl, she'd cried for forty-eight minutes. On her second night, her tears had lasted for forty-five. Did it mean that the pain was becoming more bearable? Perhaps, in the near future, she'd weep less and less, and a shorter duration of crying-time would indicate that she was getting over Paolo. Could things be that simple?

"Clara, get up." Mamma's voice was tender as she gently knocked on her door. "You've got to get ready for work."

"Coming," responded Clara with a croaky voice.

It was difficult looking forward to the day ahead. Another boring task at the office, the same useless conversation with Mr Big-idiot, and worst of all, breakfast without pastries. Where was the fun? Mamma did say that going on a diet when you're down is the worst thing someone can do, but Clara had decided to be stoical. And she had to face reality: if Paolo had left her because she was fat, she needed to be doing something about it. Perhaps, if she became slim again, he might have second thoughts.

She went to the kitchen, and sat with Mamma. They apologized to each other for having said the wrong thing the night before. Mamma looked a bit more relaxed this morning. Her brown curly hair was tidier and her forehead looked less tense. Her hazel eyes were more sympathetic and her full lips couldn't stop talking. She was wearing her stripy white and blue apron, which outlined a soft bump over her maternal breasts. Her figure was round and resembled the ladies of the Renaissance paintings. Still, she had a well defined waistline, which gave her the hour-glass shape that was so feminine.

"Mamma, you know how some people count sheep before they go to sleep?"

"Yes."

"Last night I counted butterflies. They're kind of nicer. More colours." Clara had a sip of caffelatte.

"Well, you should count how many minutes you've got left, as it's almost eight."

Clara hadn't realized that time had gone so fast. What were the clocks doing? Racing against each other? She reluctantly got ready and said goodbye.

As she left the main entrance, she noticed a few people standing right where she'd parked her car last night. She curiously approached the spot and was shocked to see the catastrophe: her cute, wonderful, silver Punto had been crushed by a Jacaranda tree. No, it couldn't be. She shut her eyes and opened them again; the scene hadn't changed. The beautiful lilac flowers were spread all over. Some were still holding on to their mini-branches, and looked like trumpet-shaped grapes joined to form purple bundles. The bulky trunk was aligned right in the middle on the roof-top, whilst its pretty mauve flowers were distributed equally all over the car, leaving no visible area on the body of her Punto. On another occasion, Clara could've admired the artistic effect, but she couldn't appreciate it at that moment.

She had to rub her eyes, perhaps she was still sleepy? That did look like *her* car. She brushed some of the lilac flowers away. Please, let it be another silver Punto, with the same car plate. Everybody was questioning how this strange thing had occurred. That Jacaranda had been there for ages. Signor Gabriele, her next-door neighbour, was in the crowd too and confirmed that he'd always known that tree, since he moved in the palazzo, which must have been a century ago.

"Is this your car?" asked a traffic warden looking at Clara.

"Yes," she managed to whisper. Her vocal chords had gone on strike.

"Any idea as to how this happened?" the man in uniform was scratching his head.

"There were no hurricanes last night, as far as I remember," commented Signor Gabriele. He was trying to be funny, but Clara wasn't amused.

A gentleman in a navy suit examined the scene. Was

he some kind of expert of trees falling on cars? "This is bizarre." He spoke like a judge pronouncing a verdict. "It looks like someone has pulled the tree from its roots, shaken its flowers off, and thrown it on top of the car."

"How likely is that?" the warden quizzed the people around him. "Has anybody witnessed anything? Any rough looking boys in the area last night?"

"Are you all right?" asked an old lady looking at Clara.

"I'll go and call your mum." Signor Gabriele hurried towards the palazzo.

Clara could hardly feel her limbs. The blood had ceased to circulate in her body, this wasn't happening. It just wasn't. It was still part of the nightmare, of which she hadn't woken up yet.

"The car is badly damaged," said the warden as he inspected what now looked like a crushed can. "Everything is shattered. All the windows and all doors." He brushed away some of the lilac flowers. "There is not one seat that is intact, and God knows what it's done to the engine."

"I can't believe that a fallen tree can do so much damage," said the gentleman in a suit.

Two hours later Clara was driving to work in Mamma's car. To her surprise, Mamma had been quite good, she hadn't fainted, and she had dismissed the incident as bad luck. Clara had called Papà who'd promptly appeared at the scene. Luckily Papà worked for an insurance company, he knew about cars and accidents, and stuff like that. He said he'd take care of that, and Clara now wondered if he meant that he could resurrect her beloved Punto. She was late for work, and wasn't proud of swiping her card that morning. She had informed them of the accident, so she wasn't expecting a telling off.

"Is there going to be a day in which you turn up and bring me good news?" asked Marcella as she saw Clara appear in the office.

"I wonder." She took her jacket off and sat at her desk. She automatically switched her computer on.

"How did this happen? Trees don't just fall on cars. At least not on a warm, tranquil May night."

"How am I supposed to know?" Clara was rather fed up now. "And, why did it have to fall on *my* car, of all cars parked in via Milano?"

"Perhaps because you parked right beside it?" Gianna entered the office and, as usual, sat on Clara's desk. "Did you have to pick that spot?"

"Well, it was the only one free at the time." Clara was feeling truly miserable now.

"And the bad news isn't over yet." Gianna was carefully examining her nails.

"Oh no, what now?" Could things actually get any worse?

"Leave her alone," said Marcella. "It's not the right time."

"No, no. I'm ready. I am so low, that I can't get any lower than this." Clara almost smiled.

"OK. I'll try to say it gently." Gianna cleared her throat. "This morning, while you were absent, Miss Shake-your-bum was chatting to Paolo in the corridor."

"Great." Clara closed her eyes.

"You should've seen her. Her skirt was even shorter than usual and she was definitely batting her eye-lids." Gianna looked disgusted.

"It's true. I've seen her too," added Marcella, with an

uneasy tone.

"And I've heard her ask Paolo if he'd join her and friends for a pizza tonight!" Gianna suddenly got up and carried on. "The cow! She doesn't waste any time, does she?"

"What did Paolo say? Did he accept the invitation?" Clara's vocal chords were playing up again.

"I couldn't hear. Mr Big-idiot stopped by in that instant and asked me something. He always picks the right time!"

Clara's phone rang. It was Papà.

"Clara," he said with a broken voice. "The expert has checked the car and said that it's not worth fixing it. It's a scrap-yard job."

"No!" Clara's scream came out without her consent.

"Please calm down. I've got worse to tell you."

"Dad, it can't get any worse, I can't believe it can!"

"Listen to me. I don't know how to tell you this, but … the insurance won't cover the cost of replacing the car."

"What do you mean? I thought we were fully insured!"

"Yes, third party, theft, fire, vandalism. But not for natural disasters. They just don't happen in Sardinia." He sounded shattered.

"No, they just happen to me." Clara's eyes were veiling with tears as she put the phone down.

It just wasn't her day. Some days are good, some are bad, but recently there seemed to have been a concentration of bad days. Clara wasn't superstitious but it did occur to her that perhaps she'd been bewitched. It was too much of a coincidence. She picked a pile of papers from her desk and went straight to the photocopier. Twelve copies of each set of documents; that would keep her occupied for the next hour, especially as the machine always played up when she used it. As she gazed at the light under the copier cover move from left to right, she felt quite lost, almost in a trance. Strange days. Wasn't there a song by The Doors with that title? What was it about? As she watched the machine spit out her copies, she was glad to have the corridor to herself, while everybody was on lunch break.

"How are you today, Clara?"

She jumped as she heard Ernesto's voice.

"You seem lost in another world." He was unloading some large boxes of paper on the floor. "I'm... almost OK. And you?"

"Good. I'm looking forward to my lunch break; any minute now." He looked at his watch.

"What's on the menu at the restaurant then?"

"I'm going home. Mum's cooking is always the best and I'd like to play some music too."

"Can you manage all that? Drive there and back, eat a whole meal, and also play music, all in one hour?" Clara was intrigued.

"Yes, with the Vespa you move faster than with a car." By now, he'd stopped unloading boxes and was standing with his arms crossed, slightly shifting his body weight from one leg to the other. Ernesto had always been shy and found it hard talking to his colleagues. "To be honest... sometimes I take longer than an hour." He winked.

"Naughty boy!" Clara waved her finger at him.

"Great sandals! What an unusual colour too. Very original," he said with a timid voice, as he stroked his chin.

"That's the best thing I've heard in days! Thank you Ernesto!" She was flattered. Finally someone had noticed her brand new sandals. And this was a guy she hardly talked to! In fact, why hadn't she spoken to him that much before? He was rather cute.

"You always wear nice clothes. I think you're the best dressed girl in Technosarda!" The instant he finished his sentence, he looked away.

"Carry on, carry on. I could do with some compliments today." Clara was laughing now.

"How much time have you got?"

"All afternoon." Clara felt uplifted; perhaps life wasn't so bad after all. But then she asked: "Have you spoken to Marcella or Gianna? Have they *paid* you to come and talk to me?"

"No, I don't talk to them. In fact, I try to avoid them. Every time I bump into them, especially Marcella, they give me loads of extra work! I've got enough to do."

"So, what do you actually do here? I mean, between lunch breaks." She had a teasing look.

Ernesto looked up and pretended to be thinking really hard. Clara was no longer paying attention to the photocopier and was just noticing his eyes for the first time. They were dark green, how unusual. And they looked perfect with his tanned olive skin. His straight hair and thick eyebrows were black, and he had a very friendly smile. She felt comfortable with him straight away. And guess what? He was taller than Paolo. But why was she comparing them now? Was it really necessary?

"I do a lot of important things. Such as going to the post office three times a day for you, and half a dozen times for the others." He was still stroking his chin. "Then I run every conceivable errand for every director we've got in this place, which includes picking up their car from the garage, collecting their dry cleaning, buying light bulbs for their desk lamps. I have no idea as to why light bulbs last such a short time in this place! Then, between unjamming the photocopier and changing the toner, I also repair leaking pipes, fix the air conditioning and the heating, destroy confidential documents and tape them back together when they get it wrong. Any more?"

"God, I thought my job was bad!" Clara was truly amused.

"It's not so bad, really. I'm glad that I've got a job. With the unemployment we've got in Sardinia, I consider myself lucky."

What a nice person. There she was, complaining about her own misfortunes, and here was Ernesto, who had a rather unpleasant job, saying that he felt lucky. Perhaps she'd just been ungrateful all this time and taken for granted the good things she had in life, and maybe these last days she was being punished for that. Maybe she ought to put everything in perspective again, she thought, as Ernesto left for lunch.

On the way home that evening, Clara decided to stop for a coffee at the bar, outside Technosarda. Since she got to work very late, she hadn't had a lunch break, and by now she needed a rest. She picked a quiet corner and was pleased to sit at a table, for a change, while sipping her espresso. Usually, when they had a break at the office, they drank their coffee standing at the bar, this time it was a real luxury to have her drink sitting down.

"Can I join you?" a familiar voice asked from behind.

Clara didn't need to turn round. She recognized Lucilla's voice. What was she doing there?

"To be honest, I quite like the idea of sitting by

myself."

Lucilla disregarded Clara's wish and grabbed a chair. She looked radiant and her blonde hair was tied up at the back. "I gather you're car-free now?"

"Anything to do with you?" Clara wondered if this charming girl, with a foreign look, could lift a tree from its roots and throw it onto her car, but it didn't seem that plausible.

"I told you that the Punto wasn't good enough." She handed Clara a set of keys and added. "But for every problem, there's a solution. Here are the keys to your new car."

Why did her voice sound so serene, so tranquil? Almost as if she'd said 'life is great'. Clara was still hearing the echo of her voice, when she realized what Lucilla had actually said.

"What's going on here? Why do you want me to have your car?" She was bewildered, to say the least.

"It's not my car. It's yours." Lucilla opened her bag and retrieved a set of papers, which she showed to Clara. "These are the registration documents. They're in your name. Just check that all the details are correct please."

"But, but... it says that the car is a Ferrari!" Clara gasped.

"Yes, it's a Ferrari Challenge Stradale. The latest model. You'll like it."

Clara was speechless; she didn't know what to say.

"I took the liberty of ordering it in red. I think it's cool; hope you don't mind." Again, her voice was so relaxed and composed. "I've parked it outside your residence. You'll find it as you get home later."

"Let me pay for my coffee and we'll discuss this outside." Clara was agitated. She frenetically headed towards the till. When she walked back to the table, she saw that Lucilla had gone. However, she'd left a set of keys and documents by the sugar bowl.

Chapter 6

As Clara drove home, she was feeling uneasy. Did the mysterious Lucilla truly buy her a Ferrari? Or was it a sick joke? Her nerves felt too fragile at the moment, for jokes of this type. What did this girl want from her anyway? As if she didn't have enough on her plate already.

The traffic was bad. Most people were leaving work now, and surely there was the odd motorist who needn't be on the road. Some people from Cagliari were truly lazy; they'd drive when they could walk, even when they knew it'd take them longer to reach their destination. These guys were Clara's favourites. It was hot and she was annoyed that Mamma's car didn't have any air conditioning. Luckily, the breeze, albeit warm, was slightly refreshing, through the open windows. She couldn't wait to be home. She was anxious to find out.

As she approached via Milano, she saw the flashy car, parked outside her palazzo. Could it be another odd coincidence? To her surprise, Papà with her brother Dino were standing next to the red Ferrari inspecting it. Clara parked and quickly joined them. She was feeling confused and still agitated.

"Hey Dino, nice to see you. Where's Ivan?" Clara approached the two men.

"Isn't this beautiful?" replied Dino, as he caressed the shiny car door.

"It's a work of art, so perfect that you're even afraid to touch it." Papà seemed mesmerised.

"Will someone take notice of me?" demanded Clara.

"Sorry sister." Dino kissed her on the cheek. "I just came to visit the family and couldn't believe what car was parked next to our flat. You don't see them very often."

He couldn't take his eyes off the Ferrari.

"I didn't even know the Challenge Stradale was for sale yet. It must be one of the first bought in Sardinia." Papà looked inside trying to capture every detail. "I wonder who it belongs to. Lucky man."

"Why do you assume this car belongs to a man?" Clara was amused.

"Well, you don't see many women driving a Ferrari," responded her brother. "And let's face it, even if you saw one, she probably would drive it like a pram, which defeats the object."

"Oh, I see." Clara was taking her time. This could truly be her latest toy; she'd better take a good look at it. The plate number was the same as the one on the registration documents. The ones which had her name on. Apparently Lucilla hadn't been joking. Clara took a deep breath. What did this mean? That this monster of a car was actually hers? The Ferrari was like a red devil, shiny, elegant, aggressive. Perhaps Dino was right, it wouldn't be the car she'd have picked. Too showy for her. But she couldn't help admire its design, it was truly a racing car, low on the ground, massive wheels, aerodynamic shape, but that white strip in the middle, running from the front to the back, well, it wasn't really her taste.

"This is the lightest Ferrari on the road, so far," commented Dino. "Not to mention the power. This devil's peak power output has been raised to 425 CV at 8,500 rpm, which gives it an exceptional rating of 118.5 CV/litre." He sounded like a car manual.

Papà was smiling, as he continued to inspect the car through the window.

"So, how fast can it go?" All those numbers didn't really mean much to Clara.

"About 300 kilometres per hour." Dino looked at her with challenging eyes.

"As if we could ever go that fast here! With those speed checks everywhere, it's no use having such a car." Clara shrugged her shoulders and handed him the keys. "Shall we take a look inside?"

Dino and Papà stopped talking, their jaws had dropped.

"It's mine," said Clara calmly.

"How on earth?" Papà's mouth was still open.

"It's a present. Someone bought it for me." She handed him the registration papers.

Papà grabbed them and read the papers carefully.

"These certificates seem real. I'll have to make a phone call. It looks like the car was bought in Modena." Papà was shuffling the papers looking stunned.

"While you make that phone call, shall we try this thing? Dino, you have to show me how to drive it."

"With pleasure!" Dino was still shaking his head in disbelief.

They jumped inside and were hit by the fragrance of leather and that 'brand new' polish. The interior was simple, almost bare, but the red seats were very supportive.

"Sheer luxury," exclaimed Dino. "Even with its simplicity in the interior, you cannot but admire the high quality of the materials." He was touching everything.

Clara grasped the leather-bound wheel and stared at the centrally positioned rev counter. It looked rather cute with its yellow graphics and red indicator.

"Come on Clara, turn the engine on, I want to hear it." He was very excited.

Clara turned the ignition key on, but nothing happened.

"You've got to push that big red button on the centre console," explained Dino.

How did he know? It sounded as if her brother had designed the damn thing. The car came to life, the sound was thrilling and made Clara put her foot down on the accelerator, just for fun.

"Come on, first gear." Dino pointed at the steering wheel and paddle to change gears.

Clara was nervous, but the sensation was phenomenal as the Ferrari charged forward, almost with a thump at the back. She could've never imagined that a car could respond so quickly to the touch of her right foot.

"Just go quickly round the block, I want to drive it now." Dino was impatient, while her father was on the mobile phone, standing on the pavement.

"Let me get the hang of it. This is *my* car, after all!" protested Clara.

She carefully tried the second and third gear, but was afraid to go any faster. It was better to stick for a tour around the block, on her first attempt. She discovered that her red devil also had a sixth gear. When would she ever be able to use it? Anyway, she was very happy in the second gear, she just liked to play tunes with that engine. And she adored it when she used the brakes. What excellent stopping power. Exactly what she needed, in case she got carried away.

"This is great. But I've had enough now." She stopped the car next to Papà, who was still examining the papers.

The passers-by were looking at them, even Signor Gabriele had turned up to admire the new toy.

"Who wants to come for a ride?" Dino's head was sticking out from the window.

"Can I? But please, I'm eighty-five, could you drive

carefully?" Signor Gabriele asked politely.

"This is no car for the faint-hearted." Dino was a bit disappointed, but then, on an impetus of good-will he added: "OK then, since it's the first time I drive it, I'll be gentle. Come on in."

"What about dad? It should really be his turn for a ride now," complained Clara.

"Don't worry, the elderly should go first." Papà smiled and helped Signor Gabriele get in, while holding his stick. He then looked at Clara, with a puzzled expression. "These registration documents are real. The car was bought new in Modena, and registered in your name."

"I thought so." Why wasn't she surprised?

"Well… the strange thing is that it was bought today… How could they get it to Sardinia so fast?"

"It's a Ferrari, isn't it?" Clara was trying to be funny, what else could she say?

Papà quizzed her intensely: "They can go fast, but they can't swim, nor fly."

"I don't know Papà. Maybe Lucilla ordered it a while ago, and it just happened to be delivered today." She raised her hands and looked up.

"Who's Lucilla?"

Clara looked away; she had no idea what to say. The truth was that she didn't know.

"Someone I met on the Bastione yesterday. She just got chatting to me, and then I bumped into her again at the bar near work today." Clara paused, and reflected on what she'd just said; it did sound out of the ordinary. "She told me that I needed a new car, so she gave me the registration documents and keys for the Ferrari, and then disappeared." She looked at Papà. "Sounds strange, doesn't it?"

"Strange isn't the right word." Her father looked confused. "I don't think the right word for this exists in the dictionary."

Mamma had invited Dino and little Ivan to stay for dinner. His wife Orietta was working at the hospital tonight, and Dino was always appreciative of Mamma's cooking.

"Why is Ivan eating his penne with tomato sauce?" asked Nonno.

"Because he doesn't like the gorgonzola sauce. Some children aren't that keen on cheese," replied Dino.

"I don't agree with cooking different dishes for different members of the family," objected Nonno as he tucked his napkin on the shirt collar. "Everybody should eat the same thing."

Valentina raised her eyebrows and winked at Dino.

"I've seen you, naughty girl." Nonno aimed his fork at her. "I also think that it isn't fair on whoever's cooking. If you have five children, and each of them wants to eat something different, should the mother cook five dishes?" He looked at Mamma.

"And who says it's the *mother* who's got to cook all the time?" objected Valentina.

"I don't mind, honestly. I always have some tomato sauce in the fridge. I just put the condiment for Ivan in a separate bowl, that's all." Mamma's voice was gentle. Nothing was ever much trouble when it came to her grandson.

"Well, I just think that youngsters today always get everything they want. They will end up spoilt when they become adults, that's all." Nonno was never easily persuaded.

"What do you think of Clara's new car?" Dino was keen to change the subject.

Nonno's eyes lit up. "What a great surprise. I loved the tour you took me on. What power that machine has, just incredible." He pushed his fist in the air.

"I loved it. There's something wild and crazy about that car. You just want to put your foot down," intervened Valentina.

"But you haven't even got your driving licence yet," pointed out Papà.

"Wait till I get it!"

"I told Zia Carmela on the phone earlier, and she's coming tomorrow to try it," Mamma was laughing. She could just picture her own auntie sitting in that car.

"Without asking my permission? Don't forget that it's my car, I may need to use it tomorrow." Clara had a mischievous look.

"Well, as your older brother... who taught you how to drive, I have a certain entitlement to use the Ferrari, occasionally."

"I suggest you draw a chart and we take it into turns." Nonno Pietro was quick. "I'm happy with just taking her for a ride once a week."

"Wait a second," interrupted Papà as he poured some wine. "Is it me, or what?"

Everybody looked at each other, while little Ivan was flying two of his penne, pretending they were airplanes.

"My daughter, Clara, goes out this morning and finds out that her Punto has been crushed by a Jacaranda tree." Papà cleared his throat and continued. "Later on, someone, a mysterious Lucilla, buys a Ferrari and gets it here all the way from Modena, only to give keys and registration documents to Clara around six in the evening.

Does this sound normal?"

"Has this Lucilla asked you to do anything for her?" Mamma questioned Clara.

"Good point. Does she want anything in return?" asked Dino.

"To be honest, I've barely spoken to the girl. She gave me the keys and disappeared within seconds!" Clara too was puzzled, to say the least.

"The good thing is that the car wasn't stolen. It's a legitimate purchase," Papà reassured everybody.

"So, what are we worrying about then?" Valentina asked naively.

"True. What is given is given. Enjoy it, for as long as you've got it." Nonno was usually quite wise, why not listen to him? He raised his wine glass and declared: "Cheers! To the new car."

"They do say that there isn't such a thing as a free lunch…" pointed out Dino.

"You're getting a free meal now, what does that tell you?" remarked Mamma as she placed the grilled sea bass on her son's plate.

As per tradition, the men of the family were enjoying a Mirto liqueur in the living room, while the ladies cleared up the kitchen. Ivan had no intention of going to sleep and was playing with the remote control. Papà, Dino and Nonno were still talking about the Ferrari and Clara was glad to be away from what had now become a boring list of engine details, kilometres per hour, revs per minute, acceleration times, and so on. The excitement had worn off. Yes, it was great having a Ferrari, and a free one came even more welcome, but the truth was that she only wanted a car to get from one place to another, and it didn't really matter what car it was. She wondered what on earth Lucilla meant with that gesture. As she rinsed the dishes she tried to imagine what could happen next, somehow there was unfinished business there. And anyway, with all this Ferrari hassle she hadn't even had the time to think about Paolo in the last few hours. *He* was the one who mattered, not that stupid car. She remembered how she'd run into him on the stairs at work, and how he'd smiled at her. His expression was apologetic, almost as if he was sorry to have made her suffer. Clara didn't want his pity; that was for sure.

"You're thinking about him, aren't you?" Mamma was drying the cutlery.

"Yes, it's still early days yet." Clara's voice was low.

"What would help you to forget him?" Valentina was adding more soap to the dishes. "The problem is that he's such a nice person, that he's difficult to dislike."

"Difficult? I hate him already," was Mamma's reaction.

"Why? He hasn't done anything wrong really. He hasn't cheated on me, he's never mistreated me. He simply fell out of love with me. Does this make him a bad man?" Clara was feeling even sadder.

"Not to love my daughter is a big fault, as far as I'm concerned."

"Come on Mum. Clara's right. Give him a break," said Valentina.

"I find it hard, the fact that we're no longer together. But the hardest of all is to imagine him with another woman." Clara was in distress.

"Has he got someone else then?" Mamma's tone was raising.

"No, not yet. But Miss-Shake-your-bum has already

asked him out," Clara spoke with a flat tone.

"Is she the bitch working in the office next-door to yours?" asked Mamma with contempt.

"Mum! I never heard you use that word before!" Valentina seemed baffled.

"For certain people, certain words are appropriate."

"I think I should go to bed. It's been a long day." Clara wiped her hands and went to the living room to say goodnight.

She smiled to see the four generations of men playing together. Papà had dug out the old Lego pieces and they were building something. Clara took a closer look, and she wasn't surprised to see that the construction appeared to be a big, what else? Nonno and Ivan were arguing as to where the wheels should go; Dino was more interested in getting the right colours to match, while Papà was inspecting the whole frame, making sure that each component was placed in the right position. Four boys working on the same project, they seemed to be doing well.

"Why can't my car have five wheels?" asked Ivan's cute voice.

"Well, it can have a fifth wheel, but it has to stay in the boot. It's called the spare wheel," Nonno patiently explained.

"But I want all the wheels to go round," insisted Ivan.

"The car can't have five wheels, four at most," clarified Papà.

"But I want five," persisted little Ivan. "And they all have to move."

"You're a stubborn little boy." Nonno was caressing the child's soft hair.

"Just like his dad," commented Clara.

"What's he to do with me? I'm just helping out here."

"With colour-coordination?" Clara winked. "If you truly want to help, explain to your son the five wheels thing."

"I thought we'd all had enough of cars today," declared Mamma as she carried coffee into the living room.

"Not for me, Mum. I'm going to bed." Clara kissed her nephew and left.

As she brushed her teeth in the bathroom, Clara was glad to be alone. She loved her family's company, but sometimes she also needed to have some time to herself. She was looking forward to going to her bedroom to think freely about Paolo, perhaps cry as well. She needed to have her forty-five minute session of mourning, before going to sleep. She also needed to try and make sense of what had happened today, with those two cars. Her old one and her new one. And, last but not least, try and figure out what this girl called Lucilla could want from her. She went to her bedroom and shut the door behind her. She switched the light on.

"I was wondering when you were going to come. I've been waiting for ages."

Clara startled. Lucilla was lying on her bed holding one of her books.

"How did you get in?" Clara's voice went faint.

"Through the window." Lucilla pointed at the open window.

"But we're on the fifth floor!"

"Long ladder?" Lucilla was calm, as usual. When she spoke, nothing seemed out of the ordinary.

Clara's heart was beating faster than normal. She was

tempted to look out of the window, but she thought better. She grabbed her chair, from under the desk, and sat down slowly, facing Lucilla, who was still lying comfortably on her bed.

"What is it with your family? You said goodnight half an hour ago, but you still carried on chatting."

"What do you want?" Clara crossed her arms and looked at the girl. She wondered if she was a foreigner, she had an unusual accent, but she couldn't quite define it.

"I'm here to ask you a favour."

"I thought so. I just couldn't expect to get a Ferrari for nothing!" Clara tried to imagine what this girl could want from her. She hoped it was nothing illegal, or immoral.

"Do you think you're ready?"

"Ready for what?" Should Clara get worried? This girl might ask her to do something dodgy, stealing perhaps?

"Why are you worried about stealing?" Lucilla looked at Clara intensely. "It's not that you're whiter than white."

"What? Stealing? I never mentioned it." Clara was perturbed. "In any case, I'm an honest person, I wouldn't do such thing."

"You're a liar. You've stolen before." Lucilla was cool.

"That's not true!"

"Easter 1990, you were twelve years old and stole an Easter-egg." Her tone was composed.

Clara had to think back, was there a blonde girl at Sunday school who could've been Lucilla? It was so long ago.

"The nuns asked us to choose between plain chocolate and milk chocolate, and I couldn't make up my mind."

"So you took the plain chocolate one in front of

them, and stole the milk chocolate egg when they weren't looking."

"But I was only twelve years-old! And it was a small egg anyway!" Clara felt vaguely ashamed.

"Stealing is bad, whether you take small or large, it's still bad."

Clara was embarrassed for having been found out. She thought she got away with it. After taking that extra egg, she'd felt guilty and somehow the chocolate hadn't tasted that good. Bad conscience could cause havoc.

She moved towards the window and looked down. There was no ladder outside. She felt a shiver down her spine. Flats were no longer safe these days. If people could get in and out as they pleased, it was bad news.

"I may have lots of faults, but I'm told that I'm a generous person." What else could she say in her defence?

No reply from Lucilla.

"Yesterday, I gave two euros and seventy-five cents to a beggar."

"If you were feeling that generous, why didn't you give him those twenty-five euros hidden inside your handbag?" Lucilla was merciless.

"Because they are part of my birthday present. I'm not giving away a quarter of my present!" Clara was getting annoyed. And anyway, how did Lucilla know about that money? She hadn't mentioned it to anyone.

"Being generous is giving something that matters to you. Something that makes a difference if you no longer have it."

Great, this was all Clara needed to hear. Not only she was accused of being a liar and a thief, the latest was being stingy. This worked wonders for her self-esteem.

"Have you come here to criticize me?" her tone was angry. "Because I'm not having it. You can go." Clara pointed at the window. "In fact, I may even encourage you to leave *that* way."

Lucilla laughed and sat on the bed, placing her hands on the soft cotton cover, close to her thighs.

"I didn't come here to upset you. I'm sorry." She looked sincere.

"Then, why have you come here?"

"I think it's time to explain."

Chapter 7

Clara decided to sit down again. "I'm listening."

"Good. You tend to do too much thinking to pay attention."

"I've now stopped thinking altogether. I'm all ears."

"I'd like you to help me stop people from committing suicide." Lucilla had spoken clearly and slowly.

Clara had to replay that sentence in her head, because it didn't sound quite right.

"Can you... rephrase that... please?" Her voice trembled slightly.

"Every day, somewhere in the world, someone kills himself, or herself." Lucilla paused, to give Clara the time to take everything in. "Soon, somewhere in Sardinia, four people will try to take their lives. I want you to stop them."

The message was clear enough now. Clara couldn't fault Lucilla for playing with words. She'd said it plainly, as it was. This didn't mean that it made sense, though. Either Lucilla was playing a joke on her, or was showing the first signs of mental illness, or she was already fully nuts. But she went along with it.

"And how am I supposed to stop people from committing suicide?"

"Simple. I will know in advance when someone is trying to take his life. I'll call you, you'll rush to the car and we'll go to the rescue together." Again Lucilla's voice was cool, as if what she'd just said was perfectly normal.

"Gosh, you've got it all worked out!" Clara laughed.

Lucilla didn't seem to appreciate the funny side of the situation, and Clara soon realized that. She stopped laughing and asked, intrigued:

"And how will you know when someone is about to commit suicide?"

"That doesn't concern you." There was a 'don't-go-there' expression in Lucilla's eyes. "I will know in advance. The problem is that sometimes I won't have enough notice, so we'll have to rush. That's why I got you a Ferrari, the fastest car."

"I see." Why hadn't Clara thought of that? She breathed in deeply. It was almost midnight and she was getting tired, and everything was feeling out of this world.

Lucilla grabbed her blue silk handbag, which was resting next to the pillow. She took something out and handed it to Clara.

"This is like a mobile phone. It's the tool which we'll use to communicate."

Clara took the device in her hand. It did look like a mobile phone, it was silver, had the right shape and a small display window. However, it had no numbers on it, just a yellow oval button in the centre.

"This is the button you press to take the call, and you press it again to hang up," explained Lucilla.

"Are you serious? If I want to get hold of you, all I have to do is to press that button?" Clara had never seen a phone without numbers before. Perhaps technology had been moving too fast?

"It's more likely to be me who contacts you, not the other way round." A serious expression appeared on Lucilla's face. "I'll call you when I need you. And make sure that you reply, otherwise I'll come and get you in person."

This sounded like a threat. Clara was gradually realizing that her visitor was serious, she had to collaborate.

"OK then. We have to rescue four people from suicide. Fine; all sounds normal. What's in it for me?"

"Fair question. I know there's something you badly want." Lucilla crossed her legs on the bed and carried on with great composure: "At the end of our mission, Paolo, the boyfriend who left you, will crawl back to you and will ask you to take him back. And you'll get to keep the Ferrari. How does that sound?"

Fantastic. How else could it sound? If you lived in another world, maybe. How was Clara to take this girl seriously? Who was she? How could she make Paolo fall in love with her again?

"The deal sounds good. But why should I believe this nonsense?"

"I told you you'd have a Ferrari, you got it. I tell you now that you'll get Paolo back, and you *will* get him back. " Her voice was uncompromising. "Not to mention the feel-good factor. That is worth more than anything else."

"What do you mean by that?"

"The fact that you'll make a difference to some people. Saving a person's life is the highest thing you can do."

"I suppose so." Clara thought of Signor Peppino; she'd felt good after helping him, it's just that it hadn't lasted that long. The break-up with Paolo, her car incident, all this stuff had been an unpleasant distraction, and she'd almost forgotten about that poor man. How could she be so uncaring?

"Why did you pick me? I'm sure there are better people at this than me." Clara was shaking her head.

"You're good at it. You'll do fine. And it won't be for long. Only four lives, and then you're off the hook." Lucilla's face was radiant, almost glowing. She inserted her hand in her bag again and took out what appeared to be a child's toy phone. "This is our emergency phone, in case something happens to the other one; if you lose it or it gets stolen."

"Come on Lucilla, this really *is* a toy phone!" Clara put the red old-fashioned style phone on her lap. It was made of plastic and was very similar to the one she used to play with as a child; however, this one had many keys instead of a spinning wheel. There were twenty-six keys, a letter from the alphabet printed on each of them, preceded by a set of numbers from zero to nine.

Lucilla seemed undeterred and carried on explaining: "This works in a different way from the other. When you want to make contact with me, you'll lift the receiver and dial the following code: 260578CSLL. This code consists of your date of birth, followed by your initials and my initials. Therefore I'll know it's you who's contacting me."

"Makes perfect sense." What else could Clara say? Was she dreaming? Everything was too strange to be normal. But if it was really a dream, would she even be able to question it?

"You ought to go to bed now. Will you show me out?" Lucilla stood up.

"But my family… they're out there." Clara realized that perhaps it was time for introductions. Shouldn't her family meet her benefactor? "Why don't you say hello to all of them?"

"I'm not a very sociable person."

"I thought so." Clara gently opened her bedroom door and quietly let Lucilla out.

79

Going to work in the morning proved to be more exciting than usual. Clara was still rather sleepy to think about her encounter with Lucilla the previous night, but alert enough to enjoy the drive in her Ferrari. She was pleased to see that her new acquisition was still there, when she left home; as she knew the car could potentially attract thieves. Also, it was good to see that it was still in one piece. Last night, it'd been impossible to find a free spot in via Milano that was nowhere near a tree. In fact, at this time of year, the Jacaranda trees along the pavement were blossoming, and her avenue looked particularly beautiful under the sun and the purple flowers. As she opened the car door, she was hit again by the fragrance of leather. She hesitated for a second, when she sat down. But when she put the car into gear, she enjoyed the kick she felt; she'd forgotten the power her new car had. As she drove along, she looked on her right, to admire the white steps coming down from the Basilica di Bonaria, which stood elegantly on top of the hill. Its architecture was a mixture of gothic and catalan styles, and she loved its white façade and wide arches. She did realize how lucky she was to be living in such a nice area of the city. In fact, she knew that one day or the other, whether with Paolo or someone else, she'd get married in that church.

The morning was bright and warm already, and both her car windows were open to let in the fresh air. Clara wondered if she could expect a hot summer. It wasn't usually this warm on the 29th May; perhaps she could go to the beach at the weekend. Some girls were already showing off their tans, and you couldn't possibly wear a skirt if your legs were whiter than mozzarella. If only her Ferrari had come as a convertible car, she would've loved it even more. In fact, she would've happily traded it in for a less flashy automobile, as long as its top could come off, and go back on, as needed.

There was one plus point though, about her red devil. Whenever she stopped at the traffic lights, she'd get noticed. Not that she particularly liked being the centre of attention, but she was keen on the idea that men, the other half of humanity, were utterly surprised to see a girl driving that kind of car. When she pulled away from the green lights in Piazza Matteotti, no-one could keep up, not even the black BMW with the aggressive driver. It had to be male, of course. And he didn't like it at all, being overtaken by a girl in a Ferrari. She could see his sullen face as she glanced at the rear mirror. Sweet revenge for the ladies.

When she finally got to work, it was 08:27; she was three minutes early. That was great, because she could park her Ferrari in a visible spot in the main courtyard. As she grabbed her bag and jacket from the passenger seat, she noticed that a smaller car had just parked next to hers. As she opened her door, the other driver did too, and they got out together. Clara recognized Miss-Shake-your-bum and smiled. The expression on her colleague's face was priceless.

"How?... What?... Who?" Teresa didn't seem to be able to speak properly today.

"Yes?" replied Clara candidly.

"Is it yours?" Miss Shake-your-bum's voice was broken.

"Of course," replied Clara with nonchalance, as she walked elegantly towards the main entrance.

"I don't believe it! Who lent it to you?" Teresa tried to follow Clara, but her tight mini-skirt didn't allow long steps.

Clara ignored her and let the door shut behind itself. She could've held it open for her colleague, but why should she? If Miss Shake-your-bum wore proper clothes to work, she'd be able to walk as fast as everybody else. The sure thing now was, give it ten minutes, the whole of Technosarda would know that Clara had driven to work in a Ferrari. Just enough time to grab a coffee from the espresso machine.

Instead of going up to the eighth floor, Clara headed down to the basement. There was a coffee machine, close to the storage room. No-one came down there first thing in the morning. She put the light on in the hallway and looked around, she was pleasantly alone. The air around her was stuffy, as that forgotten place didn't have any windows. But it was a precious spot, because it hosted an automatic espresso machine and the stationery room. Clara pressed the button for cappuccino, got her frothy drink and sat on the bottom step of the stairs. As she blew on her coffee, she tried to imagine Teresa rushing from one office to the next, announcing Clara's latest arrival. It was nice and quiet down there, she never liked too much excitement first thing in the morning. She didn't believe in being cheerful and full of energy at 08:30, that wasn't normal. Clara opened her bag to look for a tissue and spotted the new phone. It hit her; almost as if someone had physically bashed it against her face. In her waking minutes, that morning, she'd forgotten about it. She held it close to her chest and shook it. The device didn't show any life, but she dared not press the yellow button. What if it really worked and Lucilla materialized in the basement? She'd had enough of Lucilla for now. Not that she didn't like her; it's just that she wasn't exactly light company. She seemed to turn up whenever she was least expected, and always talked about strange things. Could they become friends? Unlikely. Clara had enough friends, they were cheerful, good company and above all, normal.

She took a sip of her cappuccino, it had now reached the perfect temperature. She put the phone back inside and wondered, as she gradually woke up. This Lucilla girl, who was she, really? She seemed to know an awful lot about Clara's past. Not to mention lifting a tree and dumping it on her car, that wasn't a gesture most girls could accomplish on their own. But then, she could've paid someone to do the deed. Also, who says that the jacaranda hadn't decided to uproot itself and fall *naturally* on Clara's car? The Ferrari, that could be explained, especially if your purse was loaded with euros. But how could Lucilla get inside Clara's bedroom from an invisible ladder? Or had she come through the front door? If so, how? Clara sipped the last drop of coffee and tilted her head backwards as she felt the magic liquid warm her throat.

The lift doors opened and Ernesto popped out with an empty trolley.

"Good morning Clara, where were you?" His voice was lively.

"I'm here, sitting on the stairs, having my coffee."

"No, I meant where were you when I got here. You always seem to be daydreaming." He parked the trolley by the storage room door and leaned on it.

"Do you believe in the supernatural?"

"What a question to ask first thing in the morning!" he chuckled.

"Have you ever experienced anything out of the ordinary?" Clara was serious.

"I tell you what's out of the ordinary." He came close to her. "That Ferrari parked in our courtyard. The

Challenge Stradale, it's phenomenal!" He was animated as he pointed his finger towards east.

"Oh no!" She shook her head.

"We must have some big cheese visiting here today. I wonder who he is…"

"Why do you assume that the car belongs to a man?" Hadn't she asked that same question yesterday?

Ernesto scratched his chin and looked up. "You've got a point. Never assume anything. Considering the choice of car and its colour, it could very well belong to a hot girl!" he winked.

This was getting amusing. Clara rarely had fun before nine in the morning.

"Now, let's imagine the Ferrari belongs to a girl." She got up, crossed her arms and walked in small steps in the tiny hallway. "What would the car tell you about that girl?"

"Rich, for a start." He pointed out.

"No, no. Let's imagine that she won some money, lots of it, and had to buy a car, and that was the car of her choice. What would you make of her?" she looked at him in the eyes. They were nicer than usual, this morning.

"Ehmm… Let me try to picture her." Ernesto paused, leaned his back against the wall this time almost as if he needed more support to imagine the driver of such car. "She'd be dark haired. I can't quite see a blonde in a red Ferrari." He crossed his arms and looked up. "Definitely a fiery woman, confident, with lots of personality, and I can see that she'd be very well-dressed too."

"Congratulations Ernesto! You've won a ride in the Ferrari." Clara handed him the keys.

He looked astonished, from his big wide smile no words were coming out.

"It's a gift. From a friend. Have fun." Clara was still

holding the keys and waving them in front of his face.

"What a friend! Can you introduce her to me?" He shouted as he grabbed the keys to check them.

"No. She's only *my* friend. Not to be shared. Unlike the car."

"Come on Clara, tell me the truth. How did you get this car? Did you borrow it off this friend?" His voice raised.

"It's mine. You can take a look at the registration papers."

"But... but, will you trust me to drive your Ferrari?" It was hard to tell whether Ernesto was more excited or incredulous.

"Of course, you can use it during your lunch break today. It'll make a change from your Vespa."

"Wow!" He shouted at the top of his voice and hugged Clara.

She felt his warmth running around her entire body, even her fingertips. What a pleasant sensation.

"I better go; otherwise Mr Big-idiot will wonder where I've ended up." She smiled as she went inside the lift.

Her prediction had been right. Her coffee break had only lasted fifteen minutes, but in that time Miss Shake-your-bum had advertised Clara's arrival in a Ferrari to the entire workforce. And that was over one hundred employees. This constituted proof that word of mouth was more powerful than e-mail, and that in the future, if she had any secrets that should be divulged, she could rely on a swift and glamorous messenger who occupied the office next door.

"Don't ask me about the Ferrari, please," announced Clara to Marcella as she entered her room.

"Everybody is talking about it. Gianna has already been here twice to make enquiries. Where were you?" Marcella seemed enthusiastic.

"Why can't someone have a coffee in peace and quiet nowadays?" Clara sat at her desk and switched on her computer. "Do I have to have a flashy car to get people interested in me?"

"That's what happens when you work in a dull place." Gianna appeared at the door.

"Is there some special radar under my chair? Because every time I sit here, you seem to turn up at my office!" Clara looked at Gianna with a puzzled expression.

"She's been coming here every five seconds. She's got to be the first one to know!" Marcella looked towards Gianna.

"Who told you?" asked Clara.

"Next door," said Gianna pointing at the opposite wall. "Miss Shake-your-bum must've been a town crier in her previous life. She has the voice and the attitude for it."

There was a knock on the door. Paolo appeared like a vision and asked Clara if he could have a word with her. Clara's heart started beating fast. How strange, seeing Paolo had a more powerful effect than racing the damn car. Gianna and Marcella tactfully left the office.

"I hear you have a new car." Paolo spoke with a quiet voice.

"I needed a new one, following yesterday's mishap with my Punto." So this was it, Paolo was only showing an interest in her because of the Ferrari. Why had she hoped for more?

"You didn't waste any time," he smiled and looked at

her in the eyes.

"Anyway, it's none of your business, is it?" Clara was uneasy, his gaze made her feel vulnerable.

"I thought we were still friends!"

"Oh, now that I've got a Ferrari you want to be friends!" She was angry.

He seemed surprised and hurt at her reaction. She felt ashamed, she knew better than that. Paolo could be insensitive at times, even cold, but never an opportunist.

"I'm sorry, I didn't realize you wanted to salvage our friendship."

"We were friends before we became an item. I always valued our friendship. It'd be very sad to lose it. But if you can't forgive me for what I've done to you, I'll understand. I've been a bastard after all." His shoulders went down and he headed for the door.

Clara was confused, she had to stop him. She grabbed his arm and said:

"It's early days, and it still hurts. Perhaps with time, we can become friends again."

"I hope so." Paolo smiled timidly and left the office.

What was that all about? She didn't expect Paolo's sudden interest. He'd only dumped her a few days ago. Was he being cheeky in wanting her friendship? Was he being selfish? Perhaps he was trying to ease his guilty conscience. Should she feel angry or pleased? Clara sat again at her chair. Why was life always so complicated? She'd been struggling for days to get over Paolo and this sudden request for friendship really confused her. How was she supposed to forget about him, when she bumped into him at work every single day? And when he was being so nice? If only he behaved like a jerk occasionally, he'd make life easier for her.

That night, when she went to bed, she didn't cry for Paolo. But she thought about him, for forty-minutes. The time dedicated to her ex-boyfriend seemed to be getting less and less, this was good news. She welcomed tiredness with open arms, as she lay comfortably on her bed. Sleep was vital to her, as it was the only way to shut off from the world, unplug all connections and forget everything. Also, it was the best way not to feel the pain.

In the middle of the night, she heard a strange beeping noise. The sound was very light to start with, then it became louder and louder. What on earth was it? Clara wasn't sure whether it was part of the dream, or outside in via Milano, but it seemed to be originating from her chair, close to the window. She put the light on and realized that her handbag was beeping. What was going on? She managed to open the bag and spotted the new phone. The display was pulsing with life. It was flashing a succession of different colours, but no letters, no numbers, no images. That thing was so noisy, it wouldn't stop. She pressed the yellow button automatically.

"I need you now. Come down and meet me at the car," ordered Lucilla.

Oh, how much Clara loved the 'hellos', and 'how are yous', and all those polite greetings her new friend ignored the existence of.

"But... but... it's two in the morning!" Clara was hoping the clock would be wrong.

"I know. You've got five minutes to get dressed and be at the car." Lucilla hung up.

Great, that was exactly what Clara needed now. Deep down she'd hoped that this weird mission thing was just a teaser, but now, reluctantly, she had to admit that Lucilla was never in the mood for jokes.

Chapter 8

Via Milano was quiet at two in the morning. Lucilla was already sitting in the passenger seat as Clara arrived. She opened the door and slammed it as she sat at the wheel.

"Your hair is in a mess." That was Lucilla's comment.

"What do you expect in the middle of the night?"

"Our destination is Sassari, or thereabouts." Her voice was calm, how else?

"But it's two hundred kilometres from here!" Clara looked at her in shock.

"Yes, normally it'd take two hours, but with this car you can manage in one and half."

"You must be kidding!" Clara was shaking her head. "I'm not driving like a maniac!"

"Up to you. It's two in the morning, two hours to get there, one hour to do the deed and two hours to get back, that makes it five hours in total, plus or minus a minute here and there. That means you'd be back at seven, just in time for breakfast." Lucilla paused, she always knew when to take a breather. "But if you want to get some sleep, before going to work, then you'd better put that foot down!"

Clara could see that Lucilla had a point, but she wasn't going to give her the satisfaction. She started the car and headed towards the highway SS131, the main road connecting the south to the north of Sardinia.

"Don't worry about the speed checks, no-one will stop you as long as I'm with you." Lucilla had a reassuring tone.

Clara was irritated. She never liked being woken up, especially in the middle of the night. And she didn't like driving when she was supposed to sleep, her body didn't respond that well, it wasn't designed to function during the dark hours. When she was a teenager, she had considered becoming a patissiere or a baker as an adult, but the thought of opening the business at five or six in the morning was intolerable. The two delightful professions not only involved getting up early to open the shop, but also getting up in the middle of the night, to bake the goodies. She couldn't do it. She would've gone bankrupt within days. Although, she'd considered it seriously. The experience of eating fresh focaccia and pastries as soon as they leapt out of the oven deserved serious attention and respect.

"We're going to save a human life, and all you can think of are cakes!" reproached Lucilla.

"Don't expect me to have a normal train of thought at this time."

"So, aren't you going to ask who you'll be helping?"

"I'm sure you'll tell me at some point." Clara's put the fifth gear. "By the way, could I have more notice next time? It'll make my life easier."

"If it's easy, it's not worth doing."

"Well, I happen to disagree," Clara was still annoyed. "My motto is: get the best results with the least efforts."

"Lazy cow."

"How can you say that with such a pleasant voice? It's a double insult." Clara was losing it.

"Drive."

Clara breathed in deeply. She had to have a high dose of patience with this girl. Well, there was no point in being angry, she was going to be silent now and concentrate on the drive.

The SS131 wasn't so busy and Clara felt quite happy about using the sixth gear, once out of the city. The car responded happily, and she was surprised to see how she hit the 200 km per hour, without feeling they were going too fast. The Ferrari was steady, glued to the tarmac, no matter how much she pressed the accelerator. Everything around was quiet and dark. The windows were closed as the night had become cooler. She kept staring at the black sky through the windscreen, and couldn't believe how many stars were scattered up there. She used to count them when she was little, but she'd run out of numbers. Sometimes, with her brother Dino, they used to split the sky in two, Clara would count the stars on the right of the moon, and Dino would count those on the left. And then they'd argue about the middle line. While Nonno kept telling them to stop counting stars as they would get a wart on their face for each star they spotted. They were always relieved to find out, the following morning, that no new bumps had appeared on their skin while asleep. When Clara had travelled away from Sardinia, she'd always missed her night sky. It was never so starry in other places. Paolo had showed her the various constellations, but she didn't quite believe they were for real. After all, you could draw a golden thread between all sorts of stars and design whatever shape you wanted. She just liked to look at those points of light, and admire their beauty. And if you really wanted to make a picture out of them, you could, and more so, it could be different every night.

As they approached the north of Sardinia, the road became bendier. Sometimes it was poorly lit, with sharp corners, so she had to pay more attention. Somehow though, despite her fatigue, she felt in control. There was the strange sensation that, even at high speed, she was safe. The time went by quickly, Clara always knew that during the night the clocks cheated. It was almost three-thirty and they were approaching the first exit for Sassari.

"We're going to an old people's home, in the outskirts of the city to help Giovanni, an 84 year old man." Lucilla spoke softly and slowly.

"All this fuss for an 84 year old man?"

"What do you mean by that?" Lucilla showed surprise for the first time.

"Well, I have a lot of respect for older people. But come on, the guy has already had a full life!" She'd spoken hastily, now she needed to justify herself. "If we have to save someone's life, wouldn't it be better to concentrate on the young ones?"

"I'm truly shocked by what you said. I'd never expected this from you." Lucilla sounded disappointed. That was a victory for Clara, she'd managed to remove her angelic smile for a few seconds at last.

"Well, I mean it and I don't." Clara slowed down. "You need to give me directions, that's the turning for Sassari."

The old people's home was located south of the city. From the outside it looked like a gigantic villa. It was well-lit and the walls were painted in peach. Each room seemed to have a balcony, with white railings. Some of the balconies had pots and plants, the one in the right corner, had a lovely red geranium, which occupied most of the balcony floor. All the green shutters in the windows were closed.

Lucilla went through the main courtyard, which was paved with terracotta tiles. It hosted one fig tree and a huge bougainvillea bush on one side, and a small herb garden on the other. Clara could smell the mint and the basil, and immediately thought of spaghetti with tomato sauce.

Lucilla went past the front door, and headed right, to the back of the villa.

"How are we supposed to get in?" asked Clara in a low voice.

"The back door is unlocked. Just follow me."

Natural; all perfectly natural. Why did Clara ask stupid questions at times?

Lucilla seemed to know what she was doing. There was a smaller wooden door at the back of the house, with an old-fashioned metal handle.

"Before we get in, a few recommendations." Lucilla looked at Clara seriously and whispered: "I'll take you to Giovanni's bedroom. He's already stolen various types of medicines from the nurse's room. He's now preparing to take them. He will be sitting on his bed, and all the pills will be on his bedside table. You'll go in and talk to him."

"Easy." Clara looked at Lucilla and shouted in whispers: "Are you mad? What if we get caught in there? We'll get into trouble!"

"It won't happen. I'll be outside Giovanni's door, just in case."

This was sheer insanity. Why did Clara get involved with this crazy girl? She should've known better. "What shall I tell this old man? I haven't a clue!"

"You'll think of something." Lucilla paused. "But, one word of warning. Don't say anything nasty, or immoral, or untrue. If you break the rules, the phone will beep."

"But…"

Lucilla had already walked away, and Clara was compelled to follow. The wooden door hadn't screeched when they opened it, perhaps it wasn't that old. The corridor ahead had the night lights on, and Clara was impressed by the cleanliness of the marble floors. On the cream walls there were pictures of the past Popes and saints; perhaps the house was run by nuns. There was a delicate scent in the air, a mixture of cleanliness and rose fragrance. Lucilla walked around as if it was her own home, with such spontaneity that it made Clara wonder if she should be concerned at all. Her blonde friend turned to the left, onto a narrower corridor with no pictures, and then went up one flight of stairs. The steps were so shiny that Clara was afraid she might slip over them. As they got to the first floor, she spotted a statue of the Madonna on the landing, standing on a glass pedestal. There was also a vase with white lilies, to accompany the divine figure. Clara wasn't a religious person, but she winked at the Madonna for encouragement. She continued to follow Lucilla to the second floor, and tried to be as quiet as possible, but she was sure that her heart, which was now beating like an African drum, could be heard as far as Sassari city centre.

"This is the right floor. Room 203. " Lucilla pointed at the far corner. She then realized how pale Clara was and held her arm. "Don't be afraid, you can do it. I'll be outside." She walked Clara to the door and unexpectedly pushed her against it. "Sometimes you have to resort to tough measures."

"Who is it?" asked an old man's voice from inside.

"Can I come in?" Clara gently opened the door.

The room was bright, both the main light and the small lamp were on. The old man was sitting on his bed, and was wearing a burgundy dressing gown. A dozen different packets of medicines were resting on his bedside table and he was holding a bottle full of white liquid.

"Who are you?" he asked with a husky voice.

"My name is Clara."

"Come closer, I can't see you very well."

She moved gently towards him, and sat next to him on the bed.

"I can't read the label, what's this for?" he handed the bottle to Clara.

She examined the label and burst into laughter: "This is a strong laxative. It wouldn't be a nice way to die!" she tried to look serious, but she couldn't.

"Typical luck! I just grabbed any medicine I could when the nurse wasn't looking." He glanced at Clara and continued. "Would you read the other medicine labels for me? I can't find my glasses."

Clara looked around and spotted his spectacles on top of the TV. She got up, took them and handed them to him.

"You're not going to call the police? About me, intruding here..."

"Why? Because I'm worried you might kill me?" He chuckled.

He put his glasses on and took a good look at her, until he seemed to almost recognize her. "But... you're the girl from the dream! Yes, it's you... but your hair was up and you were wearing a red dress, with a black belt."

Clara was stupefied, as she did have a dress like that, but it no longer fitted her. "Tell me about this dream."

Signor Giovanni seemed very confused. "I had it this afternoon, during my siesta. I never dream in the afternoons, it's unusual." He closed his eyes and continued. "I was walking through a forest, and I wanted to go very far, as far as possible, a place no-one could reach me. And then I realized I was being followed. I turned around and there was a young woman, with curly dark hair who was wearing a red dress. It was *you*, I'm sure. And behind you, there was this blonde girl. I can't remember what she was wearing, but she had a hat on, a light blue hat, with a veil over her eyes."

Clara gasped. It suddenly came to her. It was the same lady who had appeared on her dream about the wedding. Who else could it be, but Lucilla?

Signor Giovanni opened his eyes. "The curious thing is that I never dream colours, only black and white. But in this one dream, the red of your dress and the blue of her hat were really striking. I tried to run fast, and faster, but you finally reached me and took my hand. You smiled at me and guided me back where I started from. The lady with the blue hat was still behind us, and kept smiling."

"Yes, she smiles a lot. Far too often."

Clara got up and went towards the window. What was she supposed to make of these dreams? She'd heard of telepathy and weird stuff like that, she'd heard of premonitions, but she'd never heard of people who could interfere with other people's dreams. Was Lucilla some kind of hypnotherapist especially trained to test new frontiers? Actually, now that Clara thought of it, why hadn't she asked her who she was?

She turned around and looked at the room. It was tidy, and the pine bookcase was full, mostly of history books. The desk on the corner had a round metal lamp, with a matching pen holder. A thick note-book was left open, but nothing was written on it. There was a hint of aftershave in the air, still lingering from the morning, she assumed. Signor Giovanni looked pale, but quite young for an 84-year-old man. He still had all his hair, which was almost white, but she wasn't sure if his teeth were real, they were too perfect. He was tall and slender, and he seemed a man of culture. Her heart had stopped racing by now.

"So, what it's like? Life inside an old people's home?" Clara had to start somewhere.

Signor Giovanni seemed taken aback by her question. Maybe she should've phrased it differently.

"How do people spend their time in this type of... place?" She pointed at the walls.

"I gather this is the first time you've seen one." He adjusted his glasses. "Young people sometimes don't even know we exist."

Ehmm. Had Signor Giovanni just sounded a little sad there? Clara felt she ought to say something positive. "Of course we know that you exist. It's just that all of my old relatives are still at home, and get looked after by their family. So, I never come to these places."

He seemed put off even by that comment. Couldn't she do a bit better?

"I guess some people are luckier than others." Did that sound any better?

He got up, and slowly walked towards his desk. He was very tall and his back was arched forward, a detail she hadn't noticed before. He grabbed the chair from under the desk and sat. Perhaps it was more comfortable than the bed.

"Why do you want to take your life, Signor Giovanni?" Clara may as well be direct, since her chit-chat wasn't working.

He seemed astounded at first. Then an expression of embarrassment appeared. Almost as if he suddenly realized that what he was about to do was a foolish act. Perhaps it was the idea of getting caught. By a younger person, a girl even.

"I've had my life Clara. I've done all there is to do, I'm ready to go."

That was a difficult assertion to contend with. Clara was only twenty-five, and at times she couldn't face the possibility of living other fifty years. Life could be tough, very painful, what words of encouragement could she give to Signor Giovanni who'd already gone over *her* limit?

"I can't complain. They treat me well here. I guess it's the loneliness that is the worst. I have two children and four grand-children and they never visit me. All my friends and sisters have already died, so the only people I see are these decrepit beasts like me."

Clara was standing against the closed shutters, and could feel a fresh breeze coming from the semi-open slats. What could she say to help? Maybe silence was golden at this stage. Signor Giovanni appeared to be in distress; his forehead was crumpled, maybe with worry or doubt. Strangely enough, there was no fear on his face.

"The hardest thing of all is to outlive your friends, or family. It's not natural." He looked up and his eyes seemed sad, even through the glasses. "I lost my nephew last year. He was only fifty-nine. It should've been me." He sighed. "Nature has a funny way of working."

Clara had to agree with that. Sometimes nature, or call it destiny, or God, operated in strange ways.

"It's simple. The time has come for me to go." He seemed peaceful. This was definitely at odds with what he'd just said.

"But surely if you died, all your children would miss you. Terribly."

"Not at all. I'm rich, and all they're waiting for is my departure to heaven, or hell, so that they can cash in the inheritance." His tone was cynical.

"That can't be right, I don't believe it."

"It's the truth. I haven't seen them for years. Once a year I get a letter from my grand-children, it's usually around Christmas time. I end up buying the latest mobile phone, or Play Station, or fashionable gadget and send it to them, in the hope of a courtesy visit. But nothing, not even a thank you note."

"This is really bad. I'd never do that to my grandfather. In fact I don't expect anything from Nonno, he's only a pensioner."

"He's lucky. My family only exists to squeeze money out of me."

"Then, don't leave them anything! If you've made a will, take their names off the will and…"

A beeping noise started to rise from Clara's handbag. The damn phone had come to life again. Obviously Lucilla didn't like what she was saying. She had to change tactics.

"Have you thought of giving your money to charity?" The phone went silent. "You know, there are so many children out there, starving, sick. You see it on TV all the time. In the third world, but I'm sure even in Sardinia, there's lots of poor people. If you have all this spare cash, why not give it to them? You can't take it with you, anyway…"

"For a moment I thought you were going to ask me to give it to *you*!" he laughed heartily. "You know, you put me in a good mood."

Clara sighed with relief. It was nice seeing Signor Giovanni's forehead looking relaxed, in fact, now that she paid more attention, she noticed that for an 84 year-old man, he didn't have that many wrinkles. Some people just had very good skin. Usually men, who didn't care about it anyway.

"I thought of something else." Clara paused. "You look to me as if you're in good health, despite your age. I know that all those medicines weren't meant for you." She winked and walked towards him. "What about having some fun? What about thinking of doing things that you used to enjoy, and made you laugh? You've probably worked very hard all your life; don't you think that now it's pay-back time?"

Signor Giovanni seemed intrigued by that suggestion. She could've pushed it even further, but perhaps it was enough to just sow the seed.

"Can I take all those medicines back then?" She felt she could chance it.

He hesitated for two seconds. "Help yourself." At this point, not only his forehead looked relaxed, but the rest of his face too. What was particularly reassuring was that glimpse of life Clara saw in his eyes. "Suddenly, things don't seem so bad after all. You know what? The fact that someone cares, even someone I've never met before, actually makes a big difference." Signor Giovanni looked at her through his glasses and asked politely: "Will you come to visit me again soon?"

Clara was taken in by surprise. Sassari was a long way to drive just for a visit, but what else could she say? "I promise I'll come again. But I don't know how soon… Soonish."

"Thank you. I could consider you like a new grand-daugther." He got up and held his arms open to hug her.

"Just in case it crosses your mind… I don't want any of your money, clear? Just use it for a good cause." She leaned towards him and he put his arms around her.

"I will. Only use it for a good cause." He held her tight.

Clara imagined how Signor Giovanni could be her new grand-father. Nonno never displayed much affection, and yet she knew he deeply cared for her. She could pretend, just this time, that she was cuddling her real Nonno.

Chapter 9

"I'll drive on the way home," said Lucilla as they got back to the car.

"That's the nicest thing you said today. How did I get on?"

"You were good. I told you you'd manage."

"How do I know that he wasn't pretending? What if he changes his mind again?" Clara had found it too easy to dissuade him. Surely things weren't that simple?

"You just have to hope he doesn't."

That wasn't a satisfactory answer. "But..."

"You've done your best. And that's all that counts." Lucilla turned the engine on.

"Not really. I genuinely want to know what happens to Signor Giovanni."

"Only time will tell." Lucilla put her foot down and the car almost took off.

Clara got to work at 08:45. She was still in a trance. Sleep deprivation had a terrible effect on her. How did she manage when she used to go dancing all night and go straight to work from the disco? It wasn't that long ago, and she could do it so easily then. Was this a sign that she was getting old?

"You're late, and Mr Big-idiot has already been looking for you," announced Marcella.

"Good news always starts in the morning." Clara slumped on her chair.

"My God, you look terrible. Are you unwell?"

"What exactly about me looks terrible? I didn't have

the chance to look in the mirror this morning."

"Bad hair day, for a start. Your curls are everywhere; it's hard to tell which is the face or the back of your head."

"Thank you Marcella, what would I do without you?" Clara pushed her hair back and secured it with a clip.

"And now that I can see your face, you've got circles under your eyes. Perhaps you ought to wear your sunglasses." She laughed.

"What, inside the office?"

"It's bright enough here, the sun is shining over your entire desk!"

"Is it really that bad?" Clara was concerned.

"No, I'm just joking. It's just that… you're not at your best, in case you bump into Paolo out there."

Clara decided to ignore Marcella's comment. She stared at the blank computer screen and paused to reflect. Part of her felt happy, she didn't know why. There was a strange vital energy coming from deep inside, an optimistic vibration. But she also felt in a bad mood. She always got ill-tempered when her sleep was taken away from her, and she had to thank Lucilla for that. Now, she had to be practical. It was Friday, thank God. Only a few hours to go till the week-end, and then she could lie in bed as long as needed. She had to put a brave face to the day ahead and resist the temptation to snooze under the desk. She could start with that pile of photocopies that Mr Big-idiot had left on her desk. That task didn't require much concentration. She grabbed the papers and went out to the corridor. She heard Teresa's squeaky voice and her stupid laughter. Music for her ears.

"I adore football," Miss Shake-your-bum was saying as she touched Paolo's arm.

That felt like a vigorous slap on Clara's face. Teresa,

the temptress, was touching Paolo and flirting with him. How dare she? Clara woke up immediately as she approached the two of them.

"Since when has football become your passion?" quizzed Clara as she looked for Paolo's reaction out of the corner of her eye.

"I've always liked football. And footballers," she winked at Paolo.

Clara felt fire in her face, she could have strangled her.

"I better go, I've got loads to do." There was a hint of uneasiness in Paolo's voice. He quickly left.

"So, what's life like as a single girl?" Miss Shake-your-bum had one of those faces that you'd happily slap.

Had she suddenly become taller, or was she wearing high heels? Clara checked her shoes, she was definitely wearing high-heeled sandals, they must've been at least ten centimetres. And a mini-skirt, for a change.

"It's a refreshing novelty. And how do *you* like being a single girl?" asked Clara with a cool manner.

"I've always enjoyed it. Especially because it never lasts too long with me," replied Teresa, with her high-pitched voice.

Her lips were quite thin, but she'd made an effort to expand them with a red lip-liner. Clara wondered what could be attractive about her. She had nice legs, and large breasts, but there was nothing special about her face. Her features were pretty ordinary, that's why she had to wear make-up all the time. Her mannerism was abrupt at times, like now, the way she pressed the keys on the photocopier, she was almost fighting with the machine. No gentle touch, just a bash here and there. Was she feminine? Not really, sometimes her language was like a docker's, and the way she swayed her hips implied that she couldn't walk too easily on those high heels.

"So, why don't you tell me about the Ferrari?" Teresa spoke again.

"What about it?" Clara was pleased to have induced a dash of envy.

"Apparently it was given to you by a friend. If this is the case, why don't you introduce this friend to us?"

"I don't usually share my friends." said Clara calmly. "Nor my boyfriends."

"What about you *ex*-boyfriends?"

Clara could have grabbed her by the hair and dragged her all along the corridor, down the eight flights of stairs, through the entrance, and dumped her in the middle of the courtyard. And then run her over with the Ferrari. Two times, just to make sure.

"Ernesto, Ernesto!" shouted Teresa at the top of her voice. "I told you to bring me some more paper this morning, and you still haven't done it. Get a move on!"

Clara was amazed that this girl could have such an unpleasant attitude. She was truly a docker. Since Ernesto ignored her plea, she proceeded to go to the top of the stairs and carried on screaming:

"Ernesto! While you're at it, bring me some toner for my printer as well. I need it *now*."

"Actually, he's doing some work for me at the moment, that's why he's been unable to carry out your request." Clara explained with a polite manner.

"I always have to ask him dozens of times. Lazy git!"

"Well, he's not just here at *your* service, you know. He does work for everybody," said Clara in his defence.

"I'm done with the copier. It's all yours!" Teresa waved the papers in the air. "By the way, I'm not around on the 3rd of June. You'll have to cover for me at the board of director's meeting."

"But… it's *your* meeting to organize. How can you not be around?" protested Clara.

"Family commitments. I can't be here. You'll have to do it." She sneered as she walked away.

What a cow. What a bitch she was. Not only she was trying to get her hands on Paolo, she was also dumping her own work onto Clara. She'd done it so many times, and yet, Clara couldn't object. The two secretaries had to cover for each other, that was the rule. To be fair, when Clara was on holiday, Teresa would do her job, but she did it so badly, that on her return, Clara had to do it all again as well as correcting her colleague's mistakes. And guess what? No one seemed to notice. She'd been tempted to make an official complaint, but how could she win? Teresa was the secretary of the CEO, she was untouchable. Or perhaps, touchable only by the right men.

The copier ran out of paper and Clara headed for the basement. The storage room was open and Ernesto was shuffling boxes, while listening to hard rock music. As soon as Clara went in, he lowered the volume.

"This sounds very energetic. Who's the band?"

"AC-DC. They were very popular in the seventies." Ernesto lowered the box he was holding and came closer to Clara.

"I've heard of them, but I never actually listened to their music."

"You haven't really lived until you heard their songs! They're just great!" Ernesto seemed excited. "When I drove your car yesterday, I put the song called 'High Voltage' on top volume, as I raced Viale Poetto. It was… I can't even describe it… too good to say in words."

Ernesto was full of life. What a positive person to be around with, he always seemed in a good mood. What was his secret?

"You're not on drugs, are you?" asked Clara with a low voice.

"My only drug is rock and roll, baby!" he shouted. "Will you come to my gig tomorrow night? We're playing at the Music-Struck night-club."

"Wow! I didn't know you were in a band. What music do you play?" Was that a silly question?

"We cover the AC-DC songs, so we try to play like them. But Angus is unbeatable."

"Who's Angus?" Clara was more intrigued.

"Angus Young is their lead guitarist. He's a crazy Scotsman, and with his guitar he can do things like… Caravaggio with his paintbrushes." He played his air-guitar and made the right funny faces.

"And, is this your role? Lead guitarist?"

"Yes." Ernesto looked away shyly. Perhaps being on the spot wasn't exactly his favourite position.

"Can I borrow this CD? I want to be prepared before I see you live." Clara approached the small stereo.

"Will you really come then?" he seemed taken aback.

"I wouldn't miss it for the world." Clara took the CD, grabbed two reams of paper and left the room.

The main problem, at meal times, was that Mamma's cooking was simply the best. How on earth was Clara supposed to eat sensibly and watch her weight, when she was presented with the most delicious dishes on earth?

"Only half a portion for me," said Clara as Mamma served the porcini mushroom risotto.

Mamma ignored her request and served her a full portion.

"I asked you to give me only half a plate," persisted Clara.

"Well, I cooked risotto for five people and I'm not going to throw any away." Mamma's expression was resolute.

"Why aren't you taking me seriously? I told you I was on a diet and you're not helping!"

"I'll have your half portion," volunteered Valentina. "In fact, I can have your whole plate, if you wish. I wouldn't forego this risotto for anything."

"What's this novelty that you're on a diet? I hadn't heard that before." Papà poured a glass of wine.

"It's not a formal diet as such; it's just that I'm trying to reduce the quantities I eat. Especially carbohydrates and sweets."

"And why is that?" Nonno broke off a piece of focaccia.

"Because she's convinced that Paolo left her because she's fat." Mamma raised her arms in the air. "Nonsense. He left you because he didn't love you." She could be cruel at times, unknowingly.

"This has nothing to do with Paolo!" Clara was getting irritated. "The reality is that I've put on weight and my clothes no longer fit me. It's so … disheartening to feel that all my trousers are tight!" She bashed her fork on the table.

"Look on the bright side, sister. You can now buy yourself a whole new wardrobe!" Valentina was always full of good ideas.

"I think that Clara looks just fine. So what, if she weighs a couple of extra kilos?" Mamma's audience wasn't receptive, so she talked to Clara specifically. "Do you want to look like one of those models whose busts are flatter than a plaice? Who wants to see legs as thin as toothpicks? Just eat what you want my dear, and you'll be happy."

If only life were that simple.

"To be specific, I weigh *ten* kilos more than a few years ago. I don't expect to lose all those extra ten kilos, but at least half of them."

"Mamma, you must be at least *fifteen* kilos overweight. Perhaps you and Clara could go on a diet together?" Valentina had already finished her risotto.

"No, no, no! I like your mum the way she is." Papà touched his wife's arm. "I wouldn't change her. Or maybe, I'd just get a version of Maria who's not so talkative."

Clara sighed. She would've liked to hear from Paolo that he didn't want to change her. Instead he'd managed to give her complexes of inferiority and weight-inadequacy, which she'd never experienced before. But one thing he hadn't indented was her will power. She was able to eat only half a portion of her risotto.

When Mamma collected the plates she couldn't help herself: "I was very much hoping you'd eat it all!"

"Live and let live, Maria," intervened Nonno. "If that's what your daughter wants to do, you should respect her wishes. She's not asking you to make any sacrifice. And I'm sure that Clara is going to have two of those grilled squids now."

"You bet," replied Clara with a twinkle.

Clara retired to her bedroom early that night. It was her first Friday evening as a single girl. Up to now, her past weekends had been more exciting. She could've gone out with Marcella and friends, or with her cousin Daniela, but she'd opted for a quiet evening at home, in the company of a book. As she was lying in bed reading, she couldn't concentrate. It was warm and the window was open; through the shutters she could hear the traffic, cars and scooters racing by; via Milano was still lively at this time.

She wondered if she'd end up like Zia Carmela, an old spinster. At least her great-auntie was still slim at her age, but could Clara look forward to becoming a fat, as well as an acidic, spinster? She hoped very much that all of this was just a phase. She wasn't made to be on her own forever; she needed someone special in her life. She wondered if Paolo had gone out tonight. Was he with his friends, playing football, or ... no, that thought couldn't be entertained, with Miss Shake-your-bum? That felt like a punch in her stomach; jealousy could be lethal. It was only four nights ago that they split up, and yet it seemed like months had gone by. Time had stretched, like a thick elastic band that could be pulled even further, and it would never snap. Her recent days had been full of strange events, and each of them had lasted an eternity. Even if it felt like she'd been single for a long time, her pain hadn't subsided. Sometimes it was acute, and at others, dull and persistent. Any distraction was appreciated. When sleep finally arrived, it was welcomed with immense gratitude.

But good things never last. At 04:38 her new phone started to beep. Clara recognized the sound immediately, and cursed. She managed to get up without switching her light on, stumbled on her slippers and grabbed the obnoxious gadget. She pressed the button once, and then again, in the hope to shut Lucilla up, even before she spoke. But her newly-acquired friend wasn't easily discouraged, and kept buzzing. Clara was tempted to throw the gadget from her window. There had been a dog barking all night, she could hit him and make him go quiet for a minute. What a cruel thought; the dog wasn't to blame. She sighed, and against her wishes, she pressed the yellow button again.

"Why does it have to be the middle of the night?" she hissed.

"Don't ask me, ask your Sardinian fellows." Lucilla's voice was unmistakable. "Come down, we've got to go now."

"I can't remember where I've parked, honestly." Clara couldn't even recall her name at this time.

"Near the newsagent's booth, close to the Basilica di Bonaria."

"OK. I'm coming." Why hadn't her Ferrari been stolen yet? Cagliari was supposed to be among the top cities for car thefts. Clara sighed. She finally put the light on and grabbed the first clothes that felt comfortable, for all she knew it was going to be another long drive. She quietly sneaked out of her apartment and reached her car.

Chapter 10

Lucilla smiled, but Clara didn't return the favour. How could this blonde girl always appear happy and at ease, even in the middle of the night?

"So, what's our exciting destination?" Clara put her seat belt on.

"Sant'Antioco, or thereabouts."

"I've never been there. I've been meaning to visit for a while, fancy that."

"We should manage it in less than an hour, as you know there's a connecting causeway between Sant'Antioco island and Sardinia."

"Perhaps next time you could organize the mission during daylight? Since I have to drive all these kilometres, I may as well enjoy the view!"

"I'm not the one who decides where and when." Lucilla was cool.

Clara started the car and left via Milano. There was a strange feeling in the air, almost as if she was escaping to do something naughty. Leaving her flat as quietly as possible at this strange hour, and not telling her family of her weird mission. What would they think if they knew? No-one would believe her, or they would certainly question her mental health. In the scale of things, this whole anti-suicide operation was way out there. But again, at this time of night, anything could be normal, it was hard to tell the difference.

"People are asking questions about the car, how I got it, and stuff. What am I supposed to tell them?" Clara's voice was croaky.

"This pact between you and me is a secret. Nobody should know." Lucilla sounded serious.

"How am I supposed to lead this double life? My family and friends are getting suspicious."

"Be creative."

"I thought that you objected to lies," dared Clara.

"I didn't say you should lie."

"Does not telling the truth constitute a lie?"

"Clara, you're a resourceful creature. I trust that you'll know what to say when the moment comes."

Well, Clara had wondered a lot about Lucilla's true identity, but in that instant she was convinced that her blonde friend must be a politician. No-one else was as good when it came to evading questions. In a gesture of rebellion, she put the song It's a 'Long Way to the Top, if you Wanna Rock'n'Roll' on, and turned up the volume.

"What's that… noise?" enquired Lucilla.

"This is not noise, it's music. Perhaps not the kind of music you listen to, wherever you come from." Clara had a grin on her face.

"It's painful for my ears." Lucilla put the volume down. "Where does it come from?"

"A friend at work lent me this CD. It's from a band called AC-DC."

"Tell me about this friend. Do you like him?"

Why was Lucilla always so… direct? "His name is Ernesto, he's our office junior. He's friendly and funny."

"How does he compare with Paolo?"

Clara hesitated, and then replied: "That question is ill-posed. It'd be as if you asked how does the Pope compare with President Bush."

"Does Ernesto make you laugh?" Lucilla wasn't one to give up easily.

"As a matter of fact, he does. I always enjoy his company."

"Did Paolo make you laugh?"

"Well, sometimes. But to be honest, I wouldn't call him a joker. What I liked about him was his wisdom, his intelligence and his knowledge. He seemed to know about all sorts of things."

"A portable encyclopaedia."

"Yes, but a cuddly one."

"Why do you want him back?" persisted Lucilla.

"Because I love him. When is the third degree going to end?"

"Mine ends now. But perhaps it's you, who should start questioning things."

Clara turned the music up and declared with her body language that the conversation was over. The music was invigorating, there was nothing like hard rock to wake you up. The only problem was that it was impossible to think. Did she really want to think, anyway? The moment you thought, you started to *feel* as well, and at present, she was happy with just being a zombie at the mercy of the pounding music. The road ahead was quiet, what a pity that there was hardly anyone to overtake. But maybe it was less dangerous this way, she could go as fast as 240 km per hour on the SS130, which was a thrill in itself. At that speed, time didn't seem measurable.

The CD ran out of songs and Lucilla immediately took advantage of the silence.

"We'll get there very quickly if you continue to drive this fast."

"I'll have to slow down once we get on the SS126, as it's a narrower road."

"Don't you want to know about your mission?"

"I'm all ears." Clara slowed down and tried to listen carefully.

"His name is Mario, he has a small furniture business

and he's on the verge of bankruptcy."

"Do these people have surnames? You never told me Signor Giovanni's surname."

"The surname doesn't matter. You won't need to know that."

"Why can't I have all the information? It's always on *your* terms."

"You're only told what you *need* to know," re-iterated Lucilla.

"Well, if that's the case, don't tell me any more. I'll ask this Mario person directly."

"You really are stubborn." Lucilla still had her natural calmness.

"It's a quality all Sardinian people have."

"Quality?"

In answer to that Clara put the CD back on, as loud as possible. Lucilla smiled, as usual. What else could she do, except smirk and grin? She could've never been an actress with her lack of alternative facial expressions. Sometimes Clara felt like shaking her from top to bottom, to see if she could elicit some different type of reaction. A bit of passion here and there, either positive or negative, wouldn't go amiss. She detested people who always seemed cool, no matter what. But why was that? What right did she have to be angry with Lucilla after all? She'd done nothing wrong, except wake her up at inconvenient times. In fact, she'd given her a free Ferrari. Maybe she should be a bit more grateful and appreciative; friends like these were rare, if not unique.

It was almost 05:30 and strangely enough Clara was fully awake, was her internal clock going crazy too? She decided to enjoy the view, after all, she rarely had the opportunity to watch the dawn. The sun was timidly appearing from behind a cloud. It was the only cloud on the horizon; it almost felt like it'd been placed there to play hide-and-seek with the sun. The SS126 was now approaching the island of Sant'Antioco. Clara felt a bit ashamed for never visiting this place before. Paolo had told her about it years ago, and somehow she still remembered. She slowed down as she reached the causeway connecting the island to Sardinia. On her right she could enjoy the vastness of the open sea, while on her left she could view the large lagoon, which then opened into the wide sea. The pink flamingos were quietly standing on the lagoon; they looked so elegant with their long and slender pink legs which contrasted with their white plumage. Their necks too were extremely long and slim, even more graceful than swans'. But their pink beaks appeared chunky and pointed, almost like they didn't belong to their delicate heads. The flamingos were still, perhaps they were sleepy at this time? The only movement came from three men and a woman, in the distance, who were bending down towards the water. They were probably picking some mussels and clams. The colours of the dawn were so gentle and soft, with a variety of pinks and very pale yellows mixing with the light blue of the sky.

"You need to go through the town of Sant'Antioco, the place is just outside." Lucilla seemed to know where they were going, thank God. Clara was too distracted by the scenery and had almost forgotten why they were there in the first place. She drove over the new concrete bridge and observed the remains of the old roman bridge on the right.

She carried on, and spotted the ruins of an old factory and its chimneys, which contrasted strongly with the beautiful sea. The small marina was populated by the fishermen's boats. She was very tempted to wander away to the beaches, but opted to stick to her mission and go straight to the town centre. They reached an avenue with terraced houses and flat terracotta roofs. Clara loved the balconies with cast iron railings, and even those made of cement, as most of them hosted multi-coloured flowers. The street was rich with shops, and bars.

"Continue driving on this main street, until we leave the town." Lucilla seemed familiar with the place.

Clara obeyed, and they got to a large piazza with a roman fountain. She continued driving towards the Corso Vittorio Emanuele. The trees stood tall and provided a refreshing shade along this avenue, the singing of the birds resting on the branches was particularly cheerful. Clara spotted many bars and cafes, and noticed that despite the early hour, quite a few people had stopped for a break. They were either workers enjoying a coffee before their labour, or youngsters having breakfast after all-night fun at the local disco. Clara could imagine how lively this street would become during the evening promenade, with families and young people enjoying their ice-cream as they strolled along.

They left Sant'Antioco behind, and Lucilla pointed to an unfinished road on the right. To Clara's surprise, after about one kilometre and lots of dust gathered on the car windows, they reached an open land, with a pre-fab building, placed in the middle of it. It looked like a mushroom that had sprung up during the night. There was an old red VW Golf, parked near the entrance of the dwelling.

Clara's heart started to beat fast again. She parked next to the Golf and switched the engine off.

"I'll wait in the car for you. Go through the main metal door, you'll find an open area with bits of wood everywhere. The office is on a mezzanine floor, which you can access through a spiral staircase, once you've walked along the workshop. Mario will be there, but he can't see you, because he's holding a gun and is busy trying to figure out how to use it."

"A gun? Are you telling me that this man is armed?" Clara's heart started to race for the Olympics.

"Yes, but he won't use it on you. It's for himself," replied Lucilla, with a serenity that felt rather bizarre on this occasion.

"You told me he doesn't know how to use the damned gun! What if he makes a mistake and a bullet comes out in my direction?" Clara was now shouting.

"It *will not* happen." Lucilla looked at Clara. "Get moving, before he pulls that trigger." She pushed Clara out of the car.

"I don't like it when you get physical!" Clara slammed the door as she got out. Her poor car door had been seriously mistreated recently. She touched her own legs, to make sure they were still there, and shook them gently. The sun was now fully shining; she could feel the rays warm up her face, before she turned towards the main entrance. The building was simple, four white walls with large windows at the top, and a flat roof.

She gently opened the metal door and heard the sound of a radio coming from the distance. The room occupied the entire floor, and it looked like a huge carpenters' workshop. There were large worktops, with various types of wood, and pieces of furniture-to-be lying around. Two carved chairs, a tall wardrobe, a chest of drawers, and different sized tables. Clara was amazed by the number of tools on show, as she walked towards the mezzanine floor. Things that resembled hammers and knives, pliers and pinchers. Various types of woodworking benches and menacing electric saws with different blades. Not to mention all the other scary instruments she didn't even know existed up to two minutes ago. She decided to focus on other details, such as the delicate light coming from the upper windows and the fragrance of the different woods. In fact, she ought to be thinking of what she was going to say to Signor Mario in a minute.

There was no excuse for getting lost in this place. The broad rectangular workshop which she'd just walked through, ended on the other side with a spiral metal staircase. Clara quietly walked up the stairs, supporting her shaky body on the cold thin banisters until she was faced with a frosted glass door. She knocked. No reply, but the radio went quiet. She knocked again, grabbed every piece of courage she could find, and went in.

"I didn't say you could come in." The gentleman had a very deep, manly voice.

Clara noticed that he furtively hid something in one of the drawers.

"Is that a gun you're putting away?" she asked bravely.

"Who the hell are you?" Signor Mario's sweat was running from his temples, and yet the office wasn't hot.

"Can I sit down?"

Before Signor Mario could reply, Clara dragged a chair towards herself and sat. She breathed in deeply and coughed, as the room was full of cigarette smoke. Bad idea. She explored the office with her eyes. One wooden book-case stood on the right, stacked with lever arch files. The desk facing her was bare, not one single paper, but Signor Mario was leaning his elbows on it, with his arms crossed. The desk was made of cherry wood and it matched the shelves, and the two chairs. A second smaller desk occupied the opposite corner. The office walls were built with glass, so that you could look down to the workshop area from any angle.

Signor Mario seemed uneasy, was that surprising? He was probably in his fifties, and his hair was going grey. His face was round and his eyes small, but kind, and he sported a thick dark moustache. Clara wondered why moustaches and beards never went grey at the same time as hair did.

"So, what do you want?" He seemed annoyed. Perhaps he didn't like being interrupted?

"I've been sent here to stop killing yourself." Clara had decided not to use the chit-chat technique this time.

His jaw dropped and he managed to whisper: "Who sent you?"

"A friend."

He pushed his chair back and got up. He walked around the desk, came towards Clara and sat on the edge of the table. He put his hands in his pockets and looked at her.

"Nice workshop." Perhaps Clara ought to back-track a little.

Signor Mario grabbed a packet of cigarettes from his shirt pocket. Clara noticed that his large hands looked rough and dry. She never understood why men didn't use moisturiser. He lit a cigarette and exhaled his smoke right onto her face.

"You don't look like a smoker." His voice sounded even deeper.

"I hate it."

He proceeded to blow his next puff to his side. It didn't make that much difference, the room was already immersed into a cloud.

"Look, I'm not going to beat around the bush, Signor Mario." Clara paused. "Can you tell me what *is* the problem?"

He thought about it. Clara wondered what was going through his mind. Perhaps he didn't know where to start? He kept inhaling the smoke and exhaling it quickly, without savouring it. That cigarette wasn't going to last for long.

"This." He opened his arms and pointed to the workshop. "My father was a carpenter and taught me how to carve wood and make beautiful things. Finally a few years ago, I was able to start my own small company making traditional Sardinian furniture. Things went well, and I hired two more carpenters, and we made great things."

He paused and grabbed a second cigarette. Clara was choking, but felt it was wise not to complain on this occasion.

He continued: "We started to get more orders, not only from locals but from the main island as well, even tourists from the continent. They like the fact that each piece we make is unique and done to very high standard. Anyway, I hired three more people, who started last month and had ambitions of expanding. I talked to my bank manager who agreed to give me a loan of 150,000 euros." He exhaled his smoke, right on Clara's face. Then, he automatically waved it away with his spare hand.

"Sorry, I forgot you hate it."

"And what were you going to do with this money?" It sounded like a lot.

"I was going to build a proper workshop, a brick building with a showroom attached to it. Then I was going to put a fence around it, pay the extra salaries, buy more wood and more tools."

"Even more tools?" Did they exist?

He extinguished his cigarette. Clara noticed that the

ashtray contained a dozen butts. Was it wise to have ashtrays made of wood? Weren't wood and fire supposed to be kept away from each other, except in fireplaces and pizza ovens? Actually, shouldn't she try to concentrate now?

Signor Mario got up and went towards the glass wall. "Last Monday, the money was credited to my bank account, and yesterday, Friday afternoon, I discovered that the whole 150,000 euros had gone."

"How could that be?"

"My clerk. Clever boy." He shook his head. "I hired Roberto on a part-time basis to do my accounts, as I'm terrible with paperwork. Sometimes I'd ask him to order stuff for me, wood mostly. Since I like being down there, in the workshop making furniture, rather than stuck here in the office, I decided that he could sign the cheques as well as me. I was stupid enough to inform the bank that only *one* signature was required. He was also entitled to withdraw any amount in cash, with no limit. I just trusted him, I'd known him since he was a little boy."

"Did you inform the police?"

"Oh yes, but Roberto's gone." Signor Mario flapped his arms as if they were wings. "He left not only this island, but Sardinia too. The police found out that he was on a flight to Rome, and then from Paris to Cuba, on Wednesday afternoon, the same day that the money disappeared."

"But surely he'll get caught. Our police can liaise with the Cuban authorities."

"Roberto is smart. I bet you that he's already got a false passport and he's moved to another Country already." He squeezed his cigarette packet and grabbed another one. Surely if this guy didn't die by means of a gun wound, heavy smoking would take care of it?

"What are your options then?" Clara was alarmed.

"Well, the bank wants the money back, which is understandable. So I've got to repay the loan and I can't afford it if my business stays small. A month ago I had two employees and no debts and now I have five employees and huge debts. And I don't know what to do. I'll go bankrupt, lose everything and my carpenters' families will suffer too."

"So, this bastard has run out with your money, causing hell for you and your employees' families. He should be shot with your gun now."

The phone started beeping.

"What's that noise?" Signor Mario seemed surprised.

"In fact, you know what I really wish for him?" Clara's tone was still, as she crossed her legs. "Either that those 150,000 euros are stolen back from him by some poor Cuban kids, who proceed to beat him up and leave him lying in the gutter." The beeping was getting louder. "Or that he gets some nasty disease and he has to spend all that money on medication and surgery, and that he suffers greatly until he eventually dies *slowly* in agony." The phone was so loud now that it sounded like an ambulance siren. Clara searched in her handbag, pressed the yellow button and shouted: "I was joking!" The device went quiet and she recomposed herself.

She pushed her chair back and waved her hand in the air to get rid of the smoke. Why did it have to follow her face anyway? "Now, if this theft hadn't happened, would you be a happy man?"

"Of course! We'd be celebrating. I'd planned a party for this afternoon and … now that I think of it, I better cancel."

"So, you wouldn't be thinking of suicide, if you had that money in your account?"

"No way! I'd never thought about it until now."
Signor Mario paced around his desk. "I know it's a
cowardly thing to do, but I can't face it." His voice had
become even deeper. "Seeing my workshop and furniture
being repossessed, my house, my car, everything. Not to
mention my carpenters, when I have to tell them I've no
longer got a job for them. How can I look them straight
in the eyes again? And know that all of this happened
because I was such an idiot to trust that boy!"

Clara agreed with him. Signor Mario had been naive
to trust his clerk, especially when it came to the freedom
of withdrawing cash. Still, perhaps it was better not to
share her opinion.

Signor Mario grabbed his packet of cigarettes again,
and with great relief Clara noticed that it was empty. He
squeezed the package with anger, and managed to reduce
it to a tiny bundle of shiny paper. Then he threw it against
the glass wall.

Clara was thinking hard. The challenge that Signor
Mario posed was different from her previous ones. She
finally spoke: "Do you mind if I just go out for a few
minutes? But you must promise that you won't shoot
yourself."

"What's outside? Have you called the police? My
brother?"

"No, no. Please trust me. I know it's difficult to trust
anyone at the moment, but only on this occasion, you're
allowed to do it. I'll be back in a minute, and I'll be alone.
And, I may be able to help you."

Signor Mario nodded, his gaze was still lost on the
workshop below. Clara was happy to get out and ran
towards the exit. Lucilla was leaning on the Ferrari door.

"I know what you're thinking," she sounded angry. Great.

"OK then, fork out the cash," dared Clara.

"No. It's not supposed to work this way."

"It's the only way!" Clara was very tempted to raise her voice, but she realized she had to be cool when she addressed Lucilla. "The guy is about to kill himself because someone stole 150,000 euros. If we give him the money back, he won't do it. Easy."

"What did I tell you about *easy* things?"

"Come on Lucilla!" Clara's voice started to go up, why couldn't she control herself? "I can't tell the guy all that bullshit that suicide isn't the solution, that his family will miss him, that he should face to the consequences of his mistakes, he won't buy it!"

Lucilla shook her head in disagreement.

"He needs the money. And you can give it to him," persisted Clara.

Lucilla looked up and sighed heavily.

Clara continued: "You paid cash for my Ferrari, and you can't tell me now you don't have 150,000 euros to spare. It's not believable!"

Lucilla walked up and down and kicked at a small stone. Finally Clara was starting to get some kind of human reaction out of her. She carried on with ferocity. "If you don't come up with the cash, I'm gonna leave now, as I'm not wasting my time with Signor Mario. And he'll be dead, thanks to you!" Would Lucilla take the bait? Clara opened the door to the car, but Lucilla held her arm. How did she get so close, so fast?

"There's a briefcase behind my seat. It contains 150,000 euros."

"Hasn't your mum taught you that it's dangerous to carry that much cash?" Clara impulsively hugged Lucilla, who seemed to be taken in by surprise. It was the first time she felt that they could become friends. Possibly.

Lucilla offered to drive on the way back, perhaps she knew that Clara needed a break. It was 06:35 and the roads felt livelier. Clara would've loved to stop at one of the beaches, but she was hoping to be home before anyone got up. She watched the lagoon again, which was now shining like a blue-silver mirror as it reflected the light. The flamingos seemed to be less numerous, maybe some of them had already flown away, or maybe it was just her imagination.

She thought about Signor Mario and his ordeal. This time Lucilla hadn't paid her any compliments for managing to accomplish the mission. It'd been too easy, she'd said. People needed to face up to their problems and not be handed the solution on a golden tray. But some problems only had one solution, no matter how you looked at them. What if she'd managed to convince Signor Mario not to kill himself, without the money being offered to him. Well, he would've had a life of misery, facing huge debts, bankruptcy, and staff dismissal. And in any case, Clara made him promise that if the money did turn up eventually, for instance if this Roberto got struck by lightning, repented and returned the cash, well, Signor Mario would have to give back whatever he'd regained. She was proud for having come up with this deal. Miracles did happen occasionally.

Lucilla wasn't going too fast, the SS126 was bendy, as it followed the curves of the mountains of the Sulcis region. She could've gone faster, but she knew that no more excitement was required at this stage. Clara observed the territory and the remains of the old mines. This whole area used to be the mining heart of Sardinia. The remains of these structures contrasted remarkably with the agricultural setting. The whole view induced silence; everything seemed still, almost as if both Clara and Lucilla were suspended in time, between past and present. Amid the deep valleys and the harsh mountains, they kept appearing: the ghosts of the old mines. Edifices where people worked and sometimes lived, and which now, showed no sign of life. They were hollow, their soul had been robbed, and they must feel terribly lonely.

"Animism, that's what it's called." Lucilla had a knack for speaking at the right time.

"Pardon?"

"The belief that inanimate objects can have feelings."

"Well, those mines must've witnessed so many lives, people who worked hard, who occasionally joked, even men who died in them." Clara was reflecting.

"So have these mountains, those oak trees, these valleys. That doesn't mean they could feel it."

"Since you mention feelings, doesn't it occur to you that I may not like your intruding in my thoughts?" Clara felt provoked.

"I can't help it."

"That perhaps I might like a bit of time to myself? Apparently nowadays, I can't even sleep without having you appear in my dreams." She waved her hands in irritation.

"It won't be for long. Only two more missions and you'll be a free woman."

"I can't wait."

When they finally got back to via Milano, Lucilla found the perfect parking spot, just outside the palazzo. Naturally, Clara pondered on the fact that in all her seven years of active driving, that parking place had never been free. But she decided not to dwell on it.

"I guess you'll call me again when needed?"

Lucilla nodded.

"Make it daytime on the next occasion, please." Clara said goodbye and entered the building. When she gently inserted the key to her front door, she was hoping for silence.

But she heard Nonno and her mother having a debate on how hot caffelatte should be. Was there a point in having any conversation at this time of the morning? It was a Saturday, why were they up so early? What a stupid question to ask; Mamma and her Nonno didn't belong to the category of working people, so they didn't know how to behave sensibly. Now, how was she going to reach her bedroom, if she had to walk close to the kitchen? Were they likely to spot her during their lively discussion? There was only one way to find out.

Chapter 11

Clara took her trainers off; surely if she walked bare-footed, the ceramic tiles wouldn't betray her presence. Mamma and Nonno were still talking, but Valentina had the bright idea to get up and leave her bedroom in that instant.

"Clara, you're already up! How come?" she sounded sleepy.

"I could ask the same question about you." Clara was prompt.

"I've got to go to school, it's not Sunday. But you're usually in bed until late on Saturdays."

Mamma and Nonno appeared from the kitchen and then looked at each other in wonder.

"I've just been jogging," declared Clara.

"What? You wear jeans when you jog?" Valentina seemed confused.

"I'm not beautiful enough to wear shorts."

"I thought you hated jogging, or exercise for that matter." Her mother was also surprised.

"Well… it's part of my new get-fit regime. Lose weight, get in shape…" What else could she come up with?

"You're taking this slimming programme very seriously," commented Nonno. "It's not like you. Are you sure that everything is fine?"

"Perfect. But because I'm so unfit, I now have to go for a rest, after my jog. Will you excuse me?" Clara headed towards her bedroom, and left her family in a state of wonder.

She had a sigh of relief as she shut the door. What a nightmare; she wasn't good at lying, and she didn't like it at all. Until recently, she'd never had secrets from her family, and this situation was starting to feel uncomfortable. She had the impression that sooner or later something would go wrong, and she'd get found out. But then, was she doing anything unethical or dishonest? Not really, so why worry? She threw herself on the bed, still clothed, and closed her eyes. Images of Paolo and Teresa came to mind, then Ernesto emerged with his air guitar, followed by Lucilla withholding the briefcase with the money. The best was Signor Mario's radiant expression when he was given the cash. It'd been such a satisfaction, to see an explosion of joy in his face, after he'd been so desperate. Lucilla had been right when she'd once mentioned the feel-good factor, it definitely was worth all the effort. She smiled as she serenely fell asleep.

The Music-Struck night club was nestled in the heart of the Castello district, the oldest part of Cagliari. This historic quarter was located on one of the city's hills, and was still partially enclosed by high ramparts and protected by two medieval Pisan towers. The alleyways between the tall buildings were steep and narrow and Clara wasn't too relaxed at the thought that Rita, Valentina's friend, was driving for the first time after passing her test. Valentina was even more agitated; what troubled her wasn't so much the thought of being at the mercy of an inexperienced driver, but rather the fact that her friend was somewhat impulsive. Reckless would've been a more appropriate word for Rita, but Valentina decided to settle for impulsive.

"I remember from my history lessons that the Castello district was used as headquarters by the Spanish rulers for four centuries." Rita almost scratched her bumper on a wall, as she drove past.

"Perhaps you ought to concentrate on the driving?" suggested Clara, who was sitting next to her.

Rita carried on through the narrow street, until she had to stop on a rise behind a Fiat Panda. Her car started to slide backwards and the Cinquecento behind hooted repeatedly.

"Use the hand-brake if you can't control it with the clutch and accelerator. It'll help." Clara's heart started to pound, until the car in front finally moved. "I suggest you accelerate real fast now."

Their car skidded and finally took off.

"Remember to use the brake as well, you shouldn't be going so fast in these streets. This isn't the Imola racing circuit."

"But it's fun!" cried Rita.

"I suggest we stop somewhere near the Elephant Tower and walk."

Clara couldn't wait to get out.

Rita found a spot and managed to park her car in six manoeuvres.

"What a relief!" Valentina got out and shut the door. "You're a dangerous motorist, perhaps I'll walk home tonight."

"Do you think the elephant too was scared?" Rita pointed to the small elephant statue on the front of the white tower.

"Yes, can't you see that he's petrified? Turned to stone," said Clara.

Valentina and Rita giggled for a few minutes, perhaps they'd found the driving experience amusing. Clara wasn't sharing that feeling; in fact she wondered how on earth she'd ended up going out with two teenagers. When she'd rung Marcella and Gianna, about Ernesto's gig, they categorically refused to be stuck in a smoky hole in the Castello district, listening to a thumping beat. It wasn't their idea of fun, they'd said. Clara thought that the AC-DC album she'd listened to before, was in fact cool and energetic, even danceable at times. Perhaps her friends were getting old, or maybe *she* was acting like an adolescent. Anyway, it wasn't just about the music, she was quite intrigued at the idea of Ernesto playing his guitar, and let's face it, she could do with some distraction and entertainment at the moment.

"I lost my sandal! Ah!" Rita was laughing loudly.

"Her heel got caught in the cobbled stones and the sandal came off!" Valentina was chuckling too.

Clara walked back and rescued the shoe as the two girls kept giggling. What was so funny about it all? She then remembered how, in her teens, she used to laugh all the time, at every opportunity, even by herself; perhaps she was just that much happier then? She carried on walking ahead, the narrow streets were shadowed by the tall buildings, and someone in via Genovesi, had forgotten to take the washing from their line on their balcony. Still, it was unlikely to rain, although the air could get humid at night. But with this clear sky, and warm breeze, even a very soggy jumper would be dry by tomorrow. She wondered what these streets could have looked like in the 15th century; probably they wouldn't have been that different, except for the road signs and the occasional antique shop. Did they sell antique furniture in 1435 for instance? What was *antique* then?

"Clara, where are you going? The club is just behind this street," shouted Valentina.

"Sorry, I got distracted." Clara stopped and slowly walked backwards. She'd always liked walking backwards, since she was a child, and had gradually developed a sixth sense for unforeseen walls or other obstacles.

"What's your sister doing?" asked Rita.

"She's not all that normal," whispered Valentina, and then proceeded to shout: "One day you'll trip on something and you'll fall over."

The door to the Music-Struck was made of dark wood and was arched at the top. It was Clara's first time in this club and she didn't know what to expect. The room was small, only a dozen round tables were scattered around, and the bar area was near the entrance, to the right. At the far end, on a risen wooden floor, stood a simple stage, with lights pointing to the centre. Ernesto was meddling with various cables which looked like a bundle of black spaghetti, whilst his friends were lifting the amplifiers and carrying musical instruments. One guy in particular was assembling a drum kit. The club was busy and some jazz music was being played in the background. The smell in the air was a mixture of burning candles, cigarette smoke and freshly ground coffee. Valentina picked the only table that was free, in the middle, and they ordered drinks. Clara looked at the décor, the bar counter was made of polished wood and had a rounded shape. The various liqueurs were displayed at the back, on a mirrored wall with glass shelves. The walls were painted in ochre and the ceiling was white with an old-fashioned chandelier hanging in the middle At the back of the stage was a large circular window with stained glass, and a streetlamp behind partially illuminated the scene, through the coloured glass.

"Who are these gorgeous girls?" Ernesto appeared behind Clara's back.

"My sister and her friend," Clara introduced the girls.

"So, are you all ready to rock?" He grabbed a chair.

"Excuse me," whispered Clara, "why are they playing jazz in the background if tonight it's hard rock evening?"

"You tell me. I've been trying to get the DJ to play some other type or music, classic rock for instance, but he won't have it. He's fixated with jazz." Ernesto shook his head and frowned. "Of all music styles, did he have to pick jazz?"

"I gather it's not your favourite." Clara didn't really have an opinion on the subject.

"No; its only use is getting babies to sleep."

Valentina and Rita laughed whilst Clara wondered if she'd use jazz for her future baby. Maybe she'd pick Mozart instead.

"I've got to go and tune my guitar. We'll start in half an hour." Ernesto's face was excited and ready to have fun.

Rita lit up a cigarette and Clara felt the need to go out for some fresh air. She'd breathed in enough smoke for the day, between Signor Mario and the twenty minutes in the club. She could happily escape Rita's contribution to air pollution. She left the bar and walked towards the terrazza in via Santa Croce. The view from there was spectacular, and considering she'd hardly moved all day, stretching her legs was very welcome. How many calories could a girl burn with each step? Four, or five? How many would it take to burn off her dinner? She wondered how many calories there could've been in her plate of Sardinian gnocchetti with sausage. And that was only the first course. Perhaps it wasn't a good idea, the counting business, she hated feeling guilty after eating something delicious.

When she got to the terrazza, it was free of people. She had the view to herself. Cagliari by night was atmospheric; she could see the largo Carlo Felice, with its lights on each side, leading to the harbour behind. Beyond the lights of the port, it could only be dark, as the sea had merged with the night sky. For all she knew, there could be a massive void behind, where the world ceased to exist, or where it would go on forever. The city below was well-lit, it reminded her of a flat Christmas tree, with a few flickering lights, scattered randomly. She could watch the panorama for hours, but she'd better head back.

Clara liked the sound of her footsteps on the cobbled street. It was the first time she'd worn heels, after many years. Now that she was no longer going out with Paolo, she could freely enjoy them. The problem was that, however cute they were, her turquoise sandals were extremely uncomfortable. How could some girls wear them all day long, or all night long in discos? Still, only a few girls could walk backwards in high heels, without looking; why not try it again. Clara listened for any potential cars coming by, but the roads were silent, so she went for it. One, two, three steps, that was more than twelve calories, besides, they were backwards, so more effort on concentration and muscles. Four, five and… it happened in slow motion. Her right heel got stuck and her foot got twisted. She lost balance, her arms tried to open forward, to counteract the push backwards, but it didn't work. She found herself sitting on the tough and cold ground with her legs wide open and a sharp pain in her ankle. For just a second she appreciated having a chubby bottom. She heard some voices behind, why did people have to appear when least desired? She'd better get up soon, but how could she do it gracefully?

"Can I help you?" A guy with a familiar voice rushed towards her.

Two seconds it took, and she hoped very much to be wrong. It couldn't possibly be Paolo. This couldn't happen.

"Yes, please," Clara responded faintly.

"My God, it's you!" Paolo leaned towards her and couldn't help but smile. "You look rather funny."

The three girls behind were laughing. Could there be a more embarrassing situation?

"But... that's Clara! I can't believe it!" screeched Teresa. "You look so comic, like a cartoon!"

"Thanks very much." Clara certainly wasn't amused. Of all people, it had to be Miss Shake-your-bum.

"I guess you fell over because of your high heels? Not all girls can wear them." Teresa was looking at her sandals.

"Will someone help me get up?" What were these idiots thinking?

The two other guys came towards her, but Paolo was first. He held her arm and helped her to stand up. Clara screamed from the pain in her ankle.

"Are you OK? Where does it hurt?" He seemed concerned.

"I'm fine... it's just the shock." Clara didn't know which was more painful, the ankle or her wounded dignity.

"This is Clara, my colleague." Teresa introduced her to the other two girls and two guys.

"Are you here on your own?" Paolo asked.

"No, my friends are inside the club," she pointed in the direction of the Music-Struck. "I just came out for a breath of fresh air."

"Shall I escort you to the club?" Paolo offered.

135

"We're late Paolo, we've got to go now," Teresa hurried.

"I'll be fine." Clara pulled her navy linen skirt into place.

She made sure she didn't take a single step until the crowd of six had disappeared from her view. She couldn't risk falling again, and now it was more probable with her faulty ankle. Damn, typical bad luck. She'd gone out tonight, to forget about Paolo and have some fun. But no, this wasn't allowed. She had to be persecuted by him at every possible opportunity. And, as if it wasn't bad enough to bump into him just after she stylishly placed her own bottom to the ground, he also had to be escorted by the only woman on earth she hated. Actually, yes, that was her conclusion, what she felt for Miss Shake-your-bum wasn't a gentle dislike the way it was for Lucilla, it was a real passionate loathing. There was an element of consolation though, no matter how high Teresa's heels were, she was still shorter than Paolo.

Clara hobbled back to the club; as she entered she noticed that Ernesto was talking to Valentina and Rita. He was so friendly and always tried to make people feel comfortable. She tried to hide the pain, but it was difficult.

"You look pale, and you're hobbling." Ernesto went towards her.

"I fell and hurt my ankle."

The two girls got up and tried to help Clara.

"I told you so," Valentina commented tactfully.

Clara didn't need to reply. Her glance was enough.

"Sit down, I want to take a look at it," proposed Ernesto.

"No way, it hurts too much."

"Come on, I've done a first-aid course, I know what to do." He gently helped Clara to sit on the chair. He took hold of her leg and removed her sandal.

"What if I've got smelly feet?" Clara did wonder.

He turned towards the waiter and shouted: "Giorgio, bring a gin and tonic for Clara and a gas mask for me."

"Stop it! I'm not *that* bad." She gently hit his arm.

He held her right ankle with great care and felt the muscles and bones. He then proceeded to lightly massage her foot and ankle. His hands were quite soft for a man, and they felt so warm and soothing. The pain was becoming more tolerable.

"Nothing serious. The ankle has a light sprain, but it'll do. I suggest you raise your foot, and then when you get home put an ice-pack on it." He dragged a chair from the nearby table and delicately laid Clara's foot on it.

"Wow, you're a talented man," commented Rita.

He was still caressing Clara's ankle, when his friend called: "Ernesto! We've got a gig to get on with, stop fiddling with women's feet."

"You'd better go." Clara couldn't help smiling.

Ernesto disappeared behind the stage door. The four guys started to play a low volume tune, the drums were beating gently, as the bass and rhythm guitars were leading, still on a low note. The singer announced the song: 'Live Wire'. But where was Ernesto? Still tuning his instrument probably? The music continued to build up and when it reached its peak, *he* appeared like thunder. But what on earth was he wearing? A dark suit, with short trousers. A white shirt and a stripy tie, and to complete the gimmick, knee-high white socks and trainers. Was this guy really Ernesto? When he started to play, the music took off. His guitar was so captivating. Even the singer couldn't keep up with his attention-grabbing riff and energy. The audience kept clapping and shouting, no-one could sit still. Rita and Valentina were hysterical, the craziness was spreading like a virus among the crowd, as they played further tracks. Even the jazz-loving DJ seemed mesmerised. Clara wanted very much to stand up and cheer, but her sore ankle wouldn't allow it. She had to settle for swinging and rocking in her chair, a task which required a good dose of resourcefulness, especially with this beat.

"This one is famous. It's called 'Hell's Bells'!" shouted Rita.

No wonder Lucilla didn't approve. Those songs weren't exactly spiritually uplifting, and some of them were rather rude. That one they'd played earlier, 'She Shook Me All Night Long', was close to being distasteful, but Clara couldn't deny that the beat was contagious and just fun. And Ernesto, how could he be so different from the way he was at work? He turned from a quiet office junior to a … what exactly was that? A lion that had escaped from a cage and was now jumping up and down and around the stage. But how could he still play that guitar whilst doing all that?

"He does it very well! He looks very much like Angus Young!" yelled Rita.

"I didn't know you were a fan of AC-DC!" exclaimed Valentina.

"Of course. And look at him, he's got the outfit as well."

Clara was chuckling, what else could she do? There wasn't a single person in the club who wasn't enjoying this. Not only did they play like the real band, but apparently they also *looked* like them. During that performance, midnight went past and no-one noticed.

Time stood still again, inside a bubble of happy noise. Clara forgot about her life and worries, and she guessed that the other spectators were lost in the same experience.

"It was too good, it can't stop now." Rita was disappointed when the band disappeared behind the stage.

"They've been playing for two hours." Valentina checked her watch. "Where's the time gone?"

The DJ shouted: "I know it's a bit of an anti-climax, but we'll have to put on some more mellow music now. Otherwise who'll be able to go to sleep tonight?"

"As long as it's not jazz," yelled back Clara. After Ernesto had given the whole of himself to his audience, they couldn't possibly spoil his fun with some ordinary jazz.

"Who's talking about going to sleep anyway? It's only one in the morning," shouted a short guy from the back. His voice was so loud that it was hardly believable it came from such tiny body.

The DJ settled for 'Child in Time' by Deep Purple and then continued with Rainbow songs. Ernesto appeared behind Clara's back, how did he always manage that?

"You've gone out from the stage door and come back from the main entrance. How?" Clara was massaging her ankle.

"There's a back door. I walked through the alleyway, got some fresh air, cooled down, and here I am." He seemed in good spirits.

Valentina and Rita leaned on the table and paid attention to every single word he said. He'd become their idol.

"The gig was fantastic, unbelievable. You're all great!" Clara was still amazed. "But where did you find this suit?"

Ernesto slowly removed his tie. "It's my confirmation suit. I asked my mum to chop off the bottom part of the trousers. She took a lot of convincing."

"I bet. But how does the confirmation suit still fit you?" Clara had a moment of panic. Even her clothes from six months ago no longer fitted her.

"I got confirmed when I was twenty-two and basically I haven't changed since." He paused and looked up. "I don't know whether it's good or bad."

Lucky scoundrel, thought Clara. Some people just had it easy.

"Although I did try to wear my first communion suit, as I'd rather use an older one. But my fist just couldn't go past the sleeve hole."

"Thank God for that," she laughed.

A beeping noise was heard. Clara's heart sank. Lucilla really had no clue as to what was considered a convenient time.

"What's that beep?" asked Rita.

"My mobile phone." Clara was quick to answer.

"That doesn't sound like your mobile phone. It's rather eerie," commented Valentina.

The beeping got louder, Clara wanted to get up and leave but her ankle didn't allow sudden movements. She inserted her hand in her turquoise bag and pulled out the gadget. Clara quickly pressed the yellow button and brought the device to her ear.

"This isn't the right time," she whispered.

"First you complain I don't give you enough notice, now you whinge about me calling at this time. Did you recently become a grumpy woman, or were you born this way?" Lucilla's voice was calm; after all she was being pleasant, as usual.

"I'm with some friends right now."

"Just to let you know, our next mission is due tomorrow morning. We leave at seven from your place."

"But… it's almost two in the morning, that's less than five hours sleep. Can't we leave a bit later?" Clara was hopeful.

"Just do as you're told." Lucilla hung up.

Chapter 12

Clara was fast asleep when her phone beeped. How could it go off before her alarm clock? It was only 06:20 in the morning. She sat on her bed, and felt her ankle, it was no longer sore, the massage and the ice pack had worked. The beeping got louder, Lucilla didn't seem to understand the value of patience. Clara grabbed the device from her bed-side table and pressed the yellow button.

"I thought our rendez-vous was at 07:00!"

"I'm just calling to say that you can have a lie-in today. It's Sunday after all, and you deserve a rest."

Had Lucilla undergone a personality transplant during the night? Because she'd never been so nice.

"What happened?" Clara was secretly pleased.

"She's changed her mind."

"Oh, it's a *she*! I guess… it's a girl's prerogative to change her mind." Clara rubbed her eyes. "Does it still count as one of the missions? I mean, if the … person doesn't do it, but I was prepared to help?" She may as well give it a shot.

"What did I tell you about *easy* things?" Lucilla sounded cool. "She's still planning to do it, but not today. I guess you'll hear from me when the time's right." She hung up.

Clara looked at her phone, why was she still surprised when Lucilla just cut a conversation short with no warning? Perhaps *her* next mission could be teaching her the basics of politeness, greetings, and all those niceties that distinguished civilized human beings. Still, the good news was that now she could go back to sleep.

Why did photocopiers always break down when you had important papers to copy? Especially when they were urgent? And why the hell didn't Teresa make sure that all the documents were ready for her meeting, before she cleverly disappeared for a few days? Clara was furious. Family commitments; yes. They always occurred just after a long week-end, and she was left to pick up the pieces. She rushed down to the basement, hoping that Ernesto, her saviour, would be there. Luckily, the faint sound of music indicated his presence in the stationery store.

"Ernesto, I need a favour. The photocopier is jammed and I have thousands of papers to copy and others to print. Can you help?" she was panting.

"Of course, I'd drop anything for you!" He literally let go of the box he was carrying and proceeded to follow Clara. "As long as you tell me I'm the best guitarist in the world."

"You are. And also the best office junior on the planet, and the best Ferrari driver, of course." Clara giggled as they went up the stairs. "When things go wrong, they don't do it half-heartedly. Even the lift's broken down. And my printer ran out of toner."

"What about Marcella? Can't she help you?"

"She's sorting out the catering, and the driver for the director."

"I see. Why don't you give me the documents to copy, so I can fix the copier and get on with that part, while you sort out the other stuff that needs printing?" He climbed the last step with no effort, whilst Clara was shamefully out of breath.

"Would you like another ride in the Ferrari?" she was able to ask.

As they got to the photocopier, they found Paolo, trying to unjam the machine.

"I'll take care of it," intervened Ernesto.

"I'm dealing with it now," responded Paolo. Did Clara detect a hint of irritation in his voice?

"Clara's asked me to help with the documents, so I better get on with it. I know this machine very well," Ernesto gently pushed Paolo away and opened the front cover.

"You've asked him to help you?" Paolo was surprised.

"I had no choice. It seems that my counterpart has gone off on holiday the day we've got an important meeting. And guess what? She generously decided to leave all the work for me!" Clara pursed her lips.

Ernesto chuckled and carried on messing around with the various levers and drawers.

"That's not nice, to bitch behind her back." Why was Paolo defending her?

"I'm not bitching, I'm telling the truth. Miss Shake-your-bum knew about this meeting months ago, and yet she still took some days off and didn't prepare for it." Clara was waving her left hand.

"Is that how you call her? Suits her perfectly!" Ernesto was laughing.

"The reality is, my dear Clara, that as usual, our managers didn't have any material ready in advance. You know how they work, they're still typing their reports *now*, one hour before the meeting!" Paolo seemed displeased. "Therefore, even if Teresa wanted to copy them on time, she couldn't!"

"Fair enough. But then, she shouldn't have taken today off. She should look after her own messy meetings." Her look was defiant.

"You always want the last word!" He was cross now.

"And she's got it!" Ernesto smirked as he grabbed Clara's papers.

When the directors finally got together at 11:20 they had all their documents, their coffee, a projector, and even the sunshine in their meeting room. What more could they want? Clara was pleased that people were never punctual in Italy, as she'd needed those extra twenty minutes to print a new set of documents for a second time. As usual, Mr Big-idiot had originally given her version 12, instead of version 13, the one to be distributed. The CEO had spotted the inaccuracy, and managed to get Clara to print the correct document just in time. All was normal. Now that Technosarda commanders were in council, she could look forward to at least half a dozen interruptions on their part, demanding all sorts of unpredictable things. The last one had been a request for twelve different highlighters; which meant twelve different colours. Finding them could appear a very simple task, especially to children, but who's got twelve different coloured pens in a serious office? Highlighters only came in orange, yellow, green and fuchsia. What else could they require today? She'd stocked up on highlighters, to make sure. Also on notepads with lines of different widths, and plain notebooks. On her desk lay reams of white A4 paper as well as coloured ones, ranging from pastels to stronger shades. She'd basically made sure that every piece of modern stationery was represented by at least two samples, just in case. She'd thought of everything, but somehow, she knew that they were going to demand something she hadn't planned for. And certainly she hadn't planned for her new phone to beep at this time, on a very hectic working day. She should've left it at home.

"What's that noise?" asked Marcella.

"My phone."

"Well, what are you waiting for? It's piercing my eardrums."

Clara pressed the yellow button and listened.

"Are you ready for a drive?" Lucilla sounded cool.

"This is *definitely* not the right time. I've got work to do." Clara whispered with an angry voice.

"It's a matter of life and death. It's as simple as that."

"If I leave now, in the middle of a big-deal meeting, I'm in trouble."

"You can ask Marcella to take over. She's a good friend. See you at the car park." Lucilla hung up.

Clara sighed deeply. On the scale of things, this girl's life was more important, but whose job was on the line? And, anyway, did she have to pick the middle of a working day to commit suicide?

"You look flustered, is everything OK?" Marcella seemed concerned.

"I have to disappear for a couple of hours, can you cover for me?" Clara's eyes were imploring.

"Are you mad? We're in the middle of a board meeting. Teresa's not here and now you want to go. What if they look for you?" Marcella was shaking her head.

"Please, it's an emergency. Someone isn't well and I must go." Clara grabbed her handbag and keys. "If they look for me, just make something up. I'll return the favour at the next opportunity."

Clara left the office and quietly walked down the stairs. Luckily all the managers were at the meeting, so she was unlikely to be seen. But she bumped into Paolo on the third floor. He looked at her but didn't say a word. The last thing she needed now was a confrontation with him.

Lucilla was occupying the passenger's seat and she'd already turned the engine on. Clara kept forgetting that her blonde friend had another set of the Ferrari keys.

"Where are we heading?"

"Chia beach."

"What? But that's my favourite beach!" Of all places, did this girl have to pick her spot?

She tried to be as quiet as possible when she drove off. The board meeting was taking place on the ground floor, the windows were open in that room, and the Ferrari engine was damn noisy. Could they hear her leave? Luckily, apart from Paolo and the receptionist, no-one had actually seen her go. She was agitated, she felt out of control of the situation.

"Don't worry, nobody will look for you whilst you're gone," Lucilla declared.

"How can you be so sure?" Clara looked at her. "I really resent being called for this *mission* even during working hours. As if it wasn't bad enough being woken up in the middle of the night!"

"It's a bit like when a baby decides to be born. Mothers-to-be don't know exactly when it will happen. Sometimes it's similar when people decide to end their lives. They think about it for a while, and then it happens."

"Yes, but it looks like this girl's changed her mind once already. I've just decided that I don't like her." Clara had expressed her opinion.

"But you haven't even met her!"

"I never liked indecisive people. They're a waste of time." She huffed. "If she'd got on with it last Sunday, as planned, the thing would be over by now."

"You're showing your cruel side for the first time."

"When I say *the thing would be over*, I mean the rescue, saving her life." Clara puffed again. "Why do people misunderstand me all the time?"

"And why are you in such a foul mood?" Was Lucilla genuinely concerned?

"I don't know. Things are getting to me. These weird missions, Teresa, Paolo, everything is unsettled and undefined." Clara's voice was deflated.

"And all you want is…?"

"Normality. No more lies. I'd like to have a boyfriend, carefree days, blissful ignorance, and … wonderful desserts."

"And yet you still have great challenges to come," Lucilla's voice was barely audible.

"What did you say?"

"Nothing."

Clara didn't insist. Whatever she'd said, it didn't matter. Probably it was something that was going to annoy her anyway. As they left Cagliari, the traffic started to move faster, the windows were open and the breeze was refreshing, despite it being a warm day. The mistral was blowing, and whilst it was never welcome in winter, it provided a soothing break in the hotter season. The sea was agitated, but the mountains in the distance, seemed stable and unmoving. That's what Clara would like to feel, grounded and strong. But for some reason, her life at the moment felt like a flag, flapping in all directions.

She was pleased to reach the newly-built fast road, she was ready to put her foot down. So far no police or speed cameras had tracked her down, so why not go for it. The road was curving gently between the mountains, but it was sturdy and safe, even under the tunnel. The Ferrari never felt unstable, even on sharp corners. The fun didn't last long as she joined the old road again. The palms and the oleanders scattered everywhere were fluttering in the wind, she could smell the heat and the sea-air.

As she drove past Pula, Clara remembered how much she'd enjoyed a show at the old Roman theatre, on a summer evening last year. First, she and Paolo had walked around the remains of the Phoenician town of Nora, and had admired the ruins of the Roman *foro* and mosaics. Then they'd sat on the steps of the old theatre and enjoyed the music and the dance. Almost by magic it was a full moon that night, and its light reflected on the dark blue sea. In fact, it was so bright, between moon and stars, that there was hardly any need for artificial illumination. She'd been lost again, admiring the silhouettes of the dancers in their blue chiffons, moved by the pervasive melody. Her only touch with reality had come through the infamous mosquito bites. Of course, they'd all favoured Clara and her sweet-blooded arms. Paolo hadn't been bitten, whilst she had at least thirteen itchy blotches. Couldn't they be more democratic? He'd joked and said that the mosquitoes didn't go for sour people, but that was no consolation. After the show, they'd driven to Pula and stopped at a pizzeria. It was the best marinara pizza she'd ever tasted. It'd been baked in a traditional oven, heated by burnt wood, the dough was thin and crusty and the tomato sauce was divine.

"You really are obsessed with food," commented Lucilla.

"It wasn't just the pizza, but also their puddings. Their tiramisu…" Clara felt the need to go into detail. "They used real mascarpone and didn't add any cream. The eggs were fresh, and one of the layers between the biscuits had a chocolate/mascarpone cream, which I'd never tried before."

"OK." Lucilla was hoping to switch topic.

"And the consistency, the texture! When you tasted it, it was just right. A real semifreddo: it was cold enough to soothe your mouth with its creamy quality, but not as chilly as an ice-cream."

"Enough. You spent the last one and half minutes describing a dessert. Normal."

"I think that when it comes to the word *normal*, you're not qualified to talk."

"That's the turning for Chia," pointed out Lucilla.

Clara turned on her left and entered a narrower road. She was disappointed that her friend didn't share the same passion for food. She had no idea what she was missing.

She could feel that the sea was getting closer, despite the fact that hills were visible on both sides. The road was bendy and gently followed the contours of the land. Clara recognized the familiar Mediterranean maquis everywhere, as well as some local vineyards and orchards with fig trees and other wonderful fruits. She smiled as she noticed how the prickly pear trees stood along the edges of the road. As a young girl, she'd once tried to pick a fig; bad idea, as she got stung by the thick spikes from the fat leaves as well as by the thinner ones on the fruit's skin.

Clara noticed how new restaurants and new houses had appeared over time, she could see them from the road; although the area was still quite unspoilt. She finally got to the turning for Su Giudeu. She took this road and carried on driving until she could see the lagoon. At that point, she decided to drive very slowly, so that she could enjoy the view of the water. As usual, the large pond was populated by its pink flamingos, herons and sea-gulls. Further on, a strip of golden sand separated it from the crystal clear sea, with her favourite two rocks in the middle. Her eyes could never get tired of the blue. She could immerse herself into the shades of the light blue lagoon, the turquoise sea near the beach, and the darker blue water behind; not to mention the colour of the sky, which appeared azure, on top of the navy line of the horizon.

Clara carried on driving on the narrow road, until she reached a small hill, after which the road became unfinished. The sand dunes were visible on her left.

"I suggest you park here, in this small open area." Lucilla had spoken again.

The area was truly small, and strictly speaking, people weren't allowed to park there, but Clara wasn't in the mood to object. And anyway, there were two other cars. She turned the engine off, and opened the door. She got out and walked a little, until her beautiful sandals were covered by dust.

"I guess I'm not properly equipped for the beach!" she tried to remove the dirt from her sandals. Her black skirt was waving in the wind and the cool air was wonderfully soothing for her sticky legs.

"Perhaps you could go for a walk, near the shore?" suggested Lucilla.

Clara frowned. "I didn't come all the way to Chia, *on a working day*, to walk by the sea. Even if it's my favourite pastime."

"The girl's changed her mind again!" Lucilla uttered calmly.

"You must be joking. Tell me it's a joke!" shouted Clara.

"No joke. She's just coming back from the beach now and heading for her car, where she's going to sit for a while."

"Silly girl! What's the matter with her?"

"She'd decided to drown herself, but then as she got closer to the sea she thought it wasn't a good idea. So now she's thinking what to do next."

"Great, how long have we got? A lifetime?"

"No; to be precise she's going to decide in twenty-five minutes." Lucilla seemed to take everything literally.

"Right." Clara huffed loudly. "I'm going to go for a walk and cool down my head a little. I guess I'll see you back here in twenty-five minutes."

"Be punctual, twenty-five, not twenty-six."

"Do we need to synchronize our watches?"

Lucilla didn't have a watch.

Clara decided to reach the sea via the dunes. It was harder work, but she needed to let out some steam. In theory, she shouldn't be walking with her delicate red sandals on, but the sand was hot, hardly bearable, and she ought to pay attention to the occasional sharp leaves or small rocks and twigs buried underneath. She was amazed at how, some plants, like juniper and cyst, could grow in the sand. Especially when it rained so little in Sardinia. Junipers were scattered everywhere, and on this particular dune, they seemed to have naturally grown to make way for a sandy trail, and provide some shelter to the passers-by. Even through her sandals, she could feel the different temperature between the sun-struck sand, which almost fried her feet, and the spots shaded by the trees, which were pleasantly cool. Clara continued her climb, until she finally reached the top of the dune. She could face the open sea in front, with her favourite two rocks in the middle. The beach was wide and open and it stretched on both sides. The golden sand still had its natural undulations, probably no-one had walked on it today. Well, what was she waiting for? Someone had to leave a sign. She took her sandals off, and held them with her left hand. Counted up to three and went for it, like she used to as a child. She ran downwards, along the slope and felt the irresistible urge to roll, and transform herself into a human ball. Coming down the dune at such speed was comical, she couldn't stop laughing. From the original thrust, she kept on running even on the flat sand, for about fifty metres, until she finally reached the shore, and was able to wet her feet in the cool water.

She breathed in deeply, the scent of sea and salt was captivating; moreover, she could have the beach to herself; only a few people were dotted around, and hardly visible. A surfer was battling with the wind in the distance, like her own brown curls, which were moving in all directions. After the hard work, she could finally take it easy. She looked at the two rocks in front of her, two little islands, always next to each other. What else could they do? In the past she'd tried to climb them, but she kept slipping on the wet stone, so she'd settled for snorkeling around trying to spot any marine creature that wasn't too shy. As a child she'd wondered if sharks could be hidden behind them, but Papà had reassured her that the Sardinian sea didn't have *antipatici* girl-eating fish.

Clara started to walk on the shore. The tall waves with their foamy crests were chasing each other, and following her steps. She liked to look back at her footprints on the wet sand, toe prints looked so cute, especially the smaller ones. It was strange how, when the wave came, it would conceal them. Sometimes, it was enough for the first wave to cover them completely, especially when the mistral was blowing. Other times, the first wave would wet them, the second one would cover them, but only the third would delete them. It was just a matter of time, until all the footprints, and the sandcastles would get wiped out by the sea, leaving no sign of their existence. Perhaps this is what happened to everything, including humans? Time would gradually delete any trace of them, and in centuries to come, no-one would remember them. That thought wasn't exciting. Could there be another way? Clara looked at the dunes on her left and the hill in front, in the distance, with its Spanish tower on top, the *Torre di Chia*. That tower must've seen a lot, witnessed invasions, wars, killings, and… but no, Lucilla didn't believe in animism. She'd told her once, and yet she was the one that could give Clara the hope that it wasn't just all here and now. There must be something more. Not in the footprints, maybe, not in the tower, but somewhere else.

A strange sound was heard in the air. Like a siren, a police or ambulance, but different. At first it was faint, but it gradually became louder. The few people on the beach looked around, towards the dunes. Clara's brain started to function again, bloody hell, it was her new phone. She never realized it could get so loud. She must be late. Yes, twenty-five minutes had just passed. Why did Lucilla have to be so precise? Was one minute going to make a big difference? The signal was getting unbearable, she'd better run. She sprinted back towards the dune, she'd never climbed one so fast, not even as a child. The sand was burning her feet, and her skirt was sticking to her thighs, while her curls were seriously getting tangled. Not her idea of fun. Even more annoying was the fact that she'd just caught up on her breath. She hated being hurried, human beings weren't supposed to rush around, it wasn't like we had predators chasing us.

"You're sweaty, your face looks shiny," Lucilla's voice was heard behind a juniper tree.

Clara ignored the comment and stopped. The minute she grasped her breath, she asked: "Why aren't you at the car park?"

"Because *she*'s there, inside her own car. You know that I shouldn't stick around in the presence of others."

"Of course, no-one is allowed to see you, but everybody is allowed to *hear* you!"

"I was forced to use the phone. You were late."

"Which one?" asked Clara.

"The black Ford Fiesta. She's made up her mind now. She's going to drive towards Teulada, along the coast. She's going to pick a spot at the top, where there is no guard-rail to protect motorists. She's going to accelerate and throw herself and her car over the edge."

"Nice. What's her name?"

"Rossana."

"I guess she was born without a surname."

"Take the phone with you."

Clara tried to recompose herself, she wiped the sweat, or rather, the glow, from her cheeks and forehead. She shook the sand off her feet, put her gorgeous sandals on and walked gently towards the car. Strangely enough she was feeling calm. Perhaps she was getting used to her new role? Or was it the calm before the storm? The black Ford Fiesta was dusty and a chubby girl was sitting inside. Her gaze was lost as she looked at the windscreen, she was obviously daydreaming. Clara knocked on her window. The girl startled, and with a puzzled look let the glass go down.

"Hi, I hear you're heading towards Teulada. Can I catch a lift?" Clara bravely asked.

Chapter 13

As soon as she asked for a lift, Clara realized that it wasn't a good idea. Once she got into the car anything could happen. What if she couldn't dissuade Rossana from her unhealthy plan? The girl was looking at her, in a strange way, almost as if Clara was the mad one out of the two.

"Come in," said Rossana with a low voice.

"Actually, I've changed my mind; I don't want to go to Teulada after all." Clara spoke with a hint of embarrassment as she got into the car. But as she sat, she realized how stupid she must look. If she didn't want a lift, why was she getting in the car in the first place?

"But, you just said it, a minute ago. Do you usually change your mind so quickly?"

"Hey, no! I think that between us two, you would win the competition."

Rossana seemed puzzled and became quiet, almost lost. Clara's impression had been right, she was a rather chubby girl, but nonetheless, quite attractive. She was wearing a pair of light blue cotton trousers, with a white polo T-shirt. Her olive skin was tanned, she'd obviously spent some time outdoors, and her hair was short and dark. Despite her being rotund, she had delicate features, big brown eyes with long eyelashes, a proportioned nose and nicely shaped lips. What was strange however, was her expression; she seemed lost, as she stared at the windscreen. Almost as if she wasn't quite there. Perhaps indifferent, or unconcerned with what was going on. Clara pondered how she should deal with this girl, possibly a sharp approach might shake her up?

"No need to pretend with me," Clara said calmly. "I

know you changed your mind twice already. First you were going to do it last Sunday, and to be honest, your plans didn't agree with mine. A lie-in is sacred at the weekend. And anyway, I was annoyed at being woken up when there wasn't the need after all!"

Clara looked at Rossana, who was still silent. Dazed and confused she was, like the Led Zeppelin song.

"Then, the second time, I got dragged out of an important meeting, and had to drive all the way to Chia, which I adore by the way, only to find out that you're not going to drown yourself." Clara's voice was rising, in the hope to elicit some response.

Rossana looked at Clara and then went back to her favourite windscreen-staring position.

"To be honest, I don't think much of your choice of methods to quit this life. Drowning…" Clara shook her head. "It must be pretty unpleasant. Have you ever swallowed sea water? It's disgusting! You probably die by being sick, before you drown."

Rossana was listening and still looking away.

"Also, smashing your car and yourself over a cliff is distasteful. Imagine what it's like for the people who've got to come and fetch your battered body, as well as the car. Plus, it must be painful being bashed to pieces."

No reaction. Clara got fed up and grabbed her shoulders and started to shake her. "Hey, I'm talking to you! Wake up!"

Rossana finally smiled. "Now I remember who you are!"

"Oh, no. Another dream!" Clara rolled her eyes.

"Yes, yes, it was you. How weird." Rossana finally looked at her.

"Don't tell me please." Clara shook her head.

"I will. I must tell someone, I haven't told anyone yet. It only happened last night." Rossana seemed to come back to life and her brown eyes started to sparkle. "It was a warm sunny day, and I started to walk down a narrow alleyway made of rose bushes. The branches were tightly packed in, and almost formed a thick hedge; the bushes had roses of all colours. At some point, the alleyway forked in two directions, I just picked one by chance. I carried on along the pathway, but it kept dividing itself in other passages and I just happened to take one randomly each time. But then, when I tried to go back, I couldn't remember the way I'd walked originally, and I realized that I was very far from the entrance."

"That's not a dream, it's a nightmare."

"The rose bushes were getting taller, and the roses were starting to wither, until all you could see were dry petals and dying leaves. The more I walked, the darker it got, because the bushes became so tall that the light couldn't come through. I was starting to worry and get desperate, as I'd just realized that I was lost in this labyrinth. As I looked down at my feet, I noticed that I had a golden cord wrapped around my waist…"

"As people do," commented Clara.

"I felt something pulling me backwards through the cord, so I started to walk back following the force that was drawing me. A bit like Arianna's thread, in Greek mythology. And slowly, the bushes became shorter, the sun-rays started to come through and the roses appeared again, until I found the way out." She stared at Clara. "At the exit, you were there, with a huge roll of golden string, which you kept wrapping around, until you pulled me close to you."

Certainly Lucilla had a vivid imagination when she decided to interfere with people's dreams. "Did you notice anybody else?"

"When I came out, there was a huge garden, with thick green grass everywhere, a bit like an English lawn. As I came close to you, I spotted a blonde girl, sitting on an apple tree in the distance."

"I bet she was wearing a blue hat with a veil."

Rossana didn't seem surprised that Clara should know. "Yes, she indicated with her hand that I should come closer to her and opened her arms. But you grabbed my arm and said I shouldn't go." Rossana seemed perplexed. "Why wouldn't you let me go?"

"I don't know. To be honest, I don't think much of her."

"But she seemed so nice, and beautiful!"

"Some people can be *too* nice and *too* beautiful."

"Anyway, I woke up after that. In fact, you know the strange thing? I still have a bruise in my right arm, exactly where you held me in the dream." Rossana pulled the sleeve up, and showed the mark on her upper arm. Clara felt a shiver down her spine.

"Rossana, as much as I like hearing about your dreams, we need to do some serious talking. Shall we get out and walk a little?"

"I'm happy staying in the car."

"OK then, but let's open the doors, so we can get some air." It was one in the afternoon, not the best of times to hang around in the heat.

Clara didn't know why Rossana wanted to kill herself. Somehow today she didn't feel very inspired and she was very much hoping it'd be an easy case. Why some people chose to be uncomfortable, she didn't understand. The climatic conditions didn't help her concentration, they could be sitting in a kiosk on the beach, sipping a cool drink, but hey no, she wanted to sit and sweat in a dusty car. Different tastes.

"Why do you want to commit suicide?" she might as well be direct.

"Because I'm useless."

"Why do you think you're useless?"

"Because I'm a failure at everything." There was a tone of desperation in her voice. "My parents are very clever. My father's a university lecturer and my mother's a high school teacher. My brother is twenty-eight and he graduated two years ago in law, my sister is twenty-five and she got a degree in economics last year. They both got the top grades." She sighed. "And then I come, the idiot in the family. I'm twenty-three and I've achieved nothing!"

"Well, you've got a driving license for a start. And that's not *nothing*. The driving tests nowadays are really tough; our parents wouldn't be able to pass them!"

"I guess you've got a point. But maybe I just got lucky on that occasion." Rossana sighed again. "When I was nineteen, I enrolled at university to study economics. I took the first exam three times, and failed every time. So I changed my mind."

"I don't blame you. Economics; not exactly an exciting subject. Just numbers and money."

"Then at twenty, I enrolled on a biology degree. Again I failed my first exam, four times."

"At least you persevere, you don't just give up easily. That's a great quality." Clara was trying to see the positive side.

"At twenty-one, I decided to try physics, but I wasn't good at that either. I gave up after two attempts."

"Physics would be the last subject I'd pick."

"At twenty-two my parents picked for me: political science. That was even worse; it was enough to fail the first exam once, to put me off."

Clara didn't know what useful comment she could make at this point.

"Last Autumn I enrolled on an Italian literature course, thinking that it might be easy, since I like poetry. Guess what?"

Clara looked up. "You failed again?"

"Of course!" Rossana raised her hands in the air. "What else can I do, but fail?"

"Why do you keep doing something you're no good at?" Clara's words just came out.

"And how's that comment supposed to help me?" Rossana started to cry.

Emergency procedure. What was Clara supposed to say now? "Ehmm… if you were rubbish at all these subjects, why didn't you pick one you could pass?" Was that more helpful?

"Because I'm rubbish at everything!" Rossana was sobbing violently now. Her shoulders were shaking and she looked terribly upset. Had Clara really screwed up there? Her phone too had come to life. What a day.

"Listen, I'm sorry. I didn't mean what I've just said." Clara offered some tissues. "I guess it's the heat in here, my head is boiling." She got out of the car and stretched her legs. "Do you mind if I just disappear for a few seconds? I need to clear my thoughts."

Rossana looked at her with an air of incredulity. Her eyes were still veiled with tears and her cheeks and nose had gone puffy. Clara felt awful about leaving this way.

"I'll take your car keys with me, just in case."

Before Rossana could reply, Clara had already grabbed the keys and walked away towards the trees. Things weren't going as planned. She was too tired, too hot and bothered, to come up with a decent anti-suicide formula.

"How tactful of you." Lucilla was sitting in the shadow of a juniper. She was holding a twig, which she'd used to make some drawings on the sand.

"I need help! I just don't know what to say to this girl!"

"The girl in question has a name: Rossana."

"Tell me something I don't know." Clara was losing patience.

"You've got to keep it personal, if you want to be successful." Lucilla was rolling the twig with two fingers.

"Well, since you're the expert, perhaps you could tell me *exactly* how I should deal with her. With Rossana, I mean." Clara wiped her forehead and cheeks, her face was on fire.

"That's your problem."

Clara's hot blood started to reach boiling temperatures. "You know what? I'm going to walk away right now. I've had enough of this nonsense. I'm no bloody psychotherapist!"

Lucilla grabbed her arm. Clara hadn't even noticed that she'd got up.

"Don't be silly."

There was a thunderous look between them. Lucilla finally gave in, and her gaze became softer.

"You need to try and put yourself in her shoes. This will make it easier for you to understand her." Lucilla's voice was gentler.

"We're just too damn different! Opposite poles. She's so insecure, and such a ditherer. She doesn't know what she wants, and she changes her mind far too often." Clara raised her arms.

"But why is she like that? Try to understand. And only then, you'll be able to help."

That was easy. Everything sounded easy with Lucilla.

"Now go!"

Before Clara could even register her command, she felt Lucilla's hand, pushing strongly on her back. Good manners. She'd forgotten that her blonde friend possessed this quality, among many others.

Clara walked towards the Ford Fiesta and decided not to think too hard. Perhaps, if she was calmer, inspiration would be easier to find? The sand and dust had gathered between her clammy feet and the sandals' straps. Not the nicest of sensations.

"I thought you'd run away with my car keys!" shouted Rossana.

"No, I just took them as a safety measure."

"Who are you exactly? And what do you want from me?"

That was a legitimate question, but Clara decided to ignore it.

"Tell me more about you. What do you like to do in your spare time?"

Rossana frowned. She obviously didn't think that was the right answer. Luckily she didn't seem too upset now. "I like to play tennis, but I don't have an eye for the ball."

"It's a difficult sport. Have you tried table-tennis?"

"I found that even harder. The ball is smaller, so are the rackets."

Rossana shook her head. No. That wasn't working. And anyway, could you really get to know a person more, if they told you what their hobbies were? Paolo was a keen footballer, and so was her brother Dino. Still, they were two very different characters. How could she really get to know Rossana and her circumstances a bit better?

"Earlier you mentioned going to university…" Clara paused and opened the car door, to let more air in. "Is this something you really wanted to do?"

"No! Never. I hate studying." There was no hesitation in Rossana's reply.

"But why did you…"

"My parents forced me." She sighed deeply. "They just put so much pressure on me. You must get a degree, otherwise you're not going to get a job; if you don't have a degree you're nothing these days. Look at your brother and sister how successful they are… All this crap."

Clara was taken aback. She had no degree, and yet she never felt she was a lesser human being because of that. The rubbish that young people were told nowadays was limitless.

"But, surely you've got your own voice. Can't you speak up for yourself?" That's what Clara would've done.

"I've tried to, but they manage to twist my mind and my brain so much that they convinced me to have a go again. You see, I was useless at elementary school, at secondary school, and even at the liceo. It was thanks to their help that I managed to go through and get my certificates. So they think that if they continue pushing, I might just manage a degree!"

Clara shook her head, she couldn't believe that some parents could be so pushy, in fact, aggressive would be a better word for them. They didn't seem to have any idea of the stress they caused their daughter, and all of this, with a view to helping her.

"Now, what do *you* want to do? Have you asked that question of yourself?" Clara's voice was calm and supportive.

"It may sound strange to you, but I want to be a shop assistant."

"It's not strange at all. I love shops." Clara could've lived in a shop. Not just worked in there.

"I've got an uncle who's got a clothes shop in via Garibaldi. I asked him if I could work for him and he said he'd rather have me, his niece, than some stranger helping him out. But my parents, no way, they'd never let me work in a shop. Real snobs!"

"Rossana, can't you see that things are simpler than they seem? You can have a job that you like and don't have to study if you don't want to. Just speak to your parents and tell them." Really, things *were* that simple.

She looked away. "Things are never that easy."

"You can't possibly think of killing yourself just because your parents want you to have a degree and you'd rather not!" Clara was losing her patience again.

Rossana thought for a while and with a sad expression she spoke: "You're not helping, I feel worse now, I feel stupid."

Clara stopped for a second, how could she be so insensitive? She ought to learn to bite her tongue at times. She took hold of Rossana's arm and caressed her bruise. "You're not stupid, I am. I didn't express myself in the proper way. I… just wanted to point out that you can change things. It's your life and no-one else can, or should, tell you how to live it."

"You're right. But will I have the strength?"

"Can you see that, if you distance yourself from the problem, and become objective, it actually is not such a big deal? You have the solution in your hands."

Rossana seemed to want to reflect. Clara decided it was good to keep quiet for a while, better not to risk another botch for the day.

"Maybe it was silly of me to just surrender like that. I've got so many years ahead of me, and why should my parents spoil it?"

Clara couldn't believe her ears.

"I'll speak to my uncle, and whether they like it or not, I'll go and work for him." Rossana seemed convinced.

"Perhaps also your uncle can have a word with your parents?"

"Sure. That should help." Rossana seemed relieved. "And whether they like it or not, I'm going to do what *I* want to do."

Had it worked? Could Clara relax now? She felt a sudden affection for this girl. She could be a younger sister, and she hoped very much that she'd stand up and fight for her beliefs.

"It's really strange, I feel so light now. Almost like a big weight has come off my shoulders. In fact I feel full of life. I might go for a swim!" Rossana's voice was cheerful, and she did seem truly happy. And she was definitely *different*.

"Promise that you're not going to have any naughty thoughts while in the water…"

"No way! I just want to have fun now!"

"Before you go, can you just tell me your surname?"

The phone started to beep.

"What a funny noise, I heard it earlier too. What is it?" Rossana was showing a healthy curiosity.

"Please just tell me your surname."

The beeping got louder.

"It begins with m…"

"Spit it out!"

"Melis. Rossana Melis."

"Great, thanks." Clara hugged her new friend and said goodbye.

Lucilla hadn't uttered a word yet as they were driving back to Cagliari. Clara had expected a thank you, some form of congratulations, but it was obvious that Lucilla wasn't in the mood to pay compliments. Could she get so pissed off just because Clara had asked Rossana's surname? Was that such a big deal?

"You disobeyed me," Lucilla finally spoke.

"I've never liked the word obedience and anything related to it."

"A pact is a pact."

"Sure, but we had no pact when it came to names and surnames. In fact I don't recall you saying, explicitly, that I shouldn't ask people's surnames. You simply refused to tell me when I asked about it." Perhaps she should've been a lawyer.

"These are subtleties; nonetheless you did something that didn't meet my approval."

"So what?"

Lucilla shook her head. "You think you're smarter than you actually are."

"I don't think I'm a genius, but I'd say I've got a certain degree of intelligence, otherwise, why would you ask for my help?"

"Do you think that I carefully chose you, or that I picked you at random?" Lucilla had a defiant look this time, something Clara hadn't seen before.

"Does it matter? Surely what counts are the results, and so far I've done very well with my first three missions!"

"How can you be so sure? Have you spoken to Giovanni and Mario since your encounter with them?"

"I haven't had the chance!" What was Lucilla implying with her question?

"And how do you know that today you've truly managed to convince Rossana not to do it?"

Clara felt like someone had just punched her in the stomach. Gut feeling?

"Your pride is causing you to make two mistakes. Number one: you assume you've been successful. Number two: you assume your success is due entirely to your own efforts."

Clara's mouth was open but nothing was coming out. Not even her breath.

Lucilla laughed openly. "Do you seriously believe that just a few words here and there have persuaded Giovanni, Mario and Rossana not to commit suicide?"

Clara's ego was being smashed to pieces and she could've happily shrunk into a meaningless ball of flesh, and bones. And a bit of fat. She'd never felt so small.

"But, if I'm no good, why ask for my help in the first place?" She had a right to know.

"Help. That's the key word. You've helped, but you didn't do all the work." Lucilla paused; as usual even her pauses happened at the right time. "Remember, you're one of the actors, not the director."

"So, who's the director then?" She may as well ask.

"You already know the answer." Lucilla shut herself in silence for the duration of the return journey.

Chapter 14

Today, Mamma had prepared spaghetti alle vongole. Clara adored clams, and this time she wasn't going to ask for half a portion. Mamma was pleased to see that the pasta bowl was empty, after she served everybody; as an old-fashioned mother, she never liked to throw food away.

"Delicious clams, they taste so fresh!" Clara savoured her spaghetti. "What are you doing?" she then looked at her sister.

"I prefer to take all the clams out of their shells, put the shells aside, and then roll the clams on the fork, together with the spaghetti. It tastes better this way."

"But part of the fun is to suck them from the shell with their juice." Papà proceeded to make a lot of noise in the process.

"It can become quite messy," Clara was struggling with her spaghetti bundle. "They should genetically modify clams so that they are born and grow without a shell."

"You can buy the frozen ones, with their shells removed. But they're not as tasty," declared Mamma as she poured some white wine.

Nonno was silent, he seemed to be enjoying his food. That was usually his attitude during meals, if he was quiet, it meant the food was good.

Valentina though liked to provoke her grand-father. "Nonno, if what you say is true, about the lack of food during the war and being hungry... Did you use to eat the shells as well as the clams then?"

"That's so disrespectful, take it back!" Mamma seemed appalled.

"I was joking, come on!" Valentina looked away.

"Bad taste," commented Papà.

Nonno finished his pasta, wiped his lips with the blue cotton napkin and looked at his grand-daughter. "We certainly didn't have much food, but what we ate was genuine. None of that rubbish youngsters eat nowadays." He poured himself a glass of wine. "Therefore, girls didn't have spots on their faces in those days..." he winked.

"Nonno, that was cruel!" Clara's look was disapproving.

Valentina blushed. "I asked for it."

Mamma got up and collected the plates and then started serving the second course. Red mullets cooked al cartoccio. Clara adored mullets and started to unravel her parcel wrapped in foil, with the same excitement as a child opening a Christmas present.

"It smells divine, just the combination of olive oil, garlic and fresh parsley, together with the fish. Heaven." She sniffed twice.

"It's only fish! I do like mullets, but they're full of bones!" complained Valentina.

"I'll take the bones out for you," offered Papà.

Nonno shook his head in disapproval as the fish was passed from one side of the table to the other.

"On the way home tonight, I stopped over to admire your Ferrari. I still can't believe that we've got this car. Or rather, you've got it. What about the friend who gave it to you, what was she called?" Papà was carefully extracting the bones from the mullet.

"Lucilla. Unusual name," responded Valentina.

"Well, has she been in touch recently? When are you going to introduce her to us? The minimum we can do is to invite her for dinner." Papà seemed curious to meet this generous friend.

Clara felt the blood drain from her upper body. She wondered if she was going pale.

"Ehmm, I... haven't seen her since then." Was it obvious that she was lying?

"What? She hasn't even called you?" Mamma wasn't impressed.

"I don't think she wants to stay in touch." What else could Clara say?

"So, this Lucilla buys you a Ferrari, and then disappears." Papà passed the fish back to Valentina and started the surgery on his own mullet. "Am I being paranoid, or is something not right here?"

There was a silence, except for the cutlery rubbing on the plates.

"Also, I've noticed tonight, that there are already 750 kilometres on the clock. How did you manage to run such mileage in less than a week?" He looked at Clara the way a police inspector would. "Especially when work is only two kilometres from here."

Everybody was looking at Clara now. She hated being at the centre of attention.

"I... I've lent the car to some colleagues," she said tentatively.

"What a ride!" commented Nonno.

"You've lent your Ferrari to some colleagues? This is not your Fiat Punto!" Papà was surprised.

"But they're very nice, I know I can trust them."

"Nice? Driving your car for hundreds of kilometres for free, that's nice!" Papà shook his head. "Who's paying for the petrol anyway? That monster drinks like a sponge!"

Petrol. That's something Clara hadn't thought of. She didn't even know how to fill it up. Lucilla had somehow made sure that it always had a full tank, and now that she thought of it, the car was always clean and shiny. Did her blonde friend make sure the car got valeted when Clara wasn't looking? She did have a duplicate set of keys, after all.

"We're waiting for your answer, my dear." Mamma had a sip of wine.

Clara was lost, she couldn't remember the question.

"Are you OK? You look pale and ... tired."

Why were mums always so observant?

"I've had a bad day." Clara was happy to switch topic. "Too busy. I had to cover for Teresa, there was a board meeting and she hadn't prepared for it."

"That's nice of her," commented Papà.

"She's starting to get on my nerves, she does this far too often." Clara was fed up.

"Can't you return the favour? Perhaps you could go missing the day you've got something important?" Valentina always had bright ideas.

"I thought about it, but they won't give me any time off when *I* am organizing the event."

"When's your next meeting?" asked her sister.

"Monday, the 9th June."

"Can't you be conveniently sick on that day?"

"No way. They'd probably send the official doctor to check me out at home." Clara was amused at the thought. "The ideal thing would be for me to fall sick for real, obviously nothing too bad, like a cold, or a back-ache, but something I can demonstrate with a doctor's certificate, that doesn't cause too much pain."

"What makes you think that back-ache doesn't cause too much pain?" Nonno stroked his lower back.

"OK, something else then. I'd really like to be away from the office, unexpectedly, when there's something important. Just to see how *she* copes." She smirked.

"Pray for it then." Mamma had a mischievous look on her face.

It'd been raining that morning, only for half an hour, and yet Cagliari was in total chaos. Somehow there seemed to be many more cars around when it rained, and they all seemed to stop at the same time, possibly the same place as well? Via Roma was at a standstill. If only a few drops could cause this mess, what would happen when there was a proper storm? Clara had always believed that it should only rain at night. What was funny about the situation was that traffic could be chaotic even when not moving. Scooters and mopeds seemed to elegantly sneak between cars, vehicles kept hooting at some unknown motorist in front, pedestrians would fight with their umbrellas. And anyway, why open an umbrella when walking down the porticos?

As Clara sat at the wheel, she watched the tall palm trees, lined up on her left, the gigantic leaves waving under the strong breeze. An enormous white ferry was sitting on the sea and its pallid figure contrasted with the blue sky. Despite the rain, the sky was blue. It was one of those skies that cheated on you. It only had two or three clouds up there, and these were the only ones causing all that trouble. In fact, Clara wondered if one of them hadn't been following her all the way from home, like a personal body-guard, and it'd decided to dedicate drops solely to her and her surroundings. She smiled at the idea; the good news was that there was going to be a rainbow soon. As she crawled twenty centimeters ahead, she suddenly realized how quickly she'd fallen asleep last night. It was the first time she hadn't thought about Paolo. How could that be? If this was the man she loved, how could she forget about him so soon? But then, she'd had a very stressful day, between the meeting at work, and running to Chia, and coming back to the office, and then the third-degree from her father during dinner. Too much for one day. Probably her brain had ceased to function by bed-time. Anyway, she shouldn't be celebrating about this, after all she'd made a deal with Lucilla. There was only one more mission to accomplish and then, hopefully, she'd get Paolo back.

By the time she got to the office, it was gone nine.

"You're late," was Marcella's welcome.

"Do you think that escaped my attention?" Clara sat at her desk.

If there was a traffic jam in Cagliari, why was Clara the only affected one? When she'd arrived it seemed as if all the offices were occupied, even the car park had been full. Did some people possess special powers that enabled them to see traffic jams in advance? Or did they get to work via helicopter? Whatever it was, it annoyed her.

"Paolo came to look for you earlier." Marcella was typing very fast.

"Really? First thing in the morning?" Clara was surprised.

"Maybe for you it's first thing." Marcella looked at her watch. "But not for him."

Clara stared at her blank screen. "What did he want?"

"I didn't ask."

There was a knock on the door. Ernesto appeared and shyly looked at Clara: "I've noticed there were traffic problems in via Roma. I was just wondering how you'd managed to get to work today." He was wearing a white shirt, with big orange flowers. The right colours for a dull day.

"You're popular this morning!" Marcella looked at Clara.

"It's nice of you to check." Clara got up and walked towards him. "Yes, as you can see I managed to get in. Just." She took a closer look at one of the orange flowers. "Do you come that way too?"

"Yes, but with the vespa it's never a problem."

Marcella was silent and looked at both of them.

"I do wonder… what's the point of having such a fast car, if at the end of the day, you get stuck in traffic?" Clara waved her hands.

"Oh, I do feel sorry for you!" responded Marcella.

"You might want to swap one day. If so, just ask," winked Ernesto.

Gianna arrived and without wasting any time she asked: "Coffee time. Who's coming?"

"But it's only gone nine!" Ernesto seemed surprised.

"We always have an early one," Marcella grabbed her bag. "Do you want to join us?"

He seemed taken aback, but how could he refuse such an invitation. He nodded.

Clara made no attempt to join the party, so he looked at her. "Aren't you coming with us?"

"I can't." She pointed at her watch, "I've only just arrived!"

Marcella and Gianna were already heading for the lift, Ernesto hesitated and then whispered to Clara: "But it's not the same without you."

What a nice thing to hear. How confusing though, Clara's instincts were shouting at her, that she should just go and enjoy that coffee with Ernesto, and the girls. But reason had to prevail: "I really can't. It doesn't look good."

"OK then. Another time perhaps?" he seemed hopeful.

"Only if you wear this shirt again!"

As he left her office, she sat at her desk and switched the computer on. She noticed that she felt a hint of sadness; a strange sensation, almost of regret. That disappointed look, on Ernesto's face when she refused to go with him, made her feel uneasy.

She looked at her screen, but didn't focus. For some reason, Signor Peppino's face came to mind, and was followed by Giovanni's, Mario's and Rossana's. She suddenly remembered what Lucilla had told her yesterday, on their way back from their mission. Clara had assumed that all the people she'd tried to help were doing just fine now. But, was that the case? Why should she take this for granted? Was it to ease her conscience? She closed her eyes. Could she really hope that her involvement had actually solved the problems these people had? Shouldn't it be more of a case that when you help someone, one gesture is not enough? For instance, when she'd given that money to the beggar, maybe it helped him on that evening, perhaps to buy himself a drink, but she didn't actually contribute to resolve his long-term issues. When it came Signor Peppino, Giovanni, Mario and Rossana... was she expected to do some sort of follow-up? Or worse, should she make sure that they were still alive?

There was another knock on the door. What was going on today?

"Can I talk to you for a moment?" Paolo asked in a low voice.

"Sure, do come in." Clara could've done with being on her own for ten minutes.

Paolo shut the door behind, obviously what he wanted to tell her was confidential. She started to feel apprehensive, so decided to stay seated.

"Clara, this is a bit awkward, I don't know how to say it," he cleared his throat.

"Whatever it is, just speak." She wondered what on earth could make him so nervous. Perhaps he'd changed his mind about the split up and was... reconsidering things?

"I've been asked by the head of personnel to keep an eye on your working hours." He shook his head. "He seems to have noticed that your time keeping recently has been... slack."

Clara couldn't believe those words. She frowned.

"As his deputy, he's asked me to check what time you come in, when you go for breaks, when you leave, etc." He seemed to be very uncomfortable. "Obviously I have no intention of doing so, but I thought I should warn you."

"But... we're supposed to have flexible working hours. If you arrive late, you leave late." Clara was puzzled.

"Yes, but it seems that recently, you've tended to... arrive late and leave early." Paolo was looking edgy and kept pacing up and down the office. "Not to mention that yesterday you disappeared for almost three hours in the middle of the day."

"But I didn't swipe my card, no-one saw me leave!" How could it be?

"But I did. Obviously I said nothing about that, and maybe you think that no-one notices, but people do. I just came here to say that you should be careful."

Clara was in shock. She'd never thought of herself as someone who took advantage of work and certainly she wasn't pleased that her colleagues, including Paolo, had this opinion of her.

"I can assure you that whenever I've had to leave, it was for a very good reason," her eyes were sincere.

Paolo came close to her and touched her arm. "I know you well enough. You don't need to explain it to me. It's just that those sharks out there, they're always trying to get at someone, usually those who appear to be weak and vulnerable. Don't give them the opportunity, that's all."

"Thank you very much for the warning." Clara appreciated his gesture.

"I also want to apologize for the way I spoke to you yesterday, by the photocopier." He bit his lip. "You were right to be angry, she could've organized things better."

"Apologies accepted." Finally Clara got some satisfaction. Perhaps the charms of Miss Shake-your-bum were gradually dissipating. She secretly smiled inside, maybe Paolo got his neurons working again and was able to see her colleague for what she really was.

Mamma and Valentina were in the kitchen, preparing dinner, while rest of the family was occupied in the living room. Dino was visiting again, with little Ivan and his wife Orietta. Clara was playing with her nephew on the floor, they were involved in a battle between red and blue plastic soldiers. Somehow, Ivan's soldiers seemed to be on the winning side. Orietta was enjoying her aperitif as she sat comfortably on the sofa, while the three men were watching the local news almost in a trance.

The television was loud, as Nonno was hard of

hearing, so Clara couldn't help listening to the dull voice of the presenter. She wondered why news presenters always had that serious and solemn tone, especially the guys. The name of Rossana Melis was mentioned. She thought for a second that this name sounded familiar and then suddenly started paying attention. Apparently a twenty-three year old girl was run over by a car this morning, as she tried to cross the road to catch a bus. There were many witnesses who confirmed the accident. The girl in question died on the spot. Her photo was quickly flashed on screen, and the presenter carried on with a list of names and similar accidents which had happened so far in 2003. Clara was traumatized, this couldn't possibly be her Rossana. It just *had to be* a mistake. But the photo, it was her in the photo, perhaps when she'd had longer hair. She screamed.

"What's the matter?" asked Papà.

Clara started crying inconsolably, she was shaking. Dino and Orietta went towards her and held her and wondered what was going on. Little Ivan was pulling her jeans from below.

"I know that girl who died! She's a friend of mine," Clara could barely speak.

"Oh my God!" Mamma ran from the kitchen. "What a disgrace. How awful!" she took hold of Clara and hugged her tightly.

"I didn't know of this friend. You never mentioned her name," pointed out Valentina.

"It's someone I only met recently," Clara couldn't stop sobbing. "It's just too painful, it's too bad." She was still shaking.

"Here, have a glass of water," offered Nonno.

Valentina rescued some tissues and passed them on to Clara.

"I think I need to go to my bedroom for a minute." Clara rushed away.

When she got to her room, she shut the door. She started to breathe in deeply, in order to calm herself. She sat on her bed, stared at the wall, kept breathing until she finally became lucid. It was an accident, wasn't it? That's what the TV had said. Rossana hadn't thrown herself in front of the car. She was crossing the road and was run over. Things like these could happen, to anybody. But why Rossana? What was going on? What role did Lucilla play in all of this? Clara's head was thumping and her heart was beating fast again. She grabbed her phone from the bag, and pressed the yellow button.

"I'm here," replied calmly Lucilla.

"You'd better be," Clara responded coldly. "Meet me at the car now."

Chapter 15

Clara wiped her tears, went to the bathroom and washed her face. She headed for the living room where everyone was waiting for her. They all looked surprised and upset at the same time.

"Please have dinner without me," said Clara. "I need to go out for a walk, don't wait for me."

"But... where are you going?" Mamma was alarmed.

"Just around here for a stroll, it'll help me recover from the shock."

"I'll come with you," offered Valentina.

"No! Please, I need to be on my own." Clara was nervous. "Don't let this spoil the evening. Have dinner as planned, and maybe Mamma, keep my portion warm on the side and I'll have it when I get back."

Clara quickly left and rushed down the stairs. The lift was never available when you needed it most.

As usual, her blonde friend was waiting inside the car, which was parked on a side street off via Milano. Clara went in, slammed the door and inserted the keys.

"You've been crying." Lucilla had a caring tone.

"Cut the crap." Clara was fuming. "What happened today?"

"What happens every day, some people were born, some died." How could she be so calm and peaceful?

"Will you stop this bullshit?" Clara's look was in flames. "What happened to Rossana?"

"She was walking along via Dante and needed to catch the bus. She was late, so when she saw the bus arriving on the opposite side of the road, she tried to run across because she didn't want to miss it, and did so without looking. She was run over by a motorist, who was going too fast." Lucilla spoke evenly.

"How do I know you're telling the truth? What if she threw herself in front of the car?" Clara had started not to trust Lucilla.

"You just have to take my word for it!"

"Yes, like when you said that nobody at work would notice my absence. Guess what? They did!" Clara's eyes were piercing Lucilla's, but they didn't seem to have much of an effect.

"That's not *exactly* what I said."

"Did you have anything to do with Rossana's death?" Clara needed to know.

Lucilla seemed surprised. "Not at all, her death was natural."

"Natural? Do you call being run over *natural?*"

"By natural I mean that her death wasn't caused deliberately. It just happened." Lucilla's voice was serene.

Clara was confused. Nothing seemed to make sense now.

"Did you know yesterday, that this was going to occur today?" That was the key question.

"Possibly."

"What was the point then?" Clara started to scream, she couldn't control it. She grabbed the steering wheel so tightly that her knuckles went pale. Her shouting was intense; she felt that even the Ferrari was starting to shake. But Lucilla was still calm, perhaps she was deaf? Clara finally ran out of voice.

"That's better," said Lucilla.

"Why the hell did you ask me to stop Rossana from committing suicide, if you knew she was going to die anyway?"

"Because it's better this way."

"Better for whom?"

"For her. You should never seek your own death. Death will find you when the time is right."

Clara was mystified. What was the purpose in all of this? What had she been doing getting involved in these missions, if at the end of the day, people died anyway? She punched the steering wheel.

"Why? I need to know *why* she had to die. She was so young, she had a whole life ahead of her. It's not fair." Clara was shaking her head.

"I don't know. It's not me who decides."

"So… you're telling me that you're implicated in all of this, and even *you* don't know what it's all about?"

"I don't *need* to know. I trust that there's a good reason for it." Lucilla smiled.

"How dare you smile when someone's just died? A friend of ours! Her body's still warm in her coffin, and you smile?" Clara was enraged. She looked inside her bag and managed to find the phone. She grabbed it and threw the stupid device at Lucilla, who grasped it from the air.

"What's this all about?" asked Lucilla.

"Our deal's broken. You can have that toy back, and your damn car too! Also, don't bother about Paolo. I've had enough of you, your promises, your weird missions, and I regret the very instant I met you!"

"You're making a mistake," Lucilla spoke softly.

"The only mistake I've ever made was to come across you!" Clara slammed the door behind her and rushed home.

As she got to her apartment, she realized the consequences of what she'd just done. It'd felt good to throw the phone at Lucilla, but had that been wise? Her impulsiveness and her behaviour had caused their agreement to be terminated, that also meant that she was going to lose her Ferrari. How was she going to explain this to her family? Things were getting complicated. As if she didn't have enough to worry about. She opened the door.

"Is that you Clara?" shouted Mamma from the kitchen.

"Who else could it be?" replied Valentina.

Clara appeared and joined the rest of the family at the table.

"Are you OK bella?" Mamma touched her arm.

"Better," Clara tried to smile. "Let's talk about other stuff, please."

"Auntie, my soldiers killed half of yours earlier. Shall we fight again after dinner, so I can kill all of them?" Ivan's voice was cute.

"Of course, but you must eat all your dinner, so that your soldiers can get even stronger."

As Clara tried her seafood risotto, she noticed that it didn't taste as nice as usual. She knew Mamma's cooking was excellent, therefore, there must be something seriously wrong with her.

"Sorry we started without you Clara, but the risotto was ready and, as you know, it needs to be eaten straight away." Mamma felt the need to apologize, she always wanted the family to eat together.

"It's not a problem. I don't like it too hot anyway."

"I've promised Orietta to take her for a ride in the Ferrari. Can I borrow it tomorrow evening?" Dino was cutting a piece of ciabatta bread.

Clara felt a cramp in her stomach, what was she going to say now?

"Everybody has tried it and I still haven't had the chance! Would that be OK?" Orietta's eyes were lighting up.

Clara's cheeks became pale, almost as white as the tablecloth.

"You don't seem very pleased..." commented Orietta.

Clara looked up, her tongue seemed to be stuck and unable to move. The problem was the brain, that wasn't giving the right signal. She was holding her fork in mid-air.

"Sister! Orietta's talking to you, an answer would be polite," joked Valentina.

"I no longer have the car. I gave it back." Clara had spoken slowly.

There was some serious jaw-dropping around the table. The only one making any noise at this point was little Ivan, who was talking to an invisible soldier hidden below his risotto.

Clara felt the need to clarify: "Lucilla asked me to give her the car back. She needed it."

"Do you mean, she needed to *borrow* it?" Papà seemed puzzled.

"No, she needed to take it back. Full stop."

Everyone was shaking their heads in disbelief.

"And you just gave it to her?" Dino had an annoyed expression.

"Well, it was *her* car originally!" What else could Clara say?

"But it was registered on your name. That means that it's *your* car!" Papà seemed agitated, very rarely he would get wound up.

"Nipotina mia, please tell us that it's a joke. You still have the car, right?" Nonno was trying to make things better.

"No, not really... I've given it back." Clara looked down. She would've liked to hide under the table. She felt ashamed for lying, and to top it up, her family was now thinking that she was an idiot. Which one was worse?

"But you need a car to go to work." Mamma was in such a shock that she appeared incredibly calm.

"Which reminds me, may I borrow yours tomorrow?" Clara may as well ask the question now.

"Of course." Mamma stared at a transparent point in the opposite wall.

"What about the registration documents, and all that stuff? You need to do things properly, otherwise you may be liable for road tax, insurance, fines, etc." Papà looked irritated.

"I'll take care of it tomorrow," responded Clara.

"What kind of a friend is someone who buys something for you and then wants it back?" Dino obviously disapproved.

"There's something really odd going on here." Papà shook his head. "People just don't give you a Ferrari, for the sake of it. And then a week later take it back from you." He looked at Clara with a piercing gaze. "Are you telling us everything my dear?"

"Leave her alone!" interrupted Mamma. "She's had a bad time already with her friend dying and now you start on her."

"Auntie, shall we go and play in your bedroom? I like it there." Ivan's request was well received by Clara.

"Yes, let's go now. Sorry guys, I'm not very hungry today, do you mind if I go and play with my nephew for a while?" Clara got up and headed for her bedroom, followed by little Ivan.

She realized she was treading on dangerous grounds. No-one was supposed to get up from the table before dinner was finished. Not only had she just done so, but she'd also set a bad example for little Ivan. Pretty unforgivable. But she needed to escape from the heated atmosphere; it was a big relief to be away from the family's scrutiny. Clara and Ivan were sitting on the cool floor, in the safe haven of her own bedroom. She was caressing his soft brown hair, as he was busy lining up his soldiers on opposite fronts. There was something refreshing about the innocence of children, so liberating. Everything appeared simple to their eyes, the red soldiers were the enemy and the blue ones were the friends, they fought each other and only one army won. No-one got upset, not even the wounded soldiers.

Clara was still in shock at the news of Rossana's death. It was too horrible to believe. OK, she'd only spoken to her for an hour at most, but she did feel some affection towards her. Rossana was a nice person, nothing horrible should've happened to her. But where did all this leave Clara? Should she go to the funeral? Or was it better to cut off from it, and forget it all? Pretend that none of this had ever happened? The good news was that the deal with Lucilla was over now, life was going to get simpler. Yet, she didn't feel any better.

Clara let Ivan kill all her soldiers gradually, but she managed to knock down a few of his, which seemed to annoy him a little. After all her armed forces had perished, he asked if he could go inside her wardrobe. She let him; he'd always liked playing in there. She tried to imagine what he was doing inside, she could hear a lot of fumbling noises and laughter, how a little boy could have fun pulling skirts and trousers from their hangers, and getting entangled with jumpers, she didn't understand. Then he opened the door and appeared with a red toy phone in his hands. Clara had forgotten about this phone. It was the one that Lucilla had given her, as a back-up. She took it from Ivan's hands and he proceeded to shout in protest.

"Let me show you how to use this," said Clara.

Ivan stopped crying and listened carefully.

"You lift this thing here, it's called the receiver, and you press any of these buttons and you pretend to talk to someone." Clara put the phone close to her ear, but there was no sound. Whatever buttons she'd pressed, they hadn't worked. Lucilla had given her the right combination of keys and numbers, but who wanted to speak to her anyway? And, in any case, was this toy a real phone? She doubted it.

"Little Ivan, you can keep this and play with it as much as you want."

"Can I take it home?" he seemed thrilled.

"Sure."

Clara was glad. That was the last trace of Lucilla gone from her life.

It was hard to concentrate at work that morning. Clara was feeling deflated, her enthusiasm had gone. She'd made an effort to be at work on time today, she didn't want any unpleasant telling offs. Driving Mamma's car had felt strange, she'd got used to the Ferrari, and now everything seemed out of the ordinary. As she stared at the screen she realized that, in reality, what she'd been doing in the last week or so, had been the extraordinary thing. Perhaps, getting to work in a normal car and having a full night's sleep without undesired interruptions was that normality she'd longed for.

"You're very quiet today," Marcella was sharpening a pencil.

"I'm upset. Someone I knew died yesterday." Clara still couldn't believe it.

"I'm really sorry."

"Rossana Melis, the girl that got run over by a car."

"I saw it on television. Terrible news." Marcella was sympathetic.

"I'm still a bit shocked about it. You just don't expect these things to happen to someone you know."

Marcella got up and sat at Clara's desk, facing her. She held her arm. "Is there anything I can do?"

"No. I just need to… absorb it and make sense of it. That's all."

"The way I cope with bad news is by doing something that takes my mind off things."

"That doesn't work for me." Clara shook her head. "If I run away, the sadness chases me. I may as well face it. And get it over and done with." She sighed. "I think I'll take a long lunch hour by myself."

She needed to be alone during her lunch break, but where could she go? Home wasn't an option, as either Mamma or Nonno would be there. Bars and restaurants were normally full of people at lunchtime. She needed calm and silence, where could she find it in Cagliari? She put the car into first gear and left the courtyard. Inspiration would come, sooner or later. As she drove back towards via Roma, she realized that she was only three kilometres from the Poetto beach. The sea; that's what she needed. Surprising that she hadn't thought of it before, her own city had its own beautiful long beach. She put her foot down and raced along viale Diaz, until she reached viale Poetto, but at that point she slowed down, she remembered that the speed checks only failed when she was with Lucilla. At least, that's what she'd told her.

As she reached the area of Marina Piccola, just below the Devil's Saddle promontory, she opened the car window and breathed in the sea air, it was warm and soothing. The beach was on her right, loyal, almost as if it was standing there just waiting for Clara. She kept driving slowly and observed the little kiosks, *baretti* as they were called, some of which were already open, indicating that the summer had started. They were scattered along the beach, and always played cheerful music, served good panini and cold drinks, and offered excellent ice-creams, even the pre-packaged ones. Clara wasn't hungry, so she ignored the attractive smell of toasted focaccia and carried on driving.

The beach was quite busy for June, some girls were already showing off their tan in their mini-bikinis. How could women be so petite, when they ate lots of pasta and ice-creams? That baffled her. There she was, trying to monitor every single thing she swallowed, and yet she still weighed her whole 65 kilos. She thought about it. Wasn't it all relative? When she'd travelled to the north of Europe, she'd noticed that the women were generally taller and rounder than the Mediterranean girls. But guess what? They still looked good. What was this nonsense of having to look so skinny and fragile all the time? Who had decided that a person was attractive only when extra-slender? And what if people had a bit of fat around them? As long as they weren't obese, that should be fine.

Suddenly she remembered Rossana. She was a robust girl, and yet that's not the connection Clara would make when thinking of her. She'd remember her big brown eyes with long eyelashes, her sweet expression and her tender voice. Her insecurities and the need she had to be valued for who she was. Last but not least, her smile at the end of their conversation; it'd been so contagious.

Clara would remember the person inside that exterior. She breathed in deeply, and took her time. That was it. No more diets, she was going to be content the way she was.

The Poetto beach was very long, she continued her drive. Palms, oleanders and other bushes were dotted along the road, brushed by the wind. The sky was bright blue and the sun was high in the sky. There was no trace of clouds, not even a tiny white strip. The only contrast with the azure was the occasional seagull. She drove further and left the Torre Spagnola behind, and headed towards the town of Quartu Sant'Elena. The beach became less populated and it seemed even wider. She finally found a spot where no soul was visible. There was plenty of space to park, so she stopped and got out of the car. The strong breeze hit her face and moved her curls behind her neck. The scent of the sea was stronger now, and she enjoyed every breath of it. She took her sandals off and walked on the white fine sand, towards the shore. Some algae bundles were lying around, some even formed little balls. She picked one and remembered how she and Dino used to throw these at each other when children. They used to call them marine balls. She reached the water, and dipped her right foot first. It was cool, almost cold, and it gave her a mild shock. But then she bravely plunged her second foot, and watched the gentle waves, as they withdrew and came, and covered her up to the ankles. She folded the linen trousers up to her knees and let the water caress her skin. The sea was so clear that she could distinguish each toe when the feet were submerged. She played with the sand under the water, and tried to hide her toes beneath. The crying of the seagulls and the sound of the waves was music to her ears, it provided an oasis she'd been desperately looking for.

"If I can guess how much money you've got, can I have it?"

Clara startled. How on earth had this guy come so close without her noticing him? She turned around and recognized the beggar from last week. He was wearing the same purple trousers and yellow shirt. Was that surprising?

"You scared me," she replied.

"I'm not very attractive, but no-one's called me *scary* before." He threw his rasta hair backwards.

She looked down, around him; trying to figure out which direction he'd come from, but there were no footprints on the sand, except for hers.

"How did you get here?" She looked at the sand again. "Don't tell me you've flown."

"I'm just very light, so I leave no traces," he laughed.

"So, you want to play that money game again."

"Please."

"OK, then. Try and guess how much I've got." Somehow she knew the outcome of this.

"Twenty-five euros."

"I thought we were talking about small change." Clara was confused. She'd forgotten she still had those famous twenty-five euros hidden somewhere in her handbag.

"I didn't walk along the entire Poetto beach for some silly money." He put his hands in his pockets.

Clara turned her back on him and looked at the sea. "Why should I give you twenty-five euros?"

"Because I need them, and you don't."

That was a compelling answer. In fairness she'd forgotten about that money so probably it meant that she could go without. And what did Lucilla teach her about generosity? She looked inside her bag and noticed that the phone wasn't there. That corner felt strangely empty. Almost as if that slot shouldn't be taken by any other object. She continued to search, and moved about the lipstick, tissues, chewing-gums, diary, her own mobile phone, pocket mirror, pen. Going through that bag was like a treasure hunt.

"It's in the internal pocket, just open the zip and you'll find the three notes inside," the beggar helpfully suggested.

How dare this stranger know more when it came to her own personal handbag? Didn't he know that handbags are girls' best friends and they all contained secrets? Clara unzipped the pocket and found the money. Those three notes represented a quarter of her birthday present, and they were about to leave her now. With a tinge of sorrow she handed him the money.

"Thank you, this is wonderful," he kissed the money and jumped for joy.

Clara was pleased to see she'd managed to elicit such a reaction. Perhaps this guy was truly poor.

"Do you know what I can buy with twenty-five euros?" His eyes were sparking.

"Not much nowadays."

"There's a bar in via Sonnino and they've made a deal with me. I can get a large panino, a coke, and a cappuccino for two-euros and fifty cents." He was twirling around on the sand and his rasta hair was following him.

"That's generous."

"This means that I can have ten meals assured for the next few days." He pushed the money in the air, but still held it tight. "Thank you so much!" He came close and kissed her on the cheek.

Clara was taken aback by his sudden familiarity. What else though? She was still surprised. Had she expected this guy to smell or something? He didn't, in fact he felt rather clean, even with his old clothes on. His trimmed beard was almost soft and his skin had emanated a pleasurable fragrance, so delicate and indefinable.

"I'm glad I was of help," she smiled.

"If *you* ever need my help, here's my number: 260578CSAM"

Clara sighed. "I guessed you were a friend of Lucilla. What's AM for?"

"Alessandro."

"And the M?" she was inquisitive.

"I can't tell," he grinned.

"It looks like surnames are truly forbidden for me." She shook her head. "Nice meeting you Alessandro M, but I don't think I'll need your help, thanks." She gently turned her back on him and slowly headed towards her car. That Lucilla, she was persecuting her, either directly or via her friends. Clara hoped very much this was the last thing she'd done for her.

It was good being back home after a hard working day. Clara was drinking a cold peach tea and resting on the sofa. Valentina was studying in her bedroom, preparing for her final tests while Papà was still at work. Mamma was stuffing a rabbit for dinner, and Nonno was looking out from the balcony as he smoked his pipe. All was normal. What a wonderful thing normality was. Routine: who ever said it was boring? Clara did realize that today she hadn't actually worked that hard. It'd been very difficult to concentrate, and her life recently hadn't exactly been stress-free. Still, perhaps she shouldn't have taken two hours for lunch; she was being watched as Paolo had warned her. Perhaps the head of human resources, her own personal Big Brother, had been spying on her movements with a pair of binoculars, maybe he even knew exactly each time she left her desk to use the bathroom. She tried to picture him as she swallowed the last drop of tea.

"Someone's in trouble," shouted Nonno from the balcony.

"Why's that?" shouted back Clara from the living room.

"There's a police car, just parked outside our palazzo."

Clara got up and rushed to the balcony. "I wonder what happened."

"They're coming to our building! I bet it's the Marongiu family upstairs," Nonno exhaled his smoke. "Signor Gabriele told me that one of their sons is a drug dealer," he whispered.

The door bell rang. Clara and her Nonno looked at each other. Did the police ring the wrong bell? Or perhaps it was someone else visiting. Mamma went to the door, still wearing her stripy yellow apron and opened it.

"We're looking for Signorina Clara Serra," said one of the men in uniform.

Clara rushed from the balcony and appeared on the corridor.

"That's me."

The tallest policeman cleared his throat and spoke: "Signorina Serra, we need to talk to you."

Chapter 16

Clara gasped. What could the police want from her? Valentina rushed out of her room, Nonno and Mamma were speechless.

"Please come in," Clara managed to say.

Three officers, two men and a woman, all wearing their elegant navy uniform came in. Clara shut the door behind them and invited them to sit in the living room.

"What's the matter?" she asked timidly.

The eldest of the three, a tall and robust man, in his fifties, replied: "There was a robbery at the Banca di Roma, today. It happened around 12:40." He looked at Clara intently. "Where were you today at 12:40?"

Clara was baffled, to say the least. All these people staring at her were making her uncomfortable. "Can you please sit down? All of you?"

The policewoman looked at the eldest guy: "Is that OK inspector?"

He nodded; obviously he was the boss. The three police officers sat down, followed by Mamma, Valentina and Nonno, who took a place on the edge of their seats, almost as if they were ready to take off any minute.

Clara finally sat in front of the inspector. "Am I accused of being involved in this bank robbery?"

"*I* am the one asking the questions," he had a serious voice. "Where were you today, at 12:40?"

"I took a long lunch hour today, and I drove along the Poetto beach." Clara couldn't believe what was going on.

"Were you on your own?"

"Yes."

"Did you stop anywhere, to get a drink or a snack?" He was scribbling some notes.

"I wasn't very hungry. I just needed some time to myself, so I went further up, towards Quartu Sant'Elena and stopped at a quiet spot."

"Did you meet anyone there?"

"Yes, I did. As I was watching the sea, I was approached by a beggar."

"So, someone has seen you there, right?" He seemed inquisitive.

"Oh yes, I even gave him some money."

"How much did you give him?"

Clara thought for a little. If she told the truth Mamma would definitely think she had an extravagant daughter, giving away all that money to a stranger. But she had no option. "I gave him twenty-five euros."

Everybody in the room looked at each other, with a sense of wonder.

"Are you usually that generous with people?" asked the policeman.

"Not really. It was a one-off." Why was she feeling uneasy now?

"Would you consider yourself a wealthy person? Do you have lots of spare cash?" He almost sounded sarcastic.

"No, not at all. In fact I just about manage OK every month." Clara was definitely confused. "What's this got to do with the robbery anyway?"

"I told you that it's *me* who's asking the questions." He looked severe. "How much do you earn?"

Was he supposed to ask such indiscrete questions? "Just under 1,000 euros per month."

He looked at Mamma who suddenly felt under the spotlight. "I gather you're Clara's mother?"

She nodded.

"Can you please tell me your husband's salary?"

"1500 euros per month, unless he does some overtime," she replied timidly.

"And there's my pension," added Nonno. "I get about 700 euros!"

"Any more earnings from other sources? Donations, payments from rent, other?" He was interrogating the entire family with his eyes.

Valentina lifted her right hand. "I ... contribute to spending the money, if it's any help."

"This is not the time for jokes, Signorina." He shook his head in disapproval.

Clara had already decided that she didn't like this inspector. He was too formal, self-important and didn't have a sense of humour. But somehow she felt it was in her interest to try and get along with him.

"That makes a combined earning of 3200 euros per month. It's not bad, but I can't quite see how Signorina Clara Serra could afford to buy the latest Ferrari." His eyes were piercing Clara's again, how unpleasant.

"It was a gift from a friend." Clara's voice was firm.

"What a friend! Can I have your friend's name and address please?"

Clara felt trapped, almost like being pushed into a corner. "Her name's Lucilla."

"Lucilla... what?"

Her family and all the three police officers looked at her.

"I don't know her surname. I never asked. But even if I'd asked, I'm sure she wouldn't have told me."

"What else do you know about this... Lucilla?"

He was so nosy, this guy, so intrusive; to the point of being rude. Perhaps it went with the job.

"She's tall and blonde and very attractive. Same age as me, I believe. Also, she's got perfect teeth, you notice them whenever she smiles."

"Is that all?"

Clara was definitely feeling like her legs were immersed in quick-sand. The more she said, the deeper she went. She nodded.

"Where did you meet Lucilla?" the torturer persisted.

"At the Bastione." Clara was going to keep her answers short. She'd seen it in a movie, once, that it was the best tactic to avoid trouble.

"Did she give you the Ferrari on that occasion?"

"No."

"When did she give it to you?"

"The next day." Clara was trying to keep cool.

"How? When?"

"I bumped into her at a bar near work, she gave me the keys and told me that the car was waiting for me in via Milano. When I got home, there it was."

"It appears that the Ferrari has only ever been registered in your name." He looked at his papers.

"Yes."

"Who else knows Lucilla?"

Clara's blood stopped circulating for two long seconds. She had to think about that one. Nobody had actually *seen* Lucilla. Even when the two of them had met at the bar, they were sitting in a hidden corner, so the waiter wouldn't have seen her. Clara was the one who'd ordered and paid for the drinks. And when they'd met at the Bastione the first time, no one else was on the terrazza. Not to mention the potential suicidees, none of them had ever caught a glimpse of her. For all people knew, family, friends, and colleagues, Clara could've just invented an imaginary friend.

"As far as I know, none of my friends or family have met her," she said.

"So, you're telling me that someone that only you know, who doesn't have a surname, address, or other contact details, has bought you a Ferrari as a gift. Did she ask you anything in return? A favour, perhaps?" He looked at Clara again, trying to search the depths of her eyes.

"I'm sorry to interrupt inspector, but can you tell us what's going on? What's Clara accused of exactly?" Mamma asked courageously.

"Armed bank robbery," he replied coldly.

Clara's mouth opened automatically, but no voice was heard. She'd prompted the same reaction among the members of her family.

The inspector cleared his throat and looked at all of them solemnly. "Today, at 12:40 a lady robbed the Banca di Roma in Piazza Yenne, here in Cagliari. From the videotape recordings she looked very similar to Clara, same build and height roughly, same curly dark hair. However, she was wearing a large jacket and a mask over her face, therefore we can't be sure. The lady in question was driving the Ferrari Challenge Stradale that's registered in Clara's name."

All that information in one go made Clara feel like she'd just been run-over by a truck.

"But, I no longer have that car, I gave it back to Lucilla!" she protested.

"It's true!" confirmed Mamma. "Today she borrowed my car to go to work."

"The problem is that Clara doesn't have an alibi. She can't prove that she was at the Poetto beach with your car at 12:40. Unless she can provide name and surname of the beggar and we can go and find him. Anyway, how can she own such a car in the first place? I haven't heard anything that sounds convincing so far."

Clara was feeling trapped now. Had she been framed? But why? By whom? What was Lucilla's role in all of this? My God, what if Lucilla was a bank robber, who just used Clara as a cover? After all, how could she come up with that kind of money she'd given to Signor Mario, the bankrupt man? How could Clara explain the anti-suicide missions to the police? They'd think she was a nut case. In fact, she'd be better off not mentioning any of that, otherwise the name of Signor Mario would come up, and how was she going to account for the 150,000 euros she'd given him? Things weren't looking good, in fact the whole world was feeling rather shaky now.

"Where were you on the 26th May 2003?" The inspector was shuffling his papers.

"That was last week, Monday. I took a day off work. It was my birthday," she replied coldly.

"Where were you at 11:15 that morning?"

"Shopping." She'd decided to keep it short again.

"What did you buy?"

"A pair of peach sandals."

"Do you still have the receipt?" he was defying her with his gaze. The inspector didn't believe her.

"No, I don't keep my receipts."

"Did you pay in cash or with a card?"

"Cash."

"So you can't prove that around 11:15 on the 26th May you purchased a pair of sandals."

"But I stopped for a coffee at a bar in via Roma. I was served by a lady, surely she can confirm that?" There was hope.

"We'll check on that. Bars in that area are very popular, unless you're a regular, it's unlikely she'll remember whom she served and when."

Wow, weren't things looking great?

"Where were you on the 17th April 2003?" the inspector continued the grilling.

Clara raised her eyebrows. April was ages ago, how was she supposed to remember? She could barely recollect what she ate yesterday, and that was far more important.

"Right now, off the top of my head I don't know. I guess that if it was a working day, I must've been in the office."

"The 17th April was a Thursday. From Technosarda's print-outs of staff swipe cards, it looks like you disappeared for an hour, around 10:30."

"I can see you've done your homework," she spoke quietly. "For your information, the head of personnel hates me, so I wouldn't trust the accuracy of the data provided by him."

"That's a serious accusation," he was looking sombre.

"I think that your accusations are far more serious. What does my birthday have anything to do with a robbery? And the bloody 17th of April? I knew that 17 was an unlucky number!"

"There were two more robberies which followed the same format as the one which took place this morning. One was done on the 17th April around 10:45, the other happened on the 26th May at 11:15." He looked at Clara like an X-ray machine ready to scan her. "It appears that, on both these occasions, you can't prove where you were. Perhaps inside a bank holding a gun?"

Clara got up in anger. "This is madness. I've never done such thing!" her voice was loud. "It's pure coincidence!"

"So far you're the main suspect. We'll have to take you to the police station. But before we go…" he looked at Mamma, "we have to search this apartment. Is this

OK?"

Mamma was silent, she didn't seem to be taking it in.

"I guess that even if it wasn't OK, you'd still do it?" Clara dared to ask.

"Of course." The policeman replied.

"Why ask then?"

"We'll start with your bedroom," said the policewoman. "You must be with us as we proceed." The lady got up, and invited Clara to show them the way. The inspector followed them, while the younger policeman stayed with Mamma, Nonno and Valentina in the living room.

In a matter of minutes, her entire bedroom had been turned upside down. There wasn't a single thing that hadn't been moved, from her clothes, to her other personal belongings, to the books, stationery, hand-bags and shoes. Clara looked at the police officers in action, as she leaned against the door. She pinched her own arm, to make sure she wasn't dreaming. These guys looked professional, they'd obviously done it before. They were searching corners that Clara had never considered as hiding places, not even as a child.

"Nothing of relevance here, let's do the other rooms," suggested the inspector, as he rushed Clara along the corridor.

Clara struggled to believe this was really happening. Strange people who wore uniforms, also known as the police, suspected she was a robber and were now rummaging around her entire flat. And God, were they doing a thorough job; in each room. Everything was being brought up to full view, even very intimate things; the whole experience was humiliating and Clara felt very sorry for submitting her family to such an ordeal.

The good news was that the police found no hidden

money, nor mask, nor gun, at the end of their search. Were they also expecting to locate the Ferrari inside the flat?

"You're either truly innocent, or you're a very smart girl," declared the inspector at the end of the treasure hunt.

"I'd like to believe that I'm both." Clara's look was bold.

"We could handcuff you as we take you to the police station, but somehow I don't think that's necessary."

"I appreciate that."

"Can we come with you?" Mamma's expression was imploring.

"It's not possible. Only Signorina Serra can come with us." He seemed determined.

Mamma's eyes filled with tears, while Valentina was holding her arm. Nonno was standing up in silence, with a confused expression.

"Mamma, don't worry, it's just a mistake." Clara spoke with confidence. "I'll be back soon." She kissed her family and left with the police officers.

As they left the palazzo, her neighbours had gathered in the street to take a good look at the scene. Some were spying from their balconies, others through their windows; it was like being at the centre of a stage, under the spot light. Until now, Clara didn't know what being notorious meant. She was held on each arm by one of the officers, as they walked to the car. Each step she took felt slow and heavy, even the air she was breathing seemed charged with strong particles. As she got into the car she wondered if the siren would go off, that'd be something she could describe to her grandchildren one day, but that pleasure wasn't granted. As they drove off, she felt a pang in her stomach at the idea of causing so much embarrassment for her family, especially Mamma who cared a lot about other people's opinions. God only knew what Zia Carmela was going to say on the matter. And what could Papà's reaction be? And Dino's? They'd be terribly upset to learn of this incident.

As far as she was concerned, she ought to try and keep positive. Surely this was all a big mistake. These guys didn't have any proof that she'd actually done the robbery. The girl was wearing a mask, so it could be anyone. The police hadn't found any money, nor gun in her apartment, no sign of the Ferrari either, so what reason did they have to detain her? She was going to keep cool and collected. She was going to answer all their annoying questions again, and she'd try to be optimistic, because losing hope at this stage could only lead to trouble.

As soon as she got to the police station, she was escorted to an office where they took note of her identity details. They wanted to know if she had a lawyer, she smiled at the idea, as she'd never needed one so far. They offered to nominate a legal representative for her; she agreed to it. Apparently the police had access to a database of local lawyers. These were on call any time of day; the inspector confirmed that someone was going to arrive shortly.

Two hours wasn't what Clara called *shortly*. In fact, time had stretched enormously again, each minute had felt like an eternity, inside that cold, formal room. They didn't even have proper seating, just hard chairs.

If only she could make contact with the beggar, he could provide her with an alibi, and that would help her immensely. What was his name? Alessandro. With no surname, of course. How many Alessandros were living in

Cagliari? And who said he was from Cagliari anyway? But… he'd given her his contact number! One of those strange ones, similar to the one Lucilla had given her for emergencies. What if… and yes, it did sound crazy… but what if she could use that stupid toy phone to contact Alessandro? After all, it did have lots of letters and numbers. That was the opportunity, her winning card that could get her out of this mess. She'd better retrieve the red phone from little Ivan, so she could try and use it. A little spark was lit inside her heart, a flame of hope, something that could provide the chance to prove her innocence.

The inspector finally appeared accompanied by a short man.

"This is Avvocato Selis, your legal representative," he said.

The lawyer shook Clara's hand, but she wasn't impressed. It was a weak and sweaty shake, not at all promising.

Clara looked at him, in the hope of finding some reassuring features. He was still short, but also fat and bald, and was wearing a pair of round glasses with very thick lenses. She wondered why a professional man would wear such awful spectacles; nowadays you could get highly fashionable glasses even for the very short-sighted people.

"Would you like us to have a chat in private, before the formal interrogation?" he asked.

Even his voice was a let-down. Too high-pitched for a man, not the strong affirmative kind she was hoping for. Was there any point in talking to this guy separately? After all she wasn't going to tell him anything different from what she'd told the inspector earlier. As far as her idea of tracing Alessandro, she'd better not mention how she was going to get in touch with him. Better leave the toy phone alone.

"I have nothing to hide, Avvocato Selis. I'm happy to proceed now," she announced with confidence.

The inspector guided her to another room, his office probably. They were followed by the lawyer and the policewoman. They sat around one of the desks and the deluge of questions started again. The policeman was asking most of them, they were the same questions he'd posed before, albeit in different manner, but Clara's answers were consistent. She wasn't going to fall for any tricks. She also volunteered an accurate description of Alessandro. She tried to be honest in her answers, and told the inspector the truth, except the bit concerning her pact with Lucilla. She'd thought hard about it; she never liked lying, so she tried not to do it deliberately, but she had to omit that chapter in her life where she was involved with the anti-suicide missions, otherwise she'd lose all credibility.

"Signorina Serra, no matter how I phrase my questions, your answers are somewhat elusive." The inspector took a pause and then continued: "Let's look at the facts now. Fact one: there've been three robberies in the last two months. From the videotape images it appears that the woman committing the criminal acts looks like you. Fact two: *your* car was used in today's robbery. Fact three: you can't provide an alibi for any of the three robberies. Fact four: you own a car that costs between 170,000-190,000 euros and you can't offer a believable explanation as to how it came into your possession."

"If you put it this way, it doesn't sound too good." Clara was smart enough to see that.

He scrutinized her. "There's still a lot of research to

be done, we need to question the staff at the bank again, your work colleagues, and carry on further investigations."

Clara felt that there was hope. "So, can I go home?"

"Not yet. I need to speak to the magistrate." He seemed thoughtful. "I'll leave you in this office for a while, and I'll be back shortly."

She hoped very much that this time *shortly* meant what it was supposed to. The policewoman and the lawyer stayed in the office and kept her company. Was this out of kindness or duty? He was chewing the top of his pen.

"Is there a way we can make contact with the beggar you met today? He could supply an alibi and be of great help to us." His voice was still high-pitched.

"He told me that he's a regular at a bar in via Sonnino, but I don't know which one." Clara's voice was flat. "Perhaps we can send some policemen to look for him?"

"I'll speak to the inspector and ask him to send some of his men out."

"Perhaps I can go myself? And help to find him?"

He was shaking his head. Did he know something that she didn't?

The inspector came back in less than an hour, and was holding a piece of paper with signatures and stamps.

"I spoke to the magistrate." He paused for a few seconds, as he walked around his desk. "After considering all the facts, he recommended your detention." He waved the paper at her, which looked like an authorization for her arrest.

"What? Tell me that I misheard you." Clara's world was shattered.

"He contacted the judge in charge of preliminary investigations, and he agreed that you should be arrested.

You're the main suspect of these robberies, and in the absence of evidence that could prove your innocence we must take you into custody." He went towards Clara and held her arm.

"But I'm innocent!" she protested loudly.

"This is what's called preventative custody. In case you're the culprit, it prevents you from leaving and hiding evidence, or even repeating the crime," her lawyer tried to explain.

Clara started to cry, her tears were coming down against her will. "I have no idea how I've ended up here."

"Signorina Serra, rest assured that my team and I will continue the investigations, there are many things that don't seem quite right. If you're innocent, you've got nothing to be afraid of." He touched her arm in encouragement. "Be brave now."

So, the wicked inspector did have a human side to him after all. Perhaps deep down he believed her, but all the facts were pointing at Clara, if not at her precisely, at least in her direction.

Her lawyer seemed to be lost for words, what a great help he'd been.

"I'll come to see you in prison tomorrow." He weakly shook her hand.

Great, that was something to look forward to.

Chapter 17

It was like she'd seen on television. They took her picture and her fingerprints, and then she was handcuffed, before she left the police station. Even if she wasn't one, she felt like a criminal; what did the real criminals feel like when they got arrested? The inspector was sitting next to her in the car.

"These handcuffs…" Clara raised her hands and looked at them. "When you took me from home I didn't have any, but now I do. What's changed?"

The inspector didn't reply. Was he simply being rude, or didn't he know the answer? The fact was that in the space of four hours Clara had gone from being a happy girl, someone who'd finally got her routine back, to a very unhappy one, someone about to be locked up in jail. What was the cause for this? Had she actually done something wrong? It felt like life was just happening to her, and she had no control. Where were the certainties now? Any solid, well-rooted towers she could lean on? Not   one   on   view.

For the first time ever; she realized that no-one could help. In the past, when she'd had difficulties, she could've relied on her parents, her Nonno, her brother or sister, or even Paolo. But now, who could get her out of this trouble? Alessandro, maybe, or possibly… Lucilla. After all it's only after she'd met her that all the hassles started. But how could she trust her? How could she trust anyone? Perhaps this was the time where she was truly on her own. She had to be strong, stand up, defend herself and fight until they'd finally let her out of prison. How ironic, she hadn't even got there and she was already thinking how to get out.

The car reached viale Buoncammino; she'd always loved this part of Cagliari, with this long pedestrian avenue in the centre, its cast-iron benches and tall pine trees. There was a sensation of green and openness, since the avenue was on a hill and offered a wonderful view of the city, even at this time of night. She'd never seen the prison with the same eyes she was looking at it tonight. The building was very long, rectangular, on two levels, and had yellow walls. Each window on show had bars, even these were yellow, but of a stronger shade. Whoever designed the penitentiary did so with an aesthetic sense, as, unless you were a prisoner, you could say that it was an attractive building. The edifice was surrounded by an external tall wall, and armed guards were visible, as they walked up and down. The front had a massive arched door; the European, Italian and Sardinian flags were fluttering on the left side. The windows on the façade were arched too, and were protected by green wooden shutters, which again provided a nice contrast with the white borders and yellow walls. Why was she paying so much attention to these details anyway? Shouldn't she concentrate on the fact that, albeit beautiful, this building was going to be her prison?

"We've arrived at our destination." The inspector touched her arm.

Clara was escorted through the main entrance; it was a large arched metal gate, bullet-proof. Not very friendly. As she went through, she heard the gate being locked twice, behind. In that moment, the outside world felt shut off from her. The inspector gave her arrest papers to the prison guard, and Clara was abandoned with her new captors. The prison officer, a red-haired woman in her fifties, took Clara to a separate room, where another officer, a younger one wearing her blue uniform, explained that she had to search her. Clara agreed, after all, did she have a choice? The officer proceeded with her unwelcome task, and later asked Clara to take off her clothes. Clara thought about it for a while.

"Could you please get undressed?" persisted the officer.

Clara unwillingly took her sandals off and removed her pink tee-shirt and jeans.

"I'm afraid you have to take *everything* off," said the woman.

"Do you mean my underwear too?" Surely not.

"Naked. As mother nature made you."

Clara didn't like it. What was the need to be naked? Surely she couldn't carry anything dangerous inside her bra and knickers.

"Is it really necessary?" Her cheeks were in flames.

"I'm afraid so." The officer was still waiting.

Clara had never felt so humiliated before. It was bad enough being seen naked by your doctor, but by a total stranger, a woman in uniform, it really felt odd. She shut her eyes as she removed her bra and underpants, almost as if that gesture could protect her from the shame. In that instant, she wished she'd get sucked into a black hole in the universe and that she'd never come back.

The guard quickly searched her clothes, removed the belt from the jeans, and passed everything back to Clara. Thank God she was fast. Clara too, she'd never got dressed so quickly in her entire life.

The officer proceeded to search her handbag, which had been handed in by the policeman.

"We'll keep this and your belt. Everything will be returned to you when you're released from prison." She was still serious, almost formal. She then passed on to

Clara a soft bundle composed of two white sheets, two towels, one blanket, one tea towel and a bar of soap. This was the guard's only kind gesture, before walking away.

"What next?" asked Clara.

"Medical examination."

"Don't tell me I've got to get undressed again!"

"No, it won't be necessary."

The red-haired woman accompanied Clara to the doctor's room and left her with a man in his forties, who was wearing a white overall with a cold stethoscope around his neck. He opened another file, a medical one she guessed. He asked the usual questions about her general health and then went on to examine her. Luckily, he didn't do anything too invasive before he finally declared that Clara was in good health. He was probably referring to her physical health, as he had no idea how her mental sanity was being pushed to the limit tonight. Clara gladly returned to the care of the red-haired officer.

"What now? Surely I can go to my cell." Not that she was looking forward to be trapped in a tiny space, but she'd had enough of these intrusions.

"Normally, at this stage, you'd have to undergo the psychological examination." The woman adjusted the clip on her red hair. "But it's too late, that'll have to wait until tomorrow."

"Thank God for that!" sighed Clara with relief.

"I'll take you to the prison commander's office."

They walked along a white corridor, and Clara wondered what on earth this extra step was all about. Was he going to interrogate her? She'd had enough grilling for the day. She was escorted to a large office; this one looked and felt important. It had two wide windows, one large yucca plant in the corner, and a dark wooden desk. A delicate scent of after-shave was pervading the air, and it was perceivable despite the fact that both windows were open, and the cool summer breeze was refreshing the room. Strange, the windows had no mosquito nets, it certainly wasn't wise to open them and have the lights on, those horrible little vampires would soon invade the room.

"Signorina Serra?" called the man in front of her.

"I'm sorry!" Clara realized that he must've been speaking to her while she wasn't listening. As if mosquitoes were the things to be concerned about at that moment.

"I'm the vice commander of the prison," he announced with a grave tone.

This man looked important, even if he was just the vice. She'd better behave herself and be polite. He invited Clara to sit down, looked at some papers, and then at her through his glasses.

"You have the privilege to be able to choose between two cells," he announced.

Was he being sarcastic?

"One with a view, versus one with a balcony?" She may as well have the same attitude.

He shook his head. "The choice is about the people you're going to share with."

"What? I thought I was going to have a room to myself!" That was disappointing.

The vice-commander laughed. Clara didn't think it was funny.

"We have many rooms, but we're not a four-star hotel." He was still laughing; then he became serious. "Haven't you heard about the problems of overcrowding in prisons? Too many criminals, not enough space to lock them in."

"But I'm not a criminal… yet." By this she meant that they hadn't proved she'd done it, so she was still innocent. And, as far as she was concerned, she was innocent even if the court, through all sorts of twisting of evidence and corrupted procedures, declared her guilty. Did she need to explain it to the man?

"I'll repeat. There are two cells you can choose from. Normally we'd select the one we think is most suitable for you. But on this occasion, you can have the choice, as I believe that either of them is appropriate." He removed his glasses and placed them gently on his desk. "One of the cells hosts two women who are heavy smokers, the other has no-smokers. Which one do your prefer?"

Was there a catch? Surely things weren't that straightforward? "What have the ladies in question done?"

"The two smokers are thieves, the other ladies are…" he thought about it. "One is a drug dealer, the other is a murderess."

What was Clara expecting? Four altar girls? Neither sounded good. "How many cigarettes do the smokers go through in a day?"

"Two packets each, at least." The man crossed his arms. "It's not that they've got much else to do."

"That is 80 cigarettes a day!"

"Some of the 80 get smoked while they're outside, on their breaks." Was he trying to see the positive side, or was he giving her a hint? Clara reflected for a while. Which one was better? Or worse? First of all she didn't know how long she was going to stay in jail, so the passive smoke thing could get on her nerves, plus she'd always hated the smell, it made her eyes sting and gave her headaches. Let's face it; her quality of life would suffer if she shared a cell with two active chimneys. On the other hand, the idea of sleeping at night, in the same room as a murderess wasn't uplifting either. Still, the killer under consideration would probably have undergone some psychological treatment. The fact that she was sharing a cell with someone, must've meant that she wasn't terribly dangerous.

"How long has the drug dealer shared with the murderess?"

"Over a year now."

"I'll share with the murderess." Clara's voice was shaky.

"Fine. Just bear in mind, whoever you share with, try to get on with them. It'll make your life that much easier." That sentence sounded more like a warning than a piece of advice.

"I have no intention of making enemies here."

The man shook her hand. "Welcome to Buoncammino."

The red-haired woman touched Clara's arm and led her out of the office, into the hallway. They reached another solid metal gate. As they went through, this was locked behind them. It was strange hearing the lock going through twice, almost as to make double sure. They walked along another white corridor, for about fifty metres, everything looked clean, like a hospital. They turned to the left towards the female section of the prison and encountered another gate. This one too was made of steel, and looked very sturdy; it had nothing of the comfort and warmth of wooden doors. As they went through, the gate was locked twice again, behind them. At this point the world outside felt even further away, it'd become unreachable. It was then that Clara realized, in its full meaning, that she was being locked up.

The new corridor in front was dotted with yellowish/greenish metal doors. They stopped outside number 6. Another lady guard was waiting there.

"This your cell," stated the red-haired woman. The new guard unlocked the door, and Clara was surprised to see that there was a second one, with bars, just behind it. The officer released the barred door and invited Clara to go in. "This is your new room-mate," she announced with a lively voice to the two women inside.

"Hey Monica, wake up, we've got company!" shouted the short skinny one.

"Please let her sleep, we can do the introductions tomorrow," responded Clara.

Both guards locked the doors and said goodnight. Clara wondered if they truly meant it.

As she looked around, she felt trapped in a surreal world. She crossed her arms and secretly pinched her left elbow to make sure it wasn't a dream. It hurt.

"It feels strange, doesn't it? The first time you come inside." The skinny girl proceeded to introduce herself. "I'm Annalisa, and she's Monica."

The three women shook hands, it was all very civilized. Monica sat on her bed and didn't say a word. She was in her early forties probably, had short spiky grey hair and was wearing pink pijamas.

"She doesn't talk much," explained Annalisa. "It drives me mad because I can never have a proper conversation. Just *yes* and *no* and that's it."

That didn't bother Clara; in fact she liked people who only spoke when they had something worthwhile to say. She took a good look at her future residential suite. The room was smallish, but it seemed clean and comfortable with its white walls and tiled floors. On the left there was a single bed, and just behind it, stood a bunk-bed. On the right, was a short wall, which separated the toilet and the basin from the front of the room. She could enjoy en-suite facilities, although she wasn't pleased to see that there was no door to protect their privacy. Closer to the entrance, there was a small rectangular table with two wooden stools; and just behind, three small cabinets were hanging on the wall. These were supposed to be their wardrobes imagined Clara, luckily she wasn't expected to wear her usual fashionable clothes in this place. Probably there was one cabinet per person, and she realized that her collection of shoes wouldn't fit in all three of them. The wall facing the front door had a large window, with yellow frames and bars. Yes, it had bars; that was unusual in the windows she'd seen until today.

"Do you like it? You'll get used to it." Annalisa tried to use a reassuring tone.

She must've been in her early thirties maybe, or late twenties. It was difficult to tell her age. She was short and very skinny and had long straight brown hair, which she kept in a ponytail. Her skin was quite wrinkled and looked dry, she probably didn't use any face creams. But her brown eyes were lively and curious.

"Which one is my bed?" Clara never underestimated the importance of sleep.

"The top one on the bunk bed. I sleep downstairs, you sleep upstairs, Monica uses the single bed."

Bad news, Clara never liked to sleep on the top of bunk-beds. Once, while in her cabin on a ferry from Sardinia to mainland Italy, she'd fallen off one. It wasn't nice. And since then, she'd felt uncomfortable about sleeping on the upper floors. Still, she'd only just arrived here; it wasn't advisable to complain from the start. She continued to look at her new room to see if she'd missed something. On the wall next to Monica's bed there was a poster showing the lead guitarist of the AC-DC band, Angus Young, as he played his guitar with his tongue stuck out. On the right wall there was an image of the Madonna of the Rocks, by Leonardo da Vinci. Could there've been two more contrasting characters?

"Who likes AC-DC?" asked Clara.

Monica raised her hand. No words were uttered.

"I like them too, I think they're great." What else could Clara say to impress her? "Who likes Da Vinci then?"

"Neither of us do. That poster was left from another woman who used to be here. We couldn't be bothered to take it down." Annalisa had a coarse voice, which was strange coming from such a petite figure.

Clara was still standing up; Annalisa invited her to sit on her bed.

"So, what have you done?" asked Annalisa.

"I'm accused of armed robbery."

"Wow. No silly shop-lifting then. Just a proper, tough armed robbery." She seemed impressed.

"It was done with the aid of a Ferrari, to assure a fast escape. A Challenge Stradale." Clara may as well build-up the admiration.

"Even better." Annalisa looked towards Monica. "Have you heard? We've got someone here who deserves respect."

Monica nodded. Was she going to say something sooner or later? Perhaps she was sleeping with her eyes open.

"To be honest, I haven't done it. But people think I did." Clara couldn't lie for a long time.

Annalisa laughed. "They all say they didn't do it." She turned towards Clara. "I was a drug dealer, I got caught and now I'm here. There's no point denying it."

Clara looked at Monica, and whispered in Annalisa's ear: "Is she the murderess?"

"Yes."

"Doesn't it bother you?"

"We all have our faults." Annalisa seemed relaxed..

"What has she done exactly?"

"She was married for ten years. Her husband used to beat her up, every single night. One day, she got fed up…" She looked at Clara with a scary face. "She grabbed a huge knife and stabbed him, right through his heart."

"Wow!"

"Then she called the police and told them what happened." Annalisa looked at Monica who was still sitting quietly on her bed. "She's a good girl, really. He just over-did it with the beating, that's all."

Clara stared at Monica and said: "If I had a husband who beat me up once, he'd no longer be my husband, I'd divorce him straight away." She walked towards her. "If by chance he managed to beat me twice, I'd also stab him. Not once though. Probably two or three times, just to make sure he was dead." She looked at Annalisa again. "I just can't tolerate violence, that's all." She raised both her arms.

Clara didn't really believe what she'd just said, she couldn't even hurt an ant; but it was important to let them know that she wasn't a girl to be messed around with.

"Do you want help making your bed?" offered Annalisa.

"Yes, why not?" Clara was pleased to see that even drug dealers could be amiable.

Monica made a small movement, was she going to speak finally? No. Apparently she was just adjusting herself to lie on her right side and face the wall. She did say something inaudible, though.

"That means she's going to sleep," explained Annalisa.

"It's good to have an interpreter."

"I'm so glad you're here. I've been dying to talk to people, she's just too quiet," Annalisa said softly. "OK, we get our breaks and I can talk to the other girls, but sometimes you just want to have a chat just before going to bed, and with her it's just a monologue."

"I see."

"I was getting so frustrated. I needed to talk to someone, tell them my thoughts, my dreams, whatever runs through my head. Now you're here, that's great! Someone I can converse with, any time!"

Clara could see where this was going. "I'm happy to listen to you, but not right now, it's almost midnight." She didn't want to sound rude but sleep had to take priority.

"Tomorrow then. I hope very much you're going to be here a long time." Annalisa declared, as she switched off the lights.

Chapter 18

Sleeping on the top bunk wasn't good. Whenever Clara lay on her left side and bent her knee she could feel it hanging up in the air, suspended from a bed that was raised almost two metres from the ground. When she was a little girl she used to fall off her bed so often, that her mother had to arrange for a second mattress to be on the floor, to act as padding. Tonight, there was no security measure, if she fell down from that height, it wasn't going to be pleasant. She was especially worried about banging her head on the tiled floor; she needed to maintain her sanity, in order to survive this ordeal. Her sheets felt fresh and clean, she turned her back to the room and faced the wall. She cuddled her pillow, perhaps it could be something to grab onto in the unfortunate event of a fall.

"Can't you sleep?" asked Annalisa. "It's common on the first night."

"I'm just getting used to this bed."

"When I came here a year ago there was another woman sharing with Monica, she was called Stefania. She's the one who liked Leonardo da Vinci."

Clara didn't really care, especially at this time of night. She didn't reply, in the hope that Annalisa would be deterred from talking further. It didn't work.

"Stefania was a history of art teacher. She loved Leonardo, Michelangelo and Giotto. She was a woman of culture and taught us many things, but to be honest we didn't really care. She talked constantly on techniques, colours, styles, you name it. She went on and on about the statue of David, the painting of La Gioconda, and the Primavera of Botticelli. We almost learnt it by heart, but then she switched to Roman art, their classical statues, the mosaics, their fountains…"

"Annalisa, do we have to talk about this right now?" Clara's interest for history of art was close to zero, and at midnight, inside a prison cell, it was definitely below zero.

"I just thought we'd have a chat. You're awake, I'm not asleep." Annalisa seemed practical.

"Yes, but we're disturbing Monica." Wasn't that a good excuse?

"Sometimes I wonder whether… not only is she dumb, but maybe also deaf," whispered Annalisa.

"Still, it's not considerate; we should keep quiet at this time of night. Goodnight." Was it explicit enough?

"Goodnight."

Clara was glad to be left alone. She needed some time to think, to understand what was happening to her. Otherwise, how was she supposed to get out of this mess? Who could've taken her car and done the robbery? Most likely it was Lucilla, but it just seemed so out of character. But then, what did she really know about her? She'd never even properly introduced herself. All she knew was her other initial, an L, which was part of the number she'd given Clara when she handed over the toy phone. What else? Nothing, except her appearance and her annoying personality. Clara couldn't tell her lawyer, nor the police, that Lucilla might have some special powers. In fact, even she was starting to doubt that. Spiritual beings aren't supposed to drive Ferraris and handle lots of cash. But how did she know about those people wanting to kill themselves? Unless… this was too much to take in but… unless those people were actors and just pretended everything. Perhaps it was all part of a big plan, so that whilst Clara was being conned into helping people, she was in fact covering the robberies that Lucilla was carrying out behind her back. Still, somehow things didn't make much sense. Clara's head was hurting.

Back to reality, she needed to have a plan for tomorrow. Something that could save the day. Clara breathed in deeply and decided. She was going to make contact with her family, get the toy phone back from Ivan and call the beggar. Surely he would testify for her? After all she'd given him twenty-five euros, and he'd volunteered his phone number in case Clara needed his help. At that time it'd felt odd, but maybe he knew that she was going to get into trouble. If so, then he must be involved in this whole affair too, oh no, that wasn't good news. Everything was too much, she had to stop thinking and let go, fall asleep perhaps. She was sure that tomorrow morning, when Mamma would wake her up with a caffelatte, all of this would turn out to be just an awful dream.

Why did the sun rise so early in the summer? It was only 05:30 and the room was flooded by light. Clara tried to focus and realized that her window, the one with strange yellowish bars, didn't have any curtains, nor shutters. So, it was true, she *was* in prison. The reality was too grim to face, so she decided to go back to sleep under her sheets. Pity they weren't black. Still, nothing could keep her awake when she was entitled to a lie-in.

At some point, in her world of dreams, she heard a trolley rolling outside, she couldn't quite figure out what it was, until she heard a female voice shout: "Breakfast!"

Annalisa promptly got up and fetched three cups of caffelatte, through the tiny opening on the door, then went to sit on her bed. "If you like your caffelatte hot, you'd better drink it now."

Clara gradually woke up and stretched herself, then sat on her raised bed. Monica got up, grumbled something, took her cup and decided to stand up, leaning against the barred door. Not the best way to enjoy breakfast.

"Good morning everyone," said Clara with a croaky voice.

"Good morning," replied Annalisa.

Monica yawned loudly.

"Do they have to bring breakfast so early? It's not that we all have to rush to work afterwards." Clara was still sleepy.

"We don't have to get up now. In theory we could decide that we don't want any breakfast, but then the sound of the trolley along the corridor would still wake us up. In cell 10 none of the girls have breakfast from the trolley, they buy their own biscuits and snacks and have it whenever they want. In cell 4 they all suffer with insomnia so they're up even before dawn, they have their TV on early and loud. This really gets on the nerves of the girls in number 3, who keep complaining all the time, so to spite them, they start making a lot of noise just before midnight, when the ones in number 4 are about to fall asleep. It's called revenge, and it's only fair." Annalisa had managed to articulate the whole sentence in one breath. How could someone be so talkative at 07:30 in the morning? Clara could barely think, let alone speak. She was still trying to register what Annalisa just said when she started again.

"Monica and I on the contrary get along with everybody here. The trick is what I call *live and let live*. I don't bother you, you don't bother me. It's as simple as that. When we're out in the courtyard we talk, or rather, I talk and Monica listens, to the girls, the guards, everybody really. In particular I like to tell jokes and everybody thinks they're funny, even Monica laughs at them. Do you know the one about how many carabinieri it takes to change a light bulb?"

"No, I don't. And I don't want to know either!" Clara had spoken fast. She couldn't do with all this noise in the morning, but she noticed that Annalisa was hurt. "It's nothing against you, it's just that ... I don't function too well first thing in the morning and I need some peace and quiet around me."

"Peace and quiet?" Annalisa laughed. "I wonder what you call this."

The minute she finished her sentence, a guard unlocked their doors. She entered the room and with a metal rod she struck each single bar in their window, producing an utterly unpleasant racket. Clara tried to cover her ears.

"It's called the beating of bars. They do it to check that we haven't tried to break or crack any of them, in the hope of escaping. Apparently when a bar has been messed with, it makes a different sound." Annalisa seemed proud to know all these details.

Clara was still trying to make sense of this early morning disturbance when a second prison guard looked inside their cell and started counting very loudly.

"Just to make sure none of us has gone missing," explained Annalisa.

Clara shook her head. "I guess I'll have to forego the idea of a quiet awakening here."

The good news was that as from 08:30, they all could go out in the open. The courtyard was small, probably ten metres by five, but it provided a refreshing change of scenery and some natural sunlight. Clara noticed that, apart from some concrete benches, there were no trees, just a tall wall, on top of which armed guards were walking. It was strange to imagine that viale Buoncammino, with its fragrant pine trees, and green view, was just outside. The other prisoners were walking around in groups of three and four, some other girls were playing table-football. Clara decided to sit down, on one of the hard benches. She looked up and let the sunrays kiss her face. At this time of the morning, it felt warm, not too hot, and it was invigorating. It was good to take a break, especially from Annalisa. She'd offered to introduce Clara to the other girls, as she called them, but Clara said she preferred to stay quietly on her own. Was she being unfriendly? The reality was that she had nothing in common with a drug dealer and a murderess. The topics of conversation were very few, and in any case, Annalisa seemed to monopolize all of them. And it's not that she didn't want to talk to the other prisoners, it was just that she needed some time to herself, to reflect.

"This is our new room-mate, Clara." Where had Annalisa popped out from? She introduced three women.

Clara struggled to focus at first, as the sun light had blinded her eyes. "Nice to meet you," she said. She was disenchanted with Annalisa, she just didn't seem to get it.

"So, you're the bank robber," said a tough-looking woman. She was very tall and had lots of muscles.

"So they say."

"You got away with two bank robberies and only got caught at the third. Respect!" The masculine-looking woman patted Clara heavily on her shoulder.

"How do you know?"

"I saw your picture on television this morning."

"Wow! She's famous!" shouted Annalisa.

Clara must've misunderstood, or misheard. "Are you

sure?"

"Yes, your black-and-white photo was flashed on screen, during the news. They seemed happy to have finally caught the mysterious female robber." She winked. "The one who did it three times."

Clara hid her face between her hands. She couldn't believe it. She was officially a criminal now.

"You're not very photogenic, either. You look better face to face." The tough looking girl was examining her, top to toes.

Clara didn't know whether she should rejoice about that comment.

"I told you, she's great! How cool to share with a bank robber, there aren't many women who can boast about that," yelled Annalisa. Monica seemed to agree when she almost smiled.

"I'm not that good, otherwise I wouldn't be here," replied Clara.

"We all get caught sooner or later," concluded the tough girl.

A guard approached Clara. "Your permission to phone your family has been granted. Also, they're allowed to visit tomorrow morning."

"Wonderful news!" Clara was relieved. "Can I phone them now?"

"Yes, just follow me."

Clara was pleased to get away from the grilling of other prisoners. Was there a place in this jail where she could get some time to herself? Perhaps inside a phone box, since even using the toilet couldn't guarantee enough privacy.

She felt nervous as she dialled her home number. Almost like a child who'd been naughty and was going to be confronted with his parents, and didn't know what kind of reaction he'd get from them.

"It's wonderful to hear your voice," said Mamma over the line.

"It's great to hear yours too." Tears were rolling down Clara's cheeks.

"How are you? What's it like inside?"

"Better than we think when we're outside. To be honest I haven't had the time to figure it out myself."

"Are the other girls nice?"

What did Mamma mean by that? That wasn't an easy question to answer. "They're OK, they seem nice enough, if you don't care to look at their past."

"And your room-mates?" Mamma was eager to know.

Clara couldn't possibly tell her about the murderess. Mamma's heart was too fragile for that, so she settled for a less controversial truth. "One is called Monica, and she doesn't talk much. The other is called Annalisa, and talks for every citizen of Cagliari. To cut it short, she's doing my head in."

"At least you can have a conversation!"

Conversation? That was supposed to be a two-way thing. Monologue was more appropriate for Annalisa's natter. Clara had never met someone who talked so much, at any time, and of everything. That kind of mental torture was enough to cause her to give up the will to live. While all along, she'd thought that the murderess was the danger.

"Mamma, I've managed to get permission for you to visit tomorrow."

"Perfect, we could come just before lunch so that all the family can make it."

"I'm only allowed three visitors at a time."

"But that's not fair. We're a large family!" Mamma

sounded disappointed.

"Only three please. Just pick some names from a hat."

"I guess we'll have to split in different visits." Mamma's voice was flat.

"I'll need some clothes from home. Clean underwear, pyjamas, some jeans, t-shirts, track suits and other comfy clothes. No high fashion here."

"I'm writing it all down."

"And some nice toiletries, soaps and face creams. I don't know if food is allowed, I'll tell you tomorrow, but I could do with some chocolate."

"I'll bring you some goodies anyway. Anything else?"

"Some ear-plugs."

"OK, is that it?"

"No, one more thing. You know that toy phone I gave to Ivan?" Clara took a pause, she did realize it was an odd request. "I'd like it back."

"What? Are you teasing me?"

"No, I'm being serious." Should Clara explain that this was, in fact, the most important item?

"But Ivan may get upset if you take away his toy. After all you gave it to him."

"I know, but I'll just use it for a while and then he can have it back."

"*Use* it?" Mamma's voice sounded as if she doubted Clara's good sense.

"Play with it."

"Can't I get you something else to *play* with?"

"Please, just do as you're told!" Clara was losing her patience. Then she felt bad for shouting at Mamma. "I'm sorry. I'm just a bit on the edge here. I look forward to seeing you tomorrow. With the toy phone."

The guard told Clara that before going back to the

courtyard she had to see the prison psychologist.

"I'm not crazy," responded Clara. Although in her heart she was starting to have doubts.

"The psychological examination is done to assess whether you could be a danger to other prisoners, or even to yourself."

"Me? A danger?" That was pure irony, considering who she was locked up with.

The guard ignored her reply and accompanied her to a new office, at least one she hadn't seen before. Clara didn't like the idea of having to undergo some brain-picking activity. She just wasn't in the mood for it. She hoped very much it'd be fast and painless. In fact, she decided that she was going to be calm and collected; no emotions, no negative outbursts.

It seemed to work. She simply had to be herself, and tell the truth. The fact that she'd had a wonderful childhood, without any traumas. She was never neglected, nor beaten, nor abused in any form. Her parents had been generous without spoiling her. She'd never been jealous of her siblings and they didn't tend to compete for toys or attention. She was never bullied in school; she was successful with her studies and her job. She'd always had satisfactory relationships with people. She had lots of friends and a boyfriend who recently dumped her. But she didn't bear any grudges against him. Wasn't she a model of a perfectly sane and mature human being?

The psychologist seemed satisfied with Clara's account, and it was agreed that she was no danger to anyone.

How exciting; the next day, Clara was being taken to a new room, the visitors' one. The guard escorted her through the long white corridor, until they reached a room with minimum furnishings: a long rectangular table with a short glass panel running in the middle, and a dozen hard chairs located around the desk. Clara sat on one side, while her guard stood in the corner of the room. The door was opened and her family was taken inside.

It was lovely to see Papà, Mamma and Valentina. They hadn't changed much, whilst Clara felt she'd undergone enormous transformations. They were able to kiss each other over the glass panel, and then they all sat on the respective sides of the table. Mamma was holding Clara's hand over the glass.

"So how was your first day there?" asked Valentina.

"Not too bad. I didn't get beaten up or anything like that."

"What's the food like?" inquired Mamma.

"Good, but not as good as your cooking." Clara was sincere.

"What did you eat yesterday?"

"For lunch we had pasta with tomato sauce, meat-balls with a parsley cream, and spinach." Clara thought a little. "The pasta was a bit insipid, the meat-balls were OK and the spinach was... just spinach, boring."

"Are the portions generous?"

"I'd say they're just right."

"Can you have seconds?"

"I don't know, I didn't ask." Clara cared about food, but right now, it wasn't her priority. "Mamma, are we going to talk about something else?"

"What happened?" asked Papà. "How did you end up here?" He seemed both confused and concerned.

Perhaps it hadn't been a wise idea to switch topics. Clara didn't have an answer. "Did you bring my toy-phone?"

Valentina and Papà looked at each other, while Mamma gave Clara a blue plastic bag.

"I've brought you the things you asked for. They've all been searched by the guards."

Clara grabbed the large bag and looked inside. It was nice to touch her clean clothes again, but there was no sign of the phone.

"What about my toy?"

Mamma looked embarrassed. She bit her lips and looked down. Valentina grabbed a smaller bag which had been sitting on the floor next to Mamma, and handed it to Clara. She looked inside and was appalled to see that her toy phone had been badly bashed; it was scratched in many places and broken on one side. All the keys had been pulled out and they were lying at the bottom of the bag.

Clara went pale. "What happened to my phone?"

"Little Ivan bashed it to pieces," Valentina calmly replied.

"How's that?" Clara was still shocked.

"You know what little boys do. They always smash anything they come across!"

"But this is *not* a toy!" she shouted. Then she realized what she'd just said and tried to make amends. "What's up with children nowadays? We weren't allowed to destroy toys when we were small!" She looked inside the bag and her heart sunk even deeper when she realized that there was not a single key in its place.

"Clara, the keys can be put in back in their place. I've checked the phone and it looks like each one can be inserted into a specific slot, like lock and key." Papà was trying to reassure her. "I must admit that for a toy, it's rather complex, a small wonder of engineering. I would've fixed it myself, but there was no time. Would you like me to do it now?"

"Yes." Clara handed him the bag. "How do you know where each key goes?"

"The numbers go first, then the letters of the alphabet, all in sequence. If you get it wrong, the key simply won't slot in."

"That's probably why little Ivan smashed the phone. I suspect that he pulled them out first, then, when he tried to put them back in, he failed. He's too young to understand numbers and letters. So, he proceeded to bash the damn thing, since it wasn't doing what he wanted. Sounds like him." Valentina thought it was funny.

Papà started his tricky task, while Clara was terribly worried that the phone wasn't going to work.

"They put this toy through the x-ray machine." Papà was aligning all the keys on the table. "I wonder what it's like inside, I bet it's more complicated than it looks."

"Don't try it," commanded Clara.

"What's all the fuss with this thing sister? You must be really bored in this place."

"You're right. I've only been here one day and it seems like a century." Clara's tone was fed up. "Here time feels stretched like a long elastic. My highlight of the day is when the trolley rolls along the corridor to serve the meals."

Mamma was looking very worried.

"It's not that bad Mamma. Think that I don't have to go to work, that's a great plus. I don't need to see Mr Big-idiot nor Miss Shake-your-bum everyday. That must be worth something!" Clara smiled.

"Talking of work, one of your colleagues phoned yesterday." Papà seemed to be struggling with the letter T.

"More than just one," corrected Mamma. "We had a phone call from Gianna, one from Marcella and one from a guy called… what was his name?"

"Ernesto," said Papà.

"How sweet, that's really nice of them." Clara was truly pleased.

"This guy, Ernesto, seemed to be very concerned for you, and said that if we needed any help, he was ready." Papà was about to finish his arduous task.

"He's great. I miss him actually. He's always so much fun."

"He's the guy that plays the guitar in a band," explained Valentina to her parents. "Perhaps we could ask him to play a hard-rock serenade outside the prison just for Clara? That would cheer her up!"

Clara smiled at the idea. "Dad, have you finished?"

"Yes, but we've got a problem, three keys are missing."

"You *are* joking." Clara couldn't possibly believe it.

"No. I was searching inside the bag, but there's no trace of them. I guess we can ask Dino and Orietta to search their flat. Is it that important to you?"

Things may not have been that bad. Clara needed the keys 2 6 0 5 7 8 C S A M, which represented her date of birth, her initials and the beggar's initials. Surely she couldn't be that unlucky for one of those keys to go missing. The chances were small.

"Dad, which keys have gone astray?" her heart was pounding.

"It looks like we're missing number 1, and the letters F and M."

"Damn! Are you sure that the M is not there? Can you check again?"

Papà seemed astonished at Clara's tenacity. "I'm very sure. But can I ask you why all of this is so important?"

"Just give it to me. I'll see what I can do." Clara

grabbed the toy phone, with its bashed sides and front, bruised receiver, and the three missing slots. She then looked at her parents. "Would you mind going back to Dino's place and see if you can find the M? I don't care about the other two."

At this point Clara's family looked as if they were starting to question her sanity. They couldn't say anything.

"I have another favour to ask. The other day, when the robbery took place, I was approached by a beggar on the Poetto beach. He told me that he often goes to a bar in via Sonnino." She paused and looked at Valentina. "Do you think you could stop by every bar in via Sonnino to check if he's there?"

"Via Sonnino is long, and there are quite a few bars. But I'll do it, as long as Mamma and Papà give me some money to spend." She winked at them. "It's not polite to hang around at a bar without buying anything."

"Any excuse to squeeze some money from us," Papà chuckled.

"Also, some cash for the petrol for my scooter would be welcome. If you're going to do a job, you must do it properly." Valentina paused. "I'm going to ride along via Sonnino a few times a day, just in case I see this mysterious beggar wandering around."

"And Piazza Costituzione, there's where I met him first time," suggested Clara.

"I'll ride around all that area, and of course the Poetto. Isn't that where you bumped into him the other day?"

"Hang on a second! A full tank will never be enough to cover this running around the city a few times a day," protested Papà.

"It's for a good cause," declared Clara. Her face seemed more relaxed. She proceeded to give Valentina a description of Alessandro.

In case the missing letter M was never found, she had a back-up plan.

Chapter 19

Clara and her room companions were sipping their caffelatte. It was another bright morning, and Clara was thinking that a cloudy sky would've been more appropriate.

"What day is it?" Clara's voice was always croaky when she'd just woken up.

"Monday, the 9th June 2003." Annalisa replied promptly.

"This is the beginning of my fourth day. I've only been here three full days. It seems like a life-time."

"After one year, time goes faster."

"That's something to look forward to." Clara had her last sip of caffelatte.

"How often can we see our family? Or speak to them?"

"We're allowed four visits a month and four phone calls, that's about one a week. Although, if you're good they can give you two extra. It's a pity that we can't swap visits or phone calls, my family are fed up seeing me or hearing from me, and to be honest I've had enough of them too. I'd happily give you my slots if I could. But then what could you give me in return? It's favour for favour here. Let's suppose I could give you my time slot, what could you offer me? I do like your trainers, what's your shoe size?"

Hadn't Clara learnt? Hadn't she realized that it was a good idea *never* to ask questions, nor initiate a conversation with Annalisa? She decided not to reply. But to make sure, she quickly put her trainers on. Monday the 9th June, why was this date familiar? There was something happening today. Of course. The famous meeting at work which Clara was supposed to have organized. She smirked, there was justice after all. Hadn't she wished that she could be away today, so that Miss Shake-your-bum would end up doing all the work? Well, it looked like her prayers had been answered, although she hadn't quite envisaged such an extreme solution.

When Annalisa and Monica went outside, she opted to stay in her cell to fill in the form authorizing her to phone her family. She wondered if Papà had found the missing key, and hoped very much that Valentina had got hold of Alessandro. As she drew doodles on her piece of paper, she realized that she hadn't thought of Paolo lately. Was that because she'd been overwhelmed by the latest events, or because she started not to care so much about him? It was disappointing that he hadn't phoned her family, to find out how she was. But then, it would've been hard for him, after all he was her ex-boyfriend. Perhaps he was afraid of Mamma's reaction. How nice though that Ernesto had rung. She remembered his dark green eyes, which contrasted beautifully with his dark lashes. Yes, Ernesto's eyes had a captivating expression, a mixture of kindness and mischief. He certainly liked to have fun, and his joie de vivre was contagious.

As the guard walked by, Clara called for her attention.

"This is my request to phone my family," she handed over her form.

"But it's all scribbled! What are these doodles doing there?" the guard laughed. "I'm afraid you have to fill another one."

Oh no. What was she thinking? It was Ernesto's fault. "Can you wait for one minute? I'll fill in another one quickly."

"But, you only saw your family the day before yesterday!" observed the lady guard.

"Yes, I'm one of those pathetic prisoners who needs the comfort of their mum's voice."

"I don't think it'll be a problem. Just remember you're only allowed four phone calls a month. Don't use them up all in one go." The guard handed Clara another form.

That same afternoon, Clara was escorted by the red-haired woman to the phone booth. She liked this guard, she always smiled and she had that kind of maternal look about her. Also, she'd been very kind to Clara when she first was arrested, not a single unpleasant word was said. Even the way she led her along the corridors, she wasn't pushy or rough, she just gently touched her arm to direct her to the right places. Yes, there were some nice people, even in prisons.

Clara dialled her home number. Nonno picked up the phone.

"Hi Nonno, it's me!"

"Oh, my little grand-daughter! How nice to hear from you." He seemed emotional, for the first time.

"Perhaps next time you could come and visit me, maybe with Dino?"

"I can't wait; your Mamma said we're only allowed once a week." His voice was trembling. "Unfortunately, Nonno, I can't stay long, can you put me through to Mamma or Valentina?"

"Only your sister is here at the moment. I'll pass you through. I hope to see you soon."

"Hey Clara. Guess what? Nonno is crying!" whispered Valentina. "I haven't him shed a tear since Nonna died."

"Oh, poor Nonno!"

"We always knew you were his favourite. He hasn't been himself since you went to jail."

Was that remark comforting? Yes; but still, it made Clara feel sad. "Any news on the beggar?"

"I've been working hard for you. I've been riding twice a day around the areas we'd agreed on. No trace of him. But I found which bar he goes into. It's almost at the end, near Piazza Garibaldi."

"Was he there?" Clara's hopes were up.

"No, the owner told me that he hadn't seen him since last Friday. Apparently that afternoon he ordered double the usual amount of food and drink."

"As long as he didn't spend his twenty-five euros all in one go!"

"Anyway, I've left the owner our home number and also my mobile. I explained that it was very important for me to get in touch with Alessandro, and he seemed nice enough to want to help."

"What about the phone key? Have you found the M?"

"We searched Dino's flat high and low. We only found the missing 1. And of the letters F and M, not even a shadow."

"That's very bad news."

"Have you tried pulling out another letter you don't need and slotting it in the M hole?" Valentina had a solution for every problem.

"I've tried it, but it doesn't work. Each key fits only in the hole where it's supposed to go. Clever piece of … waste of time!"

"Orietta thinks that Ivan might have swallowed the two keys."

"Why doesn't this surprise me?"

"Come on Clara, it's not the end of the world. It's just a piece of red plastic. I can buy you another toy phone."

Valentina didn't know that it *was* the end of the world for Clara. Since Alessandro hadn't been found, that toy phone was the only way to get hold of him. What was she going to do now?

"Listen, carry on looking for the beggar. He's got to turn up sooner or later, how is he supposed to get fed? That bar is the only place in Cagliari where he gets a good deal."

"Don't worry sister. We'll get you out soon. Dad is trying to see if he can find a good lawyer for you."

"But we don't have any money saved up." Clara couldn't see how they could afford it.

"Zia Carmela has volunteered her savings. She's very generous for an acidic spinster."

"Don't talk this way; she's a good great-auntie. She even bought me an engagement present, do your remember?"

"I seem to remember, in particular, that you weren't that impressed with her gesture."

The allocated four minutes for the phone call passed too quickly, and Clara reluctantly had to say goodbye.

She could've talked to Valentina for ages, there was something very soothing about her voice. As the guard walked her back to her cell, Clara felt an immense melancholy. Perhaps it was talking to Nonno, his affectionate and caring voice. She remembered how he used to play with her when she was little and the stories he'd told her. Despite his age, he still had a sharp judgment and was one of the pillars in her family. She realized how much she missed all of them. It was strange to think how she took everything for granted, their meals together, their conversations, the sharing of problems. And only now, when this had been taken away from her, she realized how important it was. The bad thing now, wasn't simply the fact that her freedom had gone, but more upsetting was her inability to spend time with the people she loved. Phone calls and visits were scarce, and their duration short. And this was only her fourth day, how was she going to cope in the future?

When she got to her cell, Monica was reading, while Annalisa was watching some stupid programme on television. Clara sat at the small desk and stared at the wall in front. Things weren't looking too good. Between her arrest and today, she'd been visited once by the magistrate who was overseeing her case, and twice by her lawyer. Neither of them had brought good news. There had to be a way to get out of this place. Her little bashed phone was sitting on the left corner, almost in a way to suggest she should pick it up. She brought it closer to her and started playing with the keys. She looked at her poor red toy, all smashed up and bruised, and she wondered if it still worked. A quick thought passed through her mind, but she ignored it. She caressed the scratched plastic receiver, and that thought came again, sneaked inside her brain, and it wouldn't go away. It was telling her that she could phone Lucilla. No keys were missing for her. Clara tried to dismiss the sly thought, but it was stubborn and kept coming back. She'd often wondered how human beings were able to control their actions, but not always their own thoughts. Sometimes they'd appear when least expected, and the more you wanted to get rid of them, the more they persisted.

Phoning Lucilla wasn't an option. First of all because she was probably the one responsible for Clara's imprisonment. Second, because she didn't know if she could trust the blonde angelic demon, and last but not least, because she wasn't simpatica. Not to mention that they'd had a massive bust-up. Clara had thrown the phone at her, and said some nasty things. How could she even hope that she'd be willing to help?

Still, what did she have to lose? She was already in prison, what worse could happen? Luckily, Italians were civilized enough not to endorse the death penalty, so really, all in all, she was relatively safe. OK, there were worse things that could happen to her, such as being transferred to a cell where she'd get beaten up daily, or perhaps share with the equivalent of two Annalisas. But it was best not think in negative terms. Negative thinking was counterproductive, she'd heard that somewhere. Did it make any sense to call Lucilla now? Could she really do something for Clara? She automatically lifted the receiver, and almost in a trance she pressed her magic buttons 2 6 0 5 7 8 C S slowly, and the final L L very slowly. The phone started to ring, it was working. Clara's heart began its race.

"I gather you're in trouble," said Lucilla, in her usual relaxed tone.

"Just a bit."

No reply. What did Clara expect? It was *she* who'd called, not Lucilla. She'd better get on with it.

"I need your help," she whispered.

"I thought so."

"It's not very nice here." Clara didn't know what else to say.

"It's not supposed to be nice."

"You're not making it easy for me!"

"Why should I?"

Nothing had changed. Lucilla still drove her mad. Clara took a deep breath.

"I thought we were friends." Would that work?

"I think that my definition of friend is different from yours." Lucilla was serene, she didn't sound angry. Perhaps Clara could give it a try.

"I need to understand what's happened. Is there a way we could talk?" Clara's voice was rising.

"We're already talking."

"I mean *properly*! Face-to-face!"

"I'll see what I can do." Lucilla hung up.

Clara put the phone down, and suddenly felt all her strength go away. They'd only exchanged a few words, but it'd taken a lot of effort and energy. The wall in front was still there, with its Madonna of the Rocks. There was a gentle and protective expression in her face, the dark colours and strange light in the painting were captivating.

"It's a bad sign." Annalisa's voice broke the enchantment. "You've only been here a few days and you're already talking to yourself."

"Actually I was talking to the phone."

"Oh right. And what did *it* have to say?"

"It said that it didn't like what you're watching on TV."

"Oh, I see. Did it make any suggestions?" Annalisa seemed amused.

"Yes. It seemed to think that the documentary on Rai Uno would be more cultural."

"Documentaries are boring. Is there anything else it'd like to watch?"

"There's a film on Rai Tre which it said wasn't too bad."

"OK then, we're going to make your phone very happy now." Annalisa switched channels. "Make sure you ask it to sit right in front of the TV, on the tall stool. Otherwise it won't be able to see."

Clara placed her toy phone on the stool, and with a serious expression started watching TV.

Monica shook her head twice, she seemed unsure. Perhaps she didn't know what to make of them. Clara too had her doubts.

Chapter 20

Clara was lying on her bed, with her hands behind her head. She was looking at the solitary light bulb hanging off the short white cable, in the middle of the ceiling. It was dusty, but that detail didn't seem to worry her. Annalisa and Monica were out, they never missed an opportunity at break time, especially in the morning, as in the afternoons it could get quite hot.

Clara too liked some fresh air occasionally, but what she liked even more was the chance to be away from her companions and have some time to herself. She closed her eyes; the last two weeks flashed in front of her, images in black and white with no sound, nor smell, like a mute film. Signor Peppino was the first, standing next to the tree where he'd tried to hang himself. She wondered how he was feeling now. How was he coping with his grief and the absence of his wife? Were his daughters looking after him properly? God forbid, but if something like that ever happened in her family, she'd make sure that Papà would never be alone.

The image of Signor Giovanni, sitting on his bed in the old people's home, came to mind. She liked him; even in his old age, he still had all his marbles. Was he well? Was he still alive? She wondered what he'd done with his money, did he give it to charity, or was he going to leave it for his children? Then she remembered how she'd promised she'd visit him again soon. He seemed lonely, and what he was missing most was affection and love. Her last week of freedom had been too chaotic to arrange visits. Well, she'd have to be better organized next time. But... would there be a next time? And how long would it take to get out of prison? How many years did bank robbers get? What if it took ten years and Signor Giovanni was already dead, *naturally* hopefully, by the time she visited him?

What about Signor Mario? She could just picture him sitting at his desk holding a cigarette. That cloud of smoke in his office, that's the thing Clara remembered most. He was very lucky, extremely lucky. It didn't happen every day to have all that money stolen, and for someone to give it all back to you. Not the *same* money, to be precise. Clara wasn't too worried about him. He had no reason to be unhappy now. He was probably still celebrating with all his carpenters; his life's dream had come true. She wondered what had happened to the boy who stole the money in the first place. Was he still in Cuba? If the world was a just place, someone should've robbed him too, and so on. But things didn't always work out fairly.

For instance, was it fair that Rossana had died, at such young age? Was she happier now? Where was she? Did paradise really exist? Because she was too nice to go to hell or purgatory. It's true, she wanted to commit suicide originally, and that was a very bad thing in Christian terms. But, and Clara had to stress this, *but*, she'd repented of her intentions, therefore her soul should've been saved. Considering the awful death-by-car, being run over was almost like being a martyr. So, she should go straight to heaven, without any stopovers in less agreeable places. When Clara was a little girl, she had a clear idea of what paradise was like. All the people and children would walk on top of clouds, which were made of whipped cream. The houses' walls were built with thin-wafer biscuits and the roofs were made of dark chocolate. The balcony railings were actually candy sticks gums and instead of growing flowers in there, you'd grow fresh fruit, like strawberries, blackberries and cherries. And whenever you fancied some, whether it was chocolate, cream, biscuit, or fruit, you'd just break a piece and eat it, and it was the best, tastiest thing you'd ever tried. And somehow, by miracle, the piece you'd taken off would grow back, so there was always plenty for everybody. Well, if Rossana was in such a place, she was the luckiest girl in the world.

"There's a visitor for you," announced the guard as she came close to the door.

"I'm not expecting anyone."

"It's a volunteer who works for the local charities. They offer emotional support for prisoners."

Clara hesitated. She wasn't in the mood to talk to strangers. But then, maybe a conversation with someone who actually lived in the real world could provide a refreshing change.

She got up and followed the guard. When they reached the visitors' room she noticed that Monica was there too, sitting at the far end of the table, and was talking to an older lady. That's where she was; Clara had assumed that she was out in the court-yard with Annalisa.

"Where's my volunteer then?"

"She'll be here in a second." The guard moved to the corner.

Clara observed Monica. Perhaps this was the one and only opportunity to actually see her talk. She was too far for her voice to be heard. Monica was sitting with her back against the rear of the chair, her hands resting on her lap. Her gaze was lost in the distance, while her visitor was looking at her and seemed to be doing most of the talking. No surprises there.

The door opened and Clara was shocked to see who her visitor was. How did Lucilla pull this one? She looked radiant. Her blonde hair was shiny and light; it almost seemed to dance around her shoulders. She sat down and smiled. Her teeth were still perfect, and her eyes appeared to be of a darker blue this morning, the same colour as the sea when you swim away from the shore.

"This is unexpected," said Clara.

Lucilla didn't reply. She just seemed very pleased. What was there to be happy about, under the circumstances?

"This is your first public appearance." Clara was still trying to grab the implications of what she'd just said. Lucilla had always made a fuss about privacy.

"That's what you think." Her voice was serene, as always.

"How did you get permission to visit me?"

"Voluntary worker." Lucilla flashed a card with her photo on it.

Things were getting better. Her blonde friend had probably stolen someone's identity card; she was cheating the prison authorities, and God knows what trouble this could cause Clara.

"I thought that you weren't a liar."

"I'm not." Lucilla paused. "In reality my job *is* a form of charity. Helping people."

"You didn't help me much!" Clara crossed her arms.

"What do you want to talk about?"

"Can't you guess?"

"It's not polite to answer a question with another question."

Clara should've known that with Lucilla only straight-talking worked. "OK, let's start again. How have I ended up here? Was it your doing?"

"One question at a time please."

"I thought that you could multi-task, obviously you're not as gifted."

"I could reply to both questions simultaneously, but it's your brain that couldn't process the two answers together."

Smart girl. Lucilla was far too clever for her; she should just keep it simple and specific.

"Can you tell me what happened last Thursday, at lunchtime?" Was that plain enough?

Lucilla took a deep breath. She turned her head to the side and saw Monica. She looked at her for a few seconds, and then redirected her gaze towards Clara.

"A girl named Donatella stole your Ferrari."

"How could that happen?"

"Do you remember that on Wednesday night you came down to the car, had a go at me and left the keys in the car? Well they stayed there."

Clara raised her voice. "What?"

"Don't shout."

"Sorry." Clara decided to whisper. "OK, so this Donatella stole my car. I guess that after that she went to the bank and just robbed it?"

"No. She went home, got changed. She took the mask and the gun and then, only then, she drove to the bank."

"Carry on."

"She'd done it before; twice. When she got to the bank, as she was going through the doors, she put her mask on, and then pointed her gun at the staff. She ordered all the cash."

"Ordered?"

"In the sense of asked for."

Clara was trying to picture the scene.

"It was very fast, she's a professional." Lucilla flicked her hair backwards. "As soon as she collected the money, she left and drove off with the Ferrari. Then headed for her house in Pirri, where she's got a garage and could hide the car."

"Clever girl! I cannot help but admire her; I could never have done such thing." Clara was shaking her head. "Is it true that we look alike? At least, the police said so."

"She's the same build as you, similar height and hair. But so are many Sardinian girls. I guess the main thing you had in common was the Ferrari." Lucilla paused. Clara always dreaded her pauses. "Although, if I think of her properly, I'd say she's prettier than you."

"Thank you very much!"

"However, *inside*, you're more beautiful. And that's what counts."

Clara couldn't believe her ears. Lucilla had actually paid her a compliment.

"The two times she robbed the bank previously, it seems to have happened on two occasions I couldn't provide an alibi." Clara was still puzzled about that. "Was it a coincidence?"

"In human terms, yes."

What was that supposed to mean? "And in *your* terms?"

"You think that things happen by chance. I believe they happen for a reason." Lucilla crossed her legs.

"Let's imagine there is a reason as to why I've ended up in jail. Can you elucidate?"

"It's up to you to work it out."

"Of course. What else could I expect?"

Clara looked up and sighed. She then instinctively turned her head to her left and spotted Monica, who instead of listening to her visitor was staring at Lucilla.

She looked transfixed.

"I'm working hard for you. I'm trying to find a way to get you out of jail," announced Lucilla.

"Finally some good news!" Clara was relieved. "And how do you intend to achieve that?"

"Donatella isn't pleased that someone else has ended up in jail because of her. There are two elements really. Guilt and pride."

"I'm listening." Clara tried to keep her voice down, but it was hard, as she was getting excited.

"She's feeling guilty because she's fundamentally a good person. Her conscience is giving her grief, thanks to me." Lucilla paused. "She's also proud of her achievements and she doesn't want an ordinary girl like you to take all the credit."

"Ordinary girl like me? What does that mean?" Clara wasn't thrilled. How could this Donatella have an opinion of her if they'd never even met! Talk about prejudice.

"She's seen your picture on TV and they described your background. That you come from a working class family, and couldn't explain how you came into possession of the Ferrari. Your picture wasn't flattering either."

"So she's deduced from all of this that I'm an ordinary girl. I guess that's nothing wrong with that."

"Nothing wrong with being ordinary. But in your case it's factually inaccurate. You're an extraordinary girl." Lucilla paused, while Clara waited for the blow. "I would've never chosen you otherwise."

"You must be telling me this because *you* feel guilty, for putting me in this situation in the first place." Clara pointed her finger at her.

"When I said *extraordinary* earlier, I wasn't referring to your degree of intelligence."

Could Clara get offended for this remark? No, because she'd asked for it.

She suddenly became aware of a presence just behind her. Clara looked up; it was Monica, who was staring at Lucilla. Her face had lit up, almost as if she was having a vision. Clara knew that Lucilla was attractive, but to induce such a reaction in a person was a bit exaggerated.

Out of the blue, Monica held her hand towards Lucilla. "Is it you?" she asked.

Clara couldn't believe her ears. That woman had just spoken for the first time.

"Yes Monica. It's me." Lucilla took her hand.

What was going on?

"Sorry to interrupt this exchange of greetings, but this lady is actually *my* visitor!" exclaimed Clara. Time was short and she had a lot to discuss with Lucilla. And anyway, if Monica wanted to talk, for a change, why didn't she do it with *her* visitor?

The guard approached Monica and gently led her away.

"What was that all about?" Clara was intrigued.

"We were talking about getting you out of jail."

"Yes. Since you mentioned that I'm... stupid, could you explain how you intend to get me out of prison?"

"I'm working on it."

"That doesn't sound very hopeful."

"It's not meant to." Lucilla looked at Clara deeply into her eyes. "There's no way I can assure you that it'll happen."

The whole world collapsed onto Clara. "Great."

"I can only try to help, but I have no guarantees." Lucilla gently stood up and pushed the chair back into place. "I can't force Donatella." She started to walk away. "I can't interfere with free will."

As Clara was being escorted back to her cell, her legs felt weak. She felt she was carrying the entire weight of the planet, including its inhabitants. Things were looking awful. Since Alessandro had gone missing, Lucilla had been the only person she could rely on for help. But just now she'd offered no assurance. In fact, even if she'd promised Clara that she'd get her out of this trouble, why should she believe her? She'd told her once that nobody at work would notice her absence, and yet they did. She produced a Ferrari and loads of cash with no explanation, and at the same time banks were being robbed. And the latest was her visit in prison; masking her true identity with that of a charity worker. How could she trust this woman? In fact, hadn't all her troubles started after she'd met Lucilla?

Clara's stomach was churning. It looked as if there was no way out. She'd just enlisted the help of the very person who'd thrown her into this mess. How was that for morale?

When Clara got to her cell, Monica was sitting on her bed, with her back against the wall, and her legs crossed. Her face was unusually relaxed, and her eyes seemed lively. Even her short grey hair didn't seem so spiky. Clara was standing, and looking towards the window. Those yellowish bars seemed to shine under the sun, she wondered if she'll ever see a window free of bars again.

"Come and sit with me," said Monica as she patted on her bed cover.

Gosh. She'd talked again. Clara had assumed that what had happened in the visitors' room would be a one-off, one of those extraordinary events in life, like winning the lottery. She accepted the invitation and sat next to her.

Monica came closer and acted as if she was about to reveal a secret. Clara decided to pay attention.

"The night I killed my husband…" she whispered. Then Monica closed her eyes.

She breathed deeply and kept her eyes shut. Clara hoped she wasn't going to leave that sentence in mid-air. What if she decided to never talk again from this moment onwards?

Monica finally opened her eyes. "That night, he'd been more brutal than usual." Tears were starting to veil her eyes. "He came home, and was heavily drunk. Usually he'd punch me, or hit me hard, or throw me against the furniture. But that night he was very angry, for some reason."

Monica was breathing heavily, almost as if the memory was about to trigger a panic attack. "He grabbed a knife and started to chase me around the kitchen. I realized that my life was in real danger."

Clara was shocked. She'd never heard a victim describe how they'd been assaulted. And this was for real. She offered Monica a tissue. She wanted to say something, but couldn't think of anything.

"I was able to run faster than him. He chased me to the living room and he stumbled on the coffee table. He fell over, hit his head, and fainted. I guess he was too drunk." Monica snuffled and wiped her eyes.

Clara had noticed that her voice was incredibly soft, in stark contrast with her generally rough demeanour. This woman had gone through hell and yet, there was a little space for tenderness in her.

"I don't know what took me. I grabbed the knife he was holding, and without thinking I stabbed him. His blood got splattered all over his white shirt and then onto the floor. Everything around me was red!" Monica was sobbing violently at this point.

Clara could only hug her and listen.

"I suddenly realized what I'd just done and I felt like a monster. I was a vicious human being, I didn't deserve to live." Monica blew her nose and looked at Clara. "So I lifted the knife and directed it at my chest."

Clara gasped. That was a turn of events she didn't expect.

"But someone suddenly held my arm, from behind." Monica's gaze was lost at this point. "I looked back and saw a girl, a blonde girl. I had no idea where she'd come from. She wouldn't let go of my arm. She was incredibly strong for such a slim girl."

Clara realized where this was going. "Did she look like the lady who visited me today?"

"Yes. It was her!"

A slow shiver travelled down Clara's spine. This couldn't possibly be the case. Monica must've been dreaming, a post-traumatic hallucination perhaps.

"The girl told me that enough blood had been spilt. That I should call the police and explain what had happened. She waited with me until I made the phone call. And when the police arrived she was gone."

"Have you told this story to anybody?"

"No. You're the first one." Monica was looking down. "I thought that I dreamt the whole thing. I thought I was having a hallucination, caused by the shock of what I'd just done. Who was going to believe me? I didn't believe it myself!" Monica suddenly looked up, her eyes had a sparkle. "Until today, when she came to see you."

"Look... this girl, maybe, she just resembles the one in your...vision."

"You're a lucky girl Clara. She came to rescue you." The sparkle in Monica's eyes became dazzling.

"Lucky? That's not the word I'd use!"

Monica had a dreamy expression. "Now I know. Now everything makes sense."

"Look, I don't want to sound disrespectful, but your story is a bit… far-fetched."

"I don't care whether you believe me or not. I know the truth now."

And with that sentence Monica decided to lie on the bed, and stare at the ceiling. She looked happy for the first time, and Clara felt a hint of envy for not being able to share her joy.

Suddenly that prison cell felt very crowded. Maybe Monica and her newly-found happiness were filling the entire space. Clara asked to go out in the courtyard and was glad to be in the open air. She decided to stand in a corner, as she didn't want to be disturbed. All the girls seemed busy playing table-football, chatting or smoking. Clara wished there was a tree she could climb and sit on one of the branches, under the shade of its leaves.

She needed to gather her thoughts and put them in some kind of order. Lucilla's visit followed by Monica's revelation had troubled her deeply. It was becoming apparent that Lucilla wouldn't be able to help, and it was almost certain that she couldn't be trusted. But how did this reconcile with Monica's account of her drama? According to her story, Lucilla had stopped her from committing suicide. This was in line with what she'd asked Clara to do in the past. But surely, if Lucilla was some sort of angel, the logic would want her to stop Monica from killing her husband first, not from committing suicide. In the hit parade of sins, murder definitely came number one, well above suicide. No.

Nothing seemed to make sense.

The whole story told by Monica must've been the fruit of her imagination. There was no other way. Clara shouldn't even entertain it. That woman was a murderess, and yes, she was justified in stabbing that bastard; but still, if someone was prepared to kill, who was to say they weren't prepared to make up stories?

The only way to look at the situation was to accept that Lucilla couldn't help her. In fact, she might cause even more trouble for Clara. As far as Monica was concerned, Clara had to acknowledge that Lucilla's visit in prison had had an impact. It'd broken the silence for Monica. And now she was going to start talking.

But, was that a good thing?

Chapter 21

Annalisa was lecturing about something again. Clara had learned not to pay attention any more. It was a waste of energy. The secret was to nod here and there, look interested occasionally, and thoughtful at other times. Another trick was to never interrupt, as this seemed to increase the flow of words from the other side. Clara was perfecting her technique of serious listener when the food trolley rolled along the corridor.

"What's on for lunch today?" Annalisa came down from her bed and approached the barred door.

That was something else she did very well, switch topics of conversation in a matter of seconds.

"Seafood risotto for primo, and squid with peas for secondo, with fresh salad." The cell next door was being served.

"Who wants my peas?" Clara had never been too keen on those miniature green balls.

Monica raised her hand.

"Since you don't like fruit, can I have yours?" asked Clara.

Monica nodded.

Since her revelation, Clara had expected Monica to become a second Annalisa. However, she'd reverted to her old ways. It was like a bottle of spumante that had been sealed for months. It got opened at New Year's Eve, poured out all its contents, and got closed again. The only difference was that exposure to spumante usually made you feel happier, not more nervous.

Clara swapped her peas for a peach. She was looking forward to eating two peaches at the end of her meal. They looked like twins, they must've come from the same tree, therefore they were two sister-peaches. The one she was holding had a very firm shape, but it looked juicy and perfectly ripe. The skin was soft and was mostly red with shades of dark pink. Clara felt its fragrance as she held it close to her nose, there was something so nostalgic about the smell of a good peach. Her uncle's orchard in the countryside, fresh fruit salad eaten on the beach, peach slices in red wine, Zia Carmela's favourite. She'd once got drunk just by eating three peaches drowned in a carafe of wine, when her auntie had gone to answer the phone. She was only eight years old then, she didn't understand why something that tasted so good made her feel so sick afterwards.

Clara was brought back to reality when Annalisa started to talk again. She looked at Monica and wondered whether she was actually paying attention to Annalisa; she seemed more interested in picking the mussels and leaving them on the side, while carefully extrapolating any rice grain that was stuck to them. Obviously for her, the rice was more important than the fish, what a bizarre preference. But then, what could be expected from someone who liked peas?

"It's not polite to talk with your mouth full of food," Clara said to Annalisa.

"How did you know my mouth was full of food, if you weren't even looking at me? Or listening to me?"

Clara thought for a second, she really had just said it to shut her up, not to start another conversation. "Your voice is different when your mouth is full. It's best if you talk after you finish your lunch. And … don't rush, it's bad for your digestion to eat fast."

Annalisa appeared confused by her remark, but Clara detected a fleeting smirk on Monica's face.

Two days had gone by since Lucilla's visit. No breaking news. Two days weren't such a long time, but inside a prison, they felt like two years. Alessandro was still missing and Lucilla had achieved nothing. For some reason, she wasn't surprised. Clara had tried to keep positive, but whichever way she looked at it, she knew that her blonde friend was responsible for her imprisonment, so why should she help her? Perhaps it actually served a purpose to have Clara locked up? The police wouldn't have to search for the real bank robber, since they thought the culprit had already been caught. In the meantime, Lucilla could enjoy her newly-acquired wealth.

Clara had started to suspect that the robber was in fact Lucilla, not this mythical Donatella. Not bad as an invention. Probably Lucilla was wearing a wig similar to Clara's hair, when she entered the banks. And considering that they were of similar height, and from the video, she was wearing a large jacket, it was hard to tell if their body size was actually different. With the aid of a mask for better disguise, Lucilla could potentially be mistaken for Clara.

She decided to walk towards four girls who were playing table-football. It was a very bright morning and she could feel the heat of the sun on her shoulders as she watched the game. There was something relaxing about the warmth of sunrays on your body. There was also something charming about that little white ball that kept leaping from one side of the table football to the other, and the noise it made. Noise that could barely compete with the sound produced by the girls every time they scored a goal.

"Clara, could you please come with me?" The red haired guard touched her arm.

Clara hadn't seen her come close and was pleasantly surprised.

"Where are we going?"

"It's a surprise." The guard seemed pleased.

"A good one, or a bad one?"

"A good one."

The woman gently directed her inside, while the prisoners left behind seemed intrigued. They walked along the familiar corridors, until they reached the commander's office. The guard knocked on the door and they entered. Instead of the vice-commander, another man was sitting at the desk. He looked just as important, if not more. He got up, shook Clara's hand and invited her to take a seat.

"Signorina Serra, I have some good news for you." He started to shuffle his papers, several times. Then, he cleared his throat. "We've made a mistake in arresting you and you're now released from prison." His smile had a hint of embarrassment.

Clara felt too weak to get up, so she decided to stay seated. Good news was often more unbelievable than bad news.

"What happened?" she managed to ask.

He glanced his papers, then looked up. "Your lawyer will explain." He beckoned to the guard.

The red-haired lady came close to Clara and helped her get up. Clara was so overwhelmed that even getting up, at this stage, was making her dizzy. They both left the office and found Avvocato Selis waiting outside. This time she was happy to see him. "Tell me everything!" she shouted.

"It's unbelievable! Yesterday afternoon, another bank in Cagliari was robbed." His voice hadn't changed, it was still high-pitched. "Yes, the same format. The lady *who looks like you* was wearing a mask and managed to steal 18,000 euros. This time she was driving another car, which had been stolen as well."

Clara sighed with relief. "I have an alibi this time. I was in my cell with Annalisa and Monica yesterday afternoon."

"The lady in question left a note with one of the bank employees, before she ran away." He pulled a piece of paper from his pocket. "This is a copy of the post-it she left." He read it aloud: "You've got the wrong person. I'm still out and about, although I promise that this is the last one."

"Any finger-prints on the post-it?" asked Clara.

"No, she was wearing gloves. And the pen she used was a standard black biro."

"Clever girl." Clara secretly smiled. Could Lucilla have robbed a fourth bank to get her out of jail? Or had this been achieved by the mysterious Donatella? "Any news of my Ferrari?"

"No."

"I wonder if she's going to keep it." She hoped very much that either Lucilla or Donatella would have the grace to return her car.

"I hope your stay here wasn't too unpleasant." Avvocato Selis shook her hand.

"It could've been worse."

"Your family are waiting for you at the entrance," the guard informed her.

Clara's energy and vitality started to re-surface, and before she knew it, she was jumping up and down and hugging her lawyer. Should she try to keep her cool? No. It was time to celebrate.

All the important people in her family were there, ready to welcome her. The minute Clara set foot on the street, she was overwhelmed with joy, she'd never felt so happy in her life. Wasn't it strange how freedom was something we all took for granted, and only when we'd lost it, we'd realize how much it was worth. A bit like good health.

They all stopped at one of the kiosks on the avenue and had coffee and pastries. Clara's bigné filled with crème patissiere tasted like heaven, even if Ivan had touched it with his little dirty hands.

"Dino, you owe me thirty euros." Zia Carmela was sipping her cappuccino.

"Come on auntie, you don't really expect me to give you that money!" Dino had icing sugar all over his lips.

"A bet is a bet."

Nonno smirked, he knew his sister very well.

"What did you bet on?" Clara was curious. She knew that Zia Carmela had a soft spot for gambling, especially in poker.

The family members all looked at each other, like conspirators.

"Dino, are you going to tell her, or should I have the privilege?" Zia Carmela had a cheeky look.

"Tell me what?" Clara was getting suspicious.

"They've placed a bet on you." Valentina was carefully unwrapping her cornetto. "Zia Carmela said you were innocent, while Dino thought you were guilty."

Clara looked at her brother with condemnation. "Did you seriously think I'd robbed a bank?"

"I told him that it wasn't your nature," pointed out Zia Carmela.

Dino looked sheepish; he really didn't know what to say.

"He never believed your story of this mysterious friend who got you the Ferrari," intervened Orietta. "To be honest, it was highly unlikely." Was she trying to defend her husband?

"Dino? Speak for yourself." Clara was daring him.

"Come on sister, don't get angry. The bet was just a joke between Zia Carmela and me. She was so persistent that you'd done nothing wrong that I decided to challenge her with a bet of thirty euros."

"Thank you for your loyalty auntie!" Clara kissed Zia Carmela on her cheek. "And thank you for your faith in me, brother!" Her look was thunderous.

"Joke or no joke, I want my thirty euros." Zia Carmela put her hand forward. "Now."

"You've got to pay!" Nonno was having a lot of fun.

"But we're family!" protested Dino.

"Even more so." His great-auntie wasn't easily fooled.

While Valentina moved away to make a phone call on her mobile, Dino's family said good-bye.

"Ivan likes to be held by his father." Mamma was looking with affection at her two boys, son and grandson.

"Despite his bad back, Dino too likes holding his son. Especially now, since he's thirty euros lighter." Zia Carmela still had a grin on her face.

"Shall we go home and get some lunch?" suggested Papà.

The family split in two cars. Zia Carmela and Nonno were in the Fiat Punto, while the rest shared the Ford Fiesta. Clara was ecstatic. As Papà drove through Cagliari, she let the window down and breathed in the hot summer air. The city looked lively and bright, and the sky seemed endless. Somehow from the tiny court-yard in prison, the sky had felt like a limited blue rectangle, but at this moment, it had no boundaries.

As they turned into via Milano, Clara saw a group of people gathered at the entrance of her palazzo. They'd aligned themselves to form a wall and they were all holding glasses. Signor Gabriele was handling a bottle of spumante, and as Clara got out of the car, everyone applauded. Clara was touched by this gesture but felt uncomfortable about all this fuss. The neighbours started to come close to her and kissed her on the cheeks, and then proceeded to be served spumante by Signor Gabriele. Clara was overwhelmed by such warm welcome; it looked like so many of her neighbours cared about her. As she was being offered a glass, she heard the first notes of a very loud song. She turned around and noticed that Ernesto and his whole band were gathered on the pavement, with their guitars, amps, drum kit and microphones and were playing 'Whole lotta Rosie' from AC-DC. This was unbelievable; Clara had to rub her eyes to make sure she wasn't dreaming. But her senses seemed to be working fine, and while everybody was raising their glasses and cheering, she felt tears rolling down her cheeks. Now she understood why the people had formed a wall on her arrival, they'd been covering the surprise.

Ernesto was in top form; he was running and jumping around on the pavement like he'd done on stage, while the singer was screaming at the top of his voice. More and more people came out on the street, and seemed to be enjoying the music and the cool spumante. Apparently Signor Gabriele had bought a dozen bottles and was happily serving anybody, even the children.

When the first song finished, Ernesto grabbed the microphone.

"We are here to celebrate Clara's return to her family and friends! Cheers!" he shouted. "Will someone have the decency to serve a glass to the band as well?"

"Have the whole bottle!" offered Signor Gabriele.

"One bottle each!" The singer came forward.

"And now let us all sing along." Ernesto looked at the band and they all started to play and sing: "Because Clara is a good girl, Clara is a good girl, Clara is a good giiiiiiirrrrlll... No-one can deny it!"

The public cheered and screamed and requested more songs.

"We can only play one more song," explained Ernesto on the microphone. "The traffic warden there..." he pointed at the young man wearing a uniform, who was leaning against a jacaranda tree, "has told us that we're not allowed to make all this noise in public, especially at lunchtime. But he kindly agreed, on this special occasion, to let us play one more song." He paused. "Signor Gabriele, pour him a glass!"

The band started playing 'For Those About to Rock – We Salute You', another AC-DC song. Clara was amused and thrilled at the same time. She'd never been into hard rock until she met Ernesto, but she couldn't deny that this music was particularly vibrant. She was amazed to see how all these people who'd gathered in via Milano seemed to be enjoying it, despite the fact that most of them, at this time of day, were retired.

"Did you like our surprise?" Valentina had to shout, in order to be heard.

"Very much. Was it your doing?" Clara was still trying to convince herself this wasn't a dream.

She nodded. "Ernesto called us early this morning to have some news and we told him that we'd just heard from your prison that you were innocent and would be released today. We knew even before you!" Valentina had another sip of spumante. "I told Ernesto that it would've been nice to organize a welcome party for you, so he suggested the via-Milano-gig upon your arrival." Valentina looked with disappointment at her empty glass. "Who do you think I was calling on my mobile earlier?"

"Did you ever get a phone call from Paolo, while I was away?" Clara needed to know.

"No."

"Let's go inside now. I've invited Ernesto for lunch," said Mamma.

"Why only Ernesto? It's impolite to invite only one member of the band!" Valentina was disappointed, as the bass player was the cutest.

"I extended the invitation to all of them, but they've all got stuff to do." Mamma grabbed Clara's arm.

"Welcome back Clara!" Ernesto's voice came from behind. How did he always manage to do that?

She turned round and instinctively hugged him. It felt good. "Thank you for the wonderful surprise."

"Pleasure." He wasn't letting go of her.

She was suddenly feeling nervous. Where was this emotional turmoil coming from? Perhaps it was all this excitement, combined with a couple of glasses of spumante.

Ernesto looked at her. "Your mum's invited me to lunch, but maybe I shouldn't stay. It's your first meal together for a while."

"I'd love it if you stayed." Clara was still holding him.

"OK then. I'll clear up all this musical stuff and come up shortly."

What Clara had always admired about Mamma was the fact that not only she was a brilliant cook, but she could also prepare a fantastic meal in half an hour; and we're talking about a three course lunch here. The other exceptional quality that Mamma possessed was the capacity to make a meal for seven, when she'd only expected five people, and yet, provide generous portions. She'd often told Clara that a good housewife should always have plenty of food and drinks, in case she decided to invite people last-minute. On this occasion, the two extra were Zia Carmela and Ernesto, although Clara had no doubt that, if needed, her mother could've also fed the rest of the band, meaning four energetic hungry boys.

"This tomato sauce is yummy." Ernesto was rolling his spaghetti on the fork.

"I'm sure the one that your mum makes is also delicious." Mamma seemed sure.

"The curious thing when you eat pasta with tomato sauce, is that every woman uses the same ingredients, tomatoes, olive oil, basil, maybe onions and garlic, who knows? But it tastes different every time. And it's always good!" Ernesto helped himself to more.

"What happened at work while I was away?" Clara was struggling with her spaghetti bundle. It was always too big.

"Nothing much. Miss Shake-your bum, as you call her, has been huffing and puffing along the corridors, saying that she's overworked. As if anyone would believe her! And obviously lots of gossip about our Clara ending up in prison." Ernesto broke a piece of bread.

"What were people saying?" Clara was intrigued.

"Your friends, Marcella and Gianna, were defending you with their swords. Some of the other admin girls, naturally Miss Shake-your-bum was amongst them, said that a woman with a salary similar to theirs could never afford a Ferrari and nobody believed that story that it was given to you by a friend."

"And what did you think?" Clara was keen to find out.

"I thought that it was cool to have a friend who owned a Ferrari and robbed banks." He paused. "I was very disappointed to find out you were innocent."

"What do you do Ernesto? Apart from playing the guitar?" Zia Carmela got up and helped clear the plates.

"You mean, as a job?"

"Yes, what's your profession?"

"I'm an office junior."

"Do you have a girlfriend?" Zia Carmela's look was inquisitive.

"No. Not yet." Ernesto glanced at Clara.

Zia Carmela adjusted her glasses and tried to focus, while still staring at him. "Do you have any brothers or sisters?"

"Yes."

"And your parents are not divorced, or separated?"

"No." He turned towards her. "I guess I could try and guess what your profession is. Private investigator? Police officer? Or just an inquisitive great-auntie?"

"Well done Ernesto!" Nonno clapped. "My sister gets too curious at times."

"How did you like the surprise rock-concert?" Nonno was addressing Clara.

271

"Very nice. Although, I wasn't impressed by the first song they played." Clara looked at Ernesto with the corner of her eye.

"What was the song called?" asked Zia Carmela. "I don't think I ever heard it before."

"Whole lotta Rosie. It's about a fat girl," explained Clara.

Ernesto bit his lips and looked embarrassed. "It wasn't deliberate!"

"Try and get out of this one!" Valentina couldn't stop laughing.

"Honestly, I never made the association. And… anyway, what association is there to be made?" Ernesto was looking for help around the table but nobody could provide it. "I… I never think of the words, I only focus on the beat."

"Are you trying to say that this song, which talks about a fat girl, has nothing to do with Clara?" Nonno seemed to be amused.

"Oh, I'm in trouble!" Ernesto covered his face with his hands.

"Why are you all ganging up on him? I'm sure he just meant for us to have fun!" Mamma came to the rescue. "Anyway, we don't have a clue what all these pop songs are about, we're too old."

"Rock." Ernesto liked to be precise when it came to music.

Mamma was puzzled. "Pardon?"

"We don't do pop. Only rock. Or, if we want to be even more specific, hard rock." He had a sip of wine.

"Oh, it's all the same to me."

"I propose a toast to our family, which has finally been reunited." Papà raised his glass.

When Clara went to bed that night, she felt content. It was nice to have her bedroom back and a window with no bars. Mamma had tried to put everything back into its place, after the police search, but she wasn't good with books. To her they all looked the same, so Clara's first task was to put them in the order she liked: novels first, followed by poetry. Then thrillers and detective stories. The middle section of the shelf was dedicated to publications on anything, art, music, literature, with an ample space dedicated to books on chocolate. How it was made, from the cocoa beans to the stuff you eat, its history, what kind of cakes you could make with it. The pictures were breath-taking, and very inspiring. If she had a second chance again at her career, she'd become a chocolate expert, one of those people who went to the factories and tasted samples, and gave them marks and appraisals. There were wine connoisseurs everywhere; surely they would need chocolate specialists too?

She lay on her bed and thought about the day ahead. She was going to go back to work, even on a Friday when it would've made sense to take the rest of the week off. She needed to go back to normality and forget about the prison experience. For a while she'd thought that she was going to stay there forever, but thanks to Lucilla things ended up OK. In fact, she should really thank her. It wasn't fair to just take things for granted. She got up, and grabbed the toy phone which she'd placed on her desk. She dialled her friend's number.

"What now?" Lucilla spoke calmly.

"I just wanted to say thank you for helping me out." Clara was whispering.

"You've said it."

"Are you angry with me?"

"What about?"

"The nasty things I said to you in the past."

"I don't have a long memory."

Clara sighed with relief. "I… I have so many things to say, but right now, nothing comes to mind."

"Then you shouldn't be wasting my time."

"Oh, I'm sorry to trouble you!" Clara was frustrated. Really, Lucilla didn't know anything about good manners.

"Are we done?"

Clara's mind was blank. "Yes. Goodnight."

"Goodnight."

As soon as Clara put the phone down, she remembered something she was going to ask Lucilla. She'd never accomplished the fourth mission. Was their deal still ongoing? What about getting Paolo back? And the Ferrari? How annoying, this always happened to her, she'd have so many questions to ask, but they'd all vanish when the opportunity presented itself.

It felt strange driving to work with Mamma's car. This time last week she was in prison, and now she was a free woman. So much had changed in such short time. The interesting part was how human beings could adapt to new situations. That sharp, awful pain she'd felt when Paolo had left her was no longer so acute, it was more like a dull ache, which wasn't present all the time. Somehow, this morning, she hadn't debated for hours what she was going to wear. When she'd opened her wardrobe, she'd picked the first thing that grabbed her, and put it on. Obviously, the colours had to match, but apart from that she wasn't bothered about looking too fashionable or too smart. Perhaps, it was because her thoughts had gone back to the people she'd met in her anti-suicide missions. Their problems had seemed more important than what shoes or top she was going to wear, and even her prison friends had popped up in her memory. Annalisa with her incessant talk, Monica with her constant silence, *almost* constant, and the others she'd met in the courtyard. Those girls weren't having such a good time. Some might argue that it was their fault, but Clara believed that probably they hadn't been so lucky, maybe they didn't come from loving and stable families; perhaps something awful had happened to them earlier in life. It was unlikely that people chose to be criminals just for the sake of it. All of these latest events were troubling her thoughts; was the world different now, or was it the same but she was looking at it with another pair of eyes? It was hard to concentrate and focus again, when she was about to face insignificant people like Miss Shake-your-bum and Mr Big Idiot.

"We've missed you so much!" Marcella hugged Clara when she came through the door.

"It's nice to be back." Clara meant being back to normality, not at work.

"Don't lie. It can never be nice being back here!" Gianna joined them in a triple hug.

"Was your radar picking up the signal again?" Clara looked at her with curiosity.

"Yes, it's very perceptive when it comes to you." Gianna was emotional, for the first time.

"Oh, what a moving scene," shouted Miss Shake-your-bum from the corridor. "Three girls cuddling each other. The good, the bad, and the ugly."

"I guess we know which one the *bad* is…" whispered Clara to her two friends.

"I'm more concerned with who's supposed to be the ugly one." Marcella giggled.

"It was about time you'd got back to the office." Miss Shake-your-bum walked inside the room. "I've had enough of doing your work."

The three friends stopped hugging, and were looking at her from top to bottom.

"How did you like a taste of your own medicine?" Clara stared at Teresa.

"What's that supposed to mean?" She still had that squeaky voice.

"You know very well what it means." Clara was daring her.

Marcella and Gianna decided to sit on one of the desks, and enjoy the scene.

"Anyway, we all know you did it. You just got away with it!" Miss Shake-your-bum seemed very angry.

"Yes, and I can see this hasn't gone down too well with you." Clara raised her chin and looked down on her. It felt good to be taller. "What bothers you most? The fact that I too can be bad and get away with it? Or just the simple knowledge that I'm smarter than you?"

"You're such a bitch!" shouted Teresa. Her eyes were like thunder.

"You're meaningless." Clara turned her back to her, and went to her desk.

For a second she thought that Miss Shake-your-bum was going to grab her hair and start a fight, but she then remembered that it wasn't in her interest. Clara was taller and bigger, she could eat her alive. By the time she sat on her chair, Teresa had gone.

"Not bad for a start of the day." Clara looked at Gianna and Marcella. They seemed stunned.

"I didn't think you had it in you," said Marcella. "You told her exactly what she deserved."

"Oh, I knew Clara was a little tiger dressed like a lamb. She's soft and cuddly and seems very vulnerable. But if you piss her off, she shows her true nature and, really, you don't want to end up under her scratchy nails." Gianna seemed to know it all.

"I'm not that bad." Clara smiled. "But to be honest, I've often been tempted to run her over with the Ferrari."

"It's too light a car. If you want to squash her, for Miss Shake-your-Bum you need something a bit heavier, like a double-decker bus." Gianna was merciless.

"I can't believe my ears," protested Marcella. "You two are terrible." She was shaking her head.

"You know that in viale Trieste, there's a huge pot hole, where every car always gets stuck?" pointed out Clara. "Well, people like Miss Shake-your-bum should be flattened and then used to fill those kind of holes. It's the only way they can be useful to society."

"I can't believe I'm hearing this…" Marcella covered her ears with both hands.

"I've got another idea." Gianna's eyes lit up. "I suggest we…"

"Stop! Otherwise I'll tell the boss that you two are conspiring for murder. And it's not good for Clara, since she's got a criminal record." Marcella dared Clara with her stare, until they all burst into laughter.

While Clara was doing her photocopying, some of her colleagues stopped and said hello. Others, especially three of the admin girls, quickly looked at her with that kind of fugitive gaze that indicated she shouldn't be there. Some others, such as the managers, who believed they were smart, tried to crack some dreary jokes on how she'd been locked up, and how incompetent the justice system was. Still, only a few hours to go and then it was the weekend. Clara had decided that on Saturday she was going to visit Signor Giovanni, in the old people's home in Sassari. Her visit was long overdue and she was hoping very much that he'd be OK, or even better, that he'd be alive. On Sunday, she'd go to the beach during the day, and then have a relaxing evening at home.

"Welcome back Clara." Paolo came from the office behind her.

She was startled. She didn't expect to see him so soon, it was only morning. She didn't know what to say to him. Part of her was still annoyed that he hadn't even bothered to phone her family during the ordeal, but part of her had started not to care.

"I was worried for you," he whispered as he came closer to her. "I've heard awful things about prisons."

"So, your worry managed to paralyze your fingers to the point that you couldn't even make a phone call to my family? At least to find out how I was doing?" She looked back at him, but she wasn't feeling angry, just calm.

He seemed nervous and edgy. He scratched his chin and looked away. "I was terrified of your mum. What if she picked up the phone? I could just picture her screaming at me."

"So, your fear overcame your desire to know if I was OK?"

"No. I asked Marcella and Gianna, every day. They can confirm." He was sincere.

They'd told Clara that he'd done so. First thing every morning he'd be going to their office to ask if they had news of Clara. Gianna had told him that if he wanted to know he should find out for himself, Marcella had been more agreeable.

"It was terrible what happened to you. I still can't believe it. Did they treat you well?" He seemed concerned.

"I was tortured every day." Clara paused, while Paolo's jaw dropped. "It was one of the girls I shared with. Annalisa… she talked me to death."

He was suddenly relieved. "What else? What about the food? I know that it matters a lot to you."

Why did people think she was such a glutton? Food was important, but not everything. Almost. "It was a bit like in a hospital, bland. Although they served squid with peas." Her face looked disgusted.

Paolo frowned and then giggled. "And I wasn't there to eat your peas."

"No, but I negotiated them for a peach. With the other woman, the one who talked too little." Clara thought about it. "It was a good deal."

"I see, so you were sharing with a chatterbox and a quiet one. I guess one compensated for the other."

Strange, Clara had never seen it that way. For her, both Monica and Annalisa were maddening. But if you looked at it objectively, it all balanced itself out.

The copies were all done, Clara picked up the papers and made a step to move away, Paolo held her arm. He bit his lip, looked away and then managed to face her.

"I… I was wondering if you'd like to go out with me, tomorrow night." He said it very fast, almost as if he was afraid not to be able to finish the sentence.

Clara had to think, she wasn't sure she heard correctly. She interrogated him with her gaze.

"I know it sounds strange, but I was wondering if there was ever a chance that I could take you out to dinner somewhere." He spoke in a low voice.

Clara had heard correctly. Her heart stopped. What did this invitation mean? Was it a date with her ex-boyfriend? Or were they going to go out as friends? Did she need to ask?

"Why are you asking me out?" She did need to know.

"Why? I don't know. I guess I'm a fool." He looked away, then he suddenly looked back at her and realized what he'd said. "Sorry! By saying I'm a fool I didn't mean that I'm a fool for wanting to go out with you, I'd be a fool otherwise. What I meant is that I'm a fool for having left you, and now even more of a fool for having some hope that maybe you would…" he'd become pale, his forehead was sweating, he seemed in distress. "Let's just leave it." He waved his hand. "Obviously it was a bad idea."

"Wait!" Clara was still in shock. Was it because she was pleased, or because it was so unexpected? "I'm busy tomorrow night, but we can go out on Sunday night." Those words just rushed out, she didn't even have time to formulate them properly.

Paolo's face lit up, like a Christmas tree. "Great, let's go out on Sunday. What time shall I pick you up?"

Clara was still in a trance. "Eight-thirty, perhaps?"

"OK, I'll be on time." He was about to do something, perhaps hug her? But he stopped himself and rushed away.

Chapter 22

Clara was still holding her papers, but she decided to walk down the stairs. She was too puzzled to go back to the office and face Marcella's inquisitive gaze. Her colleague knew her very well, and was able to spot the tiniest change in Clara's expression. Technosarda didn't feel too busy, that was one of the advantages of going back to work on a Friday. She really didn't want to bump into anyone, and spend time chit-chatting. When she reached the first floor, she heard someone come up the stairs. Well, there were over one hundred employees; luckily she didn't know them all.

"I didn't think you'd come to work today." Ernesto was carrying a huge cardboard box.

Of all people, did she have to bump into Ernesto? She liked being with him, but right now she wanted a minute to herself.

"Why are you carrying such large box up the stairs, when we've got a lift?"

"I only have one floor to go up and anyway, it takes longer to wait for the lift, than delivering the damn thing."

He placed the box on the step where he was standing, in a position that looked rather precarious. He moved towards the right, so that he could hold the box with one hand, and grip the banister with the other. It was evident that he wanted to chat with her, and Clara felt flattered.

"That box, it looks like it could fall any minute." She wondered what it could contain.

"I don't mind. It's got glasses."

"Glasses? What for?"

"It's Teresa's birthday today. She's brought a cake and spumante and has asked me, very politely I must admit, to bring some glasses to the meeting room." He paused, and looked at Clara. "That's why I don't mind if the box falls down and they *accidentally* break."

"You're really naughty." She said pointing her finger at him. "I wonder why I haven't been invited to her little party."

"I have." He started to fold the sleeves of his stripy shirt. "I told her that I wasn't going to bring the glasses upstairs unless I got an invitation. It's not in my job description." He grinned. "Obviously I intend not to go, but I had to make a point."

"Where's the party taking place?"

"In the meeting room on the second floor."

"I wonder who's going..." Clara was pensive. Surely Paolo had been invited. What did he actually think of Miss Shake-your-bum?

"Not many people, just a few selected ones. La crème de la crème." He started to count with his fingers. "First of all anyone who's got *director of something* next to their name in their business card. Second all the admin geese."

"Admin geese?" Clara was probing. How dare Ernesto assign nicknames to her colleagues without telling her in advance?

"Yes, those three girls in the accounts department who spend all their time squawking." He pointed upstairs. "Although nobody can beat Miss Shake-your-bum's voice. That squeal can even break mirrors."

Clara laughed. It was true, Teresa's voice was quite piercing. "Who else is going?"

"I don't think he's going." Ernesto looked straight into her eyes.

"Who's *he*?"

"Paolo." He continued to look at her, his gaze was intense.

Clara felt her cheeks go in flames. She closed her eyes for an instant and then re-opened them. But she couldn't face Ernesto's look. What would he think? Why was she blushing anyway?

"Why not?" she asked, while she still looked away.

"I kind of have the impression that Paolo is not too impressed with Teresa. I don't see them much together these days."

He was still staring at Clara. Was he trying to study her reaction? What was making her feel so uncomfortable? Paolo's invitation to dinner or Ernesto's piercing gaze?

"There isn't much to be impressed with Teresa." What else could Clara say?

"I was wondering if you'd like to go out for a pizza tomorrow night." Ernesto was still looking at her, but this time there was a note of tenderness in his eyes.

"I can't, I'm in Sassari tomorrow." What a pity, she always had fun with him.

"What about Sunday night?" He seemed hopeful.

"I'm sorry, I've got another engagement." What was happening in the world today? Clara hadn't had a date since she split up with Paolo, and this morning she'd got two invitations.

"I better go now. If I don't show up, that cow will start screaming." Ernesto's look was disappointed, almost sad.

Clara felt confused. She couldn't let him go thinking that she didn't want to spend time with him, but what could she say? He'd already lifted the box and was trying to move up the stairs while Clara was in the way.

"Perhaps, we could go out another time?" She suggested timidly.

"We'll see." His voice was low, and he wasn't looking at her now. In fact he almost seemed in a rush to get away.

She moved to the side, and he walked up, past her. As she saw him leave, her heart felt like it'd just been squeezed.

When Clara left work, at 17:30, the day was still hot. Somehow, she didn't want to go straight back home, she felt like having an ice-cream. As she drove along via Roma, she decided to park her car there and walk along the Largo Carlo Felice. All the shops were open and the wide pavements were crowded with passers-by. The air was hot and sticky, there wasn't much of a breeze. The sky was a wide blue dome, occasionally dotted with birds. The traffic noise was covered by the music of a busker who was playing his guitar, a melodic love song that she'd heard at the last Sanremo festival. Clara was walking slowly uphill, there was no point in rushing when it was hot. She finally reached the small pedestrian Piazza Yenne. On her left, the bronze statue of King Carlo Felice stood high on its marble base, a tall palm tree had grown next to it, almost acting like a protective shield. Its huge leaves were motionless, on this unusually still day. Clara went inside the ice-cream parlour and debated for ten minutes which flavours to go for. Should she opt for the fruity ones, or for the creamy ones? There were at least half a dozen chocolate options. The only decision she'd made so far was settling for three balls of ice-cream. She was tempted to go for three of the chocolate varieties, but she knew that the pleasure would only last a few minutes, and then she'd be a bit sick afterwards. Was it really worth it?

"Have you decided yet?" The young and skinny shop assistant was holding the metal scoop in mid-air.

"One more minute please." How could a girl who worked in a gelateria be so thin? No law in nature could account for that.

"Is it OK if I serve the lady next to you?" she asked.

"Please go ahead." Clara could do with more time.

The fruit flavours would've worked wonders in this heat. Lemon, strawberry, fruits of the forest, mandarin, pineapple, coconut. This was a Garden of Eden. Their colours too were vibrant, and they were guaranteed to be home made, with no artificial additives. But the creams... the creams were so luscious; you could see it just from their consistency. They looked smooth, not at all icy, just like something that would melt the minute it came in contact with your tongue.

"I'll have the tiramisù, the chocolate and the zuppa inglese." Clara pronounced her verdict, but the minute the girl started to scoop the first ball, she wondered if she should've gone for the truffle instead of simple chocolate. And now that she looked at them one more time, she wondered how that ferrero rocher flavour could've escaped her attention. She shook her head. She'd have to try them another time.

When she left the parlour Clara felt close to heaven. She'd already tried all three flavours, and had no regrets. She decided to sit on one bench overlooking the small piazza. There were a few people with children, and a woman walking her dog. Some of the small flower beds had been turfed, but the grass looked dry and thirsty, only the palm trees in the middle seemed to be coping reasonably well with this high temperature. The roundabout on her left was very busy, and she sat on a bench shadowed by a tall tree. While she was wondering if it made sense to eat each ice-cream separately, or mix the flavours, a girl came and sat next to her. Of all the benches in Piazza Yenne, did she have to sit next to Clara? It was hot, and she could do with some air and space around her.

"Do you usually take so long making a decision?" asked the girl.

Was it the heat that made people so sociable? Clara recognized that this was the woman that had been queuing behind her, at the gelateria.

"Choosing an ice-cream is not to be done light-heartedly." Clara had a spoon of the tiramisù flavour.

That was it. Perhaps the stranger would leave now? She made no movement, except licking her strawberry ice-cream. She'd only picked one flavour; how strange. She suddenly turned towards Clara and looked at her, through her designer sunglasses. She had long brown curly hair, a tanned skin, and a bit of an attitude.

"I can't imagine how they could say we look alike," she declared. She turned back towards the piazza and carried on eating her ice-cream.

"Pardon?" All Clara wanted to do was to sit there and enjoy her gelato. Was it asking too much?

The girl turned again towards Clara and put her hand forward, with the intention of shaking hers. "I'm Donatella. Nice to meet you."

Clara was shocked. She unintentionally shook her hand, and tried not to look at her. She'd spotted she was holding a small pink handbag, but a gun couldn't possibly fit inside. What did she want? Hadn't she caused enough trouble already?

"I want to apologize. I never intended to cause you all

this grief. I'm really sorry you've ended up in jail because of me." Donatella was looking ahead. "Will you forgive me?"

How could Clara juggle this difficult question and her ice-cream at the same time? She had to stop eating for a minute and try to answer.

"Considering that you've managed to get me out of prison rather quickly…" Clara paused. Her ice-cream was melting, it needed attention. "I forgive you." She grabbed her spoon again.

Why wasn't Donatella going? She'd done what she was supposed to do, she'd apologized. Clara had forgiven her. Time to move on.

"Don't you want to know a bit more?" Donatella turned towards Clara and lowered her glasses.

"Not really. The less I know, the better." Clara was convinced this was the case.

Donatella pointed at the bank in front. "It's kind of funny. Robbing the Banca di Roma was the easiest of all. But I did think that things had gone too smoothly to be perfect. I certainly never intended for someone else to take the blame."

Clara hadn't realized that they were sitting opposite the very bank she was supposed to have robbed. Of all the places to enjoy her ice-cream, did she have to pick that spot?

"Have you been following me?" she asked

"Yes." Donatella had finished and was wiping her lips with a tissue. She left red lipstick marks on it.

"Don't you think it's a bit risky? For you, I mean. The police are trying to find you."

"They haven't got a clue." Donatella was looking ahead again.

"Do you do this as your main job? I mean… robbing banks?" Clara was starting to relax now.

"No, it was a temporary hobby."

"Can I ask why you chose such a hobby?" It struck Clara as an eccentric one.

"Do you really want to know?" Donatella looked at her. "You're not going to judge me?"

What a weird thing to say. She should be more concerned about the possibility that Clara might tell the police, rather than her personal judgment.

"I never judge people. I have plenty of faults myself." Sadly, Clara had finished her ice-cream and her yellow plastic spoon was now lying lifelessly inside her cup.

"I'm a qualified vet. I've graduated a few years ago and I was unable to find a job. You know, the usual thing in Sardinia. Lots of graduates, no jobs."

Clara nodded. Unemployment was a widespread plague on her island.

"My life changed one night when I was driving along the industrial area of Macchiareddu, on that wide long road. I was going very fast, over 130 km per hour and …" Donatella paused, she seemed to be getting emotional. "I… I hit a stray dog. I immediately stopped the car, got out, and realized that I'd just killed this wonderful animal." Gentle tears were coming from below her sunglasses.

"That must've been awful." Clara was sympathetic.

Donatella nodded and wiped her tears. "I took him home and I buried him in my garden."

That was surprising. Clara liked animals, but she'd never gone as far as burying a stray dog; but then, she'd never run one over.

"I often see stray dogs and stray cats in Cagliari, in the towns and villages, everywhere. It's terrible. No-one seems to care about them. There was a young mongrel running along the Poetto beach the other day, he was very thirsty, he was dying for a drink. So I rescued him and he's now living in my house. Not to mention friends and family who've all spotted abandoned animals somewhere."

This was very interesting and touching, but Clara couldn't see how it related to the robberies.

"I decided that something needed to be done. What we lack is an animal rescue centre, where we can take care of the abandoned cats and dogs, and even other animals. So I started to apply for funding to the Sardinia government and even to the European Commission, but no-one took me seriously." She sighed. "And in the meantime, lots of animals are dying!"

"So you decided to rob banks to raise the funds." Clara could see the logic.

"Exactly." Donatella looked serious. "My grand-father has left me a bit of land, just outside Assemini, and I managed to get planning permission to build the centre. The whole project would've cost about 80,000 euros. So I estimated that I should just steal that amount and possibly a bit extra to cover the running costs."

"But why didn't you simply steal that amount from one bank, rather than doing multiple robberies?"

Donatella shook her head. "No bank has that kind of cash lying around. And anyway, it's not fair to take all the money from the same place! It's more ethical to rob more, and get a little from each bank."

"*More ethical?*" Clara was bewildered.

"I knew you'd be judgmental!" Donatella lowered her glasses again and looked at Clara. She had beautiful brown eyes, very expressive. They were still puffy from the crying.

"I'm not judgmental at all. I'm just trying to understand." Clara had a gentle tone.

"Come on, look at the situation. There are hundreds of animals without a home in Sardinia. Here I am, a qualified vet who can do something to help, but have no money. Can't you see that this is the only choice?"

"Well, sort of." Clara wasn't convinced. "It just seems so dishonorable to *take* the money, rather than *ask* for it. Have you thought of fund-raising initiatives?"

"So, you think you can get 80,000 euros holding a hat outside La Rinascente?" Donatella grinned. "I had no choice. To be honest, I would've stopped at 67,000 if you hadn't ended up in jail."

"So, now it's my fault that you've had to rob another bank? I guess I'm the real criminal here." Clara smirked.

"No, it wouldn't be fair to say that. My only mistake was to *borrow* your Ferrari, but I just couldn't resist when I saw it. Parked on a side street, unlocked, with the keys inside. It was crying to be taken!"

"Talking of which, when will I get my car back?" That was the minimum compensation for all the hassle.

"I've changed the plates and I've left the Ferrari in the outskirts of Mulinu Becciu. I've dropped you a note in your post-box at home, with the keys and the exact location of the car. When you open this letter, you can go to the police, who will want to do all their forensics before giving it back to you."

"Surely you must've left some fingerprints, or other signs. How do you know they won't catch you?"

"I know what I'm doing; there's not a single print that could lead them to me. In fact, I've left a lot of misleading evidence." Donatella seemed confident.

"How did you learn all this?"

"I'll tell you another time. That story can wait until you start working for me." Donatella smiled, for the first time. Her teeth were white and shiny, a bit like Lucilla's.

"What? Working for you?" Clara did a double take.

"Yes. I need two partners. One that can do all the admin work, paper stuff, orders, filing, you name it. I think you'd be good at this. And most important, I need someone I can trust."

Clara was shaking her head. Things were really going crazy today.

"I'm not interested, thank you." She stated with calm.

"Think about it. I'll pay you more than you get now. You've got a few months. The builders have already started laying the foundations of the centre, and because I'm paying cash, they're moving fast."

"I don't believe this."

"But I also need another person and I think that a man would be better at this." Donatella paused. "I've bought a small van, especially designed to carry animals. I want to employ a guy to go round the streets of this province looking for stray animals. He should catch them, give them a drink, and then carry them to our centre. Once they get there, I can take care of them." Donatella thought for a second. "It's got to be someone who loves animals and doesn't mind driving a bright pink van."

"Bright pink van?" This was getting better and better.

"I know, lots of men object to pink. But it's my favourite colour, can't you tell?" Donatella showed off her handbag, sandals, and belt, which matched perfectly: the same soft pink leather.

Clara was still shaking her head, when Donatella handed her business card.

"I'm counting on you Clara." Her tone was solemn. "I need the help of people I can trust, so if you can help me, and if you can find someone who can round up the animals, that would be great." She unexpectedly got up and walked away, before Clara could even reply.

Chapter 23

It'd been two weeks since she'd met Signor Giovanni. People always complained that time went fast; this wasn't the case for Clara. The fortnight just gone had felt like two years, every day had been filled with some type of odd occurrence, maybe it seemed so long because nothing had been normal? As Clara approached the turning for Sassari, she pondered whether time was an absolute concept or a relative one. She was only twenty-five, and yet she felt older, could people age that much in two weeks?

Mamma's car wasn't as fast as her Ferrari; in any case, she was in no hurry. As she drove along this smaller road, she recalled how she'd spent the first half of today thinking about her encounter with Donatella. She'd thought whether she should've gone to the police or not; after all, that girl was a criminal. And yet, her instincts kept telling her she shouldn't interfere. Donatella had no further intentions to get involved in illegal dealings. In addition, she wasn't a selfish robber, in the sense that she'd done it to protect and help animals. There was a degree of nobility in her intentions. If she got locked up in prison, who'd ever take care of the problem? And surely those banks must've had some kind of insurance, so, sooner or later, probably later considering the Italian bureaucracy, they'd get their money back. At the end of the day, everybody would be happy, except perhaps the insurance companies. But, hey, they were crooks anyway, so, all in all, justice would still prevail.

Before setting off on her long journey, Clara had phoned the old people's home and asked for Signor Giovanni. She didn't want to talk to him as such; her true intent was to make sure that he was still alive. The nun couldn't hear her properly, and Clara had to shout his name quite a few times, whilst her heart beat had started to accelerate. Finally, another nun took the call, and announced that Signor Giovanni was in the courtyard, sitting on a bench, reading a book. The joy that Clara had felt was indescribable. She'd asked not to disturb him, as she really wanted to surprise him.

It was 19:15 when she finally got there. The building still looked like a villa; it was even more attractive in daylight. The peach walls seemed brighter, and the balconies with the white railings made it look like a holiday home, especially because they were adorned with plants and flowers.

Clara walked through the main courtyard; her short pointed heels were tapping against the terracotta tiles. The fig tree on the side had a few purple fruits, she hadn't spotted them last time. As she got to the main entrance, she heard some music being played in the background. She felt good about the fact that she wasn't sneaking in through the back door this time. The front door was arched and had a green frame, the same colour as the shutters. Clara rang the bell, but no-one came. The music was loud, perhaps they couldn't hear her. She tried to open the door and was surprised to see that it wasn't locked. When she entered, she faced a long corridor, with white and grey marble tiles. The cream walls were embellished with pictures of saints, in bronze frames, all lined up at eye level. Clara followed the sound of the music, which seemed to originate from the last door to the right. When she got to that room, she realized that there was a big party taking place. Four old couples were dancing a mazurka, and some ladies were dancing with each other; it was on these occasions that you took note of the fact that women outlived men. There was a live band, playing on a small stage to the left, and small groups of old people with the occasional nun, talking to each other. Two long tables had been aligned against the wall opposite the door. They looked appealing; they displayed all sorts of goodies, savoury delicacies and cakes. The room was decorated with coloured ribbons and small flags, and everybody seemed to be having a good time.

"Can I help you?" A nun approached Clara. She was short and chubby and had a lovely smile.

"I'm looking for Signor Giovanni."

"He's dancing, over there." The nun pointed at the far corner.

Clara moved forward slightly, until she finally spotted him. He was dancing with a small lady, who had curly grey hair and was wearing an elegant black dress.

"Whose party is this?" she asked.

"Signor Giovanni's." The nun pointed at him.

"Is it his birthday?" She could've got him a present, if she'd known.

"Oh no, not at all." The nun looked towards him with tenderness and then explained: "Until two weeks ago he used to be quite sad and melancholic, but then something happened. He woke up one day and went to talk to the mother superior." She paused and crossed her hands below her waistline.

"Carry on." Clara was keen to find out.

"He told the mother superior that from now on he wanted to have a party every Saturday. He was wealthy and was prepared to cover the costs. It was important that old people had fun and enjoyed the last years of their lives." The nun had a big wide smile.

Why was every day full of surprises? Clara had expected to find Signor Giovanni sitting down, watching TV, looking bored or sad. But guess what? The old man was dancing a tango with another lady now. She continued to watch them and felt a hint of frustration about the fact that he didn't take her original advice seriously. She'd suggested he should give his money to charity, not spend it on parties. She'd been so proud that night for having contributed in some small way to humanity, but she'd meant helping the poor and the weak, not encouraging entertainment for the old.

"Help yourself to food and drinks." The nun pointed to the refreshments.

Clara walked towards the table. Shiny silver trays were hosting tiny pizzas, panini, frittate, and even minute mushroom pies. The display was eye-catching, everything looked freshly prepared and appeared tasty and crusty; the scent in the air confirmed it. Clara decided to try one of each. While she took a bite at her mini-pizza, she spent some time admiring the dessert section. She carefully inspected the shape and appearance of the patisserie-mignon, the mini choux-buns with crème anglaise, the small croissants with jam, and the tiny profiteroles covered with melted plain chocolate. First the savoury, then the sweets, she decided. But she couldn't resist; she picked one of the mini profiteroles and brought it close to her face, between her nose and mouth. Yes, people could faint when they were so close to perfection.

"I prefer the choux-buns."

She recognized Signor Giovanni's voice.

"Their only fault is that they don't have any chocolate." Clara laid her profiterole on the plate.

Signor Giovanni came close to her and gave her a hug. She managed to reciprocate, whilst still holding the precious plate; not easy.

"It's wonderful that you came! What do you think of the party?" he seemed very excited.

"It's great. It looks like people are having fun." Clara tried the mini-pie; it was as good as it promised. "Have you invited anyone from your family?"

"This is my party, not my funeral. The latter is the only thing they're looking forward to." He winked.

She tried to imagine it. This long procession carrying Signor Giovanni's coffin, and his relatives just waiting to cash in his money. She'd love to be a fly on the wall the minute the solicitor read his will. *Sorry, all the money has been spent on parties, food and music. In fact, there's an outstanding bill that you should settle.* Wouldn't that be funny? It was good to see that Signor Giovanni looked quite healthy at that moment; he had rosy cheeks, probably due to the wine and the dancing, and no sign of someone about to leave this world.

"Giovanni! You promised me a waltz!" demanded a lady in a blue dress.

"No, he's already danced with you twice. It's my turn now," intervened a small woman with a large personality. She grabbed his arm and shouted: "Let's go now."

Signor Giovanni smiled at the other lady and whispered: "The next dance is yours." Then he waved at Clara as he was dragged onto the crowded floor.

Clara decided to sit down and enjoy the party.

Five hours later, she was home. She was tired, and had indigestion. Possibly it was her fault. Could she blame anybody else? Perhaps the excellence of the cooks? All her family had gone to bed, and it was nice to take refuge in her silent and cozy bedroom. She lay on her bed and remembered the hour she spent chatting to Signor Giovanni. They'd sat on the veranda facing the garden and he'd told her how much better he was feeling now, and that he'd found a new meaning to life. Apparently three ladies had asked him if they could be his girlfriend, but he'd refused. He didn't want to be single, or anything like that, it's just that the lady he liked the most had shown no interest in him. Clara was fascinated by the fact that love problems were present at any stage of life. She never thought people could fall in love past a certain age. How short-sighted she'd been. She had a lot to learn.

She wasn't sleepy yet and wanted very much to have a chat with someone, but who could she call at one in the morning? Her friends were either out or asleep. Ernesto was probably playing in a night club or having fun; he didn't seem like the kind of guy that would be at home on a Saturday night. His expressive green eyes came to mind, there was something adorable about them. Maybe she could ring Lucilla, she was the kind of girl who never went to sleep. She'd called Clara at all sorts of strange hours. Why not reciprocate? She didn't have anything specific to tell her, just wanted a chat. Considering that Lucilla's interaction skills were very basic, maybe it wasn't a good idea. Still, why not? Clara got up and retrieved the toy phone from her wardrobe. She dialled the strange phone number.

"Yes?" The usual, pacific voice had spoken.

"I went to visit Signor Giovanni today." Was she going to tell Lucilla about the wonderful food, or should she stick to the essentials? "He was in good form."

"I know."

"It was nice to see that... somehow I've changed someone's life. For the better, I mean." That thought occurred to Clara only in the moment she said it.

"You have."

"Still, part of me was a bit disappointed."

"Why?"

She'd managed to trigger some interest from Lucilla. That was something.

"You know, I'd told him that he should give his money to charity, rather than leaving it to his awful relatives." Clara was still proud about her bright idea.

"Who are you to tell people what they should do?"

Clara didn't like that tone at all. "I wasn't telling him what he should do. I was just making suggestions." Was that clear?

"I see."

"Well, anyway... He's listened to half of my advice, so he's not going to leave anything to his family. But he's sort of ignored the other half."

"And by that you mean?" Lucilla was still cool.

"Rather than giving his money to charity, he's spending it on wild parties!" Clara had raised her voice, to create a stronger effect.

"And so?"

How could Lucilla be so calm? If she were a true angel she'd be scandalized.

"So... instead of some poor children or deprived person getting help, some old people are stuffing their faces with food and dancing until dawn." Was this going to trigger a better reaction?

"As far as I know, *you* were the only one stuffing her face today."

Clara had to stop to think. Lucilla's tongue was too sharp, it'd just cut very deep. She closed her eyes, while she still held the receiver. She didn't know what to feel.

"So, you think it's OK? What Signor Giovanni is doing?" Clara managed to whisper.

"I think that you have no right to judge other people."

The good thing about Lucilla was that despite her nasty remarks, her tone always remained gentle, almost the way a mother told off her child.

"I guess you're right. Who am I to have these opinions on people?" Clara was feeling humbled.

"The thing that you don't know is that Giovanni has set aside a very large sum to donate to old people's homes." Lucilla paused and Clara waited for the blow. "In fact, what he spends on parties is peanuts. He's organizing these feasts not only for himself, but for the joy of the other people too." She paused again, to give Clara the time to take it all in. "The large sum he's set aside is already being spent to cover the costs of people who need to go into a home but can't afford one."

Clara was mortified; not only was she feeling guilty for having judged someone in the first place, but even worse for having judged them wrongly.

"You should also know that Giovanni's asked his solicitor not to mention to anyone where the money is coming from. His gift will be anonymous. He's not doing it for fame or recognition."

"Don't say any more." Clara was feeling bad enough. She was truly ashamed, and tears started to blur her vision.

"There is something more to be said."

"Could you keep it to yourself please?" Clara could take no more.

"You played a huge part in all of this. You too deserve appreciation."

Clara was still upset, nothing could console her now.

"You may have your faults Clara. But that night, what you thought was a little gesture, actually made a big change. For the better. You should be proud of yourself." Lucilla's voice was tender.

Clara couldn't stop her tears from rolling down, they were uncontrollable. She didn't know what to say.

"I think you need some time to yourself. Goodnight." Lucilla had spoken softly, with a caring tone. Even the way she'd put the phone down, had been delicate. Clara was overwhelmed; what was going on? Her feelings were so mixed; she couldn't make sense of them all. It was nice though, to hear a proper goodbye from Lucilla, for the first time. Was she starting to show the first signs of true friendship?

Clara had enjoyed her shower, after coming back from the beach. Her skin was still glowing from the sun; she was pleased to see that she hadn't gone too red; her tan had just become a bit more golden. She was facing her wardrobe and wondering what she could wear for this special Sunday evening date with Paolo. Since her old clothes didn't fit her any longer, she'd gone out and bought some new outfits, this was a good opportunity to try them on.

"You know that Paolo likes it when you wear skirts, rather than trousers," Valentina was sipping a cold drink through her straw.

"Shall I try this?" Clara pulled a black dress from the wardrobe.

"I prefer the red one; it's a good colour for you." Valentina adjusted herself on Clara's bed. "In fact, considering that this is a romantic evening, red is very appropriate."

Clara put the red dress on, but it was slightly tight around her tummy and couldn't properly hide her curved belly. She sighed; she shouldn't have eaten so much watermelon at the beach. She tried the black dress. That was much better.

"You look good. Black suits you too," confirmed Valentina.

Her evening dress was made of soft and stretchy cotton. It was semi-fitted, had a high-bib neckline which was held with wide shoulder straps. The skirt reached her knees, and was slightly flared at the bottom. The top showed off her feminine neck, and graceful shoulders, and emphasized her toned and sun-kissed skin.

"I'm going to wear my red sandals and matching handbag," she declared.

"But they've got high heels! Paolo won't be pleased!" Valentina had a naughty look in her eyes.

"Tough! I wear exactly what I want this time," Clara glanced at her sister through the mirror. "In fact, I'm about to put on my red lipstick. Whether he likes it or not."

Clara was in a rebellious mood. In the past she'd tried to please Paolo and where did it get her? Nowhere.

"Why do you think he's taking you out tonight?" Valentina had her suspicions.

"I'm not sure, but I dare not predict anything. Look what happened the last time I went out with him and thought he was going to propose!"

"Is that why you didn't tell Mamma about this date? Valentina was probing.

"You know that she hates him now. If she knew I was going out with him tonight, she'd be disappointed."

"But he's going to ring our bell! She'll find out."

A Deal with a Stranger

"He'll call my mobile when he arrives and I'll meet him outside." It was all planned. Clara didn't want to raise anybody's hopes; the only one she could tell was Valentina. Her sister could always be trusted with confidences.

Clara's mobile phone rang once.

"I can't believe it! It's 20:30 sharp. He's always so precise!" Valentina was shaking her head.

"Not exactly like me."

"You know what I believe? I think that he gets here half an hour before the time, and sits in the car waiting for the minutes to go by. There's no other way he could do it!" Valentina was certain.

Clara inspected her handbag, to make sure that everything she needed was inside. That was the problem with having multiple handbags, the transfer of objects from one to the other every time you picked a different one.

"Clara! He's waiting for you…" Valentina pointed at her watch.

"He can wait a little longer. Women should never rush to their dates, especially when the guys have been mean on occasions."

Clara tied her sandals, put her watch on, and sprayed some perfume. She faced her mirror and gave herself a final look, then said goodbye to her sister.

Chapter 24

Paolo had parked his Alfa Romeo fifty metres down the road. Obviously he didn't want to get caught by Clara's family. When he saw her, he got out of his car and walked towards her, holding a bouquet of flowers. Clara had always appreciated the fact that Paolo was a gentleman. Every time he used to pick her up from home, he'd actually get out of his car and welcome her. Marcella instead, always complained about the fact that her boyfriend would just beep the horn and sit inside his car, while he waited for her.

Paolo was wearing a nice pair of jeans, with a beige short-sleeved shirt, which had navy vertical stripes. He kissed her on the cheeks, and handed her the flowers.

"Thank you, they're beautiful." Clara liked the composition of cream and red roses.

"You look great," he said with a wide smile. He then took hold of her left arm and walked her gently towards the car. "What do you fancy tonight? A proper meal or a pizza?"

"I've had a big lunch, so I'm quite happy to go for a pizza."

"Our usual pizzeria?"

"Yes." Clara sat inside the perfectly clean car. The grey seats were spotless, the dash board, the steering wheel, and every detail in the interior had been polished. Paolo had always been a perfectionist, but on this occasion he'd gone to great lengths to … maybe impress her?

He put the radio on as they headed towards viale Poetto. The atmosphere was serene; Clara felt almost like she was seeing an old friend.

"So, what did you do today?" Paolo was overtaking a slow cinquecento.

"In the morning, I went to the beach with Valentina; then we got home for lunch and later on we went back to the Poetto. The sea was so calm this morning, so still. Not a wave on view. But by the time we came back, there was a strong breeze and the sand was flying everywhere."

"Do you still hate it when it gets too windy?" He laughed.

"Of course! What's the point of lying there under a sand storm? It gets in your hair, your ears, your nose, everywhere. You can't even eat an ice-cream without swallowing bits of sand."

"That's what makes you most angry. The sandy ice cream!" he continued to chuckle. "You know, I have a solution for a beach that works in all sorts of weathers."

"I know, I know." Clara interrupted him. "A beach with pebbles, or rocks. It's true, we have the choice here, but the idea of going to the beach is to relax. How can someone relax when lying on top of stones? They're hard, or sharp, or uneven. Not to mention walking over them. Not my idea of fun."

"Sometimes I wonder Clara…" he slowed down as he entered the car park, "which planet you actually come from." He stopped the car and caressed her cheek.

Clara wasn't having it. "What do you mean by that?"

"Just maybe… you're not from this earth. When we go to the woods there are too many buzzing insects; when we go to the beach it's too windy, or too rocky, or the sea is too salty." Paolo seemed amused.

Clara couldn't get angry at him; she knew he was teasing her. But she wondered whether she was really such a difficult person. She'd never thought of herself as someone who was too demanding or problematic.

Anyway, she hadn't come on a date with Paolo to be criticized.

"I mustn't have been that bad, if you went out with me for four years!" She raised her chin and looked ahead.

"No, you weren't bad at all." He left the car and opened her door.

The pizzeria was huge, and not too busy for a Sunday night. Clara and Paolo chose to sit outside, and picked a table on the corner which faced the back garden. It was a warm night, and the strong wind of the early evening had subsided into a gentle breeze. The garden was paved, except for a few circular areas covered with pebbles, devoted to cacti and other desert plants, as Clara called them. There were four palms on each of the corners, and a fountain in the middle.

The good thing about this place, apart from the best pizza, was that the service was friendly and fast, and the atmosphere cheerful. They were playing The Beatles in the background, which was barely audible among people's chatter.

Within forty-five minutes, the waiter delivered two large pizzas. Paolo was having a *quattro stagioni* while Clara had chosen a *margherita*. The base was crusty and golden, and the mozzarella had melted into indefinable shapes on the smooth tomato sauce. The scent of the fresh tomato with oregano was appetizing, especially on top of a very thin, fragrant dough. The simplicity of the *margherita* was what made it so special. When the ingredients were fresh and authentic, there was no need to spoil the experience with unnecessary toppings. Still, Paolo's *quattro stagioni* looked very tempting too.

They talked of everything and anything. Paolo told Clara about his football match in the morning, when his team had lost three nil. He also mentioned his friend Marco's foul play, pushing him to the side when he was about to score a goal. He now was seriously thinking whether friends and football ought to go together.

Clara told him how her Ferrari had been found and was now in the hands of the forensic police. She was in difficulty because she had to borrow Mamma's car to go to work, at least until she'd get her own car back. She told him how she didn't miss work at all when she was in prison, and how she was getting fed up with that place.

"I know; Technosarda is a tedious company to work for." Paolo poured some beer. "At least now, I don't have to spy and report on you any longer."

"How come?"

Paolo looked away. "I've... kind of... altered the data. I made the computer tell us that you were checking in earlier and leaving later." He seemed embarrassed. "So, the head of personnel realized he was wrong all along, and told me to stop checking on you."

Clara was shocked. "But Paolo! You've always been so honest and trustworthy!" She couldn't believe he'd do this. "Why?"

He bit his lip and looked down. "I wanted to protect you."

Clara was still registering his message and what it meant. She was touched by his gesture.

"Thank you very much. But I don't want you to get into any trouble because of me." Clara couldn't help but touch his hand.

"It's all done and forgotten." He smiled as he held her hand tight.

"Hello Clara!" said a familiar voice from behind her back. Who could it be, if not Ernesto?

Clara automatically pulled her hand away from Paolo, as Ernesto came to the side and faced both of them. He must've seen her holding Paolo's hand, there was no other way.

"Hi Ernesto, what are you doing here?" She suddenly felt uncomfortable, why was that?

"The same as you, I guess. This is after all, the best pizzeria in Cagliari." He was looking at her, and piercing her eyes while completely ignoring Paolo.

"It's true; they do a very good pizza here." Clara was embarrassed. It was the first time she didn't know what to say to Ernesto. And yet, she felt she had so many things to tell him, but this was the wrong place and the wrong time.

"Now I understand why you said you were busy on Sunday night." A veil of sadness covered his eyes.

Clara's heart sunk. There was something very hurtful about seeing Ernesto upset, and even more hurtful was the fact that she might be causing this suffering.

"Yes. I… I'd arranged to see Paolo tonight." Was that the wrong thing to say? She couldn't face Ernesto now. And God knows what Paolo must be thinking.

"I'd better go and join my friends. I'll see you at work." Ernesto's usual smile had gone from his adorable face, as he walked away.

Clara couldn't cope with Paolo's inquisitive gaze and looked at her plate. She'd managed to eat half of her pizza, but her appetite had gone.

"Are you and Ernesto… friends?" Paolo crossed his arms.

"Yes. We've become quite good friends at work. He's always very nice and helpful." In truth, Ernesto wasn't her friend just because he was nice and helpful. There were more appealing qualities that he possessed, but it wasn't appropriate to discuss these with Paolo.

He didn't seem satisfied. "Is your friendship very… close?"

What a cheek; that was none of his business. "I guess it's as close as… your friendship with Teresa." Clara was keen to see his reaction now.

"Nothing to worry about then. Miss Shake-your-bum and I are no longer friends." Paolo seemed relieved. "In fact, we were never friends really; I just went out with her once or twice."

Clara was surprised. "What happened? I mean, why didn't your friendship last?"

"Well, first of all I never went out with her on my own. We were always part of a group of friends. Thank God!" He finished his beer. "After you and I split up, I felt uncomfortable about going out with our common friends. I thought that if you were with them, then I shouldn't be part of the group. Especially because *I* had been the bastard."

"That made sense." Clara sat back on her chair. "Also, you weren't too popular at the time, neither with me, nor with them."

"Exactly! So I thought I should meet some new people, that's why I accepted Teresa's invitations." He paused. "What a bore! What a bunch of snobs! All they did was talk about other people, those who had money and prestige versus those who were, according to them, losers."

"That sounds about right. I was surprised you'd even consider dating Miss Shake-your-bum." Clara had a mischievous look.

"I never *dated* her. As I just said, I only saw her in company of others. Until one day she started to get on my nerves."

309

"What happened?" She was getting curious.

"It's in the past." He looked away.

Paolo didn't seem to know that whenever he looked away and avoided the question, Clara would get more inquisitive. How come, in four years of being her boyfriend, he hadn't learnt that?

"You've got to tell me. There shouldn't be any secrets between us." She crossed her arms and waited.

Paolo sighed and then spoke: "You remember that evening we bumped into you at the Castello and you'd fallen over…" He smiled. "You looked so funny sitting on that paved street!"

"I didn't find it funny!" Her face was displeased. "Carry on."

"I was worried about you. I could see you were in pain and you seemed so… fragile. So after we left you there, I just wanted to go back and see if you were OK."

"That was sweet of you." Clara was impressed.

"Well, when I mentioned this to Teresa, she started to scream! I couldn't believe my ears. And what she was saying wasn't nice at all."

"I bet." Clara was more and more interested. "What did she say?"

"No, I can't repeat what she said. But there were some nasty remarks all directed at you. I reminded her that you were my ex-girlfriend, and she should respect you."

"Come on; tell me what she said exactly."

"I can't and I won't." Paolo had made up his mind, and nothing could persuade him otherwise. "To cut it short, we had an argument and I told her that I'd had enough of her pathetic attitude, her jealousy towards you, and her snobbish friends."

"That must've gone down very well." Clara laughed.

"Now I know why she had a go at me last Friday."

As they left the restaurant, Paolo suggested they'd go for a walk along the shore. They only had to cross the road, and the beach was waiting for them.

"I know that you hate the sand on your feet at night time, but I can carry you to the seashore." Paolo had a cheeky look.

"I'm not exactly a feather. Do you really want to hurt your back?"

"It'll give me the excuse to be off work."

"Don't worry. I'll take my sandals off." Clara knew that she was wearing a smart dress, but who cared? She could never say no to a stroll near the sea.

The sand was cool and soft as they crossed the beach. The small kiosks behind provided some cheerful music in the background. The full moon was right ahead, halfway between the sky and the horizon. Its magic light was caressing the surface of the dark sea, and managed to illuminate the beach just enough for them to see where they were walking. When they reached the sea, the water was warm, and the waves were almost imperceptible, as they delicately touched their ankles.

Clara looked up, she wanted to watch the night sky and the stars above their heads; she was always fascinated by the contrast between the widespread darkness and those spots of light.

"I still have problems identifying the various constellations," she had a tone of disappointment.

"Maybe I've confused you. Every time I showed them to you, I introduced them all together. Perhaps I should explain one at a time." He gently took her free hand and with her finger he pointed at the Ursa Major.

Clara was troubled; she didn't know what this date

meant and how she was supposed to feel. She smoothly pulled her hand away. "Don't worry Paolo, I'm sure that by the time we go back, I'll have forgotten everything. I really can't see all these shapes that people make out to be there in the night sky."

"What do you mean by *people make out?*" He seemed amused.

"Well, I suspect that a long time ago, one day, or better, one night, some person woke up and started to join those bright dots in the night sky. He probably had a strong imagination and decided to have some fun drawing all sorts of pictures." She paused and bent forward to get rid of a small shell that was stuck between her toes. "This guy then proceeded to state that each picture was an animal or something else, and that they should be called constellations, and that each of them meant something profound. And since he was the first to come up with this idea, he probably got a patent for it, and now we're stuck with it."

Paolo was shaking his head and laughing.

Clara moved closer to Paolo and whispered: "I'm just trying to conceal my ignorance, that's all."

That was the wrong move to make, because Paolo swiftly grabbed her waist and pulled her close to him. They continued to walk, side to side, as if they were almost glued to each other. Clara didn't know what to do; she was inundated with conflicting emotions.

"I… I've got something to ask you, but as usual, I don't know how." Paolo's voice had become low, almost uncertain.

Clara wasn't sure whether to encourage him or not. She was afraid of what he might say. But then, why not risk it?

"What is it?"

"I've made a terrible mistake in leaving you. The stupidest thing I've ever done in my life." His voice was trembling.

Clara was confused and tried to envisage the implications of his words. "I'm listening."

"Within days of leaving you, I realized it was the wrong thing. I became aware of my true feelings for you, how much I loved you. Isn't it crazy that I had to let go of you, in order to realize how much I cared for you?" Paolo was shaking his head, and seemed in distress.

Clara was overwhelmed. Wasn't this what she'd longed to hear all these weeks?

Paolo stopped and turned her towards him. They were facing each other now, while he still held her by the waist. "I know I don't deserve a second chance. But would you consider having me back?" He was imploring her with his eyes.

Clara turned away from him and looked at the sea. "I'm... shocked. I don't know what to say."

Paolo sighed. "Can I possibly have a bit of hope? A tiny hint?" He seemed in despair.

Clara was in turmoil. She should've been rejoicing at this, she should just be kissing him and saying yes a million times. But what was holding her back? Did she want to make him pay for what he'd done to her, and keep him waiting a little longer? Not really. She'd never been a vengeful person. Perhaps she was just very surprised; to the point that her sentiments didn't have the strength to show up yet.

"I'm touched to know that you still care for me," she managed to reply.

Paolo took this as an encouragement and carried on. "If you give me a second chance, I'll marry you straight away! I know you're the woman for me." His eyes were sparkling.

"Hey, hey! Hang on!" protested Clara. "How can you talk of marriage if we're not even together yet?" She was definitely overwhelmed now. The whole world was crumbling on her, even if it felt like a good world. Still, all of this was very confusing. "Anyway, you can't ask me to marry you until you've got a ring to offer me." This could give her a bit of time.

"Well, I'm not going to buy you an engagement ring, until I know you will say yes. What's the point?" He seemed slightly embarrassed.

Some men were just too practical. A bit more of romance would've been welcome. Maybe.

"Look, I need to think about all of this. It's just so unexpected, that's all." Clara was sincere.

"I'd like to know now. But I understand that I'll have to wait." Paolo seemed disappointed.

"Well, *yes*! I had to wait three weeks to get you to come to your senses. The minimum you can do now is to wait a few days." She laughed, in an effort to lighten up the atmosphere. But her heart wasn't rejoicing.

Chapter 25

Clara got to work early that Monday morning. She'd hardly slept the night before, so she'd decided that rather than lying in bed with her eyes wide open, she may as well get up and come to work.

It was refreshing to arrive at the office when hardly anyone was around. She switched her computer on, checked her e-mail, and decided to go to the basement to grab a coffee. Her head was feeling fuzzy from lack of sleep, and she could do with an injection of caffeine. She went down the stairs, rather than taking the lift. A bit of exercise might help her too.

When she got to the second floor, she suddenly wondered why she was going down to the basement to get her coffee. Her office was on the eighth floor, and there was another machine on the fourth. She walked down slowly, and thought about it. She was amazed to discover that, possibly, deep inside, she was hoping to bump into Ernesto. Yes, his stationery room was located in the basement. When she finally got there, all the lights were off; perhaps it was too early for him. She got her espresso and sat on the stairs. Despite the fact that the coffee came from an automatic machine, it was still creamy and smooth, the aroma was captivating, and luckily it was strong enough to wake her up. The problem with espresso was that it was finished in just two sips, so Clara sat there and stared at her empty plastic cup. Perhaps Ernesto would arrive soon? With his scooter it was easy to avoid the traffic. In any case, why was she waiting for him? This was silly. She'd better face reality and start thinking about Paolo's proposal. He was the guy she loved, wasn't he? And he obviously cared very much about her too. He'd gone to great lengths to mask her inexcusable time-keeping, even to his own risk. He'd had a fight with Miss Shake-your-bum just to defend her. That was a lot of extra points in his favour. What was she doing down there? Paolo worked on the eighth floor, so she'd better get back to the office.

"You must've fallen out of bed!" That was Marcella's welcome.

"Happy Monday," replied Clara.

"You don't look too good. Is everything all right?"

"Will there ever be a time when you actually pay me a compliment?" Clara was shaking her head and smiling at the same time.

"Only when you deserve one."

"You're beginning to sound like Gianna. She's usually the poisonous one." Clara chuckled.

"Bitching behind my back?" Gianna entered the office.

"How do you do that? You've got to tell me!" Clara was waving her finger.

"Do what?" Gianna sat on Marcella's desk.

"Come to our office exactly as I'm about to say or do something of great consequence." Clara's look was curious.

"I can feel it in the air. Something's up." Gianna crossed her arms and her legs, while still sitting on the desk.

"We're all ears." Marcella crossed her arms too.

Those two friends were unmanageable. Clara decided to keep them waiting a few more seconds. "I went out with Paolo yesterday."

"He wants to get back with you!" Gianna quickly shouted.

"*I* was supposed to tell you that!" protested Clara.

"What's going on here? Can you let Clara talk for once?" Marcella gave Gianna a fiery look.

Clara got up and closed the door, and then she walked towards her friends.

"Paolo told me that he still loves me and he wants us to get together again." Clara's voice was very low, the way a child tells a secret.

"That's wonderful news!" Marcella raised her arms in a sign of victory.

"I knew it! I knew that deep down he was still in love with you!" Gianna seemed very pleased.

"So, are you... together now?" asked Marcella.

Gianna's face hinted at the same question.

"He said he wants to marry me." Clara was still taken in by this news, even as she said it.

"That's even better! Why are you being so... quiet?" queried Gianna.

"I'm perplexed. I was hoping that he'd realize that leaving me was a mistake, but now that it's happened I'm utterly confused." Clara sighed.

"It's perfectly normal. Part of you wants to hit him, I bet." Gianna seemed sure.

"That's probably true. You're probably still angry at him, and maybe that's why you can't feel happy about it." Marcella touched Clara's arm.

"Keep him waiting... let him suffer for a while." Gianna had a naughty look.

"Don't listen to her Clara. Just follow your heart." Marcella had a dreamy expression.

What her friend didn't know, was that Clara's heart wasn't speaking to her. It'd decided to go on strike, and the few messages it'd sent were contrasting and confusing. Couldn't the answer be a clear yes or no, black or white? She'd always hated greys, and all their shades.

Clara was laying the table for dinner, and whilst Valentina and Mamma were preparing the pasta, she wondered if she should tell her family about Paolo. She'd already told her sister, who'd seemed pretty amazed at the news. But was there any point in telling the others?

Clara was still annoyed with herself for not having made a decision about Paolo's proposals. Because they were two, as far as she was concerned. One was about becoming boyfriend and girlfriend again; the other was about getting married. It was important to keep them separate, as one didn't necessarily lead to the other. Her head was telling her that Paolo was a good guy, he loved her very much and wasn't afraid of commitment, which was something quite rare in men. They always feared the *m* word, *m* for marriage. But her heart, that stupid throbbing thing inside her chest, wasn't getting excited. Should that be considered alarming? Or should she just be practical and consent to the fact that her heart had been exposed to some thrilling experiences recently. Strange encounters with people that were about to die and didn't, people that were supposed to live and didn't, people who didn't quite qualify as people, and to top it up, a final vacation in prison. Perhaps her heart was so used to this roller-coaster, that a marriage proposal from the man she loved was as exciting as a rainy day.

"Why have you put out the spoons instead of the forks?" Mamma was serving the spaghetti.

"You seem to be miles away," said Papà as he sat at the table.

"Perhaps she's in love?" commented Nonno, as he tucked his napkin into his collar.

Clara felt her cheeks go in flames. She hoped very much that her tan would disguise it. It didn't.

"So, you *are* in love then!" Mamma looked at her deeply. "Who's the lucky guy?"

"Stop it! Why don't you leave her alone?" intervened Valentina. She got up and quickly replaced the spoons.

Clara was grateful to her sister, but was also aware that her family was looking at her. Was this the moment of truth, or could she avoid it? She decided to take some time, and roll her spaghetti over and over again around her fork. Nonno poured a glass of wine, while Mamma dipped a piece of focaccia on her pasta sauce. They still managed to stare at Clara while busy with their eating.

"If you carry on rolling that fork, you're going to leave a silver track at the bottom of the plate." Papà smiled.

Clara decided to eat her bundle of spaghetti; that could give her a few extra seconds. She needed to make a decision, or at least provide some kind of explanation.

"Paolo told me that he still loves me and wants us to get back together!" She said it all in one breath.

Mamma dropped the fork, while Papà's fork and its tied spaghetti were left in mid-air. Nonno was calm; he didn't seem surprised at all. Valentina looked at Clara with admiration. As if there was something to be proud of.

"Since you spilled the beans, I may as well put the finishing touch." Valentina looked at everybody with confidence. "Paolo's also asked Clara to marry him!"

Mamma's jaw dropped, while Papà slowly lowered his fork, leaving the spaghetti intact. Nonno dabbed his lips and placed the napkin on his legs.

"Is someone going to say something?" asked Clara. "Usually you offer your comments in these circumstances." Was there a hint of sarcasm in her voice?

"If you told me that Paolo wanted to be your boyfriend I'd probably suggest you should send him packing." Mamma had a sip of wine. "But the fact that he wants to marry you, changes everything."

"Why should that change everything?" asked Papà.

"Because it means that he's serious." Mamma had another sip. "It means that Clara's not just a girl he goes out with. He wants to share the rest of his life with her. Don't you think that means a lot?"

"What does Clara think? Isn't that what matters the most?" Nonno was always the wisest.

All the family decided to stare at her again; another one of those situations that Clara hated.

"To be honest, I don't know what to think. I guess I'm still shocked at his proposal." Clara looked at her plate.

"He seems serious about you!" Papà appeared happy.

"I'd say he's besotted with her!" Valentina hugged her sister.

"I think he's finally realized how special Clara is." Mamma's eyes were veiling with tears.

"All we have to see now is whether his feelings are reciprocated." Nonno poured some more wine and smartly decided to change the topic of conversation.

Clara was brushing her teeth, while the rest of her family were watching television. It was a bit early to go to bed, but she was tired from the night before, and was keen to spend some time in her own company. Her face, reflected in the bathroom mirror, looked drawn and pale. How strange that even tanned people could look pallid at times. She headed for her bedroom and wished goodnight to her family.

"You always take so long in coming to bed. I've been waiting for ages!" Lucilla was lying on her bed.

Clara quickly locked her door, just in case. Strangely, she was pleased to see her blonde friend.

"What a surprise!"

"Good or bad?" Lucilla was reading a book.

"It remains to be seen."

"You look exhausted." Lucilla was another one great for compliments.

"Can you tell me something new?"

"Come, sit here with me." Lucilla folded her book, or rather, Clara's book, and sat on the bed. Clara followed her invitation.

"Lucilla, I… I'm in turmoil," she whispered.

"I know. That's why I'm here."

"Life is strange at times." Clara took a deep breath in. "You chase a dream for a long time, and when it finally happens, it doesn't give you the happiness you were looking for."

"Happiness?" Lucilla turned towards her. "It this what it's all about?"

Clara was puzzled, she frowned. "Of course. What else?"

"No wonder you're confused." Lucilla shook her head.

Clara became impatient. "I would really appreciate it if, for once, and only once, you'd actually speak a bit more clearly to me."

"I'm not here to give you answers. Maybe I'm here to get you to ask more questions." She shrugged her shoulders.

"But I need answers! I desperately need them. Please!" Clara's eyes were imploring.

"Try again."

"You remember our deal? If I completed my missions, Paolo would fall in love with me again." Clara stared at the wardrobe opposite her. "There's one outstanding mission, and yet Paolo's come back to me already. Did he do it *naturally*, or was it your... influence?"

"Does it make a difference?" Lucilla smiled.

"It makes *all* the difference!"

"It was *natural*, as you call it. No interference on my part." Lucilla was calm.

Clara was even more confused now. Wasn't that the best news she could hear? Paolo truly loved her; it wasn't through magic intervention that he'd come back to her. She suddenly stood up and paced around her room, nervously.

"Why? Why am I having all these doubts? Why can't I simply be ecstatic about this? She clenched her fist.

"What's going on exactly?" There was warmth in Lucilla's voice.

"I'm torn. I'm completely torn apart!" Clara was still walking up and down. "Half of me wants to throw myself into his arms, and the other half is indifferent. I've never been in this situation before!" She couldn't stop pacing around. "I've always known exactly what to do in my life. I'm not one to hesitate in making a decision. Now I don't have a clue!"

Lucilla was silent, and seemed rather relaxed. That made Clara even more wound up.

"Can't you help for a change?" Clara had a daring expression.

"You know, when only a short while ago, you criticized Rossana for being an indecisive person? She's so insecure, and such a ditherer. She doesn't know what she wants… that's what you said about her." Lucilla paused. "What does it feel like?"

"Is that your way of helping me?" Clara was furious.

"What do you want me to say?"

"Well, since you seem to know me very well, why don't you just *tell* me what to do? Accept Paolo's proposal, or reject it?"

Lucilla shook her head. "I'm not telling you something that you know already."

Clara couldn't win. She was tempted to get really angry at Lucilla, but decided to adopt a smoother approach.

"Can't you give me a hint? Just a tiny little clue?" Clara had stopped, and was now standing up opposite her, with an attitude of prayer, almost.

Lucilla closed her eyes and breathed. Was that a good sign?

"As you pointed out earlier, there's still one last mission to accomplish." She opened her eyes again, and they seemed so peaceful. "When you save the life of the next person, you'll have your answer."

Clara was taken aback. OK; a deal was a deal, but this was kind of… pushing it.

"Is this the last one? I mean, the last person I have to save from suicide?" This couldn't go on forever.

"I originally said four people, and four people it is. This is indeed your last mission." Lucilla got up. She opened Clara's wardrobe and picked up the toy phone. She put it inside her blue silk bag, and took out the smaller mobile phone. She handed it to Clara. "Take this. I'll call you some time tomorrow." She walked towards the door.

Clara automatically followed her; she didn't want her to go away, not so soon.

Lucilla turned and faced Clara. "This is the last time we see each other. Goodbye."

Clara hoped she had misunderstood. "You mean, *goodbye* in the sense of arrivederci, or goodbye in the sense of farewell?"

"Farewell, my dear." Lucilla's tone was clear, still angelic, but painfully unambiguous.

Clara's world was in pieces, it couldn't possibly be. Lucilla couldn't just disappear like that. And yes, she'd annoyed her on occasions, but on the whole she wasn't so bad.

"You can't leave me now! Especially when we're finally starting to get on well!" Clara protested.

Lucilla smiled and gently touched her cheek. A tear had just rolled down Clara's soft skin.

"Say something else! Say that it was a bad joke! That's more acceptable from someone with your sense of humour!" Clara was pleading.

Lucilla kept smiling.

"I can't let you go! I won't let you go! This wasn't the deal." Clara quickly walked around Lucilla and leaned against the door spreading her arms wide open. "You're not leaving me this way. We've got so many things to tell each other, so many arguments to have! Please!"

Lucilla came close to Clara and gave her a tight hug. She felt warm and soft, like a wonderful human being. But her voice was still and pure. "I'll always be with you. It's just that you won't notice me!" She delicately let go of Clara.

Clara's eyes were full of tears, her vision was completely veiled. She heard the door open and shut gently. When she finally managed to wipe her cheeks, Lucilla had gone.

Chapter 26

It was a quiet week at the office. In the air, there was that Mediterranean feel of *too hot to do any work*. Everyone seemed to be taking it easy; even Clara's boss was away, whilst Gianna and Marcella were out on their morning coffee break.

Clara was glad about this lull, too much had happened in the recent weeks. At the moment she found it hard even to concentrate on the minor tasks, let alone the complicated requests that Mr Big Idiot could come up with.

She touched the velvety leaves of her African violet, which had been with her since she joined Technosarda. There were some new purple flowers coming up, they looked so small and fragile, perhaps they'd open up and smile at her some time soon?

"It looks as if you're trying to hypnotize that plant!" Paolo suddenly appeared inside her office.

"Perhaps it's the contrary. It's her that it's mesmerizing me. Such a delicate creature."

"Do you still talk to your plants?"

"Of course! They're the only ones that pay attention to me." Clara crossed her arms.

Paolo was about to say something back, but he stopped himself. He decided to sit on Marcella's desk instead, and put his hands in his pockets.

"Fancy a coffee?" he asked timidly.

"Ehmm... Marcella's out, and I'm not supposed to leave the office unattended." Clara was pleased with her reply. It was the safest option.

Paolo looked at her, and then directed his gaze at the window, on his right. Clara was feeling uncomfortable, she knew that he wanted an answer, but she didn't have one yet.

"Are you still thinking about it?" He finally braved the awkward question.

"Yes."

Paolo stood up and headed towards the door. "I shouldn't be putting pressure on you. Sorry." He smiled at her. "Take your time."

His last sentence didn't sound that sincere. But was that surprising? Clara had a deep sigh when Paolo disappeared from view. She shook her head, then held her face between her hands. Another deep sigh. She hated life when it got too complicated.

Her new phone beeped. She quickly grabbed her handbag from the floor and retrieved it.

"Now is the time." Lucilla had spoken again, with her celestial voice.

"I'm ready."

"The person you're trying to save is in your building. On the roof-top. This person is trying to jump. You'd better go."

"OK. What's the problem with this person?" Clara needed a full briefing. Or maybe, she just wanted to chat to Lucilla a little longer.

"You'll find out soon enough."

Why did Lucilla have to be so cryptic all the time?

"I... I just wanted to say that... I'll miss you." Again, Clara's words had come out against her will.

"I won't."

What else did Clara expect?

Lucilla finished her sentence: "I won't, because I'm always going to be with you. Good luck!" She hung up.

Clara was still trying to absorb Lucilla's last words. She wished she'd had the time to properly say goodbye, like real friends do. But it seemed as if her blonde friend was always in a hurry. Why was that? Did she have other human beings to attend to? In fact, now that Clara thought about it, hadn't Lucilla helped Monica during that infamous night? At least that's what Monica had said. Clara was feeling put off. She'd always thought that guardian angels were supposed to be *personal*, not to be shared. Why was she feeling irrationally jealous now?

Her new phone started to beep again. Clara sighed; patience had never been one of Lucilla's virtues.

In order to reach the roof-top she had to go up a small metal staircase, located behind the fire exit door. Thank God she didn't have to drive a long distance this time. Her Ferrari was still with the police. Who could possibly want to commit suicide, amongst her colleagues? She didn't know of anyone being in big trouble. But then, she didn't know all of them personally. She walked past the fire door and quietly went up the narrow metal staircase. She was then faced with a green door. She pulled the rusty handle down and pushed the door open. The hot breeze hit her face, and blew her hair backwards. She walked out in the open terrace and tried to see if she could spot anybody. The large square roof-top was paved and had a short wall all around it. In the middle stood a huge noisy metal box, probably containing the air conditioning units. Clara tried to focus, but it was hard without sunglasses. The person in question must be somewhere, maybe behind those units.

She walked around and finally noticed someone sitting on the short wall, legs dangling in the emptiness, with his back towards her. It appeared to be a man from that distance. A guy who was occupying a rather unsafe position. His hands were at his sides, placed openly on top of the wall, almost as if they were meant to provide extra thrust for the jump. How could she tackle this? There was a risk that, if she tried to talk to him, he would actually take the leap. Perhaps her best option was to grab him from behind and pull him towards the floor. She didn't think twice, she ran towards the guy, grabbed him by his waist and dragged him down. What followed was a bundle of chaos, between his full weight on top of her, the heat and the hardness of the floor, and her hair all over her face.

"What the hell…?"

Clara immediately recognized Ernesto's voice. Of all people. Her energies suddenly left her, she almost fainted. Thank God she was on the floor already.

He seemed shocked to see Clara there. He rolled away from her, but decided not to get up.

"What are you doing here?" he shouted.

"What are *you* doing here?" was Clara's response. She pushed her hair away from her eyes. She still wasn't sure she was seeing correctly.

Ernesto hid his head between his knees. Clara came close to him and touched his shoulder. She wanted to hug him and tell him that everything would be all right and kiss him better, but was that the right thing to do? She certainly didn't want to screw this one up.

"What's wrong?" she whispered in his ear.

Ernesto was shaking his head; maybe he didn't want to talk to her?

"I'd like you to leave me alone." He lifted his head and looked at Clara, with a profound sadness.

"I'm not going anywhere without you." Clara was determined.

"Can't you respect my wishes?"

"Your wishes make no sense at this particular moment. I'm staying here." Clara moved slightly so that she could sit and face him.

"You've always been a bit stubborn."

"What's the matter? Please tell me." Clara needed to know, desperately. She'd always cared about the people she'd rescued in the past, but Ernesto was extra special.

"Life! Just a bitch at times." He looked away.

Clara couldn't resist, she touched his tanned face, and his soft dark hair. Ernesto seemed very agitated and she just wanted to hold him and make sure that nothing bad would happen to him.

"I'm here." Her voice was tender.

He pushed her hand away. "I'm... just going through a bad patch." He shook his head again. "It all started the day our band played outside your home."

"It was wonderful." She grabbed his hand.

Ernesto seemed to be surprised at this gesture, but he didn't pull away this time. He bit his lip. "My guitar got stolen, while I was having lunch with your family."

"What? That's horrible!" Clara was furious. "Who would do such a thing?"

"It was my fault. I should never have left in inside the boot." He seemed gutted. "It was an exceptional guitar, I saved for years to buy it."

"I'll give you some money towards it. In fact, I should pay for a new one; it's my fault if it was stolen!" Clara was feeling guilty.

Ernesto was still holding her hand tightly. It felt so good for Clara.

"Don't worry. I won't need it in the other world." He grinned.

"Never, ever, joke about life and death!" She reproached him. "Is that why you want to … leave us?"

"Partially." He looked down.

Clara touched his cheek, inviting him to look at her. "Any other reason?"

He sighed. "The other bad news is that I'm about to lose my job."

"What do you mean?" Surely not.

"My two-year contract expires at the end of June, and I've been told that it won't be renewed." He looked very sad.

Clara closed her eyes. That was very bad news. Especially as jobs didn't come easy in Sardinia. But she had to say something helpful. "Look on the bright side Ernesto, who would want to work for Technosarda anyway?"

He looked lost. "A job is a job. No job, no money. No money, no guitar, no nothing." He seemed even sadder now. "I'm not a money-minded person, but my family's financial situation is pretty unstable."

What could Clara say to that? How could she make those beautiful green eyes smile again? They looked so enchanting, she could get lost in them. Could she give him some money? She could sell her Ferrari, buy a smaller car and give him the rest. Perhaps she could also offer him a percentage of her salary every month. Would he accept it?

"Is there anything else that saddens you?" She had to ask that question.

He hesitated before replying. "Yes."

331

What else could go wrong for Ernesto? Weren't two misfortunes bad enough?

He looked away as he spoke. "There's this girl I like very much."

He didn't realize it, but he'd just stabbed Clara's heart. He liked a girl. Another girl, obviously. Why was she feeling so hurt? She could barely speak.

He continued. "I've liked her for a long time, and recently I thought that I might have a chance with her." He looked down. "But I know now that she likes someone else."

"Unreciprocated love. That's very painful." Clara managed to say.

And yes, it did feel very painful. So sharp and cutting; so deep. Her heart wasn't speaking to her. It was *shouting*, at the top of its voice. Screaming to her that Ernesto was her true love. Clara almost stopped breathing; the unexpected had just hit her. No wonder she wasn't getting excited about Paolo. Her heart had already been conquered by someone more special. How could she have been so detached from herself and not have understood? Or was that pure stupidity? She couldn't even read her own feelings. There he was, right in front of her, the guy she really loved. Wow. What a slap in the face. She was the one who needed to be rescued now. Because with that, came the realization of her own inconsolable pain, the unbearable truth that Ernesto wanted another girl.

"Can you see now? What's the point in living?" He finally looked at her.

But it was Clara who dared not to look back. What if he found out?

"It's terrible. Everything's gone wrong for you." She had to acknowledge that. "But problems can be solved."

Ernesto suddenly got up, and helped Clara to rise. "Would you please leave me alone now?"

Clara instinctively put her arms around his waist, and held him tightly. She wasn't going to let go easily. "We're going back together," she said with confidence.

He seemed surprised and tried to pull her hands away. "Don't make it more difficult than it needs to be." His voice was cold.

She started to cry, those stupid tears were just doing what they wanted. Her vision was blurred but she categorically didn't want to lose sight of Ernesto, like it'd happened with Lucilla.

"I beg you! Come back with me and forget about this stupid idea!" She was shouting.

Ernesto gently wiped her tears with his fingers, and looked at her. "Give me one reason to live." He said with a desperate tone.

"Me! Clara! I'm a good reason!" She became angry and started hitting his chest. "If you die, then it's me who's got no reason to live. Do you understand?" She caressed his cheek and looked straight into his eyes, between her tears.

What happened in Ernesto's face was short of a miracle. That darkness that had veiled his eyes suddenly lifted, and a sparkle of pure joy appeared. He hugged her, real tight this time, to the point that Clara felt squeezed. But she liked being squashed between his arms. How long had she wanted this? People could get lost in such an embrace. If only time could stop in that instant, get sealed, and never change again...

"You're my girl, Clara." He whispered to her ear, while still gripping her. "I thought I had no chance with you." His voice was broken. Was Ernesto crying too?

"You're my guy, Ernesto."

He finally looked at Clara; he gently caressed her cheeks, her eyes, her lips, and kissed her tears. But he still held on tight to her. His smiling eyes were so captivating; she could look at them forever.

"My face must be a mess, with all my crying." Clara was embarrassed.

But Ernesto seemed undeterred. He softly raised her chin and kissed her lips with tenderness. Clara was ecstatic, that was the word that best described how she was feeling. That kiss, which was a gesture of pure love at first, was now becoming a passionate union of two souls. Again, it was easy to get lost and let go.

"I could kiss you for ever." Ernesto reluctantly pulled away.

"We've got a long time ahead of us." Clara was sure. Life couldn't possibly be short when you found true love.

She tucked her head between his chin and his chest, and he carried on squeezing her with his strong arms. It was great having a taller boyfriend, it made her feel more protected. She closed her eyes, and thought of Lucilla and their pact. She'd kept her word, her wonderful friend. Clara had no doubts now. What a source of inspiration Lucilla had been. Suddenly, an idea came to mind.

"Ernesto, do you like animals?"

"What a funny question to ask at this moment." He laughed. "Yes, I do."

Clara smiled while still resting her head on his chest; what a pity that he couldn't see her mischievous look.

"Would it be a problem for you, driving a bright pink van?" she asked with an air of innocence.

"You do say funny things at times." He carried on chuckling. "Pink is not my colour, but I'd drive anything that moves."

"That's great." She finally looked up, and stared at his charming green eyes. "No more money worries for you. I've got the perfect job in mind."

She went back to his tight hug and secretly wondered what she'd done with the card that Donatella had given her. It was probably inside one of her handbags, somewhere.

* * * * *

NOTE FROM THE AUTHOR

Thank you for reading my book. I hope you enjoyed it. Independent authors like me rely on reviews from readers to help spread the word about our work. Please consider leaving a review of *A Deal with a Stranger* on Amazon, Goodreads, or any other online book review website. Thank you.

I love to connect with readers. Visit my website www.martinamunzittu.com where you can subscribe to my newsletter and hear about new releases, giveaways and special promotions. You can also download a free copy of my ebook *Incompatible Twins*. This ebook is available as a special Christmas gift until 31st December 2013.

On my website you can also follow my blog, and connect on Facebook, Twitter and other social media.

ACKNOWLEDGMENTS

Some fabulous people have contributed to the research for this book. Among them, I must mention: Elisabetta Cauli, Vittorio Dessì, Francesco Massidda, Luisella Pili, Matteo Podda, Serafino Podda e Rita Puddu.

The picture on the book cover is taken from a painting that my brother Mariano did for me as a wedding present. It depicts Chia beach, which is one of my favourite beaches in Sardinia, and is also mentioned in the book. My friend Siv Lien, who is a talented designer, managed to create a great cover from this painting.

The book trailer was made by Mike Crowe, and most of the footage was provided by Italo Fois.

Sardinia and its people have been the real inspiration for this book. I could say a lot about my beautiful island and its inhabitants, but perhaps all that I wanted to say has been expressed in the words of "A Deal with a Stranger". I hope that that the fondness that I feel for Sardinia, which is the place where I was born and grew up, is evident throughout the pages.

ABOUT THE AUTHOR

I was born and brought in Sardinia (Italy). After studying languages, I moved to the UK and worked as a secretary for the University of London.

Later, I was offered a similar job in Sardinia, so I moved back there for a few years.

At the age of 28, I decided to come back to the UK, in Cambridge, and carried on working as a PA at Director level for another ten years.

In 2007, I founded my own Company, Essenza Solutions Ltd. I now offer freelance secretarial services.

I am married to Philip. As well as being a wife, I'm also a mother to a four year old daughter who keeps me busy, sometimes more than work itself. As I pick up potentially lethal objects scattered on the floor, or discover new stains on the sofas or walls, I try to get my little girl to speak Italian, as well as English.

Like any other woman, I'm good at multi-tasking, so while I'm doing all the above, I also dream about all those lovely characters who cannot wait to make their appearance in my future books.

ALSO BY MARTINA MUNZITTU

Incompatible Twins

Lucy and Poppy are identical twins. They are in their twenties and live in London. Even though they look similar, their personalities are quite different, if not opposite. Poppy has been travelling the world after graduating, whilst Lucy has settled down, got a job and bought a lovely flat. The only thing missing in Lucy's life is romance. Poppy offers to help. After all, she's seen the whole world so surely she knows how to handle this?

The perils of metropolitan London prove harder than those of the Columbian jungle. Poppy soon realizes that finding Mr Right for her sister will take a lot more than she bargained for, but she's not going to give up.

This is more a chick-lit novella than a romance novel. The love–hate relationship of the twins is evident in their humorous conversations, and will make you wonder who to root for – Poppy or Lucy. There's only one way to find out.

ALSO BY MARTINA MUNZITTU

The Broken Heart Refuge Series

Where can you find comfort when your heart is broken?

Nonna Pina runs The Broken Heart Refuge: the go-to place for anyone who is suffering for love. In Episode 1 – Betrayal – we meet Lisa, who has fallen in love with her best friend's boyfriend, and Mary, whose husband died recently.

What can be done to help Lisa? Should she tell her friend how she feels or should she run away and start a new life? Mary's grief seems paralyzing, but there's something more to it that bothers her and won't allow her to move on.

Will Mary and Lisa be able to find the answers they're looking for, among the lovely people who frequent the centre? As Nonna Pina says: "A cup of tea and a few kind words can work miracles."

This book will be available from 15 December 2013.

9941331R00195

Printed in Great Britain
by Amazon.co.uk, Ltd.,
Marston Gate.